A Scandalous Matter

THE PAST IS ALWAYS PRESENT

MARGARET LOCKE

To Meg—
Thank you for
the support!
Margaret
locke

A SCANDALOUS MATTER
Copyright © Anne Tjaden, 2016

Locked On Love, publisher
Harrisonburg, VA

Cover design by Lankshear Design – www.lanksheardesign.com
Edited by Tessa Shapcott – www.tessashapcott.com

This book is a work of fiction. Names, characters, places, and incidents either are products of the author's imagination or are used fictitiously. Any resemblance to actual events, locales, or persons, living or dead, is entirely coincidental.

First Edition: July 2016
A Scandalous Matter : a novel / by Margaret Locke – 1st ed.
Manufactured in the United States of America

ISBN: 978-0-9963170-4-7, Electronic Book Text
978-0-9963170-5-4, Paperback

For my sister, Donna, in celebration of her own Second Act.

CHAPTER 1

1813

*A*mara Mattersley sat within the circle of ancient stones, wondering for the hundredth time what she was doing. She'd been there for hours, barely moving, her heart warring with her head.

It was madness, this plan she'd hatched with Eliza, the idea that by coming to this sacred space and wishing to find her soul mate, it would happen. Her soul mate in the twenty-first century, that is.

She held a hand to her forehead, squeezing her eyes shut. It couldn't work. It wouldn't work. *Did she want it to work?*

She did.

At least the part about traveling to the future, to the opportunities Eliza promised. There wasn't anything for her here anymore.

Oh, that wasn't wholly the truth—she had her family. Her brother, Deveric, Duke of Claremont, and his wife, Eliza.

Their children, Frederick and Rose. Her sisters, Cecilia, Grace, Emmeline, and Rebecca. Her scamp of a brother, Chance. Her mother. She loved them, and they her. But familial love wasn't enough to overcome the hurts of her past, the bleak prospects for her future.

"That's what happens when you throw yourself away on a scurrilous bastard," she whispered to herself, Drake Evers' face floating before her. It'd faded in time, now a vague shadow of the man she'd once loved, the man who'd seduced her all those summers ago … before confessing he'd married.

Pain lanced her heart. How could it hurt, so many years later? Shouldn't she have recovered by now? Maybe she could, if people would let her forget. But forgetting wasn't possible in this society in which everyone judged everyone else. Being a duke's sister carried with it numerous advantages, but not when it came to avoiding notoriety in a scandal.

Of course being a duke's sister is what saved her from a forced marriage. Amara refused to enter an arrangement devoid of affection. Her passions burned too strongly for that. Luckily, her family, even her disapproving mother, had rallied around her, and their support, and certainly their social rank, kept her within polite society.

"I am too much, Eliza," she'd insisted when she'd revealed her longing to leave. "Too headstrong, too driven by the desires that landed me in trouble to begin with. Six years I've tried to tame my emotions in order to be the perfect daughter, the perfect sister, content with the same endless circuit of balls and house parties and morning calls, the same tedious afternoons of strolling in the gardens, or playing the pianoforte, or reading. It hasn't worked."

Not that Amara minded reading. Like her sister, Grace, she'd read nearly every book in Clarehaven's expansive library, especially any tomes related to science, particularly the stars.

She tilted her head to the heavens now, keeping her eyes closed as the sun beat down on her. The rock beneath her warmed, her fingers soaking up its energy as she grasped at its edges, thinking of Eliza.

Eliza, her brother's new wife.

Eliza, the woman from the future.

"I want more. A life of my own, like you had," Amara'd confessed to her sister-in-law after learning Eliza's secret, a secret she never would have believed had her brother not vouched for his wife, and had she not seen Eliza's telephone for herself. *Cell phone. She calls it a cell phone.*

Amara cradled the small black device in her hands. Though it was long since depleted of whatever powered it, she hadn't forgotten the pictures—*photographs*—Eliza'd shown her on it. Pictures of fantastical things. And the stories Eliza had told—not only of the objects depicted, but also of the options available to women in this twenty-first century. A full education. True independence. Neither of which Amara could acquire in 1813.

"Take it with you," Eliza had said, her eyes suspiciously bright as she'd handed Amara the phone that morning. "To show Cat my life here."

Cat was Catherine Schreiber, Eliza's friend from Virginia, owner of a magical manuscript enabling her to create love interests, and the woman Amara needed to find once she arrived.

But first, she must find the man.

"Cat can call you forward, I'm sure of it," Eliza had insisted. "But for love. That's how her powers work. She can bring people across centuries, as evidenced by your brother and me, but the love element is key. If you want to travel to the twenty-first century, you can only do so by wishing to be with your true love. And, Amara, you deserve that love. You are wonderful—intelligent, witty, caring. You've been the dearest friend to me. But I agree you've gotten the short end of the stick here. You deserve everything you want. You deserve to know a love like I have with Dev."

Amara had rolled her eyes in an attempt to disguise the sheen of moisture Eliza's kind words brought forth. "I thought I had that once, and *everyone* knows how it turned out. I want to flee this society precisely because of my troubles with men. Why should I wish to leap into a man's arms, even one you think could be my great love?"

That dilemma was why she'd sat here half the day, torn. She desperately wanted to escape, but to only be able to do so if she gave herself to another man? Oh, the irony.

She'd said her goodbyes to Dev and Eliza that morning. They were the only ones privy to Eliza's time-traveling secret, and the only ones who knew of Amara's intended destination. Thanks to the letter she'd left, the rest of the family would think she'd run off with the Royal Navy officer she'd met on their recent journey to Bath.

An unladylike snort escaped her. She *had* met an officer. A captain. Emmeline even commented on the man's attentions, but in truth Amara had wanted nothing to do with him. He'd had that oily aura to him, that essence of rogue she'd become so adept at discerning. He was a convenient scapegoat now, however.

It saddened her to think her family members were unlikely to challenge her bizarre tale. Would her mother be relieved to have her scandalous oldest daughter out of her hair? Amara's impetuous nature had got her into trouble more than once, though never so much as with Drake.

She dipped her head in shame. If only desire didn't plague her. If only she could leave it behind. Physical desire, at least. Her intellectual passions burned with equal fervor. Eliza's talk of women at university, women as doctors, scientists, even world leaders, had roused her mind from its stupor. The opportunities available to women in the twenty-first century were a far cry from Amara's current options. Here, she could marry. Manage a household. Bear children. Perhaps aid charitable organizations, or become a patroness of the arts or sciences. But she wasn't to undertake scholarly activities herself. Not as a woman. Not as a Mattersley daughter.

"In my mother's opinion, in the *ton's* opinion, I am no more than an aging spinster in a society where a woman's marital status determines everything," she'd told her sister-in-law a few weeks ago.

"Not in my opinion, for what it's worth," Eliza had said, clasping her hands over Amara's. "But give the future a chance. Give *yourself* a chance. Go. Explore. Open your heart. You never know what might happen."

This morning, as she'd said her final farewells, Eliza had gripped her in the fiercest embrace. "While I hope you give love a chance, remember, you still have a choice. Cat's stories promise that; she wouldn't force anyone into something. You don't have to marry *anyone*, even the man from your story, if you don't wish to." Her eyes had taken on a teasing glint. "If nothing else, well, you can have the kind of fun you can't have here."

"Fun?"

"Yeah. Fun. You know, making out with someone?"

"Making out?"

"Kissing!" Eliza had exclaimed with a bubbly laugh. "You must kiss whomever Cat writes you with to make the magic stick. And you can indulge in everything else, if you wish. If he's cute enough."

Amara's cheeks had caught on fire at Eliza's suggestion, yet the idea of a guilt-free liaison was one of the things that'd brought her here today, despite her doubts. She wanted no permanent connections, but to satiate her desires—all of her desires—without recriminations?

Opening her eyes, she stared at the ruined stones, stones weathered away by thousands of years, stones watching her, measuring her. *This was silly.* Had Eliza's plea on Amara's behalf even reached Cat, two hundred years in the future? If it had, could Cat truly make this work? Eliza had had a specific person on whom to focus: Deveric. Amara didn't have that advantage, had no way of knowing on whom she was supposed to concentrate.

Was it not likely, therefore, that nothing would happen, even if she *did* follow Eliza's instructions? What did she have to lose, then?

"You have to put your whole heart into it, though, or I don't think it'll work," Eliza had cautioned.

That wasn't hard to do when Amara's mind said the success of this scheme was an impossibility. Why *not* give the whole of her heart in the wishing? In all probability, she'd open her eyes and be sitting right here on this absurdly warm stone, wishing and praying life was different, fuller, better, just as she'd been doing for the last six years.

But what if it *did* work? She'd acquire freedoms she could only imagine, freedoms she'd never had. Anticipation and excitement filled her, and she pushed out the doubt. She could do this, could give her whole heart to the idea of something better, wherever it lay.

She clutched the phone to her chest. "I have nothing to

lose." *And potentially everything to gain.*

Closing her eyes one final time, she repeated, over and over, "I wish to be with my one true love; I wish to be with my one true love; I wish to be with my one true love."

CHAPTER 2

Valentine's Day, 2016

*M*atthew Goodson stretched his legs under the table, arching his back to work out the kinks. "Do you need a break?" Ben Cooper, his faculty mentor, set his coffee mug down, his eyebrows rising in casual concern.

"No, I'm good." Matt's back hurt, but that was nothing new. Hours sitting in front of his screen meant his long, lean, 6'3" frame found few comfortable positions. It didn't deter him; whatever it took, whatever was expected, that's what he would do. Including meeting every Sunday evening with Ben here in the Treasure Trove, the bookstore Ben's wife Cat owned.

Matt liked it here. The bookstore had quite the homey feel, especially with a fire crackling in the fireplace. But sometimes the distractions made it hard for him to concentrate, and he wished they could meet elsewhere—maybe the department, or, hell, even his own apartment. Somewhere a wild toddler would be less likely to interrupt.

"Dada! Dada!" shrieked a small voice, as a bundle of energy with a mop of brown curls sped past Matt and leapt at Ben. *Speak of the devil.*

"Washington!" Ben said, his face lighting up as he caught his son.

Matt watched as father and son reconnected after a few hours' absence. It was disconcerting to see respected professor Benjamin Cooper make googly eyes at a child, contorting his face in ludicrous ways to get a laugh out of the boy.

It's not that Matt didn't like children, per se. They were just so … loud. And messy. And demanding. Good for short amounts of time, perhaps, such as when he saw his nephews, but he was always happy to leave and return to his orderly, organized, *quiet* life.

"Hi, Matt," Cat said, as she walked into the room a moment later, a large plastic bag in her hand.

"Hello, Cat."

Opening the bag, she pulled out a box of Chinese take-out and set it on the table near Ben before reaching in for a second container. "I brought your favorite. Cashew chicken."

He smiled broadly as he accepted the container from Mrs. Cooper. He could see why Ben had fallen for her. She was a kind, considerate woman. Matt envied their easy familiarity with each other, the love that shone through their every interaction.

Not that he had time for a relationship, much less marriage. Even if he'd been interested. Which he most definitely was not. Not after Wendy. Plus, he was six months out from applying for a tenured professorship, which would grant him a permanent position—and security—at the University. That was his sole focus, as it had been since high school.

"You sure you don't mind me disrupting your Valentine's Day?" He and Ben met every Sunday like clockwork, but he'd been surprised and secretly pleased when Ben said they could still meet tonight. Guilt tickled his scalp, however, at the loving look Ben threw his wife.

"No, no, it's fine," Cat said, waving him off with a hand. "Ben and I went out last night."

"Good."

Matt had just opened the box of rice when a large thud disrupted the room. "What the?" He leapt out of his seat.

Ben stood, as well, exchanging a look with Cat.

"I'll go investigate," she said.

Ben merely nodded.

Were they insane? Why would Ben want his wife looking into this, instead of him? What if someone had broken in?

"No, wait, I'll go," Matt said.

"Bu—"

He held up a hand to quiet her as he strode toward the left side of the room, the side from which the noise had come. As he neared the Romance section, he could swear he heard scuffling, then a low moan. A low, female-sounding moan.

Rounding the corner, he stopped short at the sight of a young woman sitting on the floor, cradling her head. She wore a long white dress, a maxi dress, his sister Taylor would call it, with some sort of short red jacket over it, and she had a bonnet—a bonnet, of all things—on her head.

He frowned. What was going on? Some sort of cosplay gone bad? His brow furrowed as he studied the woman. A second moan knocked him out of his reverie, and he rushed to her side.

"Are you okay?" He'd figure out why and how she'd gotten here later; for now, he needed to ensure she was all right. His

EMT training never fully left him, though he hadn't gone on runs in years. He crouched down next to her and reached for her hand to pull it away from her head. At his touch, the woman yelped and yanked her hand back. She looked up, affording him his first full view of her face.

My God, she's stunning. A pair of hazel-green eyes peered out of a face that was both delicate and strong at the same time. Her curvaceous lips flattened into a line as her eyes widened. But there was no doubt about it, this was one gorgeous woman.

She shook her head, then glanced wildly about the room, her eyes darting to and fro before settling on him again. The panic in them made him want to reach for her, but at that moment, Cat approached from behind him.

"What's going—" She broke off as Matt stood and moved to the side so she could see the newcomer. Cat's hand flew to her mouth before she dropped it and pasted an unnatural-looking smile on her face. "Amara?" she said, taking a step closer to the woman.

The bonnet wielder's eyes flew open even wider, a feat he wouldn't have thought possible. She gave a nod. "Miss Schreiber?"

Huh. A British accent. He hadn't expected that. Maybe it was part of the role.

Cat nodded enthusiastically, crouching down by the woman. "Yes! It's Mrs. Cooper now, but please call me Cat. I'm so glad you're here. I know you must be—" She broke off and glanced up at Matt. "I know you must be overwhelmed, *Cousin* Amara. We have much to talk about. But first," she gestured toward him, "you must meet Matthew Goodson. *This is he.*"

Something in the way Cat spoke caught Matt's attention. Why had she emphasized his name in such a weird way?

Why wasn't she wigging out that this woman, whom Matt would swear was *not* here before, was sitting on the floor in the middle of the bookstore? The store had been closed for more than an hour. Had this Amara person been in the room the whole time, and he hadn't noticed?

It wasn't entirely implausible. His family teased him that when his face was in a screen, the rest of the world didn't exist. "And your face is *always* in a screen," Taylor claimed. "You're such a geek, Matty. An adorable geek, but a geek nonetheless. Come up for air sometime!"

"Well—" he started to say, wanting to return to Ben and his food. He wasn't needed here; the two women knew each other. Though at least one of them wasn't acting like it. In spite of them being related?

Something was off.

"Hold on." Cat reached down with one hand to take Amara's and help her to a standing position.

Dang. I should have done that. Social niceties weren't always his forte, especially when his mind was focused on something else. Which was often. It was one of the reasons he liked computers. Machines were much more predictable, much easier to understand than people. And they didn't take offense when he committed a *faux pas*. He was so good at missing signs and signals other people caught on to that Taylor called him Captain Obvious, because he so obviously wasn't. More like Captain Oblivious.

"Thank God you've got the Goodson good looks to disguise that," she'd said recently. "Women are always hitting on you, if you'd just pay attention."

In reality, he was well aware of that much, at least. But he wouldn't admit that to his sister. She'd start pressuring him to find someone, and that was pressure he didn't need.

Emotions and relationships only complicated things. As he'd learned when his dad left. When Wendy had left.

The young woman unfolded herself gracefully from the floor and stood. "Th-thank you," she said, nodding toward Cat.

"Mama?" called a voice from across the room.

"Everything okay?" Ben's words followed his son's.

"Yes," Cat called back. "Exactly as planned."

Planned? What? Cat's words made no sense.

"If you'll just give me a minute," she said, as she ducked back around the bookshelf, leaving Matt facing one very befuddled-looking woman. *Amara.* Pretty name, that.

He studied her face. Her skin was smooth, a delicate ivory, paler than that of just about anyone he'd ever seen, though perhaps that was because she'd hit her head. Those eyes, those gorgeous eyes, flashed uncertainly to his as she raised her hand to the back of her bonnet. She winced as her fingers pressed into a spot.

"I should check that." He reached over and pulled off the bonnet, which elicited a gasp from the woman. "Sorry, did that hurt?"

"N-no," she stammered. Her mouth puckered in an adorable little moue. "I'm not accustomed to a gentleman taking such liberties."

Well, that was some absurd way of talking. And liberties? Removing a silly hat? "I have medical training. But if you'd rather me not check …"

She closed her eyes for a second and swallowed. "I beg your pardon. I am merely a bit overset at the moment. You may … you may proceed."

Moving behind her, he ran his fingers carefully over the back of her head, sparking her second intake of breath in

17

as many moments. "Here?" he said, as his fingers found a small lump. Her hair was a rich honey brown and silky to the touch. She'd secured it in a severe bun, though. If his hair were yanked back that tightly on his head, he'd have a headache, too, lump or not.

She jerked slightly as his fingers probed the bump, but instead of moving her head away, she turned around, her own hand coming up to touch the stubble on his cheek. He'd neglected to shave that morning, but then again, he rarely did on weekends. It only mattered when he was teaching.

What was she doing? Maybe she needed to catch her balance. *With her hand on your face?* And why hadn't he dropped his own? It still cradled the back of her head.

They stood there, each with a hand on the other. A strange sizzle surged through him, an energy that sparked both desire and an odd sense of rightness, as if this moment had been meant to happen.

His lip curled at the thought. *What the heck was wrong with him?* That kind of dopey thinking was his sister's arena, not his. But why *did* he have his fingers laced through some stranger's hair while she stroked his cheek with her thumb? Five minutes ago he'd been discussing security algorithms with Ben. Now he was standing less than a foot away from a woman he'd never seen before, and he was battling the urge to kiss her, right then and there. What was happening?

Step off, Goodson.

As he dropped his hand from her head, she took a step closer, sliding her fingers around his neck and standing on her tiptoes to pull him down to her.

What the hell?

Half of him wanted to back away, to take a moment to make sense of the situation. The other half, the half under this gorgeous woman's spell, dipped his head closer, lured like a bear to honey. The tiny smattering of freckles across her cheeks danced before him as his face neared hers. And then, as her soft, pink lips touched his, he closed his eyes and thought about nothing beyond the feeling of her sweet mouth.

When was the last time a woman had kissed him as chastely as this? She didn't open her mouth. There was no meeting of tongues. Yet his pulse quickened and his insides jumped. He lifted his hands and cupped the sides of her head, deepening the kiss as he traced the seam of her lips with his tongue.

She gasped, as if the experience were entirely new to her, then opened her mouth, allowing him entry. He took full advantage, moving his body closer as his lips devoured hers, her taste intoxicatingly pure. He wanted to mold himself against her, wrap himself around her, absorb her very essence.

The little noises emanating from her had him aching for more, but the sound of throat-clearing disrupted him. Matt opened his eyes as he released her lips and reluctantly dropped his hands, though he didn't move back from her. Her fingers flew to her mouth, her eyes as wide and round as a robin's egg as she turned around.

Ben stood there, a smile playing at the corners of his mouth. "Sorry to interrupt," he said, "but your dinner's getting cold."

Matt had never wanted to kick somebody so badly in his life. He'd had to break off that kiss on account of food? On the other hand, why on earth had he been kissing this woman to begin with?

It wasn't as if he was against casual hook-ups—he certainly preferred them to any attempt at a relationship. This was different, though. Every other time he'd kissed someone, they'd at least had a conversation first. But this strange woman had appeared out of nowhere, garbed in peculiar clothing, dealing with a head injury, and the first thing she'd done upon rising was kiss him? *What was going on?*

"I, uh—" He walked in front of Amara, then stopped, looking over his shoulder at her.

"It's okay," Ben said. "I understand. More than you know."

Matt frowned, his gaze moving to his advisor. *More than you know?* What did that mean?

Ben chuckled. "I once kissed a beautiful woman in nearly that very spot."

Cat strolled around the corner, Wash on her hip. The boy happily munched a piece of broccoli. "I take it Cupid worked his magic again."

She pointed to the ceiling, and Matt looked up, noticing for the first time the pink Cupid hanging from a rafter, a *Kiss Me!* sign dangling from its foot. Did that explain it? She'd noticed the cupid, then kissed him?

"Amara." Cat's voice broke in on his musings. "I'm sure your journey has been … exhausting. Would you care for something to eat?"

Matt glanced back at the woman, who was staring at the cupid, looking once again like a frightened rabbit. Where had the seductive siren of a moment ago gone?

And why did he want her back?

CHAPTER 3

*I*t was all Amara could do to keep from clapping her hand over her mouth, half to hold the surprisingly delicious taste of his lips on hers, half to keep herself from casting up her accounts.

She was here. It had worked. She'd done it. She was in 2012, or somewhere near, she assumed.

She glanced around at the bookshelves. This must be the Treasure Trove, Cat's bookstore. She'd seen photos of it on Eliza's phone. That much, at least, was vaguely familiar. Everything else?

Her eyes flew to the ceiling, where disarmingly bright lights shone from numerous glass domes. The books on the shelves were bound in quite colorful covers, and the covers themselves looked paper-thin.

And the clothing people wore. Cat had on form-fitting trousers—trousers, like a man!—of a blue material the likes of which Amara had never seen. Her top was a thin fabric of some sort, with a flag painted on it resembling the American flag Amara'd once seen, only with far more stars and the words *Old Navy* underneath. Had Cat served at sea? Were women allowed even into the military in this century?

Cat's husband wore similar trousers, with a shirt of Scottish-looking plaid that buttoned down its entire front.

Then there was the man she'd kissed. This Mr. Goodson. His trousers were of a similar color to the breeches her brothers wore, though looser. Still, they accentuated his backside rather nicely. She fought to pull her eyes away from his derriere—how shocking to be staring there! Then again, the men in her era donned coats that concealed that particular part of their anatomy. Was it any wonder she wanted to look now?

Nevertheless, she forced her gaze up, then almost wished she hadn't as he turned toward her. He wore a shirt of a similar style to Cat's, though it was plain white in color, and cut close to his body. She couldn't help but admire his arms, shockingly bare and distractingly muscular. The leanness of his torso was evident through the thin material, its attractive shape sending unexpected, unwelcomed desire through her. Desire to touch.

"Good God," she murmured under her breath. It could be worse. She glanced at his thighs. He could be wearing what Eliza had called shorts, displaying naked flesh. *Or maybe that would be better.*

Her mind spun and her knees weakened as the enormity of all that had just happened hit her. Her insides hummed with energy, whether from the time traveling or the kiss she'd shared with a stranger, she wasn't sure. Probably both.

This Mr. Goodson was watching her, unsmiling, though his eyes were warm. Why hadn't he reacted more strongly to her bizarre advances? Likely women often foisted themselves upon him. He was undeniably tempting, and women were far more … expressive in this era. Or so Eliza had promised.

Amara had only kissed him to fulfill Cat's requirements, though. She didn't have intentions of pursuing Mr. Goodson in any serious manner. No, she had enough with which to contend, having miraculously leapt two hundred years into the future.

On the other hand, perhaps a mere physical association? The "fun" to which Eliza had referred?

Amara's cheeks tingled at the scandalous thought, even as she peeked at him again. His dark hair was cropped quite close to his head, with none of the tousled locks her male acquaintances prized. His jaw was squarely cut, reminiscence of her brother, but whereas Deveric's eyes were green, this man's were of a blue so light it was nearly ice. Slight hollows in his cheeks emphasized his cheekbones, and his lips looked as if some master sculptor had carved them.

He was beautiful. There was no other term for it. Her eyes returned to his again and again, as if some hidden force bound them. She touched her hand to her forehead, to the ache there. There *was* a hidden force. Cat's stories. Cat's manuscript.

Taking a quick breath, Amara turned her attention to Cat, whose face wore an open, kindly expression. She knew what Amara had gone through, at least a little.

"My apologies," Amara said, as the silence stretched uncomfortably. "To you, Mr. Goodson. I fear I knocked the sense out of myself just now. Please excuse my untoward actions."

She must move away from this handsome man lest she succumb to the absurd, pressing temptation to kiss him again. Without waiting for a response, she nodded at Mr.

Goodson, whose mouth had fallen open in comical fashion. As she passed him, the scintillating scent of pine tickled her nose.

She loved that smell—it reminded her of home, of the trees surrounding Clarehaven. Did he spend much of his time out of doors? Or was this a perfume? She sniffed the air. It was decidedly clean and fresh, Mr. Goodson's scent and the smell of food the only other odors she noticed.

"Whodat, Mama?" The child looked at her, but quickly ducked his head into his mother's shoulder.

Cat stroked the boy's hair. "That's Cousin Amara."

"Okay."

The expression, one Eliza loved to use, made Amara smile. She and her sisters had even begun to say it on occasion. But, oh, if only it were as simple as the child made it sound. *Okay.* She'd traveled two hundred years and an entire country away from everyone and everything she knew. *Okay.* She was here with only the clothes on her back, a handful of jewelry sewn into her dress per Eliza's recommendation, and one cell phone that wasn't hers. *Okay.*

This was mad. *She* was mad. Should she have done this? What had she been thinking?

Escape. Escape is what she'd been thinking. Escape from the strictures of her society; escape from judging eyes; escape from lack of opportunity for anything other than marriage. Escape is what she'd wanted. And she'd found it.

She raised her chin in the air, summoning confidence. She could do this. There was no need for panic. She'd survived scandal, survived years of knowing glances and whispers. There was no judgment in these people's eyes. Curiosity, yes, especially from Mr. Goodson. But no judgment, no rejection.

Yes, she could do this.

Her stomach rumbled. She hadn't eaten since the previous evening, her nerves having dispelled any thought of food before she'd ventured to the stones. The smells wafting from the other part of the room weren't entirely familiar, but they made her mouth water.

"I thank you for the invitation to partake in your dinner," she said as she reached Cat.

The little boy grinned at her, crumpling up his cheeks in the most adorable manner, a manner reminiscent of Deveric's son Frederick at that age. Would this child soon dissolve into a shrieking banshee, as Freddy had often done? She hoped not. The fits that boy had thrown. Those she didn't miss. Thankfully, Deveric never beat him. But the noise, oh, the noise, had been too much to bear.

Cat led her to a table across from a well-worn green sofa. A fire crackled merrily in the nearby fireplace, giving off familiar warmth, though the entire room was an even, comfortable temperature. *Indoor heat.* What Eliza had missed most.

Amara looked toward a window, but it was dark outside and she couldn't see anything. Back home, it'd been autumn. Was it the same season here? And *when* exactly was she?

As she took a seat at the table, she blurted out, "Might you tell me the year?"

Mr. Goodson stumbled at her words, nearly tripping over his chair. Amara stifled a laugh. Watching him almost land on his backside took the edge off his otherwise perfection.

"It's February 14th, 2016," Cat said, acting as if a request for the year was a normal question. She handed a plate to Amara, who set it down.

"2016?"

Mr. Goodson's brow puckered. "We should take her to the hospital," he said to Cat. "Confusion like this is a sign of

25

a concussion." He turned toward Amara. "How did you hit your head, anyway? How long were you there in the aisle? Why didn't we hear you come in?"

Amara opened and closed her mouth, like a fish gasping in air. At length, she said, "I was examining the books, and I ... tripped on my skirts, hitting my head on a bookcase as I fell." It wasn't far from the truth. She'd appeared here in the same sitting position she'd held on the rock, only with nothing to support her, so when her backside had slammed onto the floor, her head had flown back into a shelf. She avoided the other questions, hoping he wouldn't repeat them.

"Here, Matt." Ben handed the man a shiny, round something, rather like the new tin cans she'd seen in London. His quick glance at Amara told her Ben had distracted Mr. Goodson on purpose. How nice to have immediate allies here.

Mr. Goodson accepted the object, sliding his finger under a lever on the top and pulling. With a pop and a hiss, the lever came off, taking a piece of the metal from the can with it. He lifted the can to his mouth and drank. Amara couldn't tear her eyes away from his Adam's apple bobbing up and down in quick succession. She had no idea what he was drinking—had never seen someone drink in that way—but it was disconcertingly alluring.

He set the can down, his gaze meeting hers. She moved her eyes away, embarrassed to have been caught staring.

"Would you like one?" he asked.

"One what?"

"A soda."

"Er ..."

"Perhaps tea might be more to your liking?" Cat interjected.

Amara nodded gratefully as Cat walked to a side counter on which sat cups, bottles, and some sort of machine. She took a mug and set it under a smaller machine, one Amara hadn't noticed at first. Pulling a tiny cup from a drawer, Cat removed its lid and placed it inside the machine, then pushed a button. Amara sucked in a breath when, in a matter of seconds, a stream of black tea flowed from the machine into the cup.

"Might you have a spot of milk to add?"

Cat nodded in response to Amara's question, reaching down to pull a white jug from a black box.

A sound from her side drew Amara's eyes away from the tea. She turned her head and nearly leapt out of her skin. Mr. Goodson's ice blue eyes pierced hers, his face mere inches away. "Why'd you do that?" His voice was a low whisper.

"I-I beg your pardon?"

"You know what." He blew air out of his cheeks, his brow crinkling. "Why'd you kiss me?"

"Er ..." What could she say? *I had to so the magic would hold?*

"Pretty sure she was just overcome by your extraordinary good looks," Ben said from her other side, obviously having overheard Mr. Goodson's words. "The whole department knows half your female students are in love with you. Even some of the male ones."

"Ben!" Cat elbowed her husband gently before setting the cup of tea down in front of Amara. The familiar scent of the brew tickled Amara's nose as she picked it up for a sip.

"I'd blame Cupid and let it go," Cat said, gesturing toward the paper cherub. "Unless, of course, you want her to do it again, Matt."

The cup clattered back onto its saucer, liquid sloshing over its sides. "I beg pardon," Amara exclaimed, though whether referring to the spill or Cat's provoking suggestion, she wasn't sure. Her eyes shot to Mr. Goodson, whose lips curled into a half-grin.

"It was a nice change of pace from my typical Sunday night, I'll admit," he said. "No offense to you or Cat, of course." He nodded at Ben, who burst into robust laughter.

Amara took a quick sip of tea, scalding her tongue. "I do apologize for disturbing your person." What was the proper etiquette to atone for mauling a stranger? What was the proper etiquette for anything here? Her tongue hurt and her head pounded. What had she got herself into?

He nodded briskly. "No big deal." Sliding his chair away from her, he picked up his fork and took a large bite from his plate.

A strange sense of disappointment flooded through Amara. She didn't want complications, yet it bothered her how quickly he'd turned his attention away. Did a kiss such as that mean nothing?

Cat scooped a portion of food out of a container onto Amara's plate, then added rice. Picking up her fork, Amara poked at it.

Cat sat down next to her. "Beef with broccoli. Wash loves it." Sure enough, the little boy grabbed another piece of broccoli off his mother's plate and shoved it into his mouth.

The dinner certainly smelled appetizing. Amara gathered a small amount of rice onto her fork and added a piece of beef, as the others had done, before taking a hesitant bite. Heavens above, it was good, the sauce like nothing she'd tasted before. "It is delicious," she said after finishing the bite. "Is this an American delicacy?"

The noises from her left stopped, and she looked over to see Mr. Goodson watching her again, a half-scowl on his face. "You're kidding, right?"

Before Amara could say anything, Cat interrupted. "Amara had a different upbringing than most. Her parents … home-schooled her in a rural part of England, so she hasn't had much exposure to certain things. Especially modern technology."

Ben chuckled. "A little like you, my adorable Luddite," he murmured in an affectionate voice.

"Luddite?" The word burst forth from Amara before she could stop it. Why was Ben referencing a rebellion from her era? Why would an American be a Luddite?

Her head pounded again. Despite her long conversations with Eliza and the pictures she'd seen on Eliza's phone, she was largely ignorant of two hundred years' worth of history—or the future, from her perspective. Her throat constricted. She was ill prepared for this.

"Someone who doesn't readily accept new ways of doing things, new technologies," Mr. Goodson said almost absent-mindedly, as if the definition sprang from him without him paying any attention.

His words made sense, considering the protests over the mechanization of the cotton mills in her time. She studied the strange tea maker on the counter, as well as the bigger machine next to it, full of myriad buttons and levers. Were there machines now for everything?

"You could help her with understanding the tech, Matthew," Cat said, her eyes hopeful. "Amara could really use someone like you."

CHAPTER 4

*M*att gulped down the bite he'd been chewing. Not that he was always clued into undertones, but he could swear Cat was speaking at two different levels of discourse. Had she *meant* that last sentence the way he'd taken it? Because it'd sounded as if Cat weren't merely referring to computer help.

"Uh," he said, fidgeting with his napkin. "Sure, if she needs help." *Wait, what?* Why was he volunteering time he didn't have?

"Pretty much everything is new to you, right, Amara?"

Was that a wink Cat threw at her cousin?

Cat addressed Matt again. "The … area in which she lived was quite remote. No cell service or internet."

Matt's brow quirked up in disbelief. "What? Seriously? There are still places in the world—in *Britain*—where one can't get those?"

Amara pinched her lips before looking down at her plate.

Great. Had she taken offense? He wasn't trying to bash the

UK, but he couldn't imagine living without his phone, much less Internet.

Ben made a great show of feeding Wash a piece of beef, and he started babbling at his son in that high-pitched voice that grated on Matt's nerves, though his brothers did it with their kids, too.

Amara still stared at her plate, not eating, her forehead wrinkled in … in what, consternation? Damn. He'd better smooth things over, though he wasn't quite sure what he'd done. Maybe her head was bothering her?

"You okay?" His fingers settled on hers. She looked at his hand resting on her skin before meeting his eyes, her own round and huge. As he stared into those hazel-green circles, it hit him again: that physical zing, that pulse of connection.

What the hell? Imagining a literal charge between them? That was as corny as anything he'd ever read in a book or seen in a movie. It reminded him of a line from that Walt Whitman poem: *Little you know the subtle electric fire that for your sake is playing within me.*

Heat shot through him from head to toe and all the parts in between. That merely from touching a woman's hand?

Had she felt it, too?

Amara pulled her fingers away, clasping them with her other hand. "Indeed, thank you for your concern." Her shoulders tensed, but her voice was soft, sweet.

For reasons beyond his comprehension, he wanted nothing more than to take hold of her hand again. To kiss her. Cradle her. Matt grimaced. Physical desire he could handle, but the unexpected emotion, the unwelcome longing overwhelming him was too much to process.

He stood abruptly. "I must be going."

"Oh, no, Matt, please stay." Cat's eyes flashed to her

husband's, the wrinkle between her brows suggesting more concern than his departure should merit. Why did she want him to stay? He normally spent an hour tops here on Sundays, and rarely joined them for meals. It was closing in on two hours. He needed to go home, or at least back to the office, to get more done—and clear his head from this bizarre reaction to the gorgeous woman at the table.

"No, you have company, and I have work obligations."

Ben's mouth tipped down for an instant before he rose to his feet, nodding in Matt's direction. "I'm sure we'll see you again soon. Don't work too hard."

The last words came out in a wry tone. If anyone knew how driven Matt was, it was Ben. "You need a life, even in the middle of trying for tenure," he'd said just last week.

"Did you have one?"

"Well, no." Ben's self-effacing chuckle had wrought a similar one out of Matt. "And in fact, I tell Cat I'm glad I didn't, or I might have met someone before her."

"I'm sure she appreciates that."

"And I'm sure it's a lie. Few women looked at me twice before her. But it's all good now; I don't need anyone else." His eyes had grown soft, as they always did, when he spoke of his wife.

It set off heart pangs in Matt he refused to acknowledge. He needed no unnecessary distractions at this stage of his life. No more unnecessary hurt.

"But I speak with the wisdom of the elders," Ben had gone on. "Do as I say, not as I did."

"Right. I don't see you complaining from your big professor's chair."

Matt liked that he had such an easygoing rapport with Ben—when they saw each other, at least, which was mostly on these Sunday night meetings. Occasionally their paths crossed in the CS department in Rice Hall, but if he were honest, those interactions were strictly business and for the least amount of time Matt could manage. Not because he didn't like Ben, but he had things to do.

Gathering up his laptop, he stowed it carefully in his leather messenger bag. "It was a pleasure meeting you, Amara," he said. "An unexpected interaction, but pleasant, to be sure."

Damn it. Why was he alluding to that kiss again? Did he need to make everyone as uncomfortable as possible? On the other hand, the woman had leapt on him mere minutes after they'd met. That deserved some sort of acknowledgment, didn't it?

He slung the bag over his shoulder. "Are you here for long?" He didn't know why he'd asked that question, only that now that he'd announced he was leaving, something in him didn't want to.

Cat reached over and rubbed Amara's hand. Amara herself said nothing—*seriously, did the woman ever speak?*—but Cat gave him a smile. "She's relocated here because she … lost her family."

Oh, God. He couldn't imagine losing his mom, his siblings. Even Nathan, despite the Wendy issue. They were the only things tethering him to human interaction sometimes.

He fought the sudden urge to touch her, to smooth away the tiny frown of her mouth, the sadness in her eyes. Instead, he straightened his back, his hand gripping the strap of his bag, lest he give in to this strange impulse and scoop her up in his arms. "I am very sorry to hear that."

She nodded, a crisp, quick nick of the head.

"Perhaps our paths will cross again soon." *Lame.* He needed to stop talking and just go.

"We'd like that." Ben said, shaking Matt's hand. "You know you're welcome anytime."

Matt grinned, but his eyes were on Amara. When she finally looked up, he tossed her a wink, trying to set her at ease. "Thanks for shaking up my normal Sunday routine."

Cat snickered. "More than you know," she muttered in a voice so low he barely heard it.

Sometimes it was easier to walk away than to figure out the subtext in conversations like this. With that in mind, he turned and strolled out.

But his thoughts lingered on the honey-haired woman he'd left behind.

What did Cat mean?

CHAPTER 5

As the door closed behind Mr. Goodson, Amara let out a huge gush of air, a deep breath she hadn't realized she'd been holding. "This is real, isn't it? I'm truly here. In 2016."

Cat's eyes sparkled with excitement. "Yup. It's true. I can't wait to hear everything. I want to know about Eliza, anything you can share."

Ben reached over and rubbed his wife's shoulder. "Give her time to adjust, sweetie."

Cat ducked her head, a sheepish smile crossing her face as she tucked a piece of hair behind her ear. "He's right, I'm sorry. I just … I thought I'd never know a thing of my friend again. I have her letters, thank God, but letters can't capture all of life."

Nor could a picture. Eliza had shown Amara the photographs on the cell phone, yet they didn't compare to being here—and she'd only seen one place so far.

A low humming noise reverberated from somewhere outside.

"Matt's truck," Cat offered.

Two bright lights shone briefly through the window before moving off. Amara swallowed. Deveric had told her about such lights—headlights, he'd called them. So much to accustom herself to. Her head pounded, and not just because she'd hit it on a shelf.

"The good news is, you're well set here. Eliza, that smart little thing, set up an account for you, one that's held funds and grown interest ever since you left," Cat said as she fed Wash another piece of meat.

Relief spread through Amara. "It worked, then? She told me she'd arrange something with our family's solicitor, to be kept private, but I wasn't sure her plan would succeed, given the two-hundred-year time difference. It's why I sewed jewelry into this dress. For backup, as she termed it." The corner of her mouth tipped up. How she'd loved Eliza's peculiar ways of speaking.

"Yup. A few months after the trunk containing Eliza's letters arrived, a second package showed up. In it were legal papers made out in your name—a birth certificate, bank records, educational transcripts, even a pre-approved passport application. All we need to do for the last one is email a photo of you to the solicitor. I don't want to know how she did it, considering it's illegal, but my bestie had your back. You're a fully documented, extremely wealthy ex-pat!"

Amara wasn't sure what a number of Cat's words meant, but it didn't matter. Eliza had managed it. She'd provided her with true independence. Tears welled up in her eyes. It'd been so hard, so very hard to say good-bye to Eliza, to Deveric, to her family. They'd loved her, and she'd walked away.

Because familial love hadn't been enough anymore. She'd been lonely. Isolated. The spinster sister of a duke, forever scarred by one foolish mistake. Desperate for something more. Something better.

And removing herself would enable her sisters to make good matches, once the presence of their scandalous sister no longer dimmed their prospects.

Had they made good matches? She'd left them merely that morning, and yet here, now, their lives were more than a century gone. She'd have to ask Cat. But not now, not when she was drowning in change, in newness.

She sighed.

Cat reached over and touched her hand. "We'll help as much as we can. I promise. Ben's right; how absolutely overwhelming this must be for you. I can't fathom it, and I had my own weird stuff to come to terms with."

The tears pricking Amara's eyes spilled over. As they coursed down her cheeks, her shoulders shook in silent sobs.

"Why Cousin 'Mara sad, Mama?" Wash had stopped chewing his meat and his little eyes peeked at her with such concern it only made her weep more.

After a moment, she sucked in air. "I am sorry. I … it …"

"No need to apologize," Ben said. "No need at all. Believe me, I didn't react well when Cat told me about her love-creating powers, and that was within the same century."

"I don't create love," Cat gently corrected. "I create the initial spark. The couple decides the outcome. That's what happened with Eliza and your brother, right?"

Amara nodded, a smile spreading across her face in spite of herself. "Yes. And I thank you for that. Deveric was quite miserable until Eliza appeared. She was the sun to his rain, though it took him time to accept it." She poked at the rice on her plate. "But what if I decide I don't *want* Mr. Goodson?"

Her face flushed as if in midsummer's heat at the lie. She

did want him, only without attachment. But that was hardly something she would have admitted to her own sisters, much less to new acquaintances. Especially when one was a man. "Will I return to my time?"

Cat set her chin on her hand, considering. "I don't think so. I mean, I wrote myself several suitors but ultimately decided they weren't for me. I chose Ben, instead. But those men are still around. Grayson and Jill were here for dinner just a couple of days ago, in fact."

"Still around? Did you call them forth from other times, as well?"

"Uh, no."

"Then where—" Amara stopped as a particularly bad jab of pain stabbed her head. She reached back to the lump, a groan escaping.

"Goodness, do you think we *should* take her to the doctor?" Cat's gray eyes locked on her husband's.

"Modern medicine might be a bit much to absorb on her first night," Ben said, his voice calm. He walked over to Amara. "May I?"

She nodded.

Carefully, he removed the hairpins from her hair, and it fell around her shoulders and down her back. She tensed. It was an incredibly intimate act, a man letting down her hair, and yet neither Ben nor Cat acted as if anything untoward was happening. With the pressure of the pins off, though, she already felt better. His fingers located the bump. It hurt when he touched it, but not so much as she expected.

"I think an ice pack will do. Her pupils aren't dilated, and she's speaking coherently. For a time traveler, at least."

Cat's mouth quirked up at her husband's teasing words.

As Ben sat back down, Cat leaned over and rubbed

Amara's fingers again. *Did everyone touch so freely in this era?* "Tell you what," she said. "Wash needs to go to bed. How about I take you upstairs with us? I'll show you the room in which you'll be staying."

Amara nodded. Kindness. These people were kind. How much she appreciated that. Given Cat's position as a shop owner, she and Amara would not have associated with each other in Amara's era. More was the pity. Eliza was right; people whose character was of the highest caliber should be the most esteemed, not those whose position had been bequeathed on them through a happy accident of birth.

She rose, smoothing down her skirt.

Cat stood as well, lifting Wash into her arms. With one hand, she gestured toward Amara's dress. "I still have a few of Eliza's things, but they're not likely to fit you. Neither will mine. You're taller than Eliza, and curvier than I am."

Amara self-consciously glanced down at her bosom. Definitely larger than Cat's. And while Eliza had borrowed several of Amara's gowns when she'd first arrived, it was true the American was a number of inches shorter. Amara had no doubt anything of Eliza's would reveal much of her ankles.

Her cheeks burned at the thought of donning breeches or trousers like a man. She'd worn her share of low-cut gowns over the years, but was she ready for such exposure of all parts of her body?

"We have to go shopping!" Cat exclaimed. "Though I'm not sure what women your age wear these days." She shrugged. "I'm mostly a jeans and T-shirt type, myself."

Amara followed Cat to the stairwell behind the register.

"You're twenty-seven, right?" Cat asked.

"Twenty-eight now. Quite the spinster." Amara gave a self-deprecating snort.

"Honey, in this era, there are no spinsters. You marry because you want to. Or you don't. No judgment."

Amara grinned, the first fully felt smile of the evening. A bit of her spirit flowed back. She didn't have to marry, unless she chose of her own accord. As she ascended the stairs behind Cat, one thought echoed in her brain.

I believe I shall like it here.

CHAPTER 6

*M*att hummed along to the radio as he drove. He didn't live far from the Coopers—just on the south side of campus, off of Jefferson Park Avenue (or JPA, as every Charlottesvillian called it)—but far enough that he didn't usually walk. Besides, his truck needed exercise every once in a while, right? The advantage to living close to his office was he didn't need to drive to work. The disadvantage was it gave him fewer opportunities to use his pickup, and he loved the thing.

Perhaps it was an unusual vehicle choice for a computer science professor—he should probably have something more practical, like a Toyota or a Subaru, or at least sporty, like a BMW or Porsche. Not that he could afford the latter, but some day. Some day.

In the meantime, his trusty pickup never let him down, even if his colleagues joked they expected to see him in cowboy boots and a ten-gallon hat.

He didn't know why he'd wanted a truck, to be honest. He wasn't a country boy—growing up in Gaithersburg,

Maryland, definitely precluded that. He just liked the way it made him feel. Strong. Powerful. Manly. The opposite of the computer geek stereotype. *Good God, I sound like a TV ad.* He patted the dashboard. Bessie was his rock; she'd never let him down. Never abandoned him. She was the only woman he needed.

Amara's bewitching eyes danced before him. God, what a strange evening. Not that he was averse to kissing beautiful women, but what the hell had happened back there? And that strange electricity which had crackled between them?

She was sexy, that was for sure. Oddly so, given her garb. When had he ever thought a woman in a bonnet sexy?

Maybe she'd be up for a fling. A relationship didn't interest him. He couldn't risk it again. Not with how badly things had gone with Wendy.

It still hurt every time he had to see her with his brother at family events. That was why he rarely attended. Sure, it'd been ten years. Sure, Wendy and Nathan were much better suited to each other than she and he had ever been. Still, she'd left him for his brother, claiming he hadn't paid her enough attention, that she couldn't compete with his fixation on computers.

He frowned. He'd thrown himself into his studies, into his work, *more* after that. Not less. He'd ignored the painful truth in her words by burying himself in screens and research and teaching, avoiding relationships all together. He didn't need one. He had his career, his tenure quest, and his determination to make a splash in cyber security. And he had Ada Lovelace, his cat.

"A man with a pickup needs a dog, dude," his brother, Daniel, often ribbed him. But dogs required time and energy, and he didn't have enough of either to give. Not to a canine, not to a female.

42

So why did his thoughts keep flitting back to Amara? He didn't even know her last name, for Pete's sake. He didn't know a thing about her, beyond that she was his mentor's wife's cousin. Which should automatically render her off-limits. Despite the fact she was wickedly attractive. And a damn fine kisser.

He ran his hands along his thighs at the stoplight, wanting to smooth out the tension pulsing everywhere. For Pete's sake, it wasn't like he'd gone months without any action. This physical drive for a woman he'd just met was ridiculous. But there it was.

When the light turned green, he floored the truck, roaring through the intersection, determined to put more distance between himself and the strange events of the evening. An hour's more work, maybe a break for an episode of *Big Bang Theory*, a good night's sleep, and tomorrow he'd begin afresh, with all thoughts of the all-too-strange, all-too-tempting Amara What's-Her-Name firmly behind him.

Or he could call Julie. She'd made it clear she was up for another night if he wished. That was the kind of connection he liked: no strings attached, no messy involvement of feelings. No chance of potential hurt, either inflicting or suffering. It'd be easier to avoid the opposite sex altogether, but he appreciated an attractive woman and had drives, like any man. Though he shoved his sex drive on the back burner when working. And he was always working. It's what he loved to do. So what if Taylor claimed he worked so much to avoid dealing with real life? Work *was* his life.

He pulled into a space in his apartment building's lot and shut off the engine, sitting for a moment in the dark. Why hadn't Ben said they had company? They could've postponed the meeting. And what was up with this Amara? She'd acted so peculiarly, like she didn't know the Coopers, despite Cat's assertion they were cousins. Because of her head injury?

He shrugged, reaching for his phone, which had dinged while he was driving. Who was he to judge the Coopers? Matt liked Ben, but the Coopers were in a different life stage—nearly a decade older, with a young child. Ben and he were colleagues, friendly acquaintances, but not true friends.

Not that Matt had any friends besides her, Taylor often kidded. She was wrong; he lunched occasionally with Ben, or with Dave, whose office was next to his, and on rare occasion he and several other profs played pool or grabbed a beer. That was enough, wasn't it?

He glanced at the screen. Taylor had texted:

Hot date. Tell ya later. Wish me luck.

He grinned. His sister was younger by only a year, and they'd always been close. He was glad she was getting her spunk back; her divorce had finally been finalized a month ago, but she'd been down since her marriage fell apart. Further evidence matrimony didn't agree with the Goodson family.

In truth, Taylor's ex, Trevor, hadn't been a bad guy. He just didn't have any drive, spending his days playing video games and drinking beer while his wife brought home the bacon. When he'd started smoking pot, Taylor left him. Matt hadn't blamed her, had cheered her on, in fact. Their wastrel of a dad had been enough; neither one of them were willing to relive that again.

"Luck," he texted back. "Don't do anything I wouldn't."

Sticking the phone in his pocket, he climbed the stairs to his second-floor apartment. As he opened the door, a loud meow greeted him. "Hey, Lovey," he crooned, bending to pet the calico's head. "Miss me?"

After kicking off his shoes, he picked up Lovey, rubbing her chin as he walked into the kitchen. Flipping on the light, he pulled a can of food out of the cupboard, then put the feline down so he could spoon her food into a bowl. Setting it down, he surveyed the room. He liked the apartment's open layout; the main room was one big living room/dining room/kitchen combo, with only a counter blocking off the kitchen area.

Taylor complained his decorating style was Spartan, at best, but he savored the simplicity, the starkness of bare walls and few possessions.

The black tile of the kitchen floor was cold under his bare feet, so he wandered to the other part of the room and sat down at a large desk with double monitors on it. He started up his favorite playlist before settling in for a night of work in this nice, quiet space, with no fussing toddlers. And no oddly adorable bonneted women kissing him unexpectedly.

Amara rolled over in the narrow bed, blinking wearily at the sound of wailing from the next room. Sunlight peeked in around the edges of the window covering. It was morning.

"Shh," a voice urged. "Cousin Amara is sleeping, Wash."

The child continued to cry, and Amara yanked the blanket over her ears. At least at Clarehaven, the nursery had been far removed from her bedchamber. In fact, Clarehaven, her family's estate, was so large, she'd simply moved to another part of the house if something—children, siblings, her mother—disrupted her.

This home was tiny, in comparison. Clarehaven must have overwhelmed Eliza, if this was the space in which she'd lived before. Cat had promised a full tour today, but Amara doubted there was much more to see than what she'd taken in last night. The apartment had three bedrooms, though the one Amara was in was quite small.

"More a closet than a bedroom. I've mostly stored stuff in it," Cat had said with an apologetic smile. "It used to be my sister Marie's—I understand why she was anxious to get the heck out of here after high school."

There was also a living room with a sofa, a table, and other less familiar furnishings. Amara had got a glimpse into the kitchen, though it looked foreign to any kitchen she'd ever seen, and much smaller.

Discomfort in her lower region made Amara aware of pressing needs. She sat up, looking around the room. *Ah, yes. No chamber pots.* Eliza had wrinkled her nose at said pots, describing modern plumbing and something called a toilet with such a look of wistful longing on her face, Amara couldn't help but laugh.

She wasn't laughing now—she had to make use of this bathroom, as Eliza'd termed it. Cat had pointed it out last night, but Amara hadn't investigated, wanting merely to sleep. Rising carefully, she slipped her feet into her shoes and walked to the door. She'd fallen asleep in her gown, not wanting to ask for help in unlacing it. She'd been exhausted, anyway.

As she entered the main room, Wash let out another cry. Cat held him, bouncing him in her arms as she smoothed the hair off of his forehead. When she saw Amara, she grimaced. "I'm sorry if he woke you. He was fine yesterday, but this morning he's burning up. I gave him Tylenol, but he's miserable."

Amara merely nodded. She had no clue what Tylenol was, but then again, she had no clue what much around her was. A large, black rectangle hung on the wall across from the sofa, with rope of some sort hanging down behind it. Artwork? On one of the tables near the sofa sat a rectangular object like the ones downstairs the previous night. It resembled a book with its cover propped up, or a slim box with a hinged back. Suddenly, it made a noise, and she jumped.

"Sorry. That might be Ben; I messaged him earlier." Cat walked over to the rectangle and pushed something. The top half illuminated in a manner reminiscent of Eliza's telephone.

"Com-puter?" Amara gestured toward the machine, testing out the unfamiliar word.

"Uh huh. I guess Eliza told you about them? They are kind of cool, even though I fight with them a lot. Technology and I are not on the best of terms." She hoisted Wash higher on her hip. "I'll show you at some point, though Ben's a better instructor."

"Mama, my thwoat hurts." Wash ducked his head against his mother's shoulder.

"I'm so sorry, baby." She pressed a kiss to his hair. "I think I should take him to the doctor," she said to Amara. "It might be strep."

Amara had no idea what strep was, but if Cat was concerned, it couldn't be good. "The doctor does not come here?"

Cat chuckled. "If only. Sadly, no, she doesn't. House calls are a thing of the past."

A female doctor? It shouldn't surprise her; according to Eliza, women held a large variety of occupations in this period: engineers, lawyers, architects, doctors … even astronomers.

She pinched her arm. She was truly here, in the twenty-first century. Her past was behind her. There was only the future now. Euphoria and terror crashed over her, settling low in her belly and reminding her of why she'd come out of the bedroom in the first place.

"I, um, need to … "

Cat nodded, thankfully understanding to what she was alluding. Amara walked toward a door between her chamber and another room that contained a miniature bed with tall rails about it. It wasn't so different from Frederick's sided cradle, though this one more resembled a cage. A cage for a child. *Intriguing. And perhaps wise.*

Cat called after her. "Did Eliza explain modern toilets? And flushing? Toilet paper?"

Amara's ears burned. She was not comfortable discussing such private matters. Before she could answer, Cat crossed in front of her and opened the door, walking in ahead of Amara.

"Here's the toilet," she said, gesturing to a peculiar-looking white chair. "You sit on this part, and when you're done, you use the paper here to wipe. Oh, and you put the paper right in the toilet. Push this handle to flush." She pointed to a silver bar on the top of the white apparatus before turning to the side. "Here's the sink to wash your hands—pull the faucet handle up and to the left for hot water, or to the right for cold. There's hand soap right there; just push down on the handle and it'll come out."

Cat's gaze darted back and forth, as if to ascertain whether or not she'd missed anything. "If you'd like to take a shower, I can explain that, too. But I'll duck out now to let you have some privacy."

Amara nodded. "Thank you." Her head swam, but she'd decided last night she was going to do her best to accept everything as it came by pretending she was dreaming. Fantastical dreams weren't so unusual, right? Because otherwise she might collapse under the weight of all the newness—and she wasn't the type to collapse. If being caught naked in a garden didn't destroy her, no modern toilet would do so.

A few minutes later, as she held her hands under the miraculously warm water flowing into the sink, she decided interior plumbing was something she could certainly get used to. Hot water whenever you wished? And whoever invented toilet paper with such softness was brilliant.

What other delightful surprises awaited? Amara peeked behind the curtain to which Cat had gestured when mentioning the shower. A white tub, somewhat similar to the tubs in which she'd bathed at Clarehaven, sat on the floor, but was affixed directly to the wall. It had a similar knob to the one Amara had used at the sink. She turned on the water, enjoying the heat as the liquid warmed beneath her fingertips.

A knob on top of the faucet from which the water flowed drew her attention, so she pulled it, curious. Suddenly, water shot down on her head, inundating her hair and shoulders.

"Eek!" she shrieked, jumping back. She stood there, hair dripping into her face, feeling like a fool. Surely she should have expected that, should have noticed the fixture projecting from the wall above. Eliza had described the shower mechanism with longing, after all. Amara had agreed it sounded heavenly—she'd just wanted her first one to be without clothes on. Leaning back in, she quickly turned off the water.

Cat knocked on the door. "You okay?"

"Yes, yes. All is good."

"Sounds like you figured out the shower. If you need a towel, they're in the closet behind the door."

Amara opened the closet and discovered soft cloths of varying sizes stored within. She took out one of the larger ones, then eyed the shower. Should she try it? She'd only bathed in a tub, or occasionally in the pond at Clarehaven.

Well, if she was to be a twenty-first century woman, better start now. According to Eliza, most people bathed daily. Amara herself had been a frequent bather, preferring cleanliness to dirt, but full immersion in a tub had certainly not been an everyday occurrence—especially in the winter, when the rooms always held a bitter chill.

With excitement, she set the cloth on the counter, preparing to enter the falling water. *Blast.* She'd forgotten she couldn't undress herself—her gown laced up the back. Getting used to no servants was going to be more difficult than she'd thought, though she understood why servants were not as necessary with conveniences like showers and toilets.

"Cat?" Using the woman's first name on so short an acquaintance felt more intimate than was comfortable, but it was custom, and she must resign herself to it. She opened the door a few inches. "I require assistance with my gown."

"No problem. Give me a sec." Cat walked into the bedroom with the barred bed. When she walked back out, Wash was no longer on her hip, though his whimpering was audible. "Hopefully he'll be patient in there a moment."

As she fumbled with the laces at Amara's back, the child let out a large wail. Cat sighed as she worked Amara free of her gown and stays.

I am not embarrassed that a stranger is undressing me. I am not embarrassed. Her maid had undressed her every day. It was nothing of which to be ashamed.

"I'm so sorry, he's not usually fussy like this. He must really be feeling bad."

"I understand. I do hope the child returns to better health soon."

Cat nodded before racing back to her son.

Amara shut the bathroom door. Shedding her dress and undergarments, she studied herself in the mirror over the sink. They'd had mirrors at Clarehaven, of course—many of them, including a large one in her bedchamber. But with so many servants about, she'd never stood naked in front of one.

It was a luxury to examine her own skin. With a frown, she noted the wrinkles forming at the corners of her eyes. Minor, yes, but they hadn't been there a few short years ago; another reminder life was passing her by, changing her, aging her. She was no longer in the flower of youth. She rubbed her hand over her stomach. Was she still remotely desirable?

Mr. Goodson's face floated before her, those blue eyes rousing dangerous flutters in areas slightly south of her hand. What would he think of her naked? What would *he* look like naked?

Red fanned out over her skin. Why on earth was she thinking such things? Surely it was only because she'd kissed him that he was anywhere in her thoughts. It'd been eons since she'd had a good kiss. Her flirtation with Lord Hodgins didn't count—they hadn't got more than one or two light pecks in before her brother had interrupted them. The only man she'd ever truly passionately kissed was Drake Evers. Until last night, at least. Mr. Goodson had wasted no time in becoming familiar, sliding his tongue into her mouth. She'd liked it. She'd liked it a lot.

Her skin tingling, she turned away from the mirror and fidgeted with the knobs in the tub, remembering to pull up the smaller one only when the water was warm and she was ready.

"There's shampoo on the edge of the tub," Cat called loudly through the door. Amara flinched, not used to a relative stranger so close while she was bathing. The door was closed, however, and she had no doubt Cat would respect her privacy.

She stood for an untold number of minutes under the shower, letting the hot water beat down on her back. Heaven. This was heaven. She never wanted to leave. Could one spend one's life in the shower?

Eventually, she tipped her head back, letting the water cascade over her hair, marveling at the soothing touch of its heat. Reaching down, she picked up the bottle to which Cat had referred. A picture on the front showed a woman lathering her hair. Amara removed the cap and poured out an unexpectedly large amount of liquid into her hand. How strange. She was accustomed to a soap, or Cook's special paste, to clean the hair. Not something as smooth as this. As she massaged the liquid into her hair, she laughed out loud at the large volume of bubbles this shampoo produced. She rinsed the sweet-smelling stuff from her hair and squeezed out the excess water.

Finally, after what must have been a good half an hour, she reluctantly turned off the water, stepping out carefully onto the soft mat next to the tub. Reaching for the towel, she wrapped herself in it. She looked at her gown. She didn't particularly want to wear it again, but what other option did she have?

She'd do what she could. Pulling the stays and dress back on, she opened the door. Cat could help with the lacings.

"I'm so sorry," Cat called, her face pinched as she looped a reticule of some sort over her shoulder while clutching Wash, whose eyes looked red and his skin, pale. "I need to take him in right now. His fever has risen. Will you be okay here?"

Amara stopped in her tracks. Alone? Cat would leave

her alone? But the poor child needed care. She nodded. "Of course."

"Thanks. Feel free to look in the fridge for something to eat. Wait for me before you try the stove or microwave, though. I'll be back as soon as I can." With that, Cat raced out a side door different than the one they'd come through last night, shutting it behind her.

Amara walked over and peered through the window. Cat scrambled down a flight of stairs before securing her son in the back of a car. Amara had seen one on Eliza's phone and knew what it was called. She jumped, however, as Cat leapt into the front seat and then roared backward in the beast. Eliza had described these "horseless carriages" in great detail, but it was bizarre to see one in action.

The car edged into a smooth, nearly black street before moving forward. Amara remained at the window, frozen for some time as other vehicles streaked by. *Such speed.* Deveric would have loved it.

People strolled on the lighter gray path near the road. Though it was clearly cold, given the coats people wore and the fact that their breath frosted the air, few wore hats. All of the women were garbed in trousers, some of which looked painted on, so tight was the fabric.

Her mother would be scandalized. Even Amara's throat clenched and a knot of anxiety fed through her at the differences in apparel. Who knew clothing mattered so?

It mattered now. With her stays and dress loose, she couldn't leave the living quarters. Not that she'd planned on doing so. One small thing at a time was enough at the moment.

She retreated to the kitchen, her rumbling stomach reminding her it'd been hours since she'd last eaten. A large, white rectangle with handles dominated one corner of the room, a noticeable hum emanating from it. Amara pulled on the handle, and it opened to reveal numerous foodstuffs, all cold to the touch.

Most of Clarehaven's food had been kept in the pantry or cellar. They'd had ice much of the year in the icehouse, naturally, but to have coldness available directly in one's home, year round? Brilliant.

Amara inspected several items before selecting one labeled *strawberry yogurt*. That sounded good; she loved strawberries. Now, how did one eat it?

Opening various drawers, she studied their contents. A few of the implements were familiar, others were not. What did the green-handled object that turned do? Or this flat, round blade on a handle, sharp all the way round? Finally, she found a drawer with recognizable items—spoons, forks, rather dull-looking knives.

Pulling the thin metal coating off the top of the yogurt container, itself made of an unknown shiny but malleable material, she dipped in a spoon and took a mouthful. She nearly spat it out at the unexpected, extreme sweetness, but let the taste settle on her tongue. It wasn't bad, reminiscent of pie, but with a decided tang. She took additional tastes of the creamy substance as she investigated the kitchen.

"What *are* all of these things?" she asked out loud. One large boxy item held visibly soiled dishes. Why did they store such things and not wash them? Not that Amara had ever washed dishes. Perhaps it was easier to save them for one big scrubbing session.

Selecting an apple from a bowl, she ventured back into the living room and, curious, moved a narrow knob on the wall, jumping when a light overhead illuminated as a result. Instant lighting? Anytime one wished it? *Capital!*

Cat's computer rested on a little table near the sofa. Amara was tempted to push the screen to see if it worked similarly to Eliza's telephone but didn't want to risk damaging the item. Instead, she sat down on the sofa with her yogurt, exhaling loudly as she sank into the cushions. The sofa was soft, far softer than any at Clarehaven. She picked up a long black rectangle covered with buttons. *What did it do?* She pushed a button labeled Power. Suddenly, the large box across from her sprang to life, voices emanating from it as pictures flashed on the screen.

Amara screamed.

Television. This is what Eliza called television. Her eyes widened at the life-like figures moving across the box. Life-like, though cut off—only their upper halves were visible. Then the box switched and she could see all of them. One was saying something about Alex being her long-lost twin sister, and Barrett should have known that and not run off with her and had that secret baby.

What? Spoonfuls of yogurt went into her mouth absent-mindedly as her eyes remained glued to the screen. Here was another handsome young man, with his shirt off. Discomfort danced across the back of Amara's neck at the sight of so much skin, so much muscular skin. Discomfort mixed with something else, something she didn't wish to acknowledge. She squirmed in her seat and crossed her legs. This was acceptable, to be nude in public? On a television?

The man's muscles flexed as he strode around. He was an attractive fellow, with blonde hair and blue eyes, though not as light blue as Mr. Goodson's.

What would Mr. Goodson look like half-clothed? He was likely as solid as this television gentleman, at least from what she'd touched yesterday. She closed her eyes, picturing his face, his lips inches from hers, as she'd reached up and pulled him closer.

She couldn't believe she'd kissed a stranger so brazenly. The tendrils of excitement that had snaked across her skin reappeared. What fun that had been in the midst of this all. Where was Mr. Goodson today? What was he doing?

She pushed the Power button again, grateful when the machine fell silent, and rose, taking a bite of the apple as she moved the yogurt container onto a side table. She didn't want to think of Mr. Goodson at the moment, or of any man, for that matter.

A meow echoed from another room. Feline? Cat had a feline? Inside her home? How had she not heard it the previous evening? She set the apple next to the yogurt, then followed the noise, stopping at the edge of Cat's bedroom. It didn't feel right to enter her personal chamber. A sheaf of papers lying on a stool just inside the open doorway caught her eye, however, because the top paper featured a vividly colored illumination of a woman holding a book. Was this the magical manuscript whose powers had enabled Amara to come here? It didn't look old.

As a large, fluffy, striped cat wove itself in and around her feet, Amara debated. Should she peek at the manuscript? She took a step into Cat's room, guilt riding her as she did so. But she had to see it, had to touch the item that held such power.

Picking it up, she glanced at the script. Latin. She knew a few words but could not read this. Her eyes skimmed over the page, and she wondered at its history. How had Cat ended up with this? And how on earth did it work? Witchcraft?

Goosebumps erupted at the thought. That's what many in her era would say—this was black magic, something of the devil. And yet, could magic that created the kind of love her brother and Eliza shared be bad? Amara didn't think so. That kind of love was a once-in-a-lifetime love. *You could have that. The manuscript enabled it.* But she didn't want it. Did she?

Mr. Goodson's eyes shimmered before her.

Shaking her head to rid herself of his image, she studied the pictures. The illuminations were gloriously rich. She hesitantly ran her finger over one. The page was flat. She could not feel the ink, of the pictures or the words. How bizarre. Was this somehow a reproduction? She carefully turned the pages, nonetheless, not wanting to damage the artifact. The last page was an image Amara had seen on Eliza's phone of a woman with reddish brown hair who bore a striking resemblance to Cat. Peculiar.

A noise beeped behind her, and Amara dropped the manuscript pages, startling the cat, which shot into the child's bedroom. She hoped the boy was all right. When her nephew Frederick had taken so ill, they'd feared for his life. It'd been weeks of fevers, even an occasional delirium.

When the beep came again, Amara sought its source. The computer. A white square containing words had popped up, with the name Ben Cooper written across the top, and below it a message:

> Be home as soon as I can. We might want 2 find somewhere for Amara 2 stay for a day or 2. Easier on her & safer than w/a sick child. Maybe Shannon?

As she stood there, a second message suddenly appeared beneath Ben's words, Cat's name at the head of it:

> Shannon texted: both her kids r sick, too. & Jill is @ that conference. Can u ask Matt? Makes sense in many ways.

Stay with Mr. Goodson? Cat and Ben wished her to leave them and stay with a man? The hair on her arms bristled, and panic flipped her stomach. She forced herself to take a deep breath. In truth, she hardly knew her hosts any better than Mr. Goodson. It shouldn't matter they wanted her elsewhere temporarily. She could do it.

But to be under the same roof as an unrelated, unmarried man? Her sense of propriety warred with temptation. Temptation she didn't want or need.

On the other hand, if the child was to spend much of the next days crying and whining, she would rather avoid that. She was grateful for their consideration.

Was she not?

CHAPTER 7

Matt grimaced as he scrolled through email. More meetings, more committees, more everything he didn't want to do. He let out a sigh before taking a drink from his coffee mug. He hadn't slept well. He didn't want to admit it was because thoughts of Amara had run through his head half the night.

Was he obsessing over her because she was stunningly gorgeous? No. He'd kissed his fair share of beautiful women before, without this kind of reaction. It must be that his mind needed to puzzle the pieces out, to make her fit into some logical box so he could process the previous evening and put her behind him.

Unfortunately, that wasn't happening. The stained glass paperweight his sister had made for him (seriously, who used paperweights anymore?) was the exact same brilliant hazel-green as Amara's eyes, and every time he saw it, he thought of her. He picked up the paperweight and chucked it in a drawer, enjoying the loud thunk it made. If only he could dispose of his bizarre reaction to her so easily.

A knock sounded outside his office door. Ben Cooper stood there, his eyes tired and his forehead wrinkled.

Had something happened? Had Amara worsened? "Everything okay?"

"Yeah, fine—but Washington is sick. Strep."

"Oh. Sorry to hear that." *Crap. Was the kid contagious?* With a paper deadline approaching, getting sick was *not* on Matt's agenda.

"He'll be fine. Miracle of antibiotics and all. But can I ask a favor?"

Matt shifted in his chair. This didn't sound good. Why did he think this had nothing to do with covering Ben's class?

"Could Amara stay with you for a few days? I don't think a crowded apartment with a sick child is the ideal environment for her right now."

Matt's pulse leapt at the request. Amara? In his apartment? For days? An image of surprising her in the shower, running his hands over her slippery body, had him shifting in his seat again, but this time for entirely different reasons.

"Uh … " He didn't want to say yes, even though he had an extra bedroom. It was one thing to invite a woman home for an evening, but someone living underfoot? Around 24/7? He liked his solitude. "Can't she stay somewhere else? Cat has friends, doesn't she?"

Ben rocked on his heels, a wry grin twisting his lips. "Yup. She does. But one is out of town, and the other has sick kids of her own."

"She only has two friends?" Not that Matt was one to talk. "Doesn't your sister live somewhere nearby?"

Ben arched a brow. "Yes, actually. I didn't know you knew that. But Martha's way up north, past the airport. I think Amara would feel better not being quite so far from her … cousin. Plus, *you* she's met, at least. She hasn't met Martha, and I didn't feel comfortable pawning her off on a complete stranger." He held up his hands. "Look, I don't want to inconvenience you. We can figure something out."

Guilt pecked at Matt. *Ugh*. He really didn't want the woman with him. She was too damn tempting, and tempting wasn't what he wanted right now. Then again, with how much Ben had taken him under his wing, Matt owed him. And it was temporary. Very temporary.

"Yeah, okay. If it's just for a couple days."

Ben exhaled. "Thank you. It's a lot to ask, but Cat's got all she can handle right now with the bookstore and a sick kid. Speaking of which, I'm going home to help."

"No problem. I can swing by and get Amara after my class, if you'd like." Why had he volunteered to do that? But it was the appropriate action, right? Taylor would say so. The Coopers needed help. He needed to offer it. "Four-ish?"

"Sounds great. Thanks a million."

As Ben stepped away, Matt blew air out of his cheeks. *What the hell had he just gotten himself into?*

The door flung open and a harried-looking Cat rushed in. "Oh, my gosh, I'm sorry to have left you so long. The doctor's office was backed up, and then the wait at the pharmacy was interminable."

Amara leapt up off the sofa, where she'd been watching the television again, this time immersing herself in a story about a homeless man who was secretly a brain surgeon. This television was amazing. Not quite the same experience as seeing a play in Drury Lane, but then again, here she could watch and react in private, without eyes on her.

"Sorry, I, er … "

Cat chuckled as she saw the television. "Oh, goodness. American soap operas on your first day. That's probably not the best introduction to modern culture."

"Yes, but this gentleman, the dark-haired one with the brown eyes, he is living a double life. I can relate to that."

"You do realize it's fiction, right?"

Amara lifted her nose. "I'm from 1813; I'm not an imbecile. I can see this is a play."

"Sorry." Cat walked farther into the room and dropped her reticule on the sofa, Wash asleep in her arms.

"How does he fare?"

"Well, he has strep throat, as I thought. Luckily, antibiotics will have him feeling much better tomorrow."

"Anti-biotics? Tomorrow?" Wash's symptoms mirrored exactly those with which Frederick often suffered. What if Freddy had had access to these anti-biotics of which Cat spoke? Would he have avoided those weeks and months of ill health?

"Yes, but he'll likely be cranky the next few days, so …"

"You want me to stay with Mr. Goodson."

Cat's eyes widened. "How did you …?"

"I saw the words on the computer."

"I'm so sorry, Amara. I want to help you with this transition, and I will as much as I'm able, but we don't want you getting sick. And you might actually feel more comfortable elsewhere, where you're not stuck putting up with a sick, fussy kid. Just for a few days. Please understand."

"I do. But must it be with Mr. Goodson? Do you not have female relations or friends with whom I might stay?"

"My family's in Ohio. And I've checked with Shannon and Jill. It's a no-go."

"But to reside with a gentleman of no relation, alone, under the same roof …"

Cat's face lit in understanding. "Oh, I see. Well, that's not untoward, or whatever you might say, in this day and age. People do it all the time. And, well, it would give you a chance to spend time with Matt." She tossed Amara a wink.

Was that why Cat had proposed this arrangement? Under the guise of furthering an attachment? Amara narrowed her eyes. At that moment, Wash stirred, a sad whimper shaking his little body. No, the child was truly ill. And even if Cat had matchmaking plans as a secondary intent, that didn't mean she must accede to them. Though the idea of being alone with Mr. Goodson, with no one the wiser to her potential actions, sent devilish thoughts tumbling through her mind. Eliza said such liaisons raised no eyebrows here. She was free to indulge, if she wished. With her body, at least. Her heart would remain her own.

"Hold on a moment," Cat said before Amara could respond. She took the sleeping child into his bedchamber and laid him in the railed bed. Coming back out, she headed into the kitchen. "Wow, what a day. Did you find anything to eat?"

Amara trailed after her. "Yes, some apple and a yogurt, which was quite sweet."

"That's it? We'll have to take you grocery shopping to find foods you might like."

Grocery shopping? Oh, go to the market. Something with which Amara, as a member of a ducal family, had never had to contend. How exhausting it must be, to have to do everything for oneself.

Cat took a container out of the cold white box and

dumped its contents into a bowl. After placing the bowl into a rectangular apparatus above the stove and pressing several buttons, she asked, "What do you want to do now that you're here? Besides get to know Matt, of course."

"I do not wish to get to know Mr. Goodson." The words slipped out before Amara could stop them.

Cat's brow creased. "Really? But you came here for—"

Amara shook her head, interrupting the American. "Eliza wrote you my story, of what I wished to escape. My experiences with men, with love, have not been good ones. I came here to escape my past. To build a new, independent future." She crossed her arms over her chest. "It is why I asked what might happen should I not pursue Mr. Goodson; I have no desire for an attachment." *A tryst, on the other hand ...*

Cat frowned, tucking a piece of hair behind her ear. "I won't push it. But just as Eliza told me your story, I hope she told you mine. I didn't want a thing to do with love, either, after Ryan ditched me at the altar. But then came Ben, and ..." She paused as Amara cast her eyes up to the ceiling. "Sorry. I'll stop. Truly. But, Amara? I hope you don't rule it out."

The machine beeped—did every machine make noise here?—and Cat retrieved the bowl. "Ouch! Dang, that's hot." She grabbed a spoon. "Do you want some? It's leftover mac and cheese, but it's pretty good."

Amara's stomach gurgled in response. The fruit and yogurt, while pleasant, had not been enough to sate her.

Giggling, Cat grabbed a second bowl and spooned a portion into it. "I take it from your stomach that's a yes."

Embarrassed, Amara took the bowl and spoon Cat offered. Such frank acknowledgment of one's bodily functions mortified her, though Cat seemed at ease.

"I can't imagine what it was like to live in a society like

yours," Cat said as she settled at the table. "I never understood its appeal to Eliza."

"Nor I, given everything she told me of this era," Amara said as she joined her. "But she is happy with my brother. And I'm delighted she's brought him to life again."

"So glad to hear that—though I read it in her letters. She wrote tons, thank God."

Amara halted the spoon halfway to her mouth. "I forgot that you know how my family's story turned out."

"Not all of it. I only know what happened in Eliza's time. I've been meaning to research to see if her—if your—family is still in England."

That brought Amara up short. *Did* she have living descendants, in England or elsewhere? Not that they'd accept her as family, even if she did—she was as much a stranger to them as anyone else. Her heart sank.

"We'll definitely have to look into that."

Amara merely nodded before taking another mouthful. If nothing else, this pasta with cheese was tasty.

At length, Cat said, "I suppose it's silly, me asking you what you want to do. You just got here. You need time to get used to everything. I hope you'll tell me what's familiar, and what's totally new. And how I can help, of course."

Amara stood up, gesturing to her dress. "One thing that is vastly different is the clothing, as you can see."

Cat set her spoon down. "Hold on. I'll get those things of Eliza's I told you about, so you can at least try them on."

Jumping up, she ran out the door and down the stairs before returning a minute later, a large box in her arms.

"Heavens, I should have helped you!" Amara crossed to her.

"Nah. I lug books around all day. This is nothing." Cat set the box on the sofa and opened its flaps. She pulled out a pair of blue trousers similar to the ones she had on. "Here's some jeans and a sweatshirt." A gray, rather mannish, button-less shirt of a heavier material followed. "Yeah. We definitely need to go shopping."

"I shall try these for now," Amara said, picking up the items and walking with them into her room. Closing the door, she eased out of her dress and undergarments, grateful they were still loosened and she needn't request help. She lifted up the trousers—jeans, Cat called them, and examined the material, her fingers tracing the rough texture.

"I have wondered what it was like to wear breeches. Now I shall know," she murmured. Sitting on the bed, she carefully put one leg through the trousers, then the other. Pulling them over her hips, she struggled to determine how they fastened. She secured the button at the top, but the material still gaped. A small metal tab stuck out, and she pulled on it. As it raised, it locked the metal seams on either side of it together. *Capital*! This tab would make dressing and undressing much faster.

The jeans were loose at the waist, but not so much that they fell down. Thank goodness for her curvy hips. It felt awkward and uncomfortable to have fabric bunched between her legs, to have the jeans caressing her skin with each move she made. But it was also freeing not to be swathed in layers, to be able to move or sit or kick up her feet without worrying about skirts.

She picked up the sweatshirt. Should she leave on her stays? How did modern women support their bosoms? If she wanted stays, she'd need help to lace them, and she didn't wish to bother Cat again, so she left them off, sticking her arms through the armholes and pulling the sweatshirt on over her head. The insides were soft as it enveloped her skin, tickling and yet soothing at the same time. No wonder Eliza had wanted these clothes back!

She ran her fingers through her hair, which she'd left loose to dry after the shower. How was she to secure it up?

Cat didn't wear hers up. In fact, the American's hair was shoulder-length at most. The idea of shorter hair appealed, to lessen the weight on her head and the fuss of caring for it.

She returned to the living room. "Could you cut my hair?"

Cat looked up from the computer on her lap. "Hey, those fit a little better than I thought they would. But I'm, uh, not a hair stylist."

Amara's shoulders drooped. "Oh." Disappointment permeated her voice.

Cat studied her for a moment. "I suppose I could, then take you to a real stylist later to shape it up. You really want to cut such gloriously long hair?"

"Yes!" The words came out more forcefully than intended. "I've never been allowed, even though some women in my time have recently adopted shorter styles."

"Well, why not? Come into the kitchen."

Amara followed Cat and sat down on the chair to which Cat pointed.

"How short?"

Amara hesitated. "How long do most women in this time wear their hair?"

"As long or short as they want it. I'm sure you saw a variety of styles on TV." At Amara's blank look, she added, "Television. We call it TV for short."

Most of the women in the soap opera, as Cat had called it (though Amara didn't know why, as no one had bathed or burst into song), had longer hair, but she'd admired one woman's chin-length style.

"To here?" she said to Cat, indicating an inch or so down from her jaw line.

Cat took in a deep breath as she fetched a pair of scissors. "Here goes nothing."

Amara closed her eyes as hair fell around her. This was it, her transformation. No longer was she Amara Mattersley, scandalized daughter of a duke. She was now Amara Mattersley, twenty-first century woman. With mannish trousers and short hair. Euphoria shot through her.

The scissors stopped. Cat moved around to her front, scrutinizing her. With a few more snips, she smiled and stepped back. "Not bad, if I do say so myself. Why don't you check it out in the bathroom mirror?"

Amara walked into the bathroom. She froze at the sight of herself. She looked like a different person. A modern person. The clothes were ill-fitting, to be sure, but comfortable. And the hair—she liked the way it swung around her face. It enhanced her cheekbones. She addressed the stranger in the mirror. "You can do this, Amara Mattersley."

Ben's deep voice rang out in the other room. "I'm home."

"Oh, good. But lower your voice, please; Wash is sleeping."

"Oops. Sorry, sweetie. How's Amara?" His voice softened, but Amara could still hear their conversation.

"Fine. In the bathroom, checking out her new hairdo."

"New hair?"

"You'll see. Hey, did you talk to—"

"Yeah. He's coming by after his class to pick her up. Is she okay with it?"

"Shoot! She never answered. I hope so. I can't imagine how overwhelmed she must feel, but I still think putting the two together is a smart idea."

"Only if they want it that way. You can write it, but you can't force it, you know."

Cat snorted. "Oh, I know. And you should be grateful I know."

"Honey, I am."

Amara smiled at their playful banter, which reminded her of Dev and Eliza. What would it be like to have someone with whom she could so easily interact—who was her whole world, and for whom she was his?

It's what she'd imagined she'd had with Drake. Until his perfidious ways made themselves apparent. What kind of blackguard seduced a naïve, lovelorn debutante without telling her he'd married someone else?

Drake Evers, Viscount Monteith, that was who.

She grimaced. Six years. Six years she'd had to forgive herself for that mistake. She'd tried; but how could she forgive herself when no one else would? She'd gone from one of the *ton*'s most sought-after daughters to a near pariah. Thank goodness her family had rallied around her. It hadn't saved her reputation, though. Nothing could. Not in her society.

At least relations between men and women in this century were much more relaxed. Intimacies between courting couples were not only accepted, but also rather expected. According to Eliza, many people didn't bother with courtship of any sort anymore, choosing partners as often as desired, for a few months, weeks, or even just one night. Her sister-in-law's face had wrinkled in distaste at that admission. "That's never been who I am," she'd stated.

The thought came unbidden as Amara fussed with her new hair: *But it might be who I am.*

In truth, such an about-face of morals was a near impossibility to comprehend, though she had long rebelled against her era's restrictions. Not so much that she'd actually taken a lover, however, no matter how often she'd considered it.

Mr. Goodson's lean form and icy blue eyes flashed through her mind.

Why not? Here, she could interact with men more freely, could indulge in the desires that plagued her more than she cared to admit.

She might not wish an emotional attachment, but with his fine countenance and admirable physique, he'd be an ideal experiment, a first taste of what freedom in this era felt like. Guilt wrapped around her like a quilt. Only if he were in agreement as to the nature of their connection, of course— an affair of physical passion, no more. She never wanted to inflict the kind of pain she'd had inflicted on her.

A derisive snicker escaped. How arrogant, to think a man like Mr. Goodson would fall in love with her. The ease with which he'd accepted her kiss suggested a man comfortable with physical relations. The kind to dally but not to stay. Or she assumed it did. What did she truly know of him, or of twenty-first century relationships? Nothing.

She left the bathroom with purposeful stride. "I will stay with Mr. Goodson."

"Oh, good." Cat cast a quick glance at Ben, who nodded. "I hate to do that to you, but I don't want to risk you catching strep. Ben said Matt can get you around four. In the meantime, would you like to come down into the bookstore with me? Emily usually works Mondays—it's normally my day off—but she needs to go to an appointment, so I said I'd cover for her. It'd give us a chance to talk. Ben will stay here with Wash."

"It would be my pleasure." Amara forced a smile. She'd prefer to retreat to her tiny bedroom to rest; adjusting to a new century was fatiguing. Knowledge was more important, however. She had so much to learn, and she wanted to start right now, this very minute.

There was no time to waste in getting on with her new life.

The afternoon passed quickly. Cat was easy to talk to, and as comfortable with silence as she was with speaking, a trait Amara admired. No wonder Eliza loved her so much.

Amara spent some of the time perusing the Treasure Trove's bookshelves, marveling over the sheer number of titles in the shop, as well as the variety of topics. When customers came, she watched as unobtrusively as she could, listening to their speech patterns, studying their clothing styles, the way they moved. She'd become good at that in her years under scandal's shadow, observing others when there'd been nothing else to do. She'd come to know the little movements people made, to see when people were interested or disinterested, to judge the truth in a person's face.

She appreciated the skill now. People's behaviors weren't much different here. She could easily tell the children who were tired, the younger adults who were bored. A young couple flirting with each other proved entertaining—though the numerous public kisses they exchanged had her avert her eyes more than once.

She also revealed her ultimate dream to Cat. "I want an education. The kind of education denied to me in my own period."

"You never went to school?"

"I was tutored in every bit of instruction deemed appropriate for a woman of my rank, but a school such as boys attended? No. I can read and write, of course, and have more proficiency in numbers than many of my sex, since Deveric instructed me in mathematics once he knew of my interest. I am fluent in French. I can play the pianoforte, though not as well as my sister, Grace. I can sew, and paint tolerable portraits of flowers. I can dance any of the dances. Quadrille. Waltz. I can manage a large household. But I was not allowed to study topics reserved for men. Or at least topics not acceptable for a woman, in my mother's opinion. Science, for example."

"You want to be a scientist?"

"Perhaps. My father's library contained several books on astronomy, on the work of Herschel and his sister Caroline, a woman fortunate enough not to have her intellectual interests stifled by class—or her mother." Amara ran her fingers over the spines of the books on the shelf nearest her, pondering. "The vastness beyond us fascinates me. The stars are our constant companions. But what are stars? Why are they there? For what purpose did God make them? What other mysteries do the heavens hold?"

"We have astronomy books you're welcome to read. Though maybe you want to start with modern history? I don't know how much Eliza told you, but as you might imagine, a lot has happened in two hundred years."

"Indeed." Amara followed Cat to the History section. "Eliza said men have visited the moon. The moon!"

"It's true. And within the next fifty years, I bet we'll journey to Mars."

Amara's breath caught. Travel to another planet? She couldn't imagine. "But you are right; for today, it's best if I read history—or for me, the future."

"Here." Cat pulled a volume off the shelf. "This is a basic history, western-Civ style, from 1750 through today."

Amara took the volume and settled in on the green sofa before losing herself in the world that came after her. Napoleon. The Battle of Waterloo. Queen Victoria. The

American Civil War. The assassination of Abraham Lincoln. Thomas Edison. World War I. Hitler. World War II. The Cold War. Margaret Thatcher. 9/11.

She tuned everything out, the words reading like a fantastical novel. Knowing it was true launched a myriad of emotions. England itself had changed incredibly over the last two centuries. Eliza'd warned her that while the class system in England still existed, it was much altered, the power and influence of the nobility greatly reduced. At least the royal family remained. England without a monarch was unfathomable.

Was Clarehaven still there?

Hours passed, but she barely noticed. When she finished the book, she closed her eyes, her head spinning. She was grateful to know more of the major events since 1813, though many saddened her. Such violence in the world. She'd hoped that would have changed. Would humans ever stop killing each other? Reading of repeated atrocities, of battle after battle, war after war, she wanted to weep. So much carnage, so much loss of life.

At least women had secured mention. Not many, but names leapt out—Florence Nightingale, Susan B. Anthony, Marie Curie, Eleanor Roosevelt. Ada Lovelace, daughter of Lord Byron. Byron had had a daughter? Who'd become a mathematician, and was now known as one of the earliest computer scientists?

Had things changed so quickly in her society? Should she have stayed?

No. She wished to attend university, a privilege denied to women in her country until the middle of her century, according to this book.

The University of Virginia was right here in Charlottesville, and women were permitted to attend. Amara nibbled at a fingernail. How could she acquire entry?

The door to the bookstore swung open. "I'm here," called a voice.

Mr. Goodson's voice.

CHAPTER 8

$\mathcal{M}$att's long legs ate up the distance between the door and the register. He didn't want to be here, didn't want to take Amara home. He regretted saying yes. He had stuff to do, class to prep for, coding to proof. But he'd promised.

Cat waved from behind the register desk, her face easing into a warm smile.

"Hey, Cat. Where is she?"

Cat motioned toward the couch. The woman sitting on it turned toward him, and he did a double take. It was Amara, but she looked almost nothing like the woman he'd met last night. She wore no bonnet, for one thing. For another, her hair was short. Much shorter than yesterday, when it'd been secured in that bun.

"What'd you do to your hair?" he burst out.

Amara stood up, her back ramrod straight. "Cat cut it for me. Not that that is any of your concern."

Starch infused her defensive tone, and he bristled. She was right, though. It *wasn't* his business.

He couldn't tear his eyes from her face. The shorter locks framed it in a most becoming way, the edges drawing attention to her strong yet feminine jaw line, the whispers of hair near her eyes pulling him like a magnet into their rich velvety hazel-greenness. *Damn it.* What was with this woman's eyes? Was she some sort of witch, luring him in with those orbs?

His gaze went lower. Her other orbs were now well hidden in some overly baggy UVA sweatshirt. She was wearing jeans, too, though they didn't fit well.

"You ready? I've got stuff to do."

Amara nodded stiffly as she crossed to him, a book clutched in her hand.

When she just stood there, looking at him expectantly, he snapped, "You don't need any of your other things?"

Amara's lips pinched together. "I haven't anything else."

"You traveled from England with only the clothes on your back?"

Amara turned to Cat, wordless.

"The, uh, airline lost her luggage," Cat said, her eyes steady on Matt in spite of the hesitation in her words.

He blew air out of his cheeks, his hands fisting on his hips. That explained the overly large clothing. So why did he still suspect something weird was going on here? "They haven't located it yet?"

Cat shrugged before retrieving her purse. "Sometimes they never do. Here's my credit card," she said, offering him her VISA. "Could you take Amara out and help her get some new clothes?"

"You want me to go *clothes* shopping?"

Amara giggled out loud. At his glare, she said, "Men don't change. You reacted much as my brother would have."

He sighed, running his hand across his hair. "Fine. I

suppose I can take her to the mall. Briefly. But keep your card; it's just easier to use mine."

"Thanks, Matt. We'll pay you back."

"The cards are money?"

At Amara's question, his eyes swung to her. Her brows knit together in the most adorable fashion.

"You don't know what a credit card is?" He nearly snarled the words. Was she trying to pull his leg? This woman couldn't be for real.

"Remember, rural England," Cat whispered.

"Sure, right. C'mon." He gestured toward Amara.

"I'll call you this evening to check in," Cat said. "I'm sorry for this, but with Wash feeling so rotten, I think it's best for a day or two."

Before she trailed after Mr. Goodson, Amara turned to examine Cat's face. The woman was holding back a smile. Did she truly think thrusting Amara in with this man would spark a permanent connection?

She was wrong. Amara would stay with Mr. Goodson, but his gruff attitude made it clear there was no love lost between them.

She stepped out the front door, then halted. She hadn't yet ventured outside, though she'd watched through the window. But now she could take it all in—the noises, the smells, the sights.

Different colored lights flashed *OPEN* in a shop window across the street. Cars raced by at speeds that had Amara's heart racing. The air smelled different—not of coal, as in

London, but of fresh air and something less pleasant, dirty. A car drove by, black smoke billowing out of its tail end. Was that the unusual odor—whatever the cars released? Better than horse manure, at least.

Everything looked relatively clean. There were no soot stains darkening the buildings. Few houses had chimneys, for that matter. The streets held no detritus, though dried leaves rustled about.

Mr. Goodson had reached the bottom of the stairs and was stalking down the gray footpath. When he noticed she wasn't behind him, he turned, impatiently demanding, "Coming?"

She hurried after him, though half of her didn't want to stop looking about. He walked around the side of a large, strange-looking vehicle—it had tires like Cat's car but was much bigger. Opening the right door, he ushered her in, holding her hand briefly as she stepped on a side rail to reach the interior. *Not so unlike boarding a carriage.*

The direct skin-on-skin contact disconcerted her; in 1813, nearly everyone had worn gloves. This was more intimate, flesh pressed against flesh. Was it her imagination, or did his hand hold hers longer than necessary? Frissons of excitement skittered up her arms. She glanced down at his hand as he pulled it away. It was strong, heavily masculine, with veins cording up its back and dark hairs accentuating its muscles. A beautiful hand.

Since when had she given consideration to a hand? *Since it touched mine and left me breathless.* Shaking her head, she settled into the surprisingly comfortable seat as he crossed around the front and entered from the other side.

A wheel stuck out directly over his lap. What was that? And all the knobs and buttons?

He inserted a metal key into a slot, then turned it. The

vehicle roared to life with a loudness that startled Amara. She shrieked.

His head whipped toward her. "What's the problem?"

She took a calming breath. Nothing like proving herself out of time and place by overreacting to things normal for everyone else. "My apologies. I wasn't expecting the noise."

He actually gave her a grin. "Never been in a pickup before?" He patted the front of the vehicle, as if caressing a horse, and Amara nearly snorted. She could easily imagine Deveric doing similarly.

"Don't forget your seat belt," he said, as he pulled a flat rope over his shoulder and clicked it into a metal square at his side. Amara did the same, hoping he didn't notice her fumbling. The seat belt pressed into her chest, accentuating her breasts under the sweatshirt. Embarrassment stole over her when he glanced down, then jerked his head forward, apparently noticing the same.

He pushed a button, and rhythmic beats pulsed out from the vehicle. Amara clapped her hands over her ears at the surprising sounds. He chuckled as he turned a knob and the volume lessened. "I take it the music's too loud for you, too? Do you have super-sensitive ears or something?"

She stared into the blue depths of his eyes. Music? In a vehicle? If one could call it music; it sounded mostly like jumbled noise to her. "It is different from what I am used to," she said.

He nodded. "Not everybody likes guitar rock. What's your style? Pop? Please say it isn't country. I may be a man with a pickup truck, but I won't go there."

She shrugged. "Whatever you like."

He moved a lever on the side of the wheel, and the vehicle—a truck, he'd called it—edged out of the driveway backwards, just as Cat's car had. *It was wondrous.* Much easier than maneuvering a horse and carriage.

Then the truck jerked forward, and they flew down the road at a rate faster than she'd ever traveled. Her hand gripped the side of the door, the other one clutching her trouser leg, nails biting into her thigh. *This is normal. I'm not going to die. This is normal.*

"Seriously, you okay?"

Her eyes shot to his. He glanced at her briefly before returning his focus to the road—thank goodness; he needed to look where he was going, because she didn't want to perish in this thing!

"I am fine," she lied, as he pulled onto a different road. Houses flew by so quickly she caught only glimpses, but they were of brick, pleasing in form, surrounded by trees. It wasn't so bad. Then he crested down a hill to a crossroads, and her stomach lurched. This was like nothing she'd ever seen—rows upon rows of cars, lights of reds and greens hanging above, and long buildings with lit signs. Shops?

He turned to the right and sped up again. It took everything she had to keep from casting up her accounts. London had been crowded with carriages and carts and horses and people wherever one turned, especially on the busier roads, but this, this was completely foreign, all these metal boxes moving at fast rates of speed, signs flying by. She closed her eyes.

"I texted my sister," Mr. Goodson said. "She's meeting us at the mall. She lives in Staunton, so she'll be here in half an hour."

Amara only nodded, her eyes still firmly shut. A sister? She had to meet another new person? *You can do this, Amara Mattersley.* Perhaps his female relative would prove more congenial than he.

The truck suddenly slowed before coming to a halt. Amara

opened one eye. The cars around them had also stopped, as cars from a side direction crossed in front of them. He drummed his fingers on the wheel impatiently. "So, what do you do?"

His tone was casual, as if her answer mattered not; he was merely making small talk. That was an action with which she was intimately familiar, having passed numerous evenings discussing nothing of import with people of her acquaintance.

She flashed him a glance, her eyes colliding with his of icy blue. A shiver raced through her, and she moved her gaze down, unnerved by her reaction, only to have his lips seize her attention. When one side of his mouth lifted in amusement, she stared at her lap. What was *wrong* with her?

And what had he said? What did she do? Did he mean occupation? This was not a question asked of a lady in her time. Ladies married. Or didn't. They did not have occupations. *Blast, what could she say?* That as a member of a ducal family, the only things expected of her were to keep a pleasing appearance, practice beautiful manners, and talk of inconsequential matters?

"I'm going to enroll at the University. To study astronomy," she announced. She held her back straight and her head high, as if such actions lent credence to her words.

His eyebrow lifted, but his eyes stayed on the road as the stream of vehicles began moving again. "Cool. Professor Niemann is great. I've worked with him on some computational mathematics. I could introduce you." He frowned momentarily. "It's too late to apply for fall admission, though I suppose you could try for next spring. Or did you apply before you came?"

Amara's shoulders sank. Next spring? So far off? Though

that gave her more time to accustom herself to this new life. And what qualifications did one need for admittance? Likely schooling such as her brothers received at Eton, schooling not open to females. She was in over her head. Defiantly, she tilted her chin up, adopting the Mattersley stance.

No, she wasn't. She was intelligent. She'd read translated works of Copernicus, Galileo, Halley, Herschel. She simply hadn't had the access to education her male counterparts had, or that Mr. Goodson had, especially since her mother had frowned upon the idea of females pursuing science. That didn't make her stupid, it made her uneducated, and that's exactly what she'd come to acquire: an education.

She was determined to get it. And she needed to take advantage of every potential opportunity.

"No. Might you help me?"

Matt swallowed. "Help you what?"

"I am not sure how one applies."

"Yeah, I can help with that." *What?* Where had that come from? Why did he keep offering her his time? Then again, filling out the application wouldn't take too long, right?

When she flashed him a grateful smile, one revealing a dimple he hadn't noticed before, Matt's heart jumped, and he nearly groaned out loud. This was why knights stupidly agreed to take on dragons, wasn't it? They'd probably fallen under the spell of a woman like this one.

He'd never cared for the damsel-in-distress type. He found their neediness annoying and unsettling. He preferred more take-charge, independent types, ones who wouldn't demand too much, who were happy to take what they wanted—usually in bed—then move on. Yet something in this woman called to him. Something about her made him relish the idea of being the hero, the savior, the person who could rescue her from whatever ailed her.

He pulled into Fashion Square Mall's parking lot, shaking off those ridiculous thoughts. She was no more a fair maiden needing rescuing than he was a knight in shining armor. She was just a relative of a colleague who'd needed a favor. A very short-term favor. "Here we are. Let's do this. I've got stuff to do."

She stiffened.

Damn. That probably wasn't the most socially acceptable thing, to act as if he didn't want to be with her. But he didn't. Especially not shopping at a mall. This was about his least favorite activity imaginable. And yet here he was. With her.

Hopping out of the truck, he hurried around to her door, some part of him pleased with the excuse to hold her hand as he helped her from the vehicle. Once out, she clutched an arm around her stomach, her face a bit pale, but her stride determined as they entered the mall.

"I guess we walk, until something catches your eye?"

Amara dipped her head in assent but didn't look at him, stopping suddenly in front of American Eagle. "Let's try here. I see women of my similar age."

Good. This might go more quickly than expected. Maybe he hadn't needed to invite his sister. He checked his phone. "Okay. Taylor's fifteen minutes out."

Amara strolled the aisles without acknowledging his statement, touching various items. "These are clothes that are fully fashioned? Does one not need to visit the seamstress?"

Seamstress? Hadn't that gone out of style at least a hundred years ago? "Yeah, as far as I know."

She selected a few items as a saleslady approached. "Would you like to try those on?" the woman asked.

Thank God, someone had rescued him.

"I'll be over here," he said, as Amara followed the salesclerk toward the dressing rooms.

"I'd very much appreciate your opinion as to whether or not I look acceptable," she called back.

Acceptable? The woman would look acceptable in a gunny-sack. He fingered a sweater on a shelf. What was he doing here? He was in a mall on a weekday, looking at women's clothing, when he should have been home grading, or at least planning class, or writing that paper.

A cute blonde walked by and flashed him a grin. His body leapt, responding as it did to an attractive woman, but as he looked more closely at her face, the spark died. She wore too much makeup for his taste, her eyes black-rimmed in that raccoon manner he detested.

Amara's eyes needed no enhancement.

Good God, he was comparing other women to her? Why? She was nothing to him, the cousin of his advisor's wife. He was only here as a courtesy to said advisor. That was all.

Amara strolled into view, her body language hesitant. She'd clad herself in a pair of black leggings with an oversized tunic shirt on the top. "The shop clerk insisted I should place a belt around the upper garment," she said. Were her cheeks redder than usual?

He eyed her up and down. The leggings clung to her every curve, accentuating lean but not overly muscular limbs. Not that he had anything against the athletic look; he'd just always found a softer body more appealing. And Amara looked scrumptiously soft. The tunic top accentuated her breasts and narrow waist, and his pulse raced again, his groin jumping in reaction to the woman before him.

Her throat bobbed. "Not good?"

"No, you look—"

"Hey, Matty! There you are!" a female voice called from behind him. *Taylor.* He turned to his sister, grateful for the interruption.

"Thank God," he said. "I have no clue what I'm doing."

"What *are* you doing here? My brother, *shopping?*"

He gestured toward Amara. "Taylor, this is Amara, Ben's wife's cousin. Amara, this is my sister, Taylor Duncan."

Taylor grinned widely and stuck out her hand. "Nice to meet ya. Totally cute outfit. Have you thought about adding a scarf?"

Amara gave her a hesitant smile in return. "A pleasure to make your acquaintance, Miss Duncan. Many of the American fashions are new to me, so I am unsure of what to select. I appreciate any guidance you may give."

Taylor laughed. "Please, call me Taylor. Are British fashions so different? I wouldn't think so. But you're off to a great start. Some boots would make that outfit kick-ass."

"Would you mind if—" Matt said, before his sister broke him off.

"Yeah, yeah, meet us at Chick-Fil-A in an hour."

"An *hour?*"

"Good fashion takes time, bro."

He let out a large sigh, then handed Taylor his credit card. "Amara doesn't have one," he said by way of explanation. At least he had his laptop in the car. "Fine. But please, no longer."

"Dude, we got this!" She waved her hand at her brother, then selected a sweater and a skirt from a nearby rack. "Try these," she said, handing them to Amara. "You'll totally rock them, no doubt. So wish I had your curves."

Matt nearly broke into a run, so desperate was he to get his mind off Amara. But the whole way to his truck, all he could think was, *So wish I could have them, too.*

Miss Dun—er, Taylor—set Amara immediately at ease, perhaps because she reminded her of Eliza. Granted, Eliza was a short, plump blonde with sapphire eyes, and this Taylor was tall and lean like her brother, with similar brown hair and the same ice-blue eyes. But their personalities, their friendliness, felt the same. Thank goodness.

Amara had spent her life surrounded by her siblings— her four sisters and two brothers. Being completely on her own was a new experience, and while exhilarating in some respects, it was terrifying in others. Another friendly face was more than welcomed.

"If it were up to me, we wouldn't even be in the mall. I mean, really, the *mall*, Matty? But might as well make the best of it. I bet we'll find some really cute stuff at Buckle."

Taylor chatted non-stop, trailing after Amara toward the dressing rooms. "What's your budget? If you want, we could go to second-hand shops, too. Without Matty. I can't believe he brought you. My brother does *not* shop."

For some reason, it thrilled Amara he'd done something for her he'd normally never do. Not that it should. Not that she cared. She wasn't interested in Mr. Goodson. Not for his character, at least. He was brusque, almost rude, making it clear he was not with her of his own volition. No, his personality had not endeared itself to her in the least.

His body, on the other hand, evoked quite a different

reaction. The simple touch of his hand brought forth quivers, and her mind continually leapt to the image of his long, lean legs in those blue trousers, trousers a darker color than his eyes but which somehow enhanced them.

And then there was his mouth. She loved to watch it, the way those sensual lips curved into a smile, or a wry grin, or even flattened into a line, an expression reminiscent of her brother.

But the feelings Mr. Goodson evoked in her were anything but brotherly. Goosebumps raced up her skin as she shimmied out of the leggings, and if she were completely honest, it wasn't because of the coolness of the air. No, Mr. Goodson affected her. And she didn't like it. Intellectually, at least. Physically?

Forty-five minutes later, she and Taylor made their way to Chick Fillet, whatever that was, Amara's arms laden with bags. Taylor had talked her into buying a number of garments at American Eagle, then several more at Buckle, before they'd stopped at Steve Madden, where Amara had purchased boots eerily similar to those her brother wore.

She'd resisted at first, thinking them too mannish, yet something about donning footwear reserved in her time for men brought out a sense of heady rebellion. She'd kept the boots on, enjoying how they changed her stride, made her walk in a more cocksure manner. She felt stronger, fiercer, in these skin-tight breeches and equestrian boots.

Several men gave her appreciative glances as she and Taylor passed. Or maybe they were looking at Taylor. Amara didn't care. She grinned saucily, strutting in the boots. She was doing it. She was here in the twenty-first century, and she was surviving.

It's been less than twenty four hours, one part of her brain chided. *You've no idea what's happening in the next day, next week, much less the next few years.* She shrugged off the worried voice. No, she didn't, but she had the means to live independently. She had Cat. She had Taylor, to whom she'd taken immediately; the woman was *much* more approachable than her brother. Amara didn't even worry about keeping up the conversation—Taylor talked about anything and everything, about shopping and clothes and something called NASCAR … and about her brother.

"He's a good guy, you know," Taylor had said when they were trying on boots. "A little geeky, perhaps, and sometimes obtuse, but he's so sweet once you get to know him. He definitely needs someone to get him off those silly screens." She'd eyed Amara in a conspicuous manner. "I mean, the guy hasn't had a serious girlfriend in years. I know the dude's driven professionally, but come on, you've gotta live a little, right?"

Amara hadn't replied, focused as she was on fastening the boot. When she'd stood, Taylor had asked her point-blank, "Do you have a boyfriend?"

Amara'd stumbled in the boots, wanting to blame it on the heel height—she'd never seen shoes with heels so high. She associated heels with prostitutes; trying them on felt risqué, but she did it anyway. "No. I am not interested in such things."

"Oh." Taylor flipped her hair over a shoulder. "You into women, then? 'Cause I've got a friend who's single and looking."

Women? In an amorous way? "Uh, no. I … my heart has been burnt, and I would rather avoid the whole encumbrance of courtship. I am more interested in pursuing an education."

"I hear ya. That's what my mom always said to me, too—'Taylor, finish that degree before you even consider getting married.' I blew that one." She'd sighed, and her shoulders had wilted momentarily before she'd jumped up, smiling more widely than was natural. "I eventually got the degree, at least. And teaching kindergarten keeps me busy. Working with five-year-olds is not for the faint of heart, I assure you! I love it, though."

They walked together now in a relaxed fashion. Amara caught sight of Mr. Goodson at a table, one of those computers in front of him, his fingers pressing on it. His whole face radiated intense concentration.

"The man works too darn hard." Taylor stopped in her tracks and elbowed Amara. "Dare you to interrupt him in a way he won't forget."

"I beg your pardon?"

"Come on. Haven't you ever wanted to do something wild? I dare you to kiss him."

If you only knew. I've already done something wild and paid quite the price for it. And yet … yes, yes, she did. She was in a new place, no past to drag her down, only the future to embrace. And she rather relished the idea of doing something unexpected. Especially if it involved Mr. Goodson's fine mouth, which she'd been thinking of since the previous evening.

"You want me to kiss your brother? Here? In public?" The idea was outrageous. Scandalous. Tantalizing.

Taylor bobbed her head enthusiastically. "Yup. The man needs someone to shake him up."

A kiss didn't have to mean anything, right? *Be bold, Amara Mattersley. Be who you've always wanted to be—someone who takes risks, who embraces the passionate side of herself.*

There could be a price for this, some part of her whispered, but she ignored it as she strode purposefully to Mr. Goodson, her boot clicks imbuing her with confidence. He looked up in surprise.

"I see you found—" he started to say, but she cut him off

as she leaned in and fastened her mouth to his.

He didn't move, didn't respond for a moment, then suddenly, whip-fast, his hands snaked their way through her hair, holding her to him as his lips consumed her, predator becoming prey as his tongue delved into her inner recesses. She gave as good as he, though, her lips absorbing his delicious taste, a hint of coffee mixed with male, the saltiness of his skin making her crave more, more, more.

The world fell away. The noise of fellow shoppers, screaming children, and whirring machines were mere background notes in the symphony of kissing Mr. Goodson.

"Geez. I said interrupt him, but holy cow. Break it up, people!" Taylor exclaimed with a nervous giggle.

Mr. Goodson yanked away from Amara, his sudden absence like a gust of cold wind. He frowned, his brows low over his eyes. He glowered first at Taylor, then at Amara, then at his sister again. "What the hell?" His eyes found Amara's and locked there. "Do you make a habit of kissing men randomly?"

Flames shot up Amara's cheeks, a burning fueled by anger as much as embarrassment. She'd had enough castigation in her own time period. *Though you were rather brazen, kissing a man in full public view.* Perhaps that wasn't as done as Eliza had suggested? And what had come over her, launching herself at him like that? She hadn't even asked permission.

Her glance slid to Taylor, who was staring at her brother, a pleased smile on her face. Taylor had dared her, and Amara never was good at refusing a dare. As any of her siblings could vouch.

Once, she'd climbed too high in one of the trees near the lake, determined to reach a bird's nest, especially because Grace told her she shouldn't. Luckily, Deveric had been there to catch her when she fell.

He'd always been there. He'd caught her literally, he'd caught her figuratively, rushing to her after Drake had deserted her in those gardens, her clothes half-off, her hair disheveled, her reputation in tatters. It was Dev who'd sought to avenge her honor, though Drake had sneaked off in the night for a ship to America. Dev, who'd played every card and called in every favor to ensure no one gave her the cut, that the *ton,* outwardly at least, found no fault with the disgraced sister of the Duke of Claremont.

It was Dev who'd told her life still held promise, that there were still opportunities for her. And it was Dev who'd rallied behind her when she'd asked to be sent forward in time, for a new chance at life in a place where no one knew of her sullied reputation.

And yet what had she done? Immediately kissed a man in front of others, not once, but twice. A young woman and her gaggle of friends whispered among themselves, pointing at Amara. Misgivings at her own actions overtook her. So much for a fresh start. She was making the same mistakes all over again.

"I'm sorry. Your sister ... " She broke off, pushing her hair back from her face. "I have no excuse, Mr. Goodson. I promise, however, not to assault your person again."

At that, his eyebrows relaxed and his mouth tipped up. "Mr. Goodson? That's what students call me, thanks to the Jeffersonian tradition of addressing professors by Mister instead of Doctor. I think after two kisses we're most certainly on a first-name basis, don't you?"

He rose from the chair, those alluring trousers—*jeans*—hugging his thighs. After folding up his computer, he looked at Amara. His eyes widened as they scanned her from head to toe, apparently just registering she wore something new.

Taylor laughed. "So? What d'ya think? Did we do well?"

Matthew swallowed, his Adam's apple causing Amara's stomach to flutter in the oddest way. Why did she react so powerfully to this man? Yes, he was appealing in countenance, but she'd seen plenty of handsome gentlemen. Yet when she was near him, every part of her responded in a way somehow deeper than solely physical.

Frowning, she looked away. Was it the manuscript? The story?

"Yes."

It was the only word he said, but it thrilled her. He'd barely gotten it out, and a dull red now inched its way up his cheeks. At least she wasn't the only one affected by whatever was between them. In her day, given the physical intimacies they'd shared, they'd likely be betrothed at this point. Unless one proved to be already married, like Drake. Thank goodness times had changed.

She studied him, emboldened by his approval. His lean waist and the slight curve to his legs gave him an unbearably alluring, hollow-hipped appearance. His shoulders were not so broad as her brother's, but in truth, she preferred leaner, less rugged men. Not quite as trim as the dandies of her era, perhaps, but there was something to be said for an angular frame. Matthew Goodson certainly had one.

Maybe she shouldn't fight the attraction. Maybe she should give in. After all, this was a different century, one in which men and women could share every nature of physical intimacy without it necessitating marriage. Why not take advantage? She had considered it with Lord Hodgins, and the risk had been far greater then.

But what if he develops a tendre for you? She fidgeted with the belt at her waist. She never wished to hurt anyone as Drake had her. Then again, Matthew didn't seem the least bit interested. Except when they kissed. He'd taken her shopping, yes, but only at Cat's behest; he'd made it apparent he didn't wish to be with her. He'd called in his sister, in fact. That was evidence enough he held no particular regard for her, was it not?

"You guys wanna grab a bite to eat before I head back over the mountain?"

"Over the *mountain*?" How far had Taylor traveled?

"Yeah, didn't Matty tell you I live in Staunton? Luckily for him, I don't mind the drive."

"I hope we did not put you out," Amara said.

"Nah. This has been fun!"

Matthew exhaled loudly. "Sis, I really appreciate your help, but I can't do dinner. I've got a lecture to finalize, and I need to respond to email, and—"

"Yeah, yeah. Work, work, work. That's all you do. You need to get your head out of that computer and into the real world once in a while, Matty. Come up for air."

He sniggered. "Seems when I do, I'm accosted by this woman." His lips twitched. "Though I suppose worse things could happen."

Amara's cheeks burned, but she said nothing. What could she say? He was right.

"Fine. How about it, Amara? I can bring you home later. Where are you staying?"

Before Amara could answer, Matthew spoke. "At my place."

Taylor's mouth fell open in comical fashion. "You're letting a *woman* stay in your apartment?"

"It's a favor. For the Coopers." He shifted his weight onto one leg. "Wash has strep, and they don't want Amara to get it."

"Sure. Whatever you say." Taylor tossed her hair over her

shoulder. "C'mon, Amara, let's go get some pizza. And not the mall kind; something really good."

Pizza. Eliza had talked with great longing of the bread, tomato and cheese concoction. Amara was willing to try it if it allowed her to spend more time with Matthew's sister, whose welcoming, friendly manner reminded her not only of Eliza, but also of Amara's sister, Emmeline.

A wave of homesickness washed over her, and tears welled in her eyes. *No. I'm where I want to be.* Missing her family was to be expected, though. Especially with everything so new and overwhelming. In truth, her nerves were on edge, and exhaustion was creeping in. She almost wished to go with Matthew than face anything else new. But that was the wrong choice. She needed friendships.

And Taylor Duncan seemed a good place to start.

CHAPTER 9

"That was quite a kiss. Is there something I should know about?" Taylor's heels clicked on the pavement as she led Amara to her car.

Amara hesitated. What should she say? *I am considering a liaison with your brother, should he prove willing?* What would this woman think? Would it horrify her? "No," she answered after a moment. "You challenged me to kiss him. I did." *I don't know why. But I did.*

"Good enough." The bubbly brunette stopped near a yellow car with rounded curves. "Here's Buffy."

"Buffy?"

"Yeah, my Beetle Bug. I love this car, though Matty mocks me about her, especially because of her eyelashes." She waved her arm toward the front, where black curled ribbons protruded. "But c'mon. We spend so much time in our cars they start to feel like family, right? So why not give her some personality?"

Amara stifled a laugh. They'd had ornate coaches adorned with the family crest, well sprung and lavishly outfitted, but no one had ever named said coaches.

"Go ahead, get in."

Amara looked at the door. She wasn't entirely sure how to open it; Matthew had got the truck door for her before. But how difficult could it be? She reached for the bar on the side and pulled, and was delighted when the door opened.

"So, what brought you to the States?" Taylor asked as both women secured their seat belts.

Blast. What should she say? What *could* she say that would make any sense? "I come from a large family in England, but they … died, so I am here to find a new life."

Taylor halted the car halfway out of the parking spot. "You lost your whole family? Oh my God, that's horrible! What *happened?*"

Two hundred years happened.

"Uh. Fire." It was the first thing Amara thought of. People still died in fires in this era, surely?

Taylor nodded solemnly. "I am so sorry, Amara." She pulled out of the lot onto a busy road. At least she drove more slowly than her brother, though the speed still tied Amara's stomach in knots.

"So why are you here?"

Amara's brow knit. Hadn't she just answered that question?

"I mean, in Charlottesville. With the Coopers," Taylor added at Amara's hesitation. "Wait, sorry, that was a rude question." She grimaced. "I do that too often. But I'm guessing you and Cat are friends or something?"

"We had a mutual friend, yes." *Darling Eliza.* "And we're cousins," she quickly amended, remembering Cat's claim to Matthew.

"I've only met Cat a couple times, but she's great, and Ben really helps my brother out, keeps him grounded, you know?" Taylor fiddled with the radio and music filled the car. It'd take getting used to, this loudness in such close proximity. At least Amara didn't cover her ears this time. Taylor sang along, something about *Wildest Dreams*.

How apt the song's words were for how Amara felt: trapped in some wild dream, with a man so tall and handsome. But was he bad, as the song suggested?

Eliza was right. Pizza was divine. Amara ate three pieces, and was so sated she could barely move. She was thankful stays weren't restricting her abdomen, though if she'd worn them, she'd have eaten far less and would not feel quite so bovine as she did at the moment.

Speaking of stays, what undergarments *did* women wear here? Other women's bosoms didn't move about as much as hers. The loose top and scarf she'd purchased hid her chest to a large degree, but she'd have to ask. How mortifying.

As they'd eaten, Taylor shared about her job, her apartment, how there were no good men in Staunton, how she was glad her brother was close, since the rest of the family lived in Maryland, though she didn't see Matt as often as she'd like, because he was so busy.

"I'd love for him to stop, slow down, to look up from that dang screen. To enjoy life!" Taylor said, her eyes fixing on Amara a little too long. "He needs someone to get him to do that."

Amara dodged having to respond by taking a sip from the glass in front of her. The iced water was more refreshing than she'd expected; at Clarehaven, they'd drunk wine with meals. She yawned without meaning to.

"Oh, gosh, sorry. It is getting late. I should scoot back across the mountain. You ready for me to take you home?"

Amara nodded, glad her accidental yawn had deflected Taylor, though it was embarrassing she'd let it escape in public company. But home? Where *was* home?

The drive took less than five minutes. Tired as she was, they arrived far too soon for Amara's comfort. Staying alone with Matthew Goodson made her nervous. *Don't be silly.* It was for only a day or two, and the man probably wouldn't notice she was there, so much did he prefer staring at that black box. She could sleep, read, do as she pleased, and not be in his life at all.

Taylor walked her to his door, then knocked briskly. Rustling noises from within indicated he was coming.

"Have fun." She gave Amara a wink.

As Matthew opened the door, Taylor rushed down the stairs, calling goodbye. "Gotta scoot!" she yelled. "I'll text you when I'm home."

Taylor was so quick to her car, Amara had no time to answer. She stood at the entryway to Matthew's living quarters, staring into the ice-blue eyes of the man before her. He was still clad in his trousers and shirt, but his feet were naked. She couldn't stop ogling them. They, like his hands, were strong and angular, bony almost, with a smattering of dark hair.

They're feet, for goodness' sake. Women were not supposed to react to men's feet. Were they? Why *were* Matthew Goodson's feet so appealing, peeking out as they did from the trousers above? *Because you've never really studied a man's naked feet before.* Yes, it was the novelty that had her staring at his toes. The novelty, and the surprising sense of intimacy.

"Well?"

Her eyes flew to his face at the word. His brows rose as he looked at her expectantly. "Are you coming in?"

A soft meow echoed from inside, and a spotted feline padded its way toward the door. Reaching down, Matthew scooped up the cat and scratched beneath its chin. "No, Lovey, you're not going outside." He stepped back to allow Amara in, still stroking the animal.

What would it feel like if his hands touched her in such a way? The cat was purring more loudly than any she'd ever heard. *I'm guessing something like that.*

Her skin prickled and tingles chased their way around her stomach and up through her chest at the thought of those long-fingered hands stroking her.

This is ridiculous, Amara Mattersley.

She'd have to talk to Cat, to ask if Cat could rewrite the story now that Amara was here, so that this absurd attraction to Matthew Goodson would cease. Because every inch of her was aware of every inch of him, of those naked feet, those long legs, his shirt moving across his chest and arms as he snuggled his cat.

The animal protested with a mewl as he set it down. Amara empathized. She wouldn't want him to let her go, either.

"I'll show you to the guest room. It isn't much; I rarely have guests."

She followed him down the hall, her eyes soaking in the way his trousers cupped his backside, grateful she was behind him so he didn't see how her cheeks burned at the sight.

He pushed open a door and turned on a light. The room was sparsely furnished, its only items a narrow bed, a small desk with a simple chair, and a computer on top of the desk.

"Do you have one in every room?" she blurted out, as she set down her shopping bags. She'd never seen him without a computer, and now it appeared he had several. How wondrous were these machines that he had to have them around at all times?

"One what?" He glanced around.

She gestured toward the desk. "Those computers, the ones you press on."

"Press on?" He snickered. "You mean type?"

Her skin burned, even as it bristled. He needn't mock her. *Not that he knows why you don't know the terminology, Amara.* She herself had mocked Eliza about a number of things before learning Eliza's secret, that she was from the future. Just like Amara was from the past.

Not that this man would believe that. Not that Amara planned on telling him.

"And yes, I have many. One of the perks of being a computer science professor—you have reasons to have all the latest technology." He pointed out the door without waiting for her to answer. "Across the hall is the bathroom; I'll put a towel on the rack for you. Help yourself to whatever's in the fridge. I've got to get back to work." He turned and walked out the door.

That was it? Though what had she expected? It was clear he didn't wish to spend time with her, not like his sister had. She sat down on the bed with a sigh. She didn't want his attention, anyway. She needed this time to catch her breath after the whirlwind events of the last few days. She needed rest.

She did not know what tomorrow held, but tonight, she'd ignore the fact that Matthew Goodson was only a room away, that she was staying in the same home as a single male. Heavens, such a thing would give her mother palpitations. She wouldn't think about what it was doing to her own heart. No, tonight she would let all the worries go and sleep.

Too bad her body had other ideas, as attuned as it was to the man in the next room.

With a groan, she rolled over, burying her head under the blanket. Anything to block out thoughts of Matthew, with those feet, those hands. Those eyes …

Matt's eyes were on the screen, but his mind was on the woman in the next room. It was uncomfortable, having a female here overnight. It wasn't like he never had women here, but they didn't spend the night.

Amara wasn't one of those women, though. If she were, he wouldn't be out here, pretending to grade labs. He'd be in his room, Amara underneath him. Or on top of him. What would that tempting little frame look like without clothing? The leggings she wore were no more revealing than any other woman's, he supposed, and yet her legs in those black sheaths had sparked a strong reaction in him. But naked would be something else.

He hadn't quite gotten a sense of her chest—it wasn't overly large, no Dolly Parton going on, which was fine, as he didn't prefer that anyway. But he had no clue beyond that. *Not that you should have been looking, you pervert.*

No, he wasn't a pervert. He was a normal, healthy, red-blooded American male with a very attractive woman in the room next to his. It was perfectly natural he was distracted, right?

He ran his hands along his thighs, sexual frustration eating at him. Absurd. He wasn't a teenage boy whose hormones were out of control. He was a thirty-two-year-old professor who, while enjoying a healthy sexual appetite, had long learned to control it, to tamp it down, when other needs were more pressing.

Were these papers more pressing? What would she do if he went to her room, knocked on the door, asked to come in? She'd kissed him twice, after all—*she'd* kissed *him*. Interest was clearly there.

He shook his head. No, Amara wasn't an option. She was his advisor's wife's cousin, for Christ's sake. How awkward would it be if they slept together? Especially if she wanted something more, something he wasn't willing to give. Better to avoid that headache altogether.

He leaned forward, fixing his eyes firmly on the screen, determined to block out every thought of the delectable woman in the next room.

Now if only the rest of his body would obey.

CHAPTER 10

Sunlight streaming in from a window woke Amara the next morning. Disoriented, she bolted upright, alarm coursing through her before she remembered where—and when—she was. In 2016. In Matthew Goodson's house.

Noises filtered in from outside the room, like water running. Was he in the shower? She'd love another of those today. She'd love one every day, in fact, if it meant she could soak under luxuriously hot water, its steaminess trailing down her body.

Wait. If Matthew was in the shower, it meant he was not clothed. She was under the same roof as a man to whom she was not related, and he was naked. Heat flooded her body—half-embarrassment and, if she admitted it, half-desire. What would he look like without garments, warm water trickling over his face, his shoulders, his … parts beneath?

Such an image, murky though it was, given she'd only seen one man unclothed and that by dim moonlight, had her clutching at the sheets, her toes curling and uncurling, frissons of ... something ... racing through her.

What would he do if she entered the room and joined him? Her eyes popped at her own audacity, even if just in thought. As if she'd do that. She wouldn't. Would she?

Her stomach gurgled, reminding her other appetites were at play, too. Rising, she pulled on her clothing from the previous evening. Hopefully she'd be able to take her own shower at some point, but for now, food was foremost in her mind.

She crossed to the door, opening it. And ran directly into Matthew, clad only in a towel wrapped low around his waist. Heat rose from his skin, permeating the air around her. "Eek!" she shrieked, covering her eyes. "I'm sorry! I, uh ... "

She peeked through her fingers. He stood before her, rivulets of water dripping from his hair down his chest, a wicked smile sliding across his face. "No worries," he said. "Nothing you haven't seen before, I'm sure."

What did he mean by that? Did he think her a loose woman? Or was that a more general statement, an assumption that most women in this era would be well acquainted with men in states of undress? Either way, she frowned. He was not ill at ease in the least; this meant nothing to him.

So neither would she be. She raised her chin. "My apologies, I was simply startled to encounter someone in the hallway. I was going to find something with which to break my fast."

"Break your fast? They still make that into two words in Britain? It sounds so old-fashioned."

She stiffened before exhaling, letting her shoulders drop as a side of her mouth quirked up. She *was* old-fashioned, at least in terms of anyone she'd meet here. Might as well embrace it.

He gestured down the hallway. "There's cereal in the

cupboard and milk in the fridge. Help yourself."

"Thank you. And might I make use of your shower after?"

Whatever sense of calm he'd managed to hold onto after bumping into Amara while nearly nude fled at her request. He turned, angling his hips away, lest the towel betray just how much the image of her in his shower aroused him.

"Of course." His voice came out far scratchier than intended. Damn this distracting female. Irritation dug at his skin—or maybe it was frustration, frustration at being saddled with this entirely too enticing responsibility he didn't want. He'd call Ben as soon as he was dressed, to find out when Amara could go back.

He'd tossed and turned all night, sleep eluding him for the most part. When it'd come, it'd been laced with images of Amara—in that absurd outfit she'd worn that first night, in the black leggings she'd flaunted yesterday. And always her mouth before him, tempting him. He'd done untold things to that mouth in his dreams, indulging in his greatest fantasies, with her a most willing partner.

He stared at her face now, the smile he'd thought he'd seen a moment ago replaced by flat lips. Her eyes stared at a spot over his shoulder.

"The towels are in the hall closet," he said. "I forgot to get one for you."

She merely nodded and headed away from him toward the kitchen. He watched her go, those hips leaving him breathless, wanting to chase after her and tell her exactly what he wanted to do with her in the shower.

He'd better make the next one a cold one.

"Ben says Wash's fever is back up. They want you to stay one more night, maybe several," Matthew called down the hallway as she opened her bedroom door.

Amara frowned at the obvious distaste in his voice. Was she such a burden, then? She'd left him alone last night, hadn't bothered him that morning, hadn't so much as said a word after the exchange about the shower.

Now freshly showered herself, she combed her fingers through her wet hair as she walked toward the kitchen. She'd donned an outfit she'd purchased yesterday—a dress knit of thick, cabled cotton on which Taylor had insisted. If one could call it a dress, that is, considering it ended well above her knees. Taylor said she could wear leggings underneath, but that most women would pair it only with high boots and think nothing of it.

Amara hadn't planned on doing that, of course. The thought was shocking. No one in her era would have worn skirts that short, not even the lowest of prostitutes. But she wasn't in 1813, she was in 2016, and she was determined to fit in. And determined to rile Matthew Goodson, for reasons she didn't fully understand. Best not to examine that desire too closely, but it was what'd fueled her rash decision to leave the leggings off, exposing a good foot of skin between the tops of her boots and the bottom of the dress.

Her cheeks flamed hotter than coal in a stove as she walked into the living room. This was a mistake. What had she been thinking?

Matthew glanced up from his desk, and his mouth fell open.

Satisfaction swept through her. That's all she'd wanted, to set him as off-kilter as he'd set her that morning, clad only in that towel, the one hugging those lean, hollow hips, touching him in a way she'd wanted to touch him. That's all. She should return to her bedchamber now, dress more respectably.

Only she rather liked how he couldn't take his eyes off her. Unless he was judging her, was scandalized by her behavior? *That wouldn't be the first time.* But no, his tongue darted out to lick his lip, a motion that sent tingles through her as she imagined that tongue tangling with her own again.

He swallowed but said nothing. Disappointment creased her brow. Well, what had she expected?

"Uh, there's coffee in the kitchen. I have to leave for class in a few minutes. Do you want to stay here, or come with?" *Had his voice caught on those last words?*

Amara crossed the room to the kitchen, searching the cupboards for a mug before pouring herself a cup of the dark brew. She wasn't a coffee drinker, to be honest, but needed it today after a night of dreaming of things she oughtn't. Taking a sip, she nearly spat it out. It was much hotter and stronger than she'd expected.

After a moment, she cleared her throat. "I'd like to accompany you, if you don't mind. The idea of staying inside does not appeal."

At Clarehaven, she'd passed great stretches of time strolling in the gardens, walking the estate grounds, or riding. She loved the fresh air; staying inside for long periods was far too confining.

Here, she'd been indoors—at Cat's, then in a vehicle, then a loud, enclosed shopping center, then an even louder restaurant, now at Matthew's. Did people never spend time out of doors in this century?

"And I should like to see the University."

"The Grounds are amazing. Even after five years, I try to stop and appreciate the Lawn and Academical Village whenever I'm there. Which isn't often; I'm mostly in Rice, of course."

She didn't know the places to which he referred, but nodded. According to Eliza, the American president Thomas Jefferson had founded the University not long after Amara's own time. "Old for the United States," Eliza had said with a chuckle. "But not for you, I know."

"I teach until eleven, then have office hours until two. You okay exploring without me?"

She snorted. An inappropriate response, perhaps, but something in his tone provoked her. Yes, she would be fine. She didn't need him. *It's a big world out there*, another part of her said. *You saw a mere fraction yesterday, and it set you on your last nerve. Be careful what you reject.* "I shall be fine, and shall return to you at the appointed hour."

"Bring your phone in case you need to call or anything."

"Phone?" Her brow wrinkled. She'd brought Eliza's phone forward with her, but left it at the bookstore. Cat had promised to charge it, whatever that entailed.

"Oh, that's right. You don't have a phone, do you?"

She crossed her arms over her belly. "I do, but it is with Cat."

He picked up something from his desk. "Here," he said, handing her a rectangle larger than Eliza's phone but smaller than his computer as he stood up. "That tablet's got 4G, so you can text if you need to. My info's in it." He grabbed his own computer, tucking it under an arm. "Ready?"

Amara nodded. Should she tell him she had no clue what he was talking about? Perhaps, but she didn't wish to delay him when he was obviously in a hurry. And she didn't wish to rouse more suspicion. She'd carry the machine around; it might help her blend in more.

He walked to the door, whipping it open before looking for her over his shoulder. She followed him down the stairs, marveling over everything that had happened in the last few days, over the fact she was about to visit a university … dressed in less clothing than a courtesan would wear. Self-consciously, she tugged at the skirt. If he turned around on the stairs, he'd likely get a full view up her legs.

That thought should have been much more horrifying than it was.

CHAPTER 11

*A*mara ambled around the wide green expanse, not wanting to leave. The solid, white columns, the long black window shutters, the whole atmosphere of this central area reminded her enough of her century that homesickness unfurled through her.

She strolled along the colonnades, passing numerous doors. Once, a young woman exited one, giving Amara a glimpse of a bed inside. Students lived here? A number of young men and women milled about on the grass-covered lawn between the sets of buildings. One or two greeted her but made no further conversation before returning to their books or telephones.

She wanted to explore the large building she'd overheard someone call the Rotunda, but it was covered in metal pipes and poles—for renovations, the same stranger had said.

A waist-high box with a screen on its top stood to one side of the Rotunda. As Amara neared, a woman pressed her fingers to it, and the pictures and words on the screen changed. *Aha! It worked like Eliza's telephone.* After the woman left,

Amara remained, reading about the Rotunda's history before meandering across the short-trimmed grass, admiring the tall majestic trees. Did the students realize what a treasure this lawn was, how serene, how beautiful? Though a variety of sounds, especially of traffic, echoed in the distance, it was quieter than at the mall or near Matthew's office, and Amara was grateful. She was tired of all the foreign noises. Though London was hardly a haven of silence, at least its cadences were familiar.

An older gentleman entered one of the larger buildings interspersed among the single-person rooms. Amara paused before crossing to it. Could she go in, too? She'd tried to access a different such building, but it had been locked. Peering through the window, her breath caught at the furnishings, furnishings more similar to her era than anything else she'd seen.

She had to go in.

A shiny plaque near the door caught her eye. *Colonnade Club*, it read. Cautiously, she turned the knob and stepped inside. No one stopped her or asked her to leave. In fact, she was completely alone. Her eyes soaked in the area around her, her ears relishing the silence.

The interior gave her the sense of a London townhouse. Not exactly, of course—the layout and furniture differed, but the excitement at finding a place so reminiscent of home fired her blood.

Ascending a set of stairs, she discovered a small library in which someone was working, with papers spread out across a massive table, fingers pushing away at the computer in front of her. *Everyone had those.* As the gray-haired woman looked up, Amara said, "I am sorry, I did not mean to disturb you." Perhaps she wasn't supposed to be here. Was it a private residence?

"No problem." The woman pointed toward a door in the corner. "If you haven't seen the view from the balcony, you should."

Amara thanked her and crossed to the door. No one was on the balcony. She sank into a chair next to a narrow table, her eyes taking in the richness around her. Other parts of town might be loud and garish, but this—this was truly spectacular.

She still clutched Matthew's tablet. She hadn't done anything with it, didn't know how to do anything with it. She pushed a button on the side, and the screen sprang to life. After moment, a chime sounded, and words appeared on it:

> Feels weird texting my own personal account.
> Hope all is well—MG

He could send her a direct message whilst she was walking about? She'd spent hours writing letters by hand, had passed days waiting for the post to arrive. How different communication was here.

She rubbed a finger across the screen and it changed, showing his message on top but the alphabet in jumbled order at the bottom. Carefully, she pressed a letter, and it appeared on the screen. She added more.

> jl qm well. The univrrsity is breath-takking.
> Amaara Mattersley

She did not know how to correct the errors, so she left them. At least the send button was obvious. Within seconds, the machine chimed again.

> Good to hear from you. Was worried. Meet
> me at Rice at 2?

He'd been worried? A tiny thrill shot through her. A man other than a relation was worried about *her*. Not that she should read too much into that. Not that she should want to. She sent him a second message.

> Rhat is fin.e I may need instruvton on this machinw. Amara Matttersley

The machine chimed nearly instantly. How fast could the man write? Her efforts took time.

> Your wish is my command, my lady.

She giggled at his words, suddenly picturing Matthew as a genie in a bottle, like she'd read in *Arabian Nights*. Having Matthew Goodson at her beck and call held appeal.

Setting the machine on her lap, she looked out again, enjoying the crisp breeze and awe-inspiring view. If only life could feel this peaceful all the time. After a few more minutes, she rose with a sigh. According to the tablet's clock, it was time to meet Matthew. She'd return to this place as often as she could, though. It connected her to home, to things familiar. A minor connection, but one she would take.

Matt checked the time again. 2:08. She was late. He hated when people were late. He tapped his fingers on his desk. *She's okay, though, right?*

Of course she was okay. Why wouldn't she be? It's not like the University of Virginia campus was a threatening place, especially in broad daylight. She hadn't answered his last text, though—the one he'd sent five minutes ago. Was she lost? Ignoring him?

He sighed before reaching for his coffee. Why did he feel so protective of her? Sure, Ben had asked him for help, but this was something else, something different, something deeper. Maybe it was because she seemed so sheltered. Naïve. Yes, that reason made sense, given Cat's account of Amara's unusual upbringing.

Voices echoed in the hallway. "Yes, ma'am, his office is right this way. I'd be happy to show you." Grant, his teaching assistant.

A moment later, the TA and Amara stepped into his office. Grant's eyes never left her, a stupid, toothy grin plastered across his face. She gave the upstart a smile and thanked him. Something sparked in Matt. He wanted her to smile at him like that.

Grant's grin widened. "Let me know if there's anything else I can do for you. In fact, here's my number, in case you need it."

The man—boy, really, given he was all of, what, twenty-four?—yanked a piece of scratch paper from the pile Matt had on his desk and wrote down his digits, handing the paper to Amara.

Matt's mouth quirked up as her brow furrowed. She took the number but immediately looked to him, not the kid. "Thank you," she said, her voice laced with hesitation.

Grant's grin faltered as he looked at Matt. "Oh. Sorry," he said, swallowing. "I thought she—" He turned to Amara. "I thought you were just a student. I—"

Matt chuckled, holding up his hands. "No harm, no foul. Ms. Mattersley and I are acquaintances, that is all."

He'd said that as much for himself as for Grant, wanting

to dull the stab of jealousy spearing his chest. Amara was nothing to him. It was fine if someone else hit on her. And Lord knew male CS grad students would hit on anybody; females were still a rare commodity in the department, though thankfully their numbers were rising.

Grant nodded but scooted out the door, his chagrined expression proving he thought he'd stepped on his professor's turf.

Amara's expression was more unreadable. She gave him a stiff nod, then handed over the tablet.

A snicker escaped. "You're a worse typist than I am." Damn, why had he said that? He'd meant to tease, but it'd come out more like an insult.

Surprisingly, she laughed. "I assume 'typist' relates to putting words on that." She gestured toward the tablet. "In which case, yes. I am."

She was adorable when she laughed. That dimple showed, and her nose crinkled up in the cutest fashion. Matt wanted to press a kiss to it. He immediately banished the thought. Acquaintances only.

"What do you call that?" She motioned to the desktop computer in front of him.

He frowned. "The computer?"

"Oh, it's the same word as for the folding ones?" She pointed to the laptop on the edge of the desk.

"Uh, yeah. Though people generally call those laptops." He was thoroughly confused. The woman was acting as if computers were entirely new to her.

"Might you show me how one uses it?"

"You've never used a computer? For real?" His tone was unnecessarily sharp, he knew, but something didn't add up.

She swallowed, twisting her fingers together, distinctly ill at ease. "As Cat said, my upbringing was very … different." Her lips pulled into a false smile.

He shook his head. Cat *had* told him Amara's exposure to technology was limited, but never having experienced computers at all, in this day and age? Something niggled at the back of his neck, unease taking hold and squeezing.

"No kidding. It's hard for me to fathom as a computer science professor." Pausing, he tapped a finger against his mouth. "Though I suppose that makes me the perfect person to instruct you, doesn't it?" *Where had that come from?*

Her eyes lit up. "Please? I'd be very grateful. It's hard when everything feels so unfamiliar and foreign." She broke off, her thumbs dancing around each other.

"Sure, no problem." It wasn't like he was busy, or had a paper due in two days, or had a massive pile of exams to grade. "You figured out texting, even with a few typos. I'm sure you'll be a quick study."

"Texting? This is what it is called, sending those instantaneous messages?"

"Yup." He pulled up a chair next to his own and patted the seat. "Sit down. I don't have to be anywhere for a while; let's learn."

He'd planned on driving home and letting her do her thing while he got back to work. Instead, he found himself looking forward to the next hour or so, even as the strangeness of the situation pricked at his conscience. The satisfaction seeping through him surely was only because he was doing what he loved to do—teach. It had nothing to do with having an excuse to spend more time in Amara's company. Nope, not at all.

Though her head spun with the information Matthew hurled at her, Amara remained intensely aware of the man to her side, his pleasant scent tickling her nose as his fingers flew over the keyboard. The images on the screen changed with ever-increasing pace, but she said nothing, listening as he talked about things called Google and CNN and email and Facebook.

"Facebook," she murmured, the name stirring a memory of Eliza calling out the word when she'd been lost in delirium.

Matthew smirked. "Heard of that one, at least, huh? Who hasn't? Though they say mostly older people use it now. The kids have moved on to Snapchat and Instagram."

More names she didn't know.

He tapped something on the keyboard, and a new page popped up, one with a picture of his smiling face in the corner. "Here's my Facebook profile," he said, "though I don't do much on it—it's mostly to appease my sister."

Photos flew by, some of Taylor, and more of Matthew. In one, he had his arm slung around a blonde beauty. Amara started. That was not something that had occurred to her. Was he courting someone? Surely not; Cat would not have written Mr. Goodson into her story if he were married or promised to someone else. That set her at ease.

She grimaced. She shouldn't *want* to be set at ease, and yet … A sigh escaped. This was so confusing. She was fiercely attracted to Matthew Goodson. There was no denying it. And it vexed her sorely.

"Do you wanna try?" He stood up and gestured to his seat.

As she switched over to his chair, the heat radiating from it caught her by surprise. It was warm where his body had been, and his scent lingered. It was like being enveloped by him, but not.

"What should I do?"

He shrugged. "Whatever you want. Try searching for things in the box up there."

Amara hesitated, her tongue darting out between her lips as she contemplated. Finally, she typed in *Clarehaven* and hit return, as he'd instructed. To her surprise and delight, a picture of her home appeared on the screen. The house itself looked the same, but outer buildings had been added or torn down, and some of the foliage was different. It disconcerted her.

"Magnificent house."

She jumped at Matthew's voice. She'd forgotten he was there, so immersed was she in staring at the screen.

He leaned forward in his chair. "How'd you find that?"

She didn't answer. What could she say? *This was my home, two hundred years ago?* She tried to breathe, but the air wouldn't come. Did family still live there? *Not that they'd be family now, so many generations removed.* Her heart raced.

Never had she felt so much empathy for her sister-in-law.

Amara clutched her knees with her hands. Eliza had done it. Eliza had gone two centuries into the past and not only survived, but thrived. Amara could do this, too.

She clicked onto a different page, then another, not caring what flashed on the screen, just wanting to distance herself from the image of Clarehaven. Suddenly, a guttural moan echoed from the screen, and Amara shrieked at the pictures before her eyes. A man and a woman, unclothed, were engaging in acts too indelicate to mention. Her hands flew over her eyes, but the images seared into her brain.

"Oh my God, what?" Matthew leapt up, leaning across her as he did something to the computer. The noises stopped and the pictures disappeared. "So much for firewalls," he muttered.

Amara peeked at him through her fingers. His cheeks were as fiery red as hers must be. Thank God he hadn't acted as if it were normal to see people engaging in unmentionable intimacies right there on a screen. It wasn't normal, was it?

"Welcome to the Internet," he said, smoothing his hands down the front of his legs. "Porn everywhere." After a moment, he touched her shoulder. "I'm sorry; clearly that upset you."

"It didn't you?" Her gaze met his, visions of what she'd seen dancing in her head. Suddenly they mutated, and it was Matthew's body covering hers as they moved together in unison. Her breath quickened and her pulse raced. She couldn't tear her eyes from his. Did he sense it, too, this bizarre connection? Did he—was he—picturing the same things as she?

Matt counted to ten, then twenty, willing himself under control. Not that he regularly sought out porn, but the images on the screen combined with the closeness of Amara Mattersley, the smell of her skin, the curve of her neck, those intoxicating eyes—well, he was a mess of physical desire at the moment. The woman on the screen had almost the same shade of hair as Amara. It wasn't too much a stretch to picture himself engaging in those same acts with the exquisite woman next to him.

His groin pulsed, and he sat down quickly, lest Amara witness his reaction to the events of the previous few minutes. How embarrassing. How … erotic. What would she do if he locked the door to his office, if he moved back to his chair, pressed his lips to hers, delved deep into her mouth?

Would she respond? She had before. Temptation called, but he shook his head, bidding his body to settle.

She looked like a deer caught in headlights. Clearly the sexual scenes had had the opposite effect on her. Not that he blamed her. Porn was ... porn. It wasn't real intimacy, though reacting physically was within the bounds of reason, right? He was a man, after all.

After a moment, she spoke. "I think that was enough for today."

He nodded, springing to his feet again. "Yeah, I'm sorry. I can show you how to avoid that in the future."

She tipped her head, awkwardness emanating from her every pore. "That would be ... desirable."

At the word, his pulse leapt again. Desirable. Yes, Amara Mattersley was oh-so-desirable. He wished she'd chosen a different word, so he could get his mind out of the gutter and back to where it belonged, which was *not* on Amara's body. Though his hands longed to be there.

He yanked his phone out of his pocket. "I'm, uh, going to check in with the Coopers." He turned his back to Amara as he typed, not willing or able to handle looking at her anymore. After some quick back-and-forth texting, he returned the phone to his pocket, emitting a loud sigh. "Looks like they still want you to spend the night with me. That okay?"

A choking noise came from her, and he swung around. Her eyes were wide, but she stood, snapping her shoulders back and tugging on her sweater dress. That all-too-seductively-short dress. "Of course. I shall not bother you. I will remain in my room and read."

Without waiting for his response, she walked into the hallway. He could have sworn a cold wind followed her.

CHAPTER 12

As she climbed into his truck, Matthew said, "We can either grab a bite to eat, or pick something up to make at home."

She longed to simply return to his apartment, to hide in her bedchamber. The whole day she'd been in the company of newness: new people, new technology, new surroundings. At the mention of food, however, her stomach growled. She hadn't had anything since breakfast. Food was a necessity. Perhaps the market would not be too taxing. "Something for home would be nice."

He nodded as he pulled out of the parking lot. "I agree. I'm not much of a chef, but I can manage chicken and potatoes."

They wound their way through the streets to the large, crowded road Amara recognized from the mall excursion. As the cars inched along, she commented absent-mindedly, "This feels much the same as London."

"London?" A noise suspiciously like a snort emerged. "I don't think Charlottesville is any comparison to London, in size or looks."

She stiffened. She'd meant the traffic, the slow-moving vehicles, though it wasn't as if she could say London in 1813, with its horses and carriages. She had no clue what the London of today was like, but did he have to speak in such an arrogant tone?

"Have you been?" She arched an eyebrow at him.

"No, but London's about ten times the size of this town."

She swallowed, saying nothing. Ten times? Not that she'd seen much of Charlottesville, and London *was* a huge city, but ten times? "How many people live there?"

If he thought her question odd after she'd challenged him, he didn't say so. "Eight or nine million, I think."

She pulled at the material on her dress. Good Lord, that was enormous. Would she recognize any of it if she went back?

"Here, we'll zip into Kroger." He turned into a large lot full of other vehicles and found an empty spot. Shutting the engine off, he walked around the truck to open her door. Amara liked that. While she was sure she could manage the door herself, she enjoyed the courtesy.

The building before her loomed large. As they entered, Amara sucked in a deep breath. She'd never seen so much food in one place. London's markets had been vast but spread out, and though the banquets at Clarehaven fed upwards of a hundred people at a time, neither could compare to the bounty before her.

She followed Matthew mutely, her eyes trailing over food items in jars and metal tins of varying shapes and sizes. As they neared a row of meat packaged in a curious, clear material, the cold pulsating from the shelves hit her. So that's how they kept it from going bad. *Capital!*

People passed them pushing carts piled high with items. "There's so much. Everywhere," she commented.

Matthew set a package of chicken in the cart, raising an eyebrow at her.

"Restaurants on every corner. A shop this size full of food. So much food, instantly available."

A wry grin twisted up one corner of his mouth. "It's the American way."

"How do you keep from going to fat?"

He chuckled, waving an arm. "Look around. The American stereotype in action."

Amara did as told. A few of the customers were as lean as Matthew, but many more had extra flesh, some in considerable amounts. Not that there hadn't been larger people in her era—there certainly were. The Prince Regent, for one.

"But you?" she asked again, scanning him up and down. "There is no extra on you." Her skin heated as she spoke. She should not be appraising his person so intimately.

His eyes sparkled. "Thank you. Good metabolism, I guess. And I hit the Aquatic and Fitness Center daily."

"Fitness Center?"

"Yeah, the gym? Where people go to work out?"

"Work out?"

He snickered. "Are you kidding?" When she shook her head, he poked her lightly in her side. "Working out is exercising. You're a strange one, Amara Mattersley, with the stuff you don't know."

She pinched her lips, crossing her arms over her midsection. He was right, but the frank words hurt, in spite of the teasing grin he'd sent her when he finished speaking. At least she knew what exercise was. She walked over to a shelf, examining its contents, refusing to look at him.

After a moment, he approached. "Hey, I'm sorry. I didn't mean to hurt your feelings. I often speak without thinking."

He rubbed a hand along one of her arms.

The surprising touch stirred goosebumps, and she looked up. He was close, the heat of him tickling her skin. His ice-blue eyes were warm but troubled.

"No, you are right. I must seem ... peculiar ... to you."

It wasn't his fault. Not really. Half of her wanted to blurt out the truth of her origins, but she couldn't risk it. He'd have her hauled off to an asylum.

Eliza had used her phone to convince Deveric of her claims. But Dev had also *been* here. Because of the story Cat wrote, he'd come forward, albeit briefly, to meet Eliza, to kiss her, or have her kiss him, rather, which sent them both back to 1812. He'd seen things, things that forced him to be more open to Eliza's confessions.

Amara had no such advantage. True, she had Eliza's phone, which held several photos of Eliza, Deveric, and Amara. But how could she prove said photos were from the nineteenth century, when the technology that'd made them hadn't existed and wouldn't for nearly another two centuries?

Matthew dropped his hand and took a step back, his expression impossible to read. "Let's finish up. I'm starving."

"Me, too." She gave him a tremulous smile.

After picking up some potatoes and green salad in a clear box—in a box!—he navigated towards the front of the store. Grabbing something in an orangish-red wrapper from a shelf, he added it to the other items. "Do you want one? Kit Kats are my vice."

What in heavens was a Kit Kat? "No, thank you."

When the counter on which he'd unloaded the food moved, she ducked her head so he wouldn't note yet another reaction to something unfamiliar.

Once back in the truck, Matthew opened the Kit Kat's

wrapper. A luscious smell wafted Amara's direction, reminiscent of the chocolate drink their cook, Rowena, made for her. Her mouth watered as he took a bite.

Glancing at her, he stopped mid-chew. "You want some, don't you?" He broke off a piece and handed it to her without waiting for her answer. "Told you you should have gotten one. I hate those women who say they don't want dessert but then steal mine."

Her hand paused mid-air. She was fairly sure he was joking, but why did the idea of him hating her pain her so? It's not as if others hadn't disliked her. Lord knows, they had. But, she was startled to realize, she liked *him*. She liked Matthew Goodson. Underneath his occasional brusqueness, he had a considerate nature. He'd opened his home to her, asked after her welfare during the day, was even going to make her dinner. What wasn't to like?

Nothing. And that's the problem. She turned away, watching the scenery pass as she sampled the delicious Kit Kat. *His lips are even better.* Oh, her traitorous brain. She sneaked a peek at him, but he paid her no attention as he drove—which she supposed was a good thing, considering the numerous vehicles crowding the road.

"How long did it take you to learn how to drive?"

He shrugged. "Not long. My mom let me practice in parking lots, and then I took Driver's Ed in tenth grade like everyone else." After a second, he spoke again. "I'm going to go out on a limb here and assume you don't drive?"

Amara nibbled at a fingernail. "Not this type of vehicle." At his raised eyebrow, she clarified. "I have driven carriages, with horses." *There, let him make of that what he will.*

His other eyebrow joined the first. "Horse-drawn carriages? Are you Amish?"

"I don't know what that is."

"A religious group of people who live as if they were in the eighteenth or nineteenth century—they reject most modern technology. You know, like you."

Amara's hackles rose. "There's more to life than technology," she said with a huff, crossing her arms.

They coasted into his apartment lot, and he brought the truck to a stop in the same place as before. "There is? My mom keeps telling me that, too, but somehow I've yet to believe her." He chuckled as he hopped out and walked around to her door, helping her down with his warm, almost familiar hand. The contact eased her perturbation a bit.

"Where do your parents live?"

"Not parents. Mom. Just north of Washington, D.C. About two hours from here."

It only took two hours to travel from Charlottesville to the capital? Geography had never been Amara's strongest subject, but she was pretty sure that was a great distance. Then again, cars traveled very fast. Too bad Deveric wasn't here, with his fondness for speed.

"I am so sorry for the loss of your father," Amara said. She and her own father hadn't seen eye-to-eye, but she'd still mourned his passing.

"He's not dead." His abrupt tone caught Amara off-guard. He frowned, then shrugged his shoulders. "But he's also not worth talking about. Haven't seen him since I was nine."

He grabbed the bag of groceries from the floorboard and together they walked to the apartment, a silence between them.

"Lovey, I'm home," he called as he opened the door. The feline leapt down from the sofa, vocalizing her displeasure at his absence. "Yeah, I know, I'm late. We'll get you your foodies." He set the groceries on the counter.

Foodies? A grown man used such a child-like word? It was rather endearing, how much Matthew adored this cat. It reminded her of Deveric and his dogs—and her nephew, Frederick, whose love for his puppy, Pirate, knew no bounds.

"Lovey. How did you pick the name?"

"I named her after Ada Lovelace, one of the first computer scientists. Lord Byron's daughter."

"Yes. I know him." She nearly clapped her hand over her mouth. She should have said, "know *of* him." Would he wonder at her words?

Matthew handed her a can and a spoon. "Can you scoop some of that into her bowl?" He pointed to a shallow dish on the kitchen floor.

Thank heavens. No questions. Amara took the can. How was she to open it? She could ask, but the thought of being inept at one more thing, at showing her differences again, ate at her. There was a flat ring on the can's top. Maybe that? Using a fingernail, she slid a finger under the ring and pulled, exhaling a sigh of relief when the can opened. The sigh turned into a noise of dismay at the smell emanating from the can. *Ugh.*

Taking the spoon, she emptied the can into the bowl and placed it on the floor, amid Lovey's loud purrs. The feline rubbed herself against Amara's legs twice before wolfing down the food.

Matthew, who'd been unloading the bag of purchased foodstuffs, leaned over. Another chuckle escaped. "I didn't mean for you to give her the whole can, but you'll be her best friend now, for sure."

Amara grinned at him as she rose, enjoying the easy camaraderie. Matthew set a pan on the stove, then poured some sort of oil in it before adding the chicken. Amara watched in fascination. She'd been in Clarehaven's kitchens, of course, but had never learned to cook. She hadn't needed to.

Did everyone here know how? Taylor had implied people often ate at restaurants, but Matthew moved in the kitchen as if accustomed to it, scrubbing the potatoes in the sink before dicing them and laying them in a separate pan. He drizzled the same oil over them, then grabbed a different bottle and shook its contents over the chicken.

"What is that?"

"Basil. I'm sorry, I should have asked—do you like it?"

Amara dipped her head in a yes. Whether she liked basil or not, she wasn't going to nay-say this gentleman when he was cooking for her. Her stomach rumbled, and she set a hand over it. The bite of Kit Kat, while tasty, wasn't enough.

"I know, I'm hungry, too," Matthew said. "Want a beer while we're waiting?"

Beer? Her mother frowned upon women drinking beer. Which of course meant she wanted one. "Yes, please."

Opening the cold box he'd called a refrigerator, he pulled out two bottles, then grabbed some sort of contraption and popped the lids off before handing her one. She took a sip. Not the best-tasting drink, but not the worst, either—that had been her brother's whisky, of which she'd once stolen a gulp. She nursed the drink slowly.

Within twenty minutes, Matthew was dishing the meal onto plates and gesturing for her to sit. "It's nothing fancy," he said, a sheepish grin on his face, "but I hope it'll do."

She set her hand over his briefly as he took a chair next to her. "No man has cooked for me before. Thank you, Matthew."

Amara took a bite of chicken, her eyes closing and a smile hitting her face as she chewed.

Matt watched, his hand trembling from her touch. His response to her unnerved him. *She* unnerved him. She'd never had a man cook for her? How could that be? She was a puzzle that made no sense, as if he were trying to solve something for which he'd been given the wrong key.

He ought to have come straight home after office hours. Lord knew he had enough to do. Instead, he'd relished every minute he'd spent in this woman's company. And he wanted more time with her.

That disturbed him.

Not that he never thought about giving relationships another try. He did. Occasionally. Late at night, when the screens were off and he lay in bed, staring at the ceiling, insomnia his only companion. In those wee hours, loneliness edged its way in. But come morning, he pushed that aside and got back to what he was good at: work. Relationships, whether friendships or something more, had never come easy to him. When Wendy left him for his brother, he'd sworn that was the end, that life was more pleasant, less confusing, without another person in the mix.

But his time with Amara had been easy. Mostly, at least. He'd take the batting average, in spite of his few missteps. And Lord knew chemistry raged between them, a silent electricity leaping back and forth whenever they were in the same space.

His gaze dropped to her lips. A hint of oil from the chicken lent them a glossy sheen, and it made him want to lick them clean.

He liked that she wore no makeup, that her face, as gorgeous as it was, was one hundred percent natural. No subterfuge in her. He frowned. Physically, at least. He had the sneaking suspicion there was way more to Amara Mattersley than what he'd seen in the last twenty-four hours. She had secrets, he was sure of it. Everybody did.

What were hers?

CHAPTER 13

After dinner, Amara excused herself to her bedroom. She didn't wish to be rude, she'd assured Matt, insisting the meal was divine, but she was exhausted and wished to sleep.

An unexpected sense of bereftness hit him in the chest as she walked into her room, shutting the door behind her. Hadn't he wished for time to himself, to focus on his work? Why, then, did he feel her absence so keenly?

Luckily, sitting down in front of the screen erased all of that, and it was with surprise that he looked at the clock to discover it was past midnight. Standing, he patted Lovey, who'd taken up her usual perch on the edge of the desk, then arched his back to work out the kinks.

"That's how the evening is supposed to go," he mumbled to the cat. "Lots accomplished, no distractions, and no confusing mixed signals."

Because Amara sent him mixed signals, that was for sure. She'd kissed him twice, responding actively each time, then had turned around and played the demure miss. She'd talked with him animatedly at dinner, only to excuse herself shortly thereafter, pleading fatigue. At times, he'd sworn the desire coursing through him reflected back in her eyes, but then she'd move, change, and it was gone.

This was why he didn't bother with women most of the time. He'd never understood all the subtleties, the signals he was supposed to pick up on. Much easier to just hook up once in a while and leave it at that.

He smoothed his hands over his thighs, ignoring the tightening in his groin at the thought of hooking up with Amara. He'd like to. He'd really, really like to. But the complications that could bring with the Coopers weren't worth it.

And if Amara were to expect more? A tenured professorship had been his life goal since his first high school computer science class, and nothing and no one, not even a woman as perplexing, as mesmerizing, as Amara Mattersley would pull him from that.

Amara lay in bed, watching lights flicker across the ceiling. She knew they were headlights from passing cars, but if she didn't focus on them, if she let them be background, she could pretend it was candlelight, someone moving by in the hall, perhaps. Except of course it wasn't.

She'd fled. She knew it. The whole afternoon, from the time she'd arrived in Matthew Goodson's office until the minute he'd offered her mint ice cream for dessert, had been nothing but pleasure. Sure, half of her was tied in knots from the newness of it all, but Matthew made it less frightening. So much less frightening. And she didn't like it. She wasn't going to be dependent on him, on anyone. She wasn't.

So she'd fled, because the urge to kiss him had grown over the evening, while he'd told her about his decision to teach. His eyes lit up as he spoke of computers, of their power, of the amazing things people could do with them. And the scary things, he'd conceded, which is what drove his research, his determination to keep the world a little safer by keeping the Internet safe. Much of the terminology had gone over her head, but his passion for his profession had not.

What was it like to live with such passion for something? Had she ever had anything on which she'd focused so much of her self?

Drake Evers didn't count. That had been a few very shortsighted years of her very young life, and look what that obsession had got her. Or more likely what it had taken from her—namely everything. Her reputation. Her virtue. She'd still had her family, but the affair had permanently marred her relationship with her mother, and guilt over her sisters' reduced marriage prospects followed her daily. It was one of the reasons she'd wanted to leave, to come here—to give her sisters back the chances they should have had, without her there to raise eyebrows and draw whispers.

Rolling over, she glanced at the clock. 12:37 a.m. It was strange to have a clock in every room, especially one that glowed in the dark. Electrical power, in fact, still mystified her. Nearly everything here relied on electricity. What would these people do if they lost access to it?

A chair squeaked in the other room. Matthew was awake? Amara turned onto her back, irritation crinkling her brow as her traitorous mind wondered what he was doing.

Why did he have to be so finely formed? Those searing blue eyes, the squareness of his jaw, the stark contrast of his dark hair with his fair skin. He was beautiful. *Blast it*. A groan escaped her lips as she flopped over a third time, pulling the blanket over her head.

She half-hoped Washington was well tomorrow so she could return to Cat's. The temptation here was too great. The other half of her dreamed of what might happen if Matthew came down the hallway and instead of entering his own chamber, entered hers.

No one would have to know. Only the two of them were here.

The door next to hers opened and closed. That ended that fantasy; he'd obviously gone to his own room. Thank goodness he had some sense. Some self-control. Because apparently what they'd said about her was true.

She had none.

CHAPTER 14

A knock at the door startled Amara awake. The light streaming into the room surprised her; she'd thought she hadn't slept a wink, tossing and turning as she listened to the creaking of the bed in Matthew's chamber. Knowing Matthew Goodson lay in the next room was almost more than she could bear—so tantalizing and so scandalizing at the same time.

She sat up, rubbing her eyes. "Yes?"

"Sorry if I woke you," came his deep voice. "But Cat just called. Wash is doing much better. You can go back. If you want."

Had he paused at that last line? Did he want her to stay?

There was no reason for her to. Was there? Only torture, only temptation. Only distraction, and the possibility for complications she didn't want. On the other hand, there were no children underfoot here. It was peaceful and quiet, except for occasional noise from other apartments. She liked that.

No. This was not where she belonged. Not that she knew where she *did* belong in this century. But she was never going to find out if she centered her attention on a man, even a man as handsome as Matthew Goodson.

There was more to life than a pretty face. She'd learned that the hard way, through Drake. Handsome is as handsome does. She'd do better to stay away from Mr. Goodson completely. So why did every inch of her protest at the notion?

Because he's been kind to you, gone out of his way for you.

"I shall be out in a moment," she called, reluctantly leaving the warm bed. At least the room itself was a comfortable temperature. She fully understood now Eliza's love of central heat. It *was* a delight to not freeze upon rising.

Footsteps moved off and rattling echoed in the kitchen. After selecting attire for the day, she crossed the hall to shower, remaining under the water far longer than she probably ought to have. Not only was the magnificently hot water a gift from heaven, but hiding in the shower allowed her to avoid any immediate decision-making.

With a sigh, she shut off the water, toweling herself dry before sliding into the jeans Taylor helped her pick out. A moment of misgiving hit her; the jeans were quite formfitting, clinging to her thighs and derriere in a manner to which she was most definitely not accustomed, though Taylor had assured her they were very flattering. She pulled on a knitted top—Taylor called it a sweater—of a beautiful plum that complemented her eyes and hair. Not that she wanted Matthew to notice. Not that she'd thought of him and his potential reaction when he saw her in it. No, not at all.

She brushed her teeth with the toothbrush and toothpaste he'd given her, enjoying the clean feeling. She was lucky hers were full and more-or-less straight, compared to many of her acquaintance. Dental hygiene had certainly come a long way; toothpaste tasted far better than tooth powder.

Wandering into the kitchen, she found Matthew at the stove, cooking eggs. He glanced quickly at her, then back again as his eyes trailed over her from head to toe. She raised an eyebrow at his regard, and he flushed, his head bending toward the eggs as he stirred.

"Something wrong?"

"N-no," he choked out, his wrist stirring even faster.

Amara's lips curved into a smile in spite of herself. It delighted her to fluster him so much. Turnabout was fair play.

"So, should I drop you at Cat's this morning?"

The hesitation in his voice matched her own. There really was no reason for her to stay, to impose on him further. Plus, she wanted to get to know Cat better, to learn from her, to share stories about their respective times. Cat was the only one with whom Amara could be her natural self, since Cat knew the truth. And being herself, being able to confess her confusion and fear and not feel self-conscious about everything she didn't know, appealed.

Still, she paused. What would he say, what would he do if she said no? Perhaps his hesitation wasn't that he wanted her to stay. Perhaps it was that he wanted her to go but didn't want to appear overly eager to be rid of her. Matthew had only taken her in at Ben's request. He likely didn't want to disappoint his friend.

"Yes." It was the most logical course of action.

His wrist stopped for a second before he smiled widely, turning his face back to hers. "One final breakfast, then, before you're released from the bachelor's quarters. I hope it's not been too much of an inconvenience to be here."

He thought he was inconveniencing her? Or more likely, he was merely being polite.

"Of course not. It is I who have inconvenienced you."

He slid the eggs onto two plates before answering. "In all honesty, I hadn't expected this to be so comfortable. Thank you for being an easy guest." His tone was more formal, less open than before.

A strange disappointment stung the back of her throat. What had she expected? For him to beg her to stay? Such a wish made no sense. And yet … She shot him a glance as she took a plate. Why *wasn't* he interested in her? Matthew definitely reacted physically to her, as she to him. She knew her reasons for resisting. What was holding *him* back?

It's not as if he needed to, from what Eliza had said. Relationships were different in this era. Her sister-in-law had spoken plainly of premarital and extramarital sex, even as both women had blushed.

"I don't want you to be caught off-guard, Amara," she'd said. "Men can and will try to get you into bed, and they won't expect anything from it and won't think you will, either. It's not like here—people don't get married just because they've had sex. Er, relations."

"I understand sex," Amara had answered with a tinkling laugh to mask her discomfort. Half of her had been astonished by the lax nature of interactions between the sexes. In her society, men and women remained mostly segregated, and no respectable, unmarried woman would have been caught alone with a man. No man would have wanted that, either, for his hand would have been forced.

The other half of her found the idea of such freedom incredibly exciting, titillating. She had always had strong feelings of a sensual nature, feelings she hadn't wanted to reveal to anyone, feelings which had made her feel bad, shameful, even, long before her actual scandal. Women were not supposed to be driven by the flesh. Pleasure brought problems.

At least it had in 1813. But this was 2016. She could indulge with Matthew without ramifications, without remorse. If only he wished to.

No. Stop. She set her plate down more forcefully than intended, ignoring Matthew's questioning look and those eyes. Those desperately beautiful eyes.

Fleshly pleasures would not distract her from her goals.

It was time to leave, before she threw herself at this man a third time.

CHAPTER 15

"**M**ama!" Washington ran through the front door of the Treasure Trove a little over a week later, his father locking the door behind them before trailing after in a more leisurely fashion.

Cat whisked the boy up and gave him a big kiss on the cheek. "Did you have fun at the park?"

"Yes!" He hugged her tightly around the neck but then wriggled his way down from her arms and raced back to Ben. "Dada, I'm hungry. I have a snack?"

"How about supper instead?"

"Yay!" Wash charged up the stairs, not even looking behind to see if his father was following.

"You ladies okay here?" Ben asked.

"Yes, go—you know that boy when he's hungry!" Cat waved her husband off, and he gave her a salute before taking the steps two at a time.

Turning to Amara, Cat let out a big sigh. "I wish Wash didn't have to be with someone else all week. But I can't watch

140

Margaret Locke

him and run the bookstore. At least he loves Mrs. Postupak."

"And you, him." Amara twisted her mouth into a rueful grin. "I did not have such a close relationship with my parents. As a child, I spent my time with my nurse and nanny."

Cat half-chuckled, half-sniffled at that. "I don't know if that makes me feel less guilty, or just sad."

"We do that to which we are accustomed. Eliza is very involved with baby Rose, though. She won't hear of a wet nurse and has insisted the baby be across the hall from her chambers, rather than in the nursery."

Cat's eyes moistened. "Thank you for speaking of Eliza in the present tense. I miss her so much."

Both women glanced at Eliza's portrait over the fireplace. The blonde beauty's ever-present smile and joyful blue eyes soothed Amara.

Blue eyes brought unwelcomed thoughts of Matthew. Mr. Goodson. He hadn't contacted her since the morning he'd returned her here. As far as she knew, he'd not spoken with Cat, either. He'd even canceled last week's Sunday meeting with Ben.

Was he avoiding her? *As if you merit that much consideration.*

Clearly she'd been but a momentary distraction for Mr. Goodson. It bothered her that he was proving harder to forget. Would he show up this evening? It was Sunday again, after all.

Amara shook her head, determined to dislodge any thoughts of Matthew Goodson. She walked behind the large oak desk, anxious to see the photographs flashing across the register's computer screen.

Earlier in the week, Ben had transferred the pictures from Eliza's phone to the computer, to enlarge them. Amara viewed them daily and spent much time telling Cat stories of

141

her family.

One photo showed Eliza with Deveric. A second showed them with baby Rose. And Amara.

"Eliza wanted everyone in the photograph," Amara had said, "but reasoned she could not explain the machine. I was the only one, besides Deveric, who knew her truth." She bit the inside of her cheek, willing the stinging behind her eyes to dissipate. "At least she captured that painting of our family when no one was looking. I can still see my family. For that, I am grateful." She'd pointed out her mother, Grace and Emmeline, Cecilia, Becca. Chance and Frederick.

As the portrait flashed up on the screen again—a screensaver, Ben called it—Amara's fingers hovered over their faces. Oh, how she missed them.

She'd busied herself the past few days talking with Cat, reading, exploring the immediate area on foot, and with completing her application for admission to the University—UVA, as everyone called it, pleased she'd managed it without Mr. Goodson's help—and only a little from Ben. She was grateful for Eliza's far-sightedness in arranging for a set of official school records to be included among the documents sent to her. The dishonesty troubled her; the records obviously weren't authentic. But what could she do? Explain to University officials she had no such papers—transcripts—because a governess and tutor had schooled her?

"What if the University does not accept me?" Amara suddenly exclaimed, panic in her voice. She'd practically been having fits of the vapors since sending off the application yesterday, even though she likely wouldn't hear of the decision for months. She wanted this so badly.

Footfalls sounded on the steps, and Ben's voice echoed in the room. "One doesn't have to go to college to get a good education, you know."

Cat burst out laughing as she looked up at her husband, who carried Wash in his arms. "That from a professor?"

"It's true." He set Wash down before continuing. "If you're driven, you can teach yourself. Libraries often carry college textbooks and numerous other educational materials. Many colleges and universities even offer free courses online now."

Amara's face lit up. "Indeed? Oh, I should like to try one. Though my dream is to attend a true university, as that was a privilege denied to the women of my era."

"Well, UVA's a pretty big one. You could always choose something smaller."

Amara crinkled her nose. No, UVA was where she wished to learn. She'd walked the University's grounds nearly every day this week, enjoying the sense of home it stirred. Surely there was a way to make it happen.

An idea hit her. "Can you amend my story so I am already a student?"

Cat shook her head. "It doesn't work that way. I've tried. I can create potential love connections, but that's it."

Disappointment dragged down Amara's shoulders as a knock sounded at the door.

"That would be Matt." Ben strode to the front of the store.

The name hit her in the chest like a blow. She'd fought the temptation to visit his place of work, to send a greeting. Matthew Goodson was a complication her already confusing life didn't need. So why was her pulse racing, her eyes hungry for the sight of him?

How would he behave? Would he react to her, or would they be as strangers? Amara sucked in a breath, then feigned nonchalance as Cat cast her a questioning look.

The door swung open, and Matthew crossed the threshold,

his hair and blue sweater wet with the mist permeating everything outside. He ran his hand over his head as he wiped his feet on the rug. Each movement called Amara to him. Her mouth watered, as if presented with a feast after a long famine. *Ridiculous.* Still, she swallowed as he passed through the room. When his eyes fell on her, he stopped, and a smile broke out on his face.

"Hey, you."

"Hey." She offered the unfamiliar word in return, not sure what else to say.

"Well, don't let me disturb you." He gestured to the book Amara had forgotten she was holding, a biography of Ada Lovelace. Not that she'd chosen it because of Mr. Goodson and his cat. No, not at all.

"Ben and I will try to be quiet over here." He turned his back to her and walked to the table on the other side of the room.

That was it? Disappointment unfurled in her midsection, but she did her best to hide it.

"I'm going to take Wash up for his bath. Amara, you're welcome to stay here in front of the fire if you'd like. I certainly wouldn't want to leave that cozy spot." With a wink, Cat and the boy made for the stairs.

Amara probably *should* have followed her. She didn't need to interrupt the men. Wash was likely to be loud, however— bath time seemed a favorite time for him to launch into raucous yelling—and she *was* quite comfortable here. Surely if she read, she wouldn't bother them. She cast a quick glance toward Matthew. To her surprise, instead of sitting with his back to her, as she'd expected, he'd rounded the table and was seated where he had a direct view, if he wanted one. Which apparently he did, as those icy blue eyes were fixed on her.

She gasped, and Ben, who'd settled in next to Matthew, looked up. "Everything okay?" He looked from Matthew to Amara.

"Absolutely," Matthew said, his tone business-like. Breaking his gaze with Amara, he whipped open his laptop. "Now about those algorithms you've been testing regarding the security loophole in … "

Amara tuned the words out, though she peeked at the men once in a while. This was silly. She was making calf's eyes at Mr. Goodson like a love-struck girl, and he wasn't paying her the least attention, completely focused on the work in front of him. She didn't even *want* to be fixated on him.

Cat had said the attraction, while strong, was not insurmountable. Amara didn't have to choose Matthew for anything just because Cat had written the two of them into a magical story. After all, when Cat had chosen her love, it hadn't been any of the men about whom she'd written. She'd picked Ben, instead. And from watching them in the short time Amara'd been here, it was obvious Ben was Cat's true love.

Amara gnawed on her cheek, pretending to be lost in her book, when in reality she wasn't absorbing a single word. If Matthew Goodson *was* her soul mate, was it wise to ignore that? Look at what happened with her brother and Eliza. Amara had never seen two people more in love, regardless of the bumps they'd hit on the road to get there. Should she pass up the opportunity of a love like that?

A groan escaped her lips, much to her mortification, and when Matthew's eyes flew to hers, her cheeks burned. Perhaps he'd attribute it to the fire.

She squirmed on the sofa seat. She *was* warm, but it had nothing to do with the flames behind her but more the sparks with the man across the room. Had it really only been two weeks since she'd arrived? Two weeks ago, she'd left behind everything she'd ever known. Two weeks ago, she'd traveled forward in time—in time!—to 2016. Two weeks ago, she'd kissed that man. And enjoyed it most thoroughly. She wanted to do it again.

She wanted to do it now.

She stood up, setting the book on the sofa. She'd put it away later; what she needed now was escape. "Pardon me," she whispered before running up the stairs and disappearing through the door at the top to the Matthew-free apartment within.

Matt's eyes remained glued to the screen, but he was intensely aware of every movement Amara made. And she made a lot, her hands flipping pages too quickly to be reading them, her head turning toward him with amusing frequency. He'd had the strangest urge to plant a kiss on her the minute he came through the door, though he hadn't seen her since a week ago Wednesday.

What was it about her? It'd taken all he had to settle himself in with Ben and pretend he didn't care one whit about the woman across the room, didn't wonder what she'd been up to. He'd told her to contact him if she needed anything. She hadn't. He'd gotten the message.

On the other hand, technology baffled her. Had he misread her silence? Had she not known *how* to contact him, despite his instruction? He shook his head. *Ludicrous.* There was nothing between him and Amara Mattersley. She'd made that clear. Especially now that she'd darted up the stairs.

Away from him.

"You disagree?" Ben's voice broke him out of his reverie. "I think students might like that type of seminar."

"No, sorry, that wasn't directed at you."

Ben leveled a gaze at him over their laptops. "You could ask her out, you know."

"What? Me? No. I'm not interested."

Ben shrugged, though a smile teased at his lips. "If you say so."

Matt tapped his fingers on the edge of the table. "Seriously, I'm not interested. I don't have time to be interested, even if I were, which I'm not. I just wanted to make sure she was okay. She seems a little like a fish out of water."

Ben muttered something under his breath, which to Matt sounded suspiciously like, "Understatement." With a grin, he added, "Just saying, better to step up to the plate than wait. I nearly missed out on Cat because I didn't make a move."

Matt's eyebrows rose. He'd never heard how the Coopers met. Not that he'd asked. Colleagues didn't normally share such info. Did they?

Ben waved a hand. "Long story. Just remember: life is short. Prioritize what truly counts."

"Like tenure?" Matt's chuckle sounded more forced than he'd intended.

Ben didn't laugh with him. "I'd be lying if I said that hadn't been important to me or isn't important to me now—but in some ways I wished I'd let myself have more of a life earlier." He took a sip from a mug near his elbow. "On the other hand, had I done that, maybe I would have missed Cat, too." With a wink, he set the mug back down. "Some things are just fate, I guess."

"Fate. Right." Amara's hazel-green eyes danced before

him. He didn't believe in fate. He believed in choices and hard work. That's what brought results and success. Not chance. Not luck. Not anything as absurd as fate. Would fate be so cruel as to give a kid a dad who gambled away the family's entire life savings and more, digging them into tremendous debt? Who left and never looked back, leaving behind six devastated kids and one furious wife?

And yet, some part of him wondered if he'd met Amara for a reason. *Absurd. She's your colleague's relative who happened to get stuck in your apartment for two nights. That's it.* "Let's get back to the seminar," he said to change the subject.

Ben nodded, and the two fell into friendly but professional conversation about classes for the fall semester. The subject of women didn't come up again. Though that didn't mean Amara didn't pop into Matt's head. She did, with alarming frequency. His eyes occasionally drifted to the top of the stairs, though she didn't return. Finally, after a frustrating hour in which he'd accomplished little, he stood up. "Guess we should call it a night."

Ben rose, too. "Guess so. Wanna come up and say good night?"

Matt shook his head. "No need."

If only he believed it.

CHAPTER 16

"Amara, these are my friends, Jill and Shannon."

Amara nodded at the two women, both of whom wore friendly expressions. Jill, the shorter, heavier one, said, "It's a pleasure to meet you. Cat has told us … nothing about you." Her chuckle suggested she wished she hadn't said that.

Amara merely smiled. "I'm a well-kept secret."

"British?" Shannon said upon hearing her voice. "Awesome. How do you know Cat?"

"Uh, Eliza's a mutual friend," Cat interjected.

Jill's eyes widened. "Really?" She studied Amara.

Amara bristled at the close inspection. Did Jill know of Cat's powers? Did she know about Eliza?

"Well, glad to meet you, too," Shannon said. "Are we ready? Sorry to rush, but it's rare I get a night out without the kids, much less on a Saturday, and I'm ready to dance!"

Cat had mentioned dinner out, nothing more. Amara grimaced. "Dancing?" She wasn't particularly fond of dancing, with its intricate steps and posing interactions with men.

"You don't have to if you don't want to," Cat assured her. "The dancing is different from what you're used to."

Shannon rolled her eyes. "It's '80s night, Cat. It's not like we're dancing however they did in the 1880s, or whatever."

Cat's hand flew to her mouth as she covered a snort, though her eyes sparkled with merriment. Amara grinned, too. If Shannon only knew she needed to go back another seventy years.

"You an '80s fan?" Jill asked.

Amara hesitated. "I am not familiar with that music."

"Yeah, I guess you're a bit young. You look younger than the rest of us, at least."

Was the woman asking her age? Was that not gauche?

When Amara said nothing, Cat spoke up. "I don't know. There's not such a huge difference between twenty-eight and thirty-nine. Right? Tell me there isn't!" She pushed up her cheeks with her hands.

Everybody in the group laughed as they walked out the door.

The drive was a short one, and soon they pulled into a parking lot in front of a building marked Scooter's Bar and Grill.

Shannon bounced up and down in the seat next to Amara. "Man, I love dancing!"

Amara had sat quietly during the trip. Though it'd only taken five minutes, she'd enjoyed the amiable chatter between the women. She missed female companionship. She missed her sisters and Eliza.

Shannon had two kids and worked as a dental hygienist.

Amara wasn't sure what that was but didn't want to expose her ignorance. She'd query Cat later.

Jill worked in the Rare Books School at the University and had recently married. "Though he was happy to let me have a girl's night. Mostly because he wanted to get together with the guys and drink," she said, rolling her eyes.

"Maybe they'll recite poetry to each other," Shannon quipped. Amara didn't understand Jill's blush, but it amused her nonetheless to imagine men spouting verse as a form of evening entertainment.

"Looks crowded," Cat said, as they exited the car.

"Good. More people on the dance floor." Shannon shook her hips to the pulsating beat audible through closed doors. Heavens, how loud was this going to be?

Cat opened the door and ushered the women through. As Amara passed, Cat touched her arm. "Are you going to be okay?"

Amara nodded, despite the uncertainty bubbling in her midsection. *Yes.* She was.

Lights flashed from the ceiling—oranges, greens, and reds—in the otherwise dark room. Bodies moved on the dance floor, but the "dancing" was unlike anything Amara had ever seen—disorganized and uncoordinated. Several couples touched in ways that would have had the matrons of her era swooning in horror.

The music itself wasn't much better. Amara wanted to shield her ears but forced herself to keep her arms at her sides. If the others found the cacophony pleasing, she would feign the same.

"Ugh. AC/DC. I never did like this song," Cat called out with a frown. "Should we grab a drink?"

Shannon nodded. "Frozen margarita for me!"

"Ooh, that sounds good." Jill fished in her reticule—purse, as Cat called such a thing—pulling out some money.

Cat turned to Amara. "Would you like to try something? You don't have to."

With all three women watching her, Amara wasn't about to say no. "Yes. I shall try what your two friends have mentioned."

Cat's brows knit together. "Did you drink stuff like that in—" She broke off. "Okay, four margaritas." Leaning in to Amara, she said, "I'd suggest drinking it slowly."

"We'll get them; maybe you guys find a table?" Jill motioned to the dining tables nearby.

"A table? Are we gonna sit, or are we gonna *dance?*" Shannon protested.

Jill rolled her eyes. "Both. But I need to warm up first."

As the two women went to fetch the drinks, Cat nudged Amara. "If this is too much, if you need to go home, just let me know."

Amara's eyes darted around the room. "I have been in large crushes before. I shall be fine." *I shall be fine.*

Jill and Shannon returned, handing over two large glasses filled with a dark pink liquid. "Remember: slowly," cautioned Cat as Amara accepted a glass and took a sip. *Lud, that's sweet.* Did every American dish consist of half sugar, even the drinks? Her mouth puckered, though she raised the glass for a second taste. *Sweet, but delicious.*

Shannon motioned them over to a table that had just emptied. "I'm going to get some French fries. Anybody want anything?"

Amara didn't feel like eating. Watching the people around her was satisfying enough. Groups of women sat or stood together, talking and laughing, some with drinks in hand, some not. Men jostled each other, their eyes often drifting to the women around them. A few brave souls danced strange steps without particular rhyme or reason around the dance floor.

"There will be more as the night goes on," Cat said.

"And people drink more." Jill chuckled to herself, then sipped her margarita.

"Ever run into Derrick here again?" Shannon asked Cat.

"Once, a year or so ago. He was with Candy; they'd gotten married."

"Well, good to know there were no hard feelings."

"After one date? I'd hardly think so."

The song switched to something new, and Cat's face visibly brightened. "This was Eliza's and my favorite song." Her eyes went sad for a second before she hopped up from the table. "I gotta dance in her honor. Wanna come, Amara?"

Amara set her drink, which was now somehow more than halfway empty, on the table. A curious, relaxed feeling had settled over her, and the music no longer bothered her. In fact, whatever was playing had an enjoyable sound.

"*Wake Me Up Before You Go-Go*," Cat sang as Amara stood. The two women made their way onto the dance floor. Nerves ate at Amara's stomach—was she truly going to try to "dance" like these people, in front of these strangers? But the languor steeping through her veins had her moving before she knew it, bouncing around in a way that was freer than anything she'd ever done.

"This is capital!" she called to Cat, who smiled in return.

"Ben was right, I needed a night off."

More and more people trickled onto the dance floor. Soon Amara and Cat were surrounded. She didn't care, though. She was having too much fun. As the music switched again, Cat screamed out, "Yes! *Take On Me*," mouthing the lyrics as she moved.

Amara could see why people did this. In her era, dancing was a common recreational activity, as well, since it gave men and women an opportunity to interact. But it was much rehearsed, the steps and patterns determined by masters of dance. Here, men and women mostly ignored each other, dancing in their respective groups in whatever manner they wished.

When the song ended, Cat exhaled. "Whew! Let's take a break. Plus, we gotta get Shannon and Jill out here."

As they pushed their way through the crowd, a young man in a wide-brimmed hat put his fingers to its edge and tipped his head at Amara. She stared for a second; he was the first man she'd seen in such a hat.

"Woo, girl, you got an admirer! Look at him in that cowboy hat!" Jill whispered once Amara reached the table, tilting her head toward the man.

"What?" *What was a cowboy?* Amara glanced over, and he shot her a smile. She couldn't tell the color of his hair on account of the hat, but his eyes were a friendly green, and his chin held a slight cleft. Heat crept up her neck at his regard. He tipped his head again but then turned as someone called to him.

Amara took another sip from her drink, images of Matthew suddenly flooding her brain. Why? Why did she have to think of him now, when she was having fun, when another gentleman was expressing interest? Not that she *wanted* interest, necessarily, but it was flattering to have a man look at her in such a manner.

Matthew looks at you like that. She shook her head. *Blast it, stop thinking about Matthew Goodson!* She hadn't seen him since last Sunday, when she'd fled the room. He'd made no effort to contact her. Clearly she did not appeal to him. That was fine. That was the way it should be. She didn't need him, didn't need his distracting presence.

"Would you like another?" A young waitress with her hair in pigtails gestured to Amara's glass.

"Yes, please."

Cat shot her a concerned glance, but she didn't care. That stuff—that margarita—was tasty. And she loved how much it relaxed her. It'd been three weeks now of being on edge, of trying to acclimatize herself to this impossible future, with all of its changes, its differences. Three weeks of learning about washing machines and drive-thrus and ATMs and the Internet.

The images on Matthew's computer of the naked couple flashed before her. It bothered her, how often she thought of that, of him. How much it made her squirm when her mind pictured Matthew and her in the bed, instead.

When the waitress arrived, Amara quaffed down half the drink in a few seconds.

Cat's eyes widened in alarm. "Seriously, Amara, slow down. Tequila has quite the kick. Unless you normally drank a lot in—" She broke off, tucking a piece of hair behind her ears.

"Of course not. Perhaps a spot of sherry, but spirits were for men only. As was everything." When Shannon and Jill both looked at her, she shrugged. "I'm from somewhere extremely … old-fashioned."

The song changed again, and this time it was Shannon who stood up. "*Billy Jean*! I *love* this song!" Grabbing Jill's hand, she pulled her onto the dance floor. Cat looked at Amara.

"Of course!" Amara leapt through the crowd to the dance floor. Who knew dancing in such a wild, almost animalistic manner could feel so good? The colors swirled around her, the people swirled around her, and she laughed as she writhed her body, feeling freer than she ever had.

An arm caught itself around her waist, and she looked up, startled. The cowboy hat man hovered next to her, his eyes devouring her. "You move well," he said, his voice husky. "Wanna dance?"

Dance with him? How did one dance *with* someone in this madness? She peeked around. A few other men and women moved with each other, not really touching but definitely in communion. She threw her arms up in the air. "Why not?"

He pulled her into him until their chests brushed. Unease slithered up her spine, but she merely smiled as she edged back a few inches. He let her, the grin never leaving his face. "You are one sexy little lady."

Her brow wrinkled, even as she swayed to the rhythmic drumbeats. The man was quite forward.

Cat stepped over so that she was almost in between them. "You okay, Amara?" She cast a frown toward the man with the hat.

He touched the brim with his fingers again. "No worries, ma'am. I'm taking good care of your friend, here."

Cat's eyes narrowed, and she looked to Amara.

"I'm fine. I'm great!" Amara insisted, despite her own reservations. She was in a public room, not a private garden. Nothing untoward could happen here. Could it?

After a long pause, Cat nodded. "If you need me … "

Amara waved her off. "Don't worry. I know you've got my back." She'd heard that phrase on a television show and had wanted to use it. She whipped her head around, her body one big expanse of liquidness.

Suddenly, the music changed, a much slower, softer melody hitting her ears. The hatted man tugged her close, looping his arms around her waist. She tensed, but noting other couples in similar positions, laced her arms loosely around his neck, looking up into his eyes, which swam before her. Did he have three of them?

"You seem like you're having a good time." His expression was friendly, but his lip turned up in a way that didn't make Amara entirely comfortable. "Tell me about yourself."

He's making pleasant conversation, Amara. This is fine. Being in such close proximity with a stranger felt wrong, though. He didn't smell as nice as Matthew, and he was much shorter. *Not that that should matter.*

"Um, I …" She couldn't think of what to say. What did one share with a stranger?

"It's okay if you don't want to talk. I can think of other things we can do." His head dipped, and he captured her lips with his, his hat tapping her on her forehead. Surprised, she froze. Half of her wanted to leap back, to crack him across the face with her hand for taking such liberties. The other half, the half under the influence of the margarita, found the pure physicality of the touch as intoxicating as the alcohol. She liked kissing. No, she *loved* kissing, a fact she'd discovered when kissing Matthew.

As the man widened his mouth over hers, his tongue seeking entry, Matthew's blue eyes flashed before her, and she stilled, opening her own. Green peeked back at her.

She broke off the kiss, pushing against him, but he didn't release her. "No."

"Aww, c'mon, we're just having a little fun." He ducked his head towards her again.

"No, stop," she repeated more loudly, breaking his grip by stepping back. She wanted to run, but dancers surrounded her on every side.

The man flattened his lips and stepped toward her. Desperately, she thrust her head side to side, looking for Cat. Where had she gone? Panic gripped Amara. Surely this man wouldn't harm her, not in front of all of these people.

How had she given him the wrong idea? Why did men assume they could take liberties with her? *Was* she the loose woman everybody accused her of being? She *had* let this stranger kiss her, after all. Shame settled on her like a hair shirt, scourging her in its unwelcome embrace.

"Hey, I'm—" An arm against her pursuer's chest stopped him from speaking further.

Amara followed the lean, muscular arm up to the blazing eyes of one Matthew Goodson. "You are bothering the woman. She asked you to stop."

The man puffed up his chest, glowering at Matthew. After a heated moment of intense eye contact, he tipped his head, touching his fingers to his hat. "My apologies, ma'am." Like a snake in grass, he disappeared into the crowd.

Amara's mouth fell open. Matthew was here. He had rescued her. Gratitude warred with irritation. She didn't *want* a man rescuing her. She could fend for herself. Except the hatted man had been disrespectful to her and hadn't stopped when she asked. "Thank you," she finally said.

His eyes flashed. Was he vexed with *her*? "You're welcome." His tone was gruff, frosty. "What the hell are you doing, making out with a guy like that?"

Her gratitude exploded in a hot flare of anger. She threw her arms up. "What does it matter to you what I do?" She pointed to a couple whose bodies mashed together as if a single entity, then to a second whose mouths devoured each other nearly whole. "I'm simply trying to be part of the crowd," she said with a huff. That wasn't entirely the truth, but her head was spinning, and she couldn't think straight. "Besides," she added, almost as an afterthought, "*he* kissed *me!* I didn't want him to!"

Matthew's shoulders softened, and he put a hand at her back, guiding her from the dance floor. "You're right. He was the aggressor. I watched the whole thing."

"What are you doing here?" She stiffened at his touch even as his fingertips sent tendrils of awareness up and down her spine. She hadn't seen him come in. Then again, there were at least fifty people in here, perhaps closer to one hundred. She stumbled slightly as they exited the floor—whether from nerves or the delicious pink drink, she wasn't sure.

He gestured toward two men at a table a few feet away. "Here with colleagues, celebrating Doug's new grant. They insisted. But I think I'd better take you home."

Home? When she was having fun? "I don't think so. You are not my keeper."

His cheeks unexpectedly crinkled into a grin. "No. Most definitely not. But you need one at the moment, to save you from yourself. You're drunk."

He nodded in greeting to Cat, who'd returned to Amara's side. "Sorry, I had to hit the ladies' room," she said. "I didn't know you were here, Matt. Nice to see you getting out. Did I miss anything?"

Amara's eyes flew to Matthew's in silent entreaty. *Please don't tell her I was kissing a strange man.* She didn't want to disappoint Cat, not when the woman had been nothing but kind and generous. Plus, Cat believed Amara and Matthew to be a perfect fit. If Amara kept company with someone else, would it upset her?

"Nope, but Amara was telling me how tired she is, and how much she wants to go home for some peace and quiet."

Amara's mouth fell open as Matthew shot her a pointed glance. *The nerve!* Though her head *was* spinning.

Cat grimaced. "Well, Ben just texted to say Wash is awake and throwing a tantrum about not getting ice cream. At eleven o'clock at night. No peace and quiet to be found at the moment, I'm afraid."

"I'll take her to my place."

Both Cat and Amara's heads whipped up, Cat's face mirroring Amara's surprise.

"What?" Amara's voice was a squeak. She didn't want to spend the night with Matthew Goodson. She didn't. First of all, the man had essentially ignored her for more than two weeks. He didn't want her, and she didn't need him. Second of all, he was entirely too tempting, standing there in those blue jeans with that fitted black sweater that outlined all of him a bit too nicely. The man was too attractive for his own good, and in her discombobulated state, going home with him was not a good idea. Not a good idea at all.

So why did it thrill her so much?

CHAPTER 17

The drive to Matthew's apartment passed in silence, his jaw clenched and eyes firmly on the road. Amara held her head in her hands, the quickly moving scenery not helping her already nauseated stomach. Cat was right; those margaritas were far more powerful than she'd known.

As they pulled into the parking lot, she murmured, "I'm sorry for taking you from your companions. I have ruined your evening."

He moved a lever and turned off the engine. "On the contrary," he said, finally looking at her. "This gives me the chance to get more done."

Her shoulders deflated. *Of course. Work.* He didn't want her there, hadn't invited her for an ulterior reason. He just wanted to work. Disappointment coursed through her, though that was stupid. But the alcohol in her veins, combined with the feel of that cowboy's lips on hers—a kiss that in no way equaled the ones she'd shared with Matthew—plus the images of the naked Internet people flitting through her head, had her desiring nothing more than to throw herself at Matthew, consequences be damned.

She needed to feel connected to something, someone. Cat and Ben had welcomed her with open arms, doing all they could to help her acclimate to an entirely different century. But it wasn't the same. They had each other. She had no one. No true friends outside of Cat, who had obligations of her own. No family. The loneliness crashed over her like the waves on Brighton's beach. Was it so wrong to want to connect, to feel, to be intimate with another person?

That's what led you into scandal, echoed her mother's shrill voice in her head.

That desire for connection had propelled her into Drake Evers' arms, desperate for the emotional as well as physical communion. It hadn't come. Much of the experience, the intimacies, had been enjoyable. Some had not. But she'd thought it worth it, for them to be combined into one for all eternity.

"I love you," Drake had vowed after their ardent encounter. "I couldn't give you up. But … I've married, Amara. Some months ago, in Charleston. Father made me."

Shocked and dazed, she'd gaped at him, clutching her gown to herself in the middle of the garden. If only she hadn't, if only they hadn't. If only no one had come along. But they had, and Amara'd been discovered there, in complete *dishabille* in a garden. With a man.

The damage had been done. She was ruined.

Yet the carnal urges that had led her to the garden in the first place never left. She still desired, longed, wanted, both physically and emotionally. She'd beaten it down as much as she could, not wanting to give in to the side of herself that proved her a wanton, a slave to her own evil flesh.

Until finally, she'd kissed Lord Hodgins. It'd been an act of desperation, an attempt to embrace life on the other side, carry on affairs, and have a different sort of existence, regardless of society's disapproval. She'd been twenty-seven, for Pete's sake. Was she to live a drab, passionless existence because of one mistake made years ago?

Then Eliza had come. Joyful, exuberant Eliza, with her absolute faith in true love and her adamant belief Amara had done no wrong, who asserted that sex, as she'd so plainly termed it, was a wondrous thing to be shared between two people, without shame or guilt involved. It was a gift, not a sin.

Amara could choose to lie with a man purely for physical pleasure in this century, Eliza promised. But she'd maintained people could and did form deep, permanent, intimate attachments—and she hoped Amara would find such an attachment. "I want you to have what I've found with your brother," she'd insisted. "A love like this is worth opening yourself up for."

That was obviously true for Deveric, who'd changed into a man barely recognizable. Gone was the stoic, dark, brooding brother she'd grown accustomed to over the course of his unhappy first marriage—and the devastating loss of his wife and daughter.

Now Deveric radiated happiness, his eyes lighting up whenever his wife was near, his love and affection for her obvious to anyone who saw them.

Amara sighed. That Deveric had finally found the love he deserved thrilled her. Of course it did. But it wasn't for her. Love in 1813 meant marriage, meant giving up everything for one's husband, meant having children and spending one's life on trivial things: planning menus, supervising servants, choosing the next ball gown.

She wanted more.

A woman could have both love *and* career in this time. Many did, including Cat, who'd found great happiness with her husband and her child, but also in running her bookshop.

Amara's brows knit together. *Could* she have that kind of relationship? Love *and* independence?

"Are you coming?"

Matthew had exited the truck and circled to her side, opening the door for her, all while she was lost in thought. He held out his hand. She placed her fingers around his and squeezed, perhaps more forcefully than necessary, but she wasn't feeling particularly steady on her feet.

His eyebrow quirked up. "Just how much *did* you have to drink?"

She clutched one arm across her stomach even as she kept hold of his hand. "I am unaccustomed to margaritas."

"Obviously." He grinned, but dropped her hand.

Her mouth tipped down. Why did the absence bother her so? When she touched him, it was as if a candle flared brightly. When he removed his hand, the flame dimmed, coldness following it.

Amara Mattersley, what is wrong with you, thinking such maudlin thoughts? She was foxed. That was it. That had to be it. An unexpected giggle burst forth. She was well and truly foxed.

She'd wanted to experience the world like men did. She was off to a good start. Or at least an inebriated one. She took a step, but stumbled sideways. Matthew caught her immediately, her body pressing into his as she fought for balance. "Whoa, there."

She clutched his shirtfront and looked up into those icy blue eyes illuminated by a streetlamp. "Sorry, I, uh … "

"We'd better get you to bed."

At his words, her eyes widened, plagued by sudden visions of herself and Matthew entwined upon a mattress, his mouth in the places she'd seen oh-so-briefly in that video.

His own pupils flared. "I'm not sure I want to know what you're thinking, with how red your cheeks just went," he muttered, "but I assure you, I didn't mean it like that." He tucked her arm through his, and she toddled next to him toward the apartment door.

"Like what?" she asked, as they carefully climbed the stairs.

He scowled as he inserted his key in the lock and turned it, the door swinging open in front of them. "You know exactly—"

The meow at his feet interrupted his words, and he reached down to scoop Lovey into his arms, nuzzling her fur.

What I wouldn't give to be that cat. She sighed, blowing the hair out of her face. Envious of a feline? Absurd.

He carried the cat into the kitchen. "Why don't you have a seat? I'll feed her, then get you some ibuprofen. You're going to need it."

She kicked off the heeled shoes Taylor had convinced her to buy. They were far less comfortable when on the feet for hours. Sinking into the sofa, she stared dully into the odd-looking flames of the fireplace on the opposite wall. How had she not noticed a fireplace before? "What's—what's wrong with that fire?"

A chuckle emanated from the kitchen. "I'm guessing you've never seen an electric fireplace?"

Electric fire? She stood up and wobbled to it, sticking her hand near the flame. Heat roared against her palms, but the fire was all wrong, the colors not right, the crackling noise artificial-sounding. She wrinkled her nose.

"Not your thing, huh?" came his voice at her ear.

When had he entered the room, much less got so close to her?

"Taylor makes fun of it, but this apartment complex has no gas fireplaces, much less real wood-burning ones, so I did what I could."

She nodded, unsure what to say. Swaying lightly on her feet, she tugged at the neckline of her sweater, uncomfortably warm. Everything spun around her, though in a less pleasant way than an hour ago. She moved toward him and leaned into his shoulder, longing for the support.

He stiffened, but didn't remove her. After a moment, she wound her arms up around his neck, much as she had with the cowboy. Only with Matthew, she could barely reach; he was much taller than she. His eyes darkened, but his hands flew up to cover hers, keeping them from clasping together around his neck.

"What are you doing?"

She should have been embarrassed. She should have pulled away. And yet, she didn't. She couldn't. She was the proverbial moth, and he the flame drawing her ever closer. *But the flame scorches the moth in the end, Amara.*

She didn't care. She wanted to burn, burn with him, at least for tonight. She wet her lips with her tongue, and his Adam's apple pulsed as he swallowed. *Good.* He wasn't as unaffected as he pretended. "I … " she said, her voice hesitant.

He didn't break the awkward silence, his blue eyes fixed on hers, his mouth unsmiling. Standing on tiptoes, she pressed into him, pulling his head down. He hesitated at first, and then those lips, those entirely luscious masculine lips met hers. The connection was so intense, Amara nearly lost her balance, but his arms reached around, pulling her closer as their mouths moved over each other in a most delicious dance of their own.

His tongue flickered out, and she opened for it, welcoming it, her tongue dueling with his in a battle she didn't care who won. He groaned, a low noise in the back of his throat, and every inch of her skin stood at attention, her nipples puckering against his chest. His fingers traced their way over her derriere, molding, clasping, holding her against him, and she reveled in it, in the raw need, in the physical sensations racing through her, in the heat and flame and undeniable passion burning between them.

He broke off from her mouth, and she murmured in protest, until his lips traced a path from her jaw to her ear, his warm breath tickling in a way that made her lower regions quiver, sensation pooling low, low in her belly.

"Yes," she whispered, her fingers clasping his head, holding him to her.

He continued his explorations, his mouth kissing its way down the side of her neck until her breath came in tiny pants, every sense finely attuned to the caress of his lips, those fantastic lips. She moved one of her arms, her hand tracing its way from the rough planes of his cheek along the corded expanse of his neck down to his chest, his hard musculature palpable through his shirt. The man sat at a desk all day long—how did he possess such a chiseled physique? She pushed the errant thought out of her mind as he moved up again, his lips capturing hers as his hands molded her flesh.

"My God, Amara," he murmured against her mouth. She moaned in return. His hand shifted around to her front, up under her sweater, but before he reached her breast, an irritated meow sounded through the room. Matthew abruptly ended the kiss, breaking the circle of her arms as he stepped back. The cat butted his leg, meowing again.

He clasped the back of his head as he stared at her. "No."

"No?" He didn't want her? Her eyes drifted down his front, taking in the bulge in his jeans. He *did* want her, or at least one part of him did. Why had he said no?

"No. You are drunk. I don't sleep with drunk women incapable of making an informed choice." He exhaled a heavy gush of air. "And I don't want to sleep with you, anyway."

The minute the lie left his lips, he wished he could take it back. Amara's face crumpled, pain creasing her brow as she cradled her stomach with an arm. *Harsh much, Goodson?*

He hadn't meant to be so blunt. But he'd had to put the brakes on. Lord knew he *did* want to sleep with her. He wanted nothing *more* than to sleep with her, to bury his hands in that rich honey-brown hair, to lift her up and carry her to his bedroom like a caveman, to lay her across the bed and claim every inch of her. It startled him, this primal response. It scared him, to be honest.

Regardless of how willing she was, he couldn't. She was drunk, true, and that definitely went against his moral code. But every bit of him screamed that if he slept with this woman, there'd be no going back. She wouldn't be a quick lay he could forget about by the next evening. No, there was something more to Amara Mattersley, something more to whatever was between them. And that frightened the bejesus out of him.

"I'm sorry, I didn't mean it like that."

She held a hand up, as if to keep him away. "It is good. You are quite correct; relations between us would be a grave error. I had already convinced myself of such; I do apologize for my brazen behavior this evening."

Convinced herself? She'd thought of the two of them together? He had, late at night when sleep wouldn't come, but hadn't wanted to admit it, had wanted to chalk it up to sexual frustration and an attempt to relieve himself of the stress he was under.

Something in her voice caught at him, some undercurrent he didn't care for. Shame. Shame is what he heard.

"Hey now," he said, his hand reaching up unconsciously, his fingers dropping just before they brushed her cheek. "You weren't brazen. I just … we can't. Cat, Ben … "

She nodded stiffly. "If you don't mind, my head is spinning. I think it best if I retire."

Guilt slammed into him. Of all the times to stick his foot in his mouth, why did it have to be now? How had he managed to make such a gorgeous woman feel so rejected?

Because you rejected her, you idiot.

He said nothing as she stumbled to the guest room. She didn't look back.

They could talk about it in the morning. If she even remembered. In the meantime, she needed to sleep it off, and he …

He needed to work it off.

Chapter 18

When Amara woke the next morning, her head pounded like thundering cannons, a steady rhythmic pain she'd rather do without. *Why did men drink, if the aftermath was like this?* Her body ached, her stomach roiled. She never wanted to move again. Perhaps if she closed her eyes, she could go back to sleep and forget where she was, forget what had happened. She'd made advances to Matthew Goodson, and he'd told her outright he didn't want her.

She didn't know which upset her more, his rejection, or her own behavior, which went against everything she was trying to do. Didn't it?

No, a different inner voice said, one obviously clothed in red and carrying a pitchfork. *There's nothing wrong with a liaison—or fling, as Eliza'd termed it.* And if she was going to indulge in a fling, Matthew's physical beauty made him the ideal candidate. There was no denying it; she was wildly attracted to him. That thick, closely cropped brown hair. Those eyes, the way they burned right through her. That chiseled mouth. Those cheekbones, high and prominent. Yes, his face did everything to her it shouldn't.

Then there was his body. His height excited her, made her feel petite, dainty, a way she'd never felt before, considering she towered over her sisters. And the very maleness of him, with the ridges of muscle across his chest and shoulders …

What would it be like to touch the rest of him, to feel his naked skin under his shirt or, heavens, lower, in his trousers?

Heat spread across her skin, unfurling in her belly, vying against the upset there. She chuckled weakly. What an odd combination; the desire to cast up her accounts alongside the desire to have her way with Mr. Goodson.

Noises in the kitchen indicated he was up, and the smells drifting in her room roused a surprising rumble of hunger, considering how nauseated she'd felt but moments before. Now all she felt was hungry. A hunger of many types.

She sat up but immediately regretted it when the pounding in her head multiplied tenfold. It was then she noticed she was stark naked. Her skin flushed to nearly the color of the cherries Cook baked in her tarts. She'd removed her clothing and slept without a stitch on? Mortification warred with excitement, the pleasure at having done something so … forbidden.

After a moment, the pain in her temples abated slightly, so she stood, retrieving her sweater off the floor. Pulling it on over her head, she reached for the leggings, but her arm bumped into the nightstand, knocking over a cup of water Matthew must have placed there sometime in the night. Next to where the glass had been were two small, round objects and a note: *Take these,* it said. *They'll help your head.*

He'd come into the room? While she was sleeping? *Had he seen—?* She had no time to contemplate that, for it only took a second to realize the water had saturated her leggings.

What should she do? Donning wet clothing held no appeal, but she couldn't go out without trousers. She glanced down, tugging at the sweater with one hand. It hung low, nearly to the middle of her thighs. There wasn't much difference between it and the sweater dress she'd worn here on that first day. Surely it'd be all right, at least until the leggings dried?

Bending down, she picked up the soggy leggings and spread them out over a chair. Her head pulsed, but it was tolerable, so she made her way to the door, taking the tiny round objects with her. As much as she didn't wish to face Matthew—his rejection still stung—she *was* hungry. Besides, food might help settle her stomach.

She padded her way into the kitchen and raised an uncertain hand in greeting to Matthew, who was at the stove cooking something in a pan. "Good morning." Her voice wavered.

His eyes were earnest. "How are you feeling?"

"I've felt better." She stood, hesitating. If she sat down, would the sweater rise too much? *Not that he'd notice. He'd made it clear he wasn't interested.*

He took a plate and flipped a golden circle from the pan onto it, then held the plate out to her. "Pancake?"

As she reached for it, his gaze traveled down her body, his face reddening as he saw her legs. He cleared his throat.

Perhaps he wasn't as immune as she'd thought. The idea satisfied her. If Matthew Goodson must possess the ability to throw her off kilter, she'd only like the same in return. Plate in hand, she sat at the table, not bothering to adjust the sweater when it rose higher on her hip.

Hussy, her mind screamed. *Scandalous jade.* Yes. And she was "okay with that," as Eliza would say. She'd spent years

172

bottling up her desires. Why not let them loose? Why *not* seek out physical companionship? That's all it had to be.

She swallowed the medicinal objects from her hand with the help of the water, then took a bite of the pancake. It was tasty, if somewhat bland.

"The syrup's right there," Matt said, indicating a bottle on the table.

Syrup? Amara reached for it, pouring a small amount over the bready circle. It looked and smelled a bit like treacle. She took a second bite. "Goodness, this is heavenly!"

He chuckled, but his eyes didn't meet hers. "I'm glad. Secret Bisquick family pancake recipe and all." He placed a cup of water in front of her before he set his own plate down, laden with several of the round pancakes. They ate in a not-uncomfortable silence.

After a minute, he rose and crossed the living room. "Mind if I play some music?"

Her head hurt, but she wasn't about to confess that. "Of course not."

He pushed buttons on a black box sitting on the shelf to the side of his desk, and the room filled with a rich, heady voice crooning about heartbreak and a hotel. She paused mid-bite, listening. This music differed from what she'd heard last night—simpler, the focus on the voice rather than the accompaniment. She liked its slower cadence, its less frenetic pace. "What song is this?" she asked as Matthew returned to the table.

His eyebrows rose as he sat. "*Heartbreak Hotel*, by Elvis Presley. King of Rock and Roll." When she didn't respond, he rattled off more words. "*Jailhouse Rock*, *Suspicious Minds*, *Love Me Tender*?"

She ducked her head, toying with her pancake before

setting the fork down and looking him full in the face. "I was not raised with this kind of music. Most of the songs last night were new to me." She paused, an idea forming. "Could you teach me?"

"Teach you?"

She leaned over the table, excitement threading through her. "About modern music? Today?"

Matt took another bite of pancake, debating. He'd had great plans of grading, then writing the midterm. A typical Sunday—work, work, work. Yet the idea of spending the morning with Amara, listening to music? Nothing sounded more appealing.

You're treading on dangerous ground, Goodson. She hadn't brought up last night, thank goodness, though it left him not knowing if she didn't remember, or just didn't want to acknowledge it. But if she stayed here for the day, wearing only that soft-looking sweater, would he be able to resist?

His groin pulsed, and he shifted in his seat. Yes, she was a damn temptation. On the other hand, when did he have the opportunity to share his love for music with anyone? When would he ever find someone who'd never heard Elvis, or the Beatles, or disco? Duran Duran, U2, hell, even Justin Bieber?

His music library was vast, cultivated over years, and collected into playlists by genre, artist, and era. Music had always been there, even when work left him time for little else. It was his constant companion, sometimes his only companion, and one of his great passions.

His eyes met hers. Did she have an ulterior motive? Was

she trying to seduce him again? *Again? You should be so lucky.* Maybe he *should* have said yes last night, the way he'd throbbed for her. But no, he could never be with a woman who didn't truly want to be with him, and alcohol precluded the ability to know that.

He'd made the right decision. He'd just expressed it poorly. And the Coopers *were* a factor. Matt couldn't sleep with his advisor's wife's cousin, not without potential repercussions he'd rather avoid.

He rubbed his forehead. He was overthinking this, like he overthought everything. But there was one thing he had to know. "Where are your leggings?"

She yanked on the sweater, her cheeks flushing a darling apple red. "I, uh, knocked the glass of water on them. They are drying."

That answered that. She *wasn't* trying to seduce him. She was just clumsy.

"Do you want to borrow a pair of sweats?"

"Sweats?"

"I'll grab them and you can decide. I'm sure they'll be way too big, but, well ... " He gestured toward her legs. *Great, make her feel self-conscious.* He stole a glance at her. One corner of her mouth inched up, as if she were amused.

Wonderful. Now *he* felt self-conscious, having revealed how much those naked legs got to him. He hopped up and practically ran to his room, grabbing a pair of navy sweats from the closet. Returning to the kitchen, he handed them to her.

She rubbed the cloth for a moment but then said, that side of her mouth still quirked up, "No, thank you. I'm quite warm, so I'd rather stay like this, if you don't mind. *Do* you mind?"

He reared back before he caught himself. Did he mind? Did he mind having to stare at those creamy thighs, thighs his fingers itched to stroke, to slide up, so that he could stroke her even higher? He sat down quickly, lest his body betray how much at least one part of him didn't mind. "No, just didn't want you to be cold."

His voice had *not* squeaked on that last word. Had not.

Despite the music, a strained silence enveloped the room as he took another bite of pancake. Looking up, he caught her watching him, and he gulped down the mouthful without thinking. What was her game? Her eyebrows rose, and he popped one in return.

"Well, will you?" she said.

Would he what? Ravish her right here on this table, his hands roaming over every enticing inch, clothed or unclothed? Hell, yes. *Good Lord, Goodson. Knock it off.* He shook his head. What had she been asking him?

She folded in on herself, like a flower in a drought. "My apologies for having taken up so much of your time. If you'll return me to Cat's, I shall be—how do you say it? Out of your hair."

"Wait, what? Oh, no, that wasn't at you. I, um, yes. Yes, I'd be happy to play you music. I'd love to, in fact." Because he loved music. Not because he wanted to extend his time with her.

He walked to his desk. "The best way to experience music, in my opinion, is through headphones." He held up a pair. "I have two sets, so we can listen together."

She eyed the headphones dubiously, but came over to him. Opening them up, he carefully settled them down onto her ears. It felt surprisingly intimate. He could hear her breathing, see the rise and fall of her chest. His fingers grazed her cheeks as he adjusted the headphones. "That good?"

Her own hands moved up, clasping the earpads. "Yes," she said, a bit louder than necessary. Well, those were his high-quality, noise-canceling ones, the most expensive pair he had.

He grabbed a second pair, then motioned for her to sit on the couch. Reaching over to the end table, he picked up his phone and plugged in his headphones. "Yours are wireless. Bluetooth," he said when he caught her looking at the cord dangling across his lap. At least he thought that's what she was looking at.

Amara giggled. "Music from a phone? How is that possible?"

He didn't question how she could be unfamiliar with iPods and the like. The girl didn't even know rock or pop. Something tugged at him again, an uneasy curiosity about how anyone could be in the dark about so much, but she'd said it herself; she'd lived an incredibly sheltered life. He nearly made another Amish joke before scrolling for his '50s playlist and hitting play.

As music flooded through the headphones, Amara yelped, leaping a good six inches off the sofa. He reached over and pressed on the side of her headphones to turn the volume down. It hadn't been all that loud, but perhaps her ears were particularly sensitive. Or she had one hell of a hangover. Chagrin hit him; he should have thought of that.

"Can you hear that?" she yelled. Her eyes rounded in astonishment and wonder as the cutest little grin settled on her face. She pulled one of the headphones off, as if testing the atmosphere around her. "It's only in *my* ears?"

He had to chuckle as he put on his own headphones; he couldn't help it. Her reaction was delightfully endearing, like a newborn foal walking for the first time, or a child's first ride on a merry-go-round: half-joy, half-fear.

"This is Elvis. Same singer from earlier. The song is called *Teddy Bear*." They sat side by side on the couch, the bouncy tune and unmistakable voice saturating their ears. "Next up, Buddy Holly."

They listened their way through several more '50s songs, then moved on to the Beatles. He had to ask. "Heard of the Beatles, by any chance? British, biggest band of all time?"

Her eyes looked troubled as she shook her head, but she quickly turned her nervous expression into a big grin. "But I like what I hear. '*I Want to Hold Your Hand!*'"

Both of their gazes fell to their hands, which resided within inches of each other on the sofa. She yanked hers up and made a show of adjusting the headphones.

Holding hands. When was the last time holding hands had sounded remotely sexual? Remotely appealing? In an era where sex on the first date wasn't out of the question, holding hands didn't carry the weight it once did. And yet, the idea of sitting here holding Amara's hand consumed him. Just the chance to touch her skin, to touch her.

Instead, he sat as the music flowed, letting it be the bond between them. He couldn't say how much time had passed. Song after song played, and he told her the band, the artist, maybe a few words about them. She listened to everything, rapidly soaking it in, though she admitted Jimi Hendrix wasn't her favorite. "Too much screeching."

"Wait until we get to the '80s hair bands," he said, laughing.

At one point, he wondered if she'd fallen asleep. Her head lolled against the sofa, and her eyes were closed. It gave him the chance to study her face, her fine features, that sexy arch of her neck. A tendril of hair curled in front of her ear, and it was all he could do not to brush it back.

Lovey padded into the room and flopped down on the carpet in the block of sunshine streaming in from the window. The fact that the sun was there told him it was nearly noon; any earlier and that window didn't catch the light.

He should take her home. Get to work. And yet, he didn't want the morning to end.

Her eyes popped open. *Crap. She caught me watching her.* "What does this one mean? What is *Afternoon Delight*?"

Sure. Don't ask him about Three Dog Night or ABBA. Ask him about *this* song. "It refers to having sex in the middle of the afternoon."

Her eyes widened. "They're singing about intimacies?"

He bellowed, a full belly laugh. "Most of this music is about 'intimacies,' as you put it. Have you not been listening?"

She flushed as her eyebrows crumpled. Was she angry? Embarrassed? "You needn't mock me," she muttered.

He reached out and touched her leg. "Sorry. I wasn't trying to mock. In truth, when I was a kid, I never caught on to the lyrics, either."

"Yes," she said with a sigh, "but you were a child. I am not, and I'm hopelessly ignorant." She tugged at her sweater, looking so forlorn he nearly laughed again.

"No. Not hopelessly. We're remedying that right now."

She moved her head so that she looked at him full on. "Can we? Can we remedy *all* of it? Now?" Her hand moved to his cheek. "I'm sober, Matthew."

CHAPTER 19

He stilled.

It was beyond the pale, propositioning him in such a way. But she couldn't fight this physical desire anymore, this overwhelming need whenever he was around. It ate at her, settling under her skin, never letting go. She wanted Matthew, wanted his mouth, his hands on her.

When he said nothing, she dropped her hand, embarrassment and shame coursing through her. Twice. Twice now, she'd offered herself fully to this man. Twice now, he'd rejected her. She leapt off the couch, tearing the headphones from her ears and throwing them on the cushion. "I want to go home."

Home to Cat's. Home to Clarehaven. This was too much: the technology, the foreign customs, the people. Matthew Goodson.

He grabbed at her hand. "Amara." His thumb rubbed her skin. She looked down at his fingers. He stood, keeping hold of her hand, moving until less than an inch separated their bodies.

"I lied last night. I want you," he said, the force of the words nearly bowling her over. "Hell, yes, I want you. But have you thought this through?"

She bit her lip, her eyes entranced with his, with the storms raging through the ice.

"I'm not looking for a relationship."

His words brought a bitter chuckle from her. "I'm not, either. I just want … " She couldn't bring herself to say the words, so she raised her other hand and settled it against his chest, which heaved, his breath coming in shorter and shorter gasps.

"But if things were to go south, to go sour, you, me, Cat, Ben … "

"Who says they have to know?"

His pupils flared, and his grip on her hand tightened. "One time only." Turbulence clouded his eyes.

"One time only," she agreed with a firm nod.

He snickered. "This sounds more like a business deal than a sexual one."

She raised her free hand to his face, her pulse pounding as she traced the hard line of his jaw. "We can be in the business of pleasure."

The words shocked her. People had called her brazen for years, but she'd never really acted so, as much as she'd secretly wanted to. It didn't have to be a secret anymore.

Standing on tiptoes, she pressed her lips into his, and the dam of restrained desire broke. He growled into her mouth, a deep, visceral sound that thrilled her to her toes. His tongue traced its way across her lip, and she opened her mouth, welcoming him in. *Yes. Yes.*

He let go of her hand and wrapped a long, lean arm around her, pulling her in close, his fingers tracing her side. He moved them down slowly, slowly, his mouth never leaving hers as he found the edge of the sweater and pulled it up, tracing her skin underneath. As his fingertips trailed over her hip, he drew back. "You're not wearing underwear." His voice reflected his surprise.

Her cheeks burned. "I, uh … Cat bought me some, but I don't like wearing it." What would he make of that? Should she blurt out they didn't wear such undergarments in her time?

Half of her wanted to tell him the truth, to stop pretending, to confess she was a stranger here in so many more ways than one. But if she did, that would be the end of this, likely the end of their entire acquaintance. For he wouldn't believe her. She didn't have proof, not the way Eliza had with her phone. She only had her word. She looked up at him.

His eyelids were lowered, his pupils wide. "I'm not complaining; I just wasn't trying to move quite that fast."

She smiled, grateful he wanted to savor the experience. If it were the only time for them to be together, she didn't want to rush, either.

His hands moved back up to her face, letting the sweater drop. He fixed a long gaze on her. "I don't know what it is about you, Amara. It's not like I haven't had other women, but you're different."

She winced. His talking about other women wasn't exactly what she wanted to hear at this moment, though she shouldn't be surprised. Men in her era certainly sought out companionship, whether fleeting, or more permanent, via a mistress. And she herself had had a lover. If one could call him that. One time in a garden did not truly an affair make, did it?

His own face contorted. "That's not how I—"

She leaned into him, pressing light kisses to the base of his neck. She *was* different. But she didn't want to think about that right now. She wanted to revel in the masculine form of the man in front of her.

He exhaled and laced his fingers through her hair, pulling her face back up to his. "You're better," he breathed against her cheek before kissing her again.

The taste of Matthew was beyond anything she'd ever experienced, a heady combination of sweetness and spice, a taste of which she would never get enough. Little sounds of pleasure emanated from her throat, and she pushed into him, luxuriating in the connection, the intoxicating feel of skin on skin. She wanted more.

Her fingers slid down the front of his shirt, admiring the play of muscles underneath. Finding the shirt's edge, she moved her hand beneath it, over the firmness of his stomach. It flexed as he trailed his arm down her back, kneading her side through her sweater.

"I love your softness," he murmured against her hair, breaking the kiss. "So glad you're not super muscular, like some women."

Women? Muscular? She'd seen women running, their defined leg muscles rousing envy; women in her era were not expected to be physically active beyond walking and riding. Yet now, with him, she was grateful for her curves, if that's what he liked.

"Whereas I admire the opposite on you," she whispered into his neck, her fingers dancing over his ribs and higher, skimming across the fabric of his shirt.

"Shall I take it off?" His breath came in short pants.

He was asking permission? Drake had never asked. He'd only taken. "Yes. Please."

He dropped his arm from her waist to pull off the shirt, and she immediately rued his absence, the lack of him, wanting him back. That is, until she saw his chest. The man was a marvelous creation—leaner, perhaps, than the statue of David she'd seen in etchings, but of similar musculature, a light smattering of hair drawing her attention and her fingers. She liked how it narrowed and darkened the farther it descended on his abdomen, leading her eyes lower, lower …

The bulge in the front of his jeans made his arousal obvious, and for a second, Amara hesitated. Everything in her entire upbringing said this was not proper. And yet, what had being proper ever got her? One night of scandal and years of repentance. She was *finished* with being proper.

She leaned in and pressed her lips to his chest above one of his nipples. "You are—what was the word Cat used the other day?—*yummy*. Yes, yummy."

His chest bounced with laughter against her mouth as she moved down, bending to kiss his stomach. "God, Amara, much more of that and I'm going to want you to go lower right away. Can we slow down?"

Lower? He wanted her to go lower? Her cheeks flamed, though this time as much from embarrassment as from titillation. The idea was half-frightening, half-exhilarating. Would he do that to her, too? Would she let him?

She nodded, rising back up to her full height. "What do you want to do?"

"Well, first, let's play some more music. Set the mood." He moved back to the sofa, taking the headphones out of his phone before hooking it up to some sort of box. Music floated through the room, someone's voice singing of getting it on.

She giggled. "That's not a phrase with which I'm familiar, and yet I think I comprehend his meaning."

He raised an eyebrow. "Marvin Gaye will get you every time."

"I don't want Marvin Gaye," she said, padding across the floor to press her full length against him. "I want you."

"God, Amara, you are so damn hot. I can't believe I'm here, touching you, kissing you."

"You're not if you're still talking."

"Good point." His mouth took hers again, as the music echoed around them.

She tasted like heaven, cinnamon and vanilla and sweetness and goodness. A small voice in the back of his head insisted this wasn't the best idea, but a much louder voice coming from places farther south told that other one to shut up.

He wanted to go slow, to savor every inch of her, and yet his hands itched to reach under that sweater, to clasp her ass to him, to feel his way up to her breasts. The sweater with its deep folds had them well hidden, but he knew they were in there, tempting him, taunting him.

She smoothed her fingers over his skin, one hand stroking around to his back and up his shoulders, cupping him to her. He moved back, taking her with him onto the sofa, leaning to the side so that he lay on it length-wise, with her on top of him. Her weight, the softness of every inch of her, fired his blood, and it was all he could do not to rip open his jeans right then. Thank goodness she was on top, so he couldn't.

He could, however, get his hands on her rear, that delicious ass. He squeezed it, wanting to slide his hands in between and forward, to dip his fingers inside her, but he held himself back. She moaned and pressed her hips into his. *God, I feel like a teenager, fumbling around for the first time.* He couldn't remember the last time he'd been this excited.

"Can I remove this?" he asked, tugging at the sweater. Slowness be damned.

Her cheeks pinked, but she nodded, sitting up. He tried to yank it, but the angle was awkward and he made no progress, so she grabbed the ends and pulled it over her head, tossing it on the floor.

Holy shit. She wore no bra, either. No undies and no bra? Had she grown up in a nudist colony? Perhaps an Amish nudist colony?

Those cheeks deepened from pink to red. "Part of me wants to throw my arms across my front," she confessed.

"Please don't. You are glorious. Glorious."

The music shifted, Madonna's *Erotica* pulsating in his ears. He hadn't heard the song in years, but it definitely fit the mood.

He tried to ignore the fact that her naked pelvis was pressing into him. No, he wasn't ready for that. Not yet.

His hands moved slowly up her sides, across her stomach, to cup the fullness of her breasts. "Like manna from heaven." He squeezed them gently, his thumb flicking across one nipple.

She started, a gasp escaping her lips.

"Did you like that?"

"Yes. Do it again."

"With pleasure." He ran his thumb over her nipple a second time, enjoying the way she arched her back into his touch, her eyes closing to revel in the sensation. "But you might like this even better."

His hand pressed against her back, coaxing her forward, down to him, and he shifted slightly, leaning up to capture the luscious bud in his mouth.

"Oh. Oh … Oh my heavens," she gasped. "I've never … Oh."

He paused at those last words, his mouth releasing her nipple as his brow furrowed. "You've never?" He looked up at her face. Her wide eyes stared back at him. "Amara, you're not a virgin, are you?"

Good God, he hoped with every inch of him not. He couldn't take her virginity. But she couldn't possibly be, such a stunning woman of her age. Could she?

"No."

He relaxed, even as his groin pulsed.

"I've had one … lover, but he did not linger."

"Bad lover, then." His eyes jerked to hers. Great. Another thing he shouldn't have said. But, really, how could one ignore the magnificence of those breasts, no matter how in a hurry one was? The man must have been an idiot.

Man. Not men. Man. *One lover?* That was almost as bad as being a virgin—because he no longer felt he couldn't, but yet, she had limited experience. Very limited.

Her laugh interrupted his thoughts. "Yes, I rather think he was, now that I know a little more." She leaned forward, dangling her breasts over his mouth. "I want you to teach me the rest. Teach me everything, Matthew."

His name on her whispered breath was his undoing. Screw being as bad as being a virgin—it was *better*. He got to introduce her to all of the pleasure, with none of the guilt. He slammed the door on the inner voice screaming, "Caution, maybe some guilt!" as his mouth closed over a nipple again and suckled, her mewling response firing his blood ever higher.

She writhed against him, and his hands feasted on her

flesh, tracing their way up and down her back, over her bottom, between her legs. "Ooh," she murmured as a finger stroked its way along her inner thigh, close to her center.

"I'd like to," he said, breaking off from her breast, "switch this up."

"What do you mean?" She frowned, panting.

"You underneath. I need to reach more of you, all of you."

"All right," she said, slowly. "But I want to see all of you, too. I feel … exposed."

"Darlin', you *are* exposed, and I love every single inch of it."

She stood up, and he hesitated, his eyes taking her in head to toe. The hair, softly tousled. Her eyes, sparkling with excitement and, he supposed, a bit of nervousness. Understandable. He was nervous, too.

Her skin was so pale, so creamy. Her breasts, firm and high and full—not too large, not too small, and bedecked with the most intoxicating rose-colored nipples, nipples puckering now in the cold. Or in anticipation, perhaps.

Her narrow waist and slightly rounded belly were all woman, the embodiment of sensuality. And the triangle at the top of her thighs—how frickin' sexy that was, instead of the shaved parts several other women had sported. He'd never understood the alleged allure. He wanted a woman, not a girl.

He had one.

Slowly, he rose, his eyes never leaving hers, and he reached for the snap on his jeans. "What do you want?"

She hesitated, her tongue darting out to wet her lips. "You, if you don't mind."

The corner of his mouth tipped up as he freed the snap and lowered the zipper, pushing the jeans down over his thighs and stepping out of them.

She wrinkled her nose. "Smalls."

"Small? Um, no, I'm not small." Momentary doubt coursed through him. He might not be the best-endowed man on the planet—he left that to the porn stars—but surely he wasn't *small*. No other woman had ever said anything.

She pointed to his boxers. "No, I meant those. I'm sorry, I don't know what you call them."

"You mean my boxers? Yes, some of us *do* wear underwear," he teased. Parts that had softened slightly sprang back to attention as she moved closer.

"Take them off."

The combination of surety in her voice with the flushing of her cheeks was one seductive elixir, and he pulled the boxers down, flicking them off, and stood before her, buck-naked. She didn't say anything, didn't move. What was going through her mind?

"You are beautiful," she breathed. "So different. So beautiful. I never saw … " She broke off, biting her lip.

She'd never seen her lover naked? What kind of yokel had he been? "Beautiful is not a word a man usually wants to hear applied to himself, but if you're saying you like what you see, I'll take it."

"Oh, yes. I like it."

Matt reached for her hand, yanking her to him. "I like it, too." He pressed the full length of himself into her, relishing her intake of breath as she pressed back.

"There's something I'm dying to do," he whispered into her ear, delighting at the shivers his breath induced.

"What?" Her own breath was thin, reedy.

"I'll show you. Sit down."

Amara hesitated. His hands guided her, though, and as the sofa scraped the back of her legs, she sat. What was coming next?

He fell to his knees on the floor in front of her, his hands gripping her thighs as he leaned in to kiss her. "I want to taste you," he murmured against her lips. His tongue darted in again, a quick caress, before his mouth moved down, dropping kisses on her chin, then her neck. He stopped at her breasts for some time, laving each nipple with his tongue until she cried out, some need deep inside her questing for more.

At long length, his head moved down, the kisses trailing over her stomach, and lower, lower …

"Matthew!" she shrieked, panic in tandem with anticipation. Surely he wasn't going to? And then she had no more time for thought as he parted her lower lips and pressed his mouth against her, his tongue stroking the tiny nub at their apex.

She clutched first at the cushions, then at his head, holding him to her as his tongue worked its unbelievable magic. This was sinful. This was divine. He traced a finger lower, dipping it into her entrance, and she bucked against him, seeking more. He drove the finger deep inside, moving it in rhythmic motion with his mouth, and she was off, her body racing, climbing, questing for a summit she'd only ever reached alone.

"Matthew," she cried out again, but this time it was no protest, it was an entreaty, begging for more, and he gave, his tongue loving her until she fell over the precipice, her world bursting into a thousand colors, sensation surging through every part of her. The spasms went on and on, and she reveled in them, holding him close until the shudders had died away.

"Oh my God," she breathed, and he looked up, a saucy smile on that mouth, that mouth that had just … Her cheeks flushed thinking about it, even as part of her wanted him to do it again. But no, though she floated languidly on a cloud, some part of her said it was his turn, now.

"Should I?" She gestured toward him, her pupils enlarging as he pulsed up and down in reaction to her words.

"Oh, yes, indeed," he ground out. "But only if you want to."

Please say you want to. Please, God, want to. Some women found giving head distasteful, but he hoped and prayed Amara wasn't one of them. If she felt uncomfortable reciprocating, that would be okay. *Seriously, it would.*

"Yes." The word was soft, hesitant, but it was there, between them, and he nearly leapt to his feet, so eager was he at her response.

She stood, pointing to the couch. "Sit down." The command was stronger, more certain, and the wickedly delighted expression on her face had him wanting to bury himself in her now, skipping any more foreplay. He hoped he could hold on.

"You'll have to tell me if I do it wrong, though."

He groaned. The combination of innocence with unabashed sexuality was a bigger turn on than he'd ever thought imaginable.

"Oh, I'm sure anything you do will be … *good.*" The last word came out a moan, as she'd fastened her lips over him, licking and sucking, her enthusiasm making up for her lack of experience.

"Oh, God, Amara, that feels so … " He closed his eyes, giving over completely to the sensations enveloping him. She continued, her tongue and mouth hot everywhere. He showed her how to add her hand, increasing the pressure, but the combination of the two had him so close to the edge he had to yell out, "Stop!"

She immediately backed up, her eyes wide. "Did I make a mistake?"

"No!" He pushed her down onto the carpet, his mind barely recognizing Chris Isaak's *Wicked Game* playing as he widened her legs, touching her skin. She was wet. Thank God. He couldn't wait another minute. He slid into her, her muscles spasming around him as he sank deeper, and he nearly came on the spot, so delicious was the warmth in which he'd buried himself.

She bucked up against him, urging him deeper, giving every time he thrust. "My God, Matthew, I never … " she breathed, before she bit his shoulder, clinging to his back as he drove them both forward to paradise. As his orgasm neared, he captured her mouth with his as he thrust into her.

"Amara," he panted against her lips, his hips pounding a frantic rhythm. When it hit, his body exploded, the spasms stronger, deeper than he'd ever felt. He sank into her, savoring the absolute intensity of their connection, marveling first-time sex could be so good.

It was only moments later, when he'd rolled off to the side and pulled her close, that he realized they were lying in the middle of his living room, on the floor.

And that he'd forgotten a condom.

CHAPTER 20

*A*mara lay in Matthew's arms, replete with satisfaction despite the hard surface beneath her head. Did people typically have relations outside of a bed?

She smiled to herself as her fingers traced over his abdomen. That had been marvelous. Heavenly. She wanted to do it again.

The sudden tension in his arm took her by surprise, and worry trickled in. Was he regretting it? She certainly didn't. He'd said he didn't want a relationship; did he fear she would now pressure him to offer for her, or at least pursue a further connection?

"Amara," he whispered, his fingers lazily drawing a pattern on her arm. Well, he was still caressing her—that was a good sign.

"Mmm?"

"I'm so sorry. We—I forgot a condom."

Her hand stilled. *Condom*? She'd heard the word, something men used to protect against pregnancy and disease, usually associated with houses of ill repute. She'd never actually seen one, though. Did he think her possibly diseased? Or was he more concerned about getting her with child?

Her own muscles tensed. *Blast!* She hadn't fully considered that, though she ought; conceiving out of wedlock was the height of scandal, and every woman was on guard against it, against seduction, to avoid that potential consequence.

What had she been thinking? She hadn't, of course; she'd been governed by lust, just like that summer so long ago, in the garden, with Drake. Would she never learn?

"I'm clean," he said, though she hadn't a clue what he meant. "So let's hope one time won't result in an, uh, ... accident."

"Yes, let's hope," she murmured, though she didn't hear her own words. The euphoria evaporated in an instant. Surely God wouldn't be so cruel.

He'd mentioned condoms. Better to focus on that than on a possibility too fearful to consider. Mayhap condoms were common here. If so, she and he could engage again, without risk. "Teach me about these condoms," she said, injecting lightness into her voice. "I need to know for future encounters."

If his body had gone any more rigid, he'd be dead. "Future encounters? We said—"

"Oh, I didn't mean with you." The insouciance in her voice was faked, but he didn't have to know that. It stung that he was already trying to rid himself of her moments after they'd shared such a fantastic experience. Or had it not been so for him? "Though I would be up for it again, if that didn't satisfy you. I still have much to learn."

A harsh, guttural noise emerged from his throat. "You're killing me. That was one hundred percent amazing, and from

194

your responses, it was for you, too. But—"

"There's no pressure from me, Matthew," she interrupted, sitting up and smoothing her mussed hair. "I think I shall make use of the shower. I find myself a little soiled." She rose, but before disappearing down the hallway added, "I was seeking physical pleasure only. If you'd like to keep sharing it, I would be a willing pupil. But I expect no more from you than you from me."

Matt lay on the floor long after the shower started, his thoughts—and feelings, if he were being truthful—a mess. He'd just shared the most exquisite sexual experience of his life with this woman. Half of him—no, quite a bit more than half—wanted to do it again. The other part, the rational, logical part, told him to stop. They shouldn't have slept together this time; future times invited trouble. Eventually, one of them would develop feelings for the other and that could only lead to problems.

Maybe not, the lust-driven part of him whispered. Friends with benefits could work, couldn't it? Amara said she was no more interested in something serious with him than he was with her—though he had to admit that hurt more than expected.

Still, what could be the harm in a few weeks of mutual satisfaction? And using protection—from here on out, at least—would ensure no unwanted pregnancy. That was the last thing he needed and one of his biggest fears; something like that would derail his entire life plan. But sex ... sex was welcome on the menu.

Condoms. Amara had asked to see one. She'd never used a condom before? He raked a hand over his hair. Well, she'd only had one lover; he supposed it plausible she'd never been exposed to them. But in this day and age? So many things about her didn't add up. He'd joked about the Amish thing, but was there something else going on? Could someone really be *that* sheltered?

He could ask Cat for more information. Taylor'd tell him to talk to Amara directly, but the idea made him uncomfortable. He frowned. No, he shouldn't ask. He didn't like people prying into his business; he shouldn't pry into theirs. And Amara's history was none of his business. He wasn't invested in her, nor she in him. He didn't need to know her entire backstory.

He sat up, glancing at the clock. 1:20 p.m. *Whoa.* Where had the day gone? He had so much to do. Yet what he *wanted* to do was crawl in the shower with Amara, run his hands across her skin as the water sluiced over the two of them, press her up against the wall, and—

The sound of his phone ringing interrupted his thoughts. He eased himself up, grabbing it off the music dock. "Hello?"

"Hey, Matt, it's Cat. Sorry to bother you, but I was just checking in. Is Amara okay? I thought for sure you'd bring her home by now. Is she really sick or something? I can come get her, if you need me to."

"She's fine. She slept in late and is in the shower now." Could she hear the catch in his voice? "I'll bring her home. She said she wanted to run some errands, but I'll have her back by the time I meet with Ben, if not before." *Liar. LIAR.*

"Oh. Okay. Thanks, Matt. I appreciate you helping her out."

"My pleasure."

His pleasure, indeed. What was he doing, trying to buy more time with Amara? This was exactly what he didn't want.

And exactly what he did.

Minutes later, Amara walked into the living room, leggings on, but bare-chested, rubbing her hair dry with her towel. Her movements made her breasts bounce in the most adorable fashion, and Matt nearly groaned aloud. He'd pulled his clothing on after talking with Cat but could feel himself rise again, straining against the jeans.

"Sorry," she said. "I left my sweater out here."

"No problem," he muttered, as she retrieved the garment and pulled it over her head. He was sad to see those breasts go but relieved at the same time; there was only so much temptation he could stand. Not that clothed Amara was any less tempting, especially since he knew she wore nothing under the leggings. They clung to her, hugging her thighs, nestling against her …

He turned away, desperate for some distance.

"Now what?" she said, draping the towel over a dining chair to dry.

"What do you mean?"

"Do you want to return me to Cat's?"

He couldn't read her expression. Did she *want* to go back? Or was she trying to determine if *he* wanted her to leave? "I could," he said, hesitating. "Though she just called, and I told her you might want a little more time to recover, so she's not expecting you home right away."

Her shoulders relaxed. *Good. She didn't want to leave yet.* "I was rather hoping …" She paused as she shoved a piece of wet hair off her forehead.

Was she suggesting …? Already?

" … We could listen to more music. I'm truly enjoying that."

Oh. He felt oddly deflated, though he kept his face neutral. "Sure. We were up to the '80s. Horrible hair, but great music."

She nodded and took a seat on the couch. "I'm ready."

His heart caught at the sight of her, all innocence and excitement. Was this the same woman who half an hour before had been as wild as he in their lovemaking?

You may be ready. But I'm not.

Amara's insides tingled as Matthew retrieved his headphones and phone, then sat next to her. He was closer this time, his thigh nearly grazing hers. He smelled so good, so masculine. A hint of their intimacies lingered in the air.

"I heard this one last night," she yelled, as *Karma Chameleon* played. She shifted on the sofa to lean against him. If he didn't care for it, he'd let her know, surely.

He said nothing, moving his arm up so her head fit more comfortably against his shoulder. "Yeah, Culture Club is great. Can't always make sense of their lyrics, though."

A new, different song echoed in her ears, its beat and odd cadences sparking unexpected desire in her. How could a man singing about crying doves do that? Or was it Matthew?

"Prince," he said, lifting one of her headphones so she could hear him. "Icon of the '80s. You can't know that decade's music until you know him."

She nodded in acknowledgment, wishing she could see Matthew's eyes, see if he was truly as casual, as nonchalant as he sounded. They'd shared intimacies on this very spot. Yet now they sat as if old friends, listening to music.

She rather liked that, actually—the idea that passion

---

and friendship could go hand in hand. In her era, men and women were so often separated it was hard to form any true depth of relationship, unless officially courting.

She'd enjoyed her brother's friends, Arth and Coll, but they'd been careful to observe the bounds of propriety, engaging in conversation only in the presence of others. Never would they be alone with each other, sitting on a sofa, listening to music, to voices pouring so intimately into their ears.

As a new song started and the words *I Want Your Sex* hit Amara's ears, she tilted her head to look at him, her skin burning furiously. Matthew merely chuckled. People sang so blatantly about sex! She couldn't imagine it in her own time, though there were likely bawdier songs to which she, as a young woman of a certain social standing, had never been exposed.

The day drifted on in easy companionship. Occasionally one of them got something to drink or used the bathroom, and yet they each returned to their spot on the sofa, nestling into each other. After several hours and innumerable songs, Amara peered up at Matthew. "Do you have a song called *Home*?"

"*Home*? The one by Michael Bublé?"

Amara shifted, her eyebrows puckering. "I don't know. Eliza sang it once. It was so beautiful."

"Eliza? Cat's friend who moved to England? You know her?"

Blast. He knew of Eliza. Of course he knew of Eliza. Did he know the full story? She doubted it. "Yes," she said, hedging. "She married my brother." That was truth, at least.

"Your brother? Cat said you're here because you have no other family."

"I have family, but none with whom I currently have relations." Not a lie, right? They were all, even the children, more than a century gone.

He smoothed the hair off her forehead, sending a shiver through her at the unexpected, tender touch. "Family dynamics can be hard. I get it. I haven't spoken to my dad in years."

She had no idea what family dynamics were, but nodded nonetheless, relieved he didn't press for more about her family. She wanted to ask about his father, but he might reciprocate, and what could she tell him? He'd never believe her time-travel story. He'd likely run, never wishing to see her again. And in spite of her assertions of wanting nothing from him, she enjoyed his company, at least for now. She'd hate to lose it.

He grabbed his phone. "Shoot, it's nearly 4:00. We missed lunch. I'm starving. You hungry?"

Her stomach rumbled in answer, and he chuckled. She was hungry, hungrier than she'd realized. Only half of it wasn't for food.

"Wanna grab a bite to eat? I have time before I have to meet with Ben. If you do, that is."

He wanted to spend more time with her? She rose from the sofa. "Yes. I want pizza. I find it quite tasty."

He chuckled again as he pocketed his phone. Crossing to the door, he reached for a sweatshirt on the hook near it, then pulled off a coat, as well. "How about you take this? It's getting cold."

He held the coat for her, and she slid her arms into it, suddenly enveloped in his smell. She raised the lapels up near her face and closed her eyes, breathing deeply. When she opened them again, he was watching her, a half-smile on his face, confusion in his eyes.

"You smell pleasant," she offered, shrugging. Might as well downplay her odd behavior. She didn't want him to think she was forming an attachment to him.

Because she wasn't. She most certainly wasn't.

Chapter 21

Matt held up the keys. "I should teach you to drive," he said, as he unlocked the front passenger door.

Her eyes lit up. "Would you?" She gave the truck a dubious glance. "Though the speeds these machines go is rather terrifying."

"Sure," he said with a laugh. Her unusual combination of spirit and inexperience amused him. He couldn't imagine not knowing how to drive, not having the freedom to go where he wanted when he wanted. How constricting that must be.

He assisted her into the truck, then walked around to his side. His stomach knotted. He'd just offered to spend more time with her. What was wrong with him? He couldn't afford all this time away from his work.

On the other hand, he'd be helping someone out. No one could fault him for that, right? He was being a model citizen. As he settled into his seat, that damn voice in his head whispered, *Someone else could teach her. Cat. Ben. Doesn't have to be you.*

With a vicious yank on the gearshift, he banished that thought. He *wanted* to teach her. He'd be providing her with a useful skill. Besides, Cat and Ben were busy with a toddler. They didn't have time.

Nor do you. Stupid voice. He'd make time, somehow. He liked serving, being helpful. He looked over at her, her face animated as she exclaimed over the song on the radio, Pharrell William's *Happy*, obviously thrilled to recognize it. Her eyes flashed and her cheeks crinkled in that dimpled grin, before her mouth rounded in the most delectable O as she sang along.

No, it had nothing to do with wanting to spend more time with her. Nothing at all.

Dinner was a lovely, casual affair. Amara peppered him with questions about his family, his upbringing, and his job. To her surprise, he answered every one of them.

"Explain this tenure to me," she said at one point. "You talk about this as your life goal, but I don't know what it means."

"Tenure means job security. Once I'm tenured, the University can't fire me. I've got a job for life."

A job for life. She'd never thought of that, of the worry of not having employment, a source of income. Her brother had chafed at his ducal responsibilities, occasionally confiding he felt trapped, with so many obligations and so little opportunity for escape, but it was a title granted to him at birth, with its requisite social position and wealth.

She'd understood his frustrations. As a woman of high

birth, her future had been determined from the moment she was born: comport herself as a duke's daughter ought, bring respect to the family name, marry well. To have life so prescribed, so proscribed, was difficult to bear.

Difficult, yes, but not half so much, perhaps, as the stresses of providing for oneself, for one's family. She'd been born into wealth, born into privilege. That didn't mean, of course, that she and those of her station didn't face real struggles, real pain. But perhaps she should more readily acknowledge the cage in which she'd thought herself imprisoned was a gilded one.

"Do you not fear you shall grow tired of the same occupation for all of your life?" Sameness, to Amara, was not the goal. It's what she'd been desperate to escape: the monotony of days never changing. The same people, the same social events, the same fashion, the same daily activities. The only thing that changed was the gossip, and she'd had enough of that to last several lifetimes. She *wanted* change. New challenges. New adventures.

"No. I relish it." He tapped his fingers on the table, his eyes not quite meeting hers. Silence stretched for a moment before he heaved a sigh. "My dad lost his job when I was nine. Then my mom discovered he'd gambled away our life savings, gambled our family into extreme debt. He left. Left my mother with the entire mess. We struggled financially for many years. I don't ever want to repeat that."

Oh, how terrifying to be without funds. To be poor. Amara had landed here with nothing, and yet the reality of that had never hit. Eliza had kept her promise of provisions. With the fund Deveric and Eliza established for her at Lloyds bank, a fund acquiring interest for two centuries, she was in no danger of poverty. In fact, she'd never have to work a day in her life if she didn't want.

She was beyond grateful, of course. She wouldn't have known how to earn money. Because of Eliza's foresight, Amara had the freedom to pursue whatever she wished. She could get the education she'd always wanted. A true, broad education like that of men.

"Wow, it's close to seven." Matthew's words disrupted her musings. "We should go."

Amara fingered her glass, staring into those heavenly blue eyes, her tongue moistening her lips. "Do you have to go to said meeting? Could you not tell Ben you need to help me … shop for groceries?"

He snorted. "You want me to blow off my advisor to go grocery shopping? Can't Cat take you? I mean, not that I don't want to help, but … "

"No," she said slowly, her gaze dropping pointedly to his mouth. "I don't want to shop. But I do want to give that bed of yours an actual try."

Matthew stared at her for a moment, eyes wide. He swallowed, his Adam's apple bouncing in comical fashion. "One time. I thought we agreed."

"Yes, I know. But I'm willing to amend that agreement if you are."

His lips pinched.

"Do not worry; I expect nothing of you beyond your body."

At that, he gulped again, then flagged down the waiter. "Check, please."

The words came out so quickly, she laughed. "I take that to be yes?"

"Yes. And we'll remember the condom."

She nodded quickly, ducking her head. As bold as she'd just been in inviting a man into her bed—or herself into his, rather—some things still embarrassed her.

"No strings attached, right?"

"No strings."

"Okay. I texted Ben. Told him I'd bring you home later. Let's go."

He hopped up from the table, his long legs bumping against its edge, rattling the dishes on it. Other patrons looked at them, but he didn't care. He only had eyes for Amara, his pulse pounding at her frank invitation, an invitation he'd been only too ready to accept.

Dinner had been pleasant, but his thoughts had continually strayed to the afternoon, to his mouth on hers, her mouth on him. Luckily, Amara had kept the conversation going, her questions making it easy for him to find something to say. He'd been more open than usual, but it'd been better than silently fantasizing about the woman across the table, his fingers itching to touch her, his mind on the things he wanted to do to her, with her, for her.

As he grabbed her hand and yanked her along behind him, she laughed, a full, throaty laugh that hit him in the stomach. God, she was sexy. He didn't know what he'd done to deserve this, such an attractive woman wanting sex and nothing more, but he'd take it.

The drive home was interminably long, though it probably took less time than usual, considering he'd hit every green light. Still, it wasn't fast enough. Pulling into the lot, he'd barely thrown the truck into park before he leapt out of the seat. Amara hopped out of hers, as well, not waiting for him to come around to her door, as had been their habit.

She grabbed his hand and pulled him to the stairs, the sauciest grin on her face. "You *are* going to have to take me home one day, though," she said as she climbed. "I need clean clothes."

Never. I never want her to leave.

What the hell? The thought brought him up short, but he shook his head, dismissing it. It was his cock talking, not his intellect. He'd satisfy himself with her, and the craving would diminish. He'd never cared for having someone in his bed for anything other than sex. Sleeping next to a woman felt foreign, uncomfortable. He liked his space, his freedom.

He liked Amara's ass, which swayed as she bounced up the stairs. He liked her other parts, too. Whipping out his house key, he unlocked and threw open the door, ignoring Lovey's impatient greeting as he and Amara entered. He slammed the door shut, then turned to her, his hands grasping her face, his mouth finding hers as he pushed her up against the door.

"Oh my goodness, yes," she breathed when his mouth left hers, tracing a trail to her jaw, to her neck. His hands slid up the insides of her sweater, stroking the soft skin of her stomach, the smoothness just under her breasts. Her hands wound themselves around his head, holding his face to hers. As if he'd ever want to leave.

He flexed his hips into her, delighting in her guttural moan as his hardness pressed against her softness. She lifted a leg, hooking it over his hip to allow him better access, and they moved together, their mouths simulating the action below.

A shrill meow interrupted them, and Lovey batted at Matt, sinking a claw into his foot. "Yeouch!" he cried, leaping away from Amara. "Lovey!"

Amara clapped her hand over her mouth, though the crinkling of her eyes betrayed her silent giggles. Matt glared at the cat, but then let out a chuckle himself. "Guess she's hungry."

"Guess she's jealous." Amara smirked at him. "And, well, I *did* actually want to make it to the bed this time."

He ran a hand over his head, willing his body to slow down. "You're right. Let me, uh, feed the cat, lest she interrupt us again. Meet me back there?"

Amara wasn't sure what to do. She'd never been in a man's bedchamber like this before and didn't know the protocol. Should she disrobe? Wait for him to do that?

The room was sparsely furnished, like the rest of his apartment, though a massively large bed with a black frame took up the center of the space. She walked to it, running a hand along the foot post. Metal? Not nearly as appealing as wood, though the blackness was stark against the white of the walls. One wall, the wall opposite the bed, was taken up by a television screen larger than any she'd ever seen. How odd, to give screens such a prominent place in one's sleeping area.

The door swished, and Matthew walked through. He stopped at the threshold, hooking his thumbs in his jean pockets. "You still sure, Amara?"

"I'm sure. But are you?"

"Hell, yes." He strode to her, his hands coming around to grab her backside, squeezing it as he pebbled her face with small kisses. It was playful, affectionate, sexual, and yet also unexpected. She liked it. She looped an arm around his neck, pulling him in for another deep kiss, deciding kissing was among one of the best things ever invented.

He danced her over to the side of the bed, maneuvering her until the backs of her knees hit the mattress, and she fell onto it, taking him with her.

"Ah," she exhaled, giving him a playful nip on his lower lip. "*Much* more comfortable than the floor."

Chagrin flashed across his face, but before he could say anything, she pulled his mouth to hers and lost herself in the kissing, the touching, the exquisite feel of his full weight on her. It was almost better this second time, knowing what was coming, what could come.

She wriggled against him. "I think we're wearing too many clothes."

He propped himself up on his elbows. "I agree. A smart observation." With a grin, he rolled off her and sat up, pulling his shirt over his head.

God, he was delicious, that leanly muscled chest with its smattering of hair making her heart thump. She reached out a hand to touch him, but he swished a finger at her, grinning. "Oh, no, no, no. If I have to be topless, so do you."

She laughed. "It's different for a man."

"Not at all. I am for complete equality in toplessness."

The man was hilarious, his icy blue eyes twinkling with humor as he looked at her expectantly.

"Fine." She sat up, pulling the sweater off.

He fell to a knee in front of her. "Fair maiden, I offer myself as your champion, here to protect your breasts from harm." He took one in each hand. "I must guard them closely."

She pushed at him. "First you say we're equals, now you're trying to make me a damsel in distress? I think not."

He bowed his head, but did not release her breasts. "I defer to you, oh, my queen."

Queen. As if. Though she did like this playful Matthew; he was far more relaxed and less serious than he'd been upon their first acquaintance.

"And now for those." He motioned to her leggings with his chin. "I've envied them all night, how intimately they've sat on your thighs, your … " He cocked up a brow, neglecting to finish the sentence.

"You shall have to release me, first."

With a heavy sigh, he let go, sitting back on his heels.

She pulled the leggings off slowly, inch by inch, watching his eyes fire. "And I've wished to be those blue jeans, wrapped around your legs, your … derriere." She flushed as she said the word, her modest upbringing at war with the brazenness flooding through her, a brazenness she fully embraced. It was so much more fun than being virtuous.

"Derriere?" He snorted. "What are we, French?" He unzipped his jeans, pulling them and his smalls off much more quickly than she'd done her own apparel, kicking them to the floor before crawling to her and burying his head into her stomach, his hands reaching around to clasp her backside again. "Call it what it is. Ass. And my God, Amara, do you have a fine ass."

Silence fell after that, broken only by sweet murmuring and sounds of pleasure. After some time exploring every inch of each other's bodies, Matthew groaned. "I think I'd better get that condom now."

Amara bit her lip, suddenly shy. She watched with interest as he grabbed a small square package out of the drawer to the side of his bed and ripped it open. He pulled out a thin-looking membrane. Lying back on the bed, he said, "I'll do it, since you're unfamiliar."

She managed the briefest of nods, her eyes wide as he unfurled the condom down over his length. It was incredibly erotic, watching him touch himself. "And that protects from pregnancy? Something that thin?"

"Yes," he said, his breath ragged. "Now, come here."

She rolled to his side, stroking his belly, her eyes on his manhood.

"I was hoping you'd sit on top."

"Oh!" Women did that? Fire burned through her veins as she moved over him. How intoxicating, to have him beneath her and her in complete control. She sank down on him, marveling for a second at how she didn't notice the condom. Then she was lost in sensation, the fullness of him filling her, stretching her, the only thing on which she could focus. Soft sounds escaped her as he took her to the hilt, every inch of him deep inside her.

"Oh, yes. I do say this is a most delightful position," she murmured when she'd caught her breath. He bucked beneath her, and she spasmed around him. "Do that again!"

He complied, thrusting his hips up to bury himself even deeper. She moved her hips in return, reveling in the power it gave her, watching his face contort with pleasure as she ground against him. She braced her arms on either side of his shoulders and moved, up and down, faster and faster, until her breath was nearly forgotten, and sweat pearled between her breasts.

He grabbed her hips, his hands clasping the flesh firmly as he moved up against her, deepening the connection, the rhythm. "Touch yourself," he ground out.

Touch herself? Part of her hesitated. It wasn't that she never had. It's that it seemed so … intimate, not something to be done in front of another. On the other hand, when he'd donned the condom, she'd had to suck in a breath at how it excited her, seeing his hands on himself. Her fingers reached down, finding her own center, and she pressed against it, moving in rhythmic circles, rivers of sensation flooding between her fingers and the feeling of him inside her.

"Oh, God, yes," she cried out as ecstasy overtook her, her body convulsing around him, stars every color of the rainbow bursting behind her eyelids. His own groans greeted hers as he thrust a final time, his hands kneading her skin.

Their harsh breathing echoed in the room, the only sound as she draped herself on top of him, languor filling her every limb.

Chapter 22

"Everything okay?" Cat hurried across the room. "I was getting wor—" She stopped, her mouth popping into an O. "Oh. No groceries?"

Amara ducked her head, avoiding Cat's knowing gaze. Was it so obvious what she and Matthew had been doing? Matthew cleared his throat behind her, his hand straying to the small of her back, touching her as if to reassure her.

"Nope," he said, his voice too bright. "Store was too crowded, so we decided to try later. Sundays aren't the best days to shop, you know."

Something suspiciously close to a snort came from Cat. "Yes, I know *exactly* what you mean. Well, glad you're here now. Matt, can you stay a minute? Ben had something he needed to talk over with you. And Amara, maybe you want to come up and, uh, help me load the dishwasher?" She walked toward the stairs.

Subterfuge was clearly not Cat's forte if her attempt to be discreet was to invite one to do dishes. Amara, however, dutifully followed, not wanting to rouse further suspicion. As she hit the first step, she couldn't help but glance at Matthew. His face was serious as he watched her. Until he noticed her looking at him, that is, at which point he winked and cracked a wide grin.

Oh, goodness. What have I got myself into? Memories of the last hour, the earlier part of the day, streamed through her brain, and half of her wanted nothing else but to go back down, grab him, and head to bed. The other half, the more rational half, gave her a stern talking to. *Amara Mattersley, you yourself said it: There is no relationship here. He does not want one. You do not want one. It is a physical connection, nothing more.*

So why did a tiny part of her heart ache?

Cat barely made it through the apartment door before she spun around, her eyes dancing. "Okay, spill. Something obviously happened between the two of you."

Spill? What did she mean? Share intimate details? Did people *do* that? Even if they did, Amara didn't wish to. Intimacies were a private affair. "I don't know what you mean. I wasn't feeling well after last night's overindulgences, so Matthew kindly let me sleep in his apartment. Then we … took care of tasks and such."

Cat tucked a piece of hair behind her ears. "Okay, you don't have to share. But you can't tell me there isn't some sort of connection. It shows all over your faces."

"Even if there were," Amara said, following Cat into the kitchen, "I don't want there to be."

"Ah, but sometimes what we want and what we need are two different things. If I've learned anything in this life, it's that."

Ben walked into the kitchen and settled Wash in a chair at the table. "Matt's finally here, huh? I'll be back up shortly." He dropped a brief kiss on Cat's lips. "I hope you had a nice time," he said to Amara, no hint of anything other than sincerity in his tone.

Cat snorted again after he left. "You don't really have to do dishes, of course," she said, opening the refrigerator. "I was hoping you'd feel comfortable confiding in me. But if you don't want to, I understand."

She pulled out an apple and sliced it into pieces, sliding the pieces from the cutting board onto a plate that she set in front of Wash. He grinned, his chubby hands grabbing a slice.

Amara sat down in a chair near the little boy, her shoulders slumping in a way she'd never have got away with at Clarehaven. "I am unaccustomed to having friendships beyond family," she said at length. "And in my era, one does not discuss such things."

That wasn't entirely true. She and her sisters had had conversations, and other young women had on occasion pestered Amara for details of the intimate act, details she'd declined to give. Plus, she hadn't really known the truth of it, the grandeur of it, until today. With Matthew.

"Got it. I won't say another word, unless you want to talk—with the exception of the fact you'd make the cutest couple." Cat put a bowl of something in the microwave as she spoke, pushing buttons to heat it up.

Wash held his hand out to Amara. "Wan' apple, Cousin 'Mara?" His cheeks crinkled with his big grin. She had to admit, he was winsome.

"No, thank you."

His smile disappeared, though he didn't look angry, just confused. Turning his head toward his mother, he picked up the remaining apple pieces and dropped them on the floor with a wicked giggle. "Washington Jefferson Cooper!" Cat's voice was firm but laced with love.

Amara, on the other hand, made a face. *And that's why I don't want a child.*

"Want to watch *Pride and Prejudice* after I get Wash to bed?" Cat said, stooping to pick up the apples. "You can tell me everything they get wrong."

"*Pride and Prejudice?* Oh, yes, Eliza's favorite book. Miss Austen is most delightful. We called on her several times before I ... left."

Cat clapped her hands in excitement. "I'm so thrilled she got to meet her idol. I can hardly believe it. Pretty sure Jane Austen would agree Colin Firth is eye candy in any era. So, what do you say?"

"Yes. That sounds like a pleasurable way to spend the evening." Not as pleasurable as how she spent her day. She didn't know who this Colin Firth was, but she doubted he could be anywhere as attractive as Matthew Goodson lying naked on the bed, his ice-blue eyes ablaze with desire.

"I wish to take a shower, if that is agreeable," she said, rising from her chair. *A very cold one, perhaps.* For her body was still on fire, burning for the man one floor beneath her.

Matt did his best to concentrate on Ben's words, but his mind kept drifting to the woman upstairs. What was she doing? What was she thinking?

They'd made love twice in one day. Was she truly okay with that? Had he taken advantage of her? The idea didn't sit well with him. He was all for a good time, but only if both people were on the same page. *She said she was—said she wanted it as much as you.*

"You seem tired." Ben's words interrupted Matt's thoughts. "Should we talk about this some other time?"

"I'm sorry."

"No big deal." Ben stood. "I'll see you tomorrow. Thank you for taking such good care of Amara."

Matt's eyes whipped to Ben's. *Was that a look? Did Ben suspect?* The older man's face revealed nothing, though a corner of his mouth twitched.

Matt didn't trust himself to say anything more. Any longer here, and he might fess up to everything. He had to go. With a nod at Ben, he rose and stretched his back. While he was in good shape, there were muscles twingeing right now he hadn't even known he had. Walking to the door, he fought the urge the entire way to look back, to look for her.

Ridiculous. It was a fling.

Nothing more.

Chapter 23

The week passed slowly. Amara spent as much time as possible reading to expand her knowledge. But she couldn't focus, her mind often drifting to Matthew, to the night at the bar and the day afterward. Occasionally, she'd hear songs on the bookstore's radio she'd listened to with him, and she'd be right back in his living room, leaning against his shoulder, breathing in his lovely smell.

He'd texted once to Eliza's phone, the number of which she'd given him.

Driving lessons Saturday?

It'd taken her several minutes to reply.

Yes, pleaase. I thankk you foir yur time. Amara.

Nothing personal. A message more business-like than friendly on both their parts. But that's how they'd said they wanted it.

So why did she lie awake at night, thinking of him, wondering what he was doing?

Likely working. The man reminded her of Deveric in his single-minded dedication to his goal, his total commitment to achieving this tenure. His need for security made sense, given what he'd shared about his father.

What was her greatest need? She didn't know. She'd come here because she longed to break out, to rebel, to defy expectations and conventions and forge her own path on her own terms. On the other hand, she wanted a place she belonged, a place she could be accepted for exactly who she was.

The struggle between the two opposing desires had dogged her days at Clarehaven, and sadly, she hadn't escaped it here, as she'd hoped. Her dream of being an independent woman, of achieving whatever level of education she wished, of pursuing whatever she chose, was within her grasp. She never had to be beholden to anyone again, much less a man. So why didn't it feel enough?

Because I'm lonely.

Loneliness was an emotion to which she was long accustomed, her constant shadow even before the scandal. She'd never completely fitted in to her family, to her society.

She'd hoped to eradicate that loneliness here.

These things take time, Amara. Her friendship with Cat was deepening, though she'd yet to confide about her day with Matthew. She'd spent another evening in company with Cat's friends, Jill and Shannon, who were entertaining companions. But all were a good ten years older than she. Not that their difference in age precluded friendship, but all three were also married, and Cat and Shannon spent much time discussing their children.

Amara needed friends of her own, friends to replace her sisters, whom she missed dearly. Her thoughts flitted to

Taylor, Matthew's sister. They'd only met that one evening, but she'd liked the woman, had enjoyed her easy-going nature. Too bad Taylor did not live in town.

Saturday. She'd ask Matthew about Taylor on Saturday.

She glanced at the phone at her side. No messages. She could text him, of course. But what could she say that wouldn't be misconstrued as meaning more than it did?

Saturday. Saturday was fine.

Saturday couldn't come soon enough.

Matt threw himself into work, attempting to drown out the constant thoughts and memories of Amara underneath him, over him, with the mound of papers, emails, and requests he had to deal with.

It was good on the one hand; he'd fallen behind on the goals he'd set earlier in the semester. And working was easy, familiar. He spent his days and evenings in front of the screen, rising only to teach, attend meetings, eat, and work out at the gym. Just like he always had. And yet, it felt emptier, hollower.

His hands itched toward his phone, wanting to text her, to say hi, to see if she'd like to come over. But he wasn't about to sink to a booty call text. He wouldn't disrespect her in such a way. He could call, but that felt more intrusive, more personal. It'd suggest more than he wished to. And besides, maybe their one day had been enough for her. Maybe she didn't need or want to repeat it.

But, God, he hoped she did. He'd never found such pleasure with a woman. It'd been perfect right from the start.

Except for the lack of condom. He cursed under his breath, angry again he'd been so negligent. He'd never forgotten before. Ever. But he'd studied biology, knew down to the percentage how unlikely it was one encounter would produce a pregnancy.

He ran his hands down his thighs, breathing out hard. No, focus on the fun parts, not the fear. Or on work. He'd see her Saturday, could gauge her level of interest at that point. Until then, he had tons to do. He needed all the time he could get.

Saturday couldn't come soon enough.

CHAPTER 24

"We should go somewhere you're not likely to run into anything on your first try," Matt said as Amara clambered into the truck Saturday afternoon. He hoped his voice reflected nonchalance, nonchalance he certainly didn't feel. The minute he'd spied her descending the outside stairs from the Coopers' apartment, he'd wanted to leap out of the truck, to swoop her up and plant a kiss on that scrumptious mouth.

He hadn't, of course, just like he'd merely texted her he was here instead of going up to the door. He didn't want her to see, didn't want to acknowledge to himself, how nervous he felt, how much his pulse raced when she appeared.

Sex. That's what this was about, why his heart was pounding, his groin aching. She was the best sexual partner he'd ever had, and his body was anxious to repeat the experience. That was all.

But first he had to teach her how to drive. He sighed. What would his brothers say if they knew he was about to let a woman drive his beloved truck? He'd never hear the end of it.

"Oh, sure," Jared would tease. "Let some chick behind the wheel but not your favorite brother."

Well, as he'd said, they'd go somewhere open. Wide open. He glanced at her, and she nodded. He'd nearly forgotten to what she was agreeing, so lost he'd gotten in his own thoughts. His own fantasies. He started the truck, preparing to head out, but his eyes stole back to her involuntarily, and he exhaled. He couldn't read her face, had no clue what she was thinking. She wasn't smiling, but she didn't look sad or angry, either. He focused on the tiny v between her brows. *Nervous?*

"You ready for this?"

She swallowed and nodded again, the kind of quick nod one gave when they meant exactly the opposite. He reached over and squeezed her knee. "You'll be fine. I promise. I'll take good care of you."

Her forehead furrowed at his words, but she flashed him a smile, her eyes drifting down to her knee, where fingers still rested.

"Oh. Sorry." He yanked his hand away, shifting the car into reverse without looking at her again.

"It's okay. I rather like it," she said, and he hit the brakes, jolting both of them. Laughter bubbled out of her, and he couldn't help but wing a grin in return. "I do hope I do better than that," she said after a moment.

"You could hardly do worse." He eased the truck out of the driveway, his thoughts on her words. She liked it. How was he to take that? Was she open to a repeat of last Sunday's activities? Half of him thrilled to the notion. The other half worried about how much he'd enjoyed that brief touch, how much the idea of driving along with his hand resting on her thigh appealed to him. A mark of familiarity. A mark of comfort.

A mark of possession.

He kept both hands on the wheel.

A few minutes later, they pulled into an empty parking lot.

"It's the high school. Everybody stays away on the weekends, kids and teachers alike." He sucked in a deep breath. "Okay, before we put you behind the wheel, let me describe things. It's not that complicated—basically, you've got the steering wheel and two pedals."

She nodded, but said nothing, her eyes wide and mouth flat.

She's really nervous. It shouldn't surprise him; he'd been petrified the first time he'd driven. He resisted the urge to squeeze her thigh again in reassurance. "Always use your right foot. That's rule number one," he said. "It helps you keep the brake and accelerator separate."

Her cheeks were paler than usual, but her face was a study in concentration, her brow creasing as she watched intensely. He gave details on the pedals, the wheel, and the gearshift. Thank goodness it was sunny; windshield wipers and turn signals could wait.

At length, he stopped, running his hands along his thighs. He was really going to do this. He was going to let a woman drive Bessie, his baby. *But not any woman.* Amara.

He jumped down from the driver's seat as she left the other side. He wasn't doing this because she was special to him. He was doing this because she needed help, and he liked to help, liked to teach. If he didn't, he wouldn't have become a professor.

They met at the front of the truck, nearly walking into each other.

"Sorry," she bit out, as she made to move around him.

He grabbed at her arm, not sure why. "You scared?"

She nodded, her eyes meeting his before quickly sliding away. She stared off into the distance for a moment before admitting, "Yes, but not just about the driving."

That caught him off guard.

"You. Me. We're not—I don't want … And yet, I find myself very happy to see you." Her eyes, those stunning eyes swung back around, fixing firmly on his. "And I find myself desperately wanting to kiss you."

He moved in before she'd finished the sentence. "Thank God," he said. "It's all I've been thinking about since you walked down those damn stairs."

His arms crushed her to him as she wove her wrists around his neck, her fingers into his hair. His mouth smashed onto hers, an impatient, aggressive meeting, but she gave as good as she got, the little noises escaping her throat driving him mad with desire. His hands roamed over her sides, her back, her ass, pulling her in tighter, seeking more of her. Hers stroked along his hair, his eyebrows, his face.

At last, they pulled apart.

"What …?"

"I don't know."

They didn't need to explain. Each somehow knew what the other was asking. What *was* this overpowering attraction, this underlying need whenever she was near? He'd made it through the week fine, focusing on what he needed to focus on, what he was *supposed* to focus on: work. But five minutes in her presence, and all he could think about, dream about, was her.

She straightened her shoulders, standing tall. Perhaps she was trying to instill confidence in herself, but the effect was to thrust her breasts out. He swallowed, hard.

"Perhaps if we agreed we would like to end today's encounter in a more intimate way, we could focus on the task at hand?"

Wait, *what*? She thought telling him she wanted to have sex would make him think about it *less*?

"Absolutely." He eyed the truck. There wasn't room in the cab, but maybe if they climbed in the back? *Chill, Goodson.* It was broad daylight, and though the parking lot was empty, that didn't mean it'd stay that way. Plus, sex in public had never been on his bucket list. He exhaled. He could do this. He could focus on teaching, and after that—reward. For both of them.

The next hour passed more quickly than expected. Amara managed to stall the truck several times—an amazing feat, considering it was an automatic. When she did move the thing forward, she refused to go above ten miles an hour, but she did it. The excitement on her face when she successfully pulled into a parking space made him laugh. "Try doing it when there are cars on either side."

Her hands maintained their vise-like grip on the wheel, but she'd shot him a small glare that ended in a chuckle.

"Wanna try going in reverse?"

She shook her head. "Not today. In truth, I am overwhelmed. This is much different from driving a carriage."

"Are you *sure* you're not Amish?" he quipped. Because, seriously, who else drove carriages in this day and age? He sighed. Amara Mattersley was an enigma, no doubt about it. But what he wanted most at the moment was not to figure her out, but to get his hands on her. "My place?"

"Yes, please."

He reached over and turned the engine off before alighting from the passenger side. This time, they didn't stop at the front, but raced past each other in their desire to get back to the vehicle.

The drive home never felt so long.

Amara traced her fingers along the contours of Matthew's back, marveling at the differences between them. Where she was soft, he was hard—all muscle underneath that skin, moving under her fingertips. He lay slumped over her, breathing heavily, trying to catch his breath after a most delightful hour, perhaps two, that had ended with ecstasy so intense, she could hardly bear it. She ran her hand down to his derriere, squeezing lightly.

"That was … "

"Yes."

She didn't finish her sentence, and he didn't ask her to. It'd happened in the parking lot that afternoon, that sense they knew what the other was thinking, that words weren't necessary. It unnerved her. She leaned in and bit his shoulder lightly, as much to distract herself from those uncomfortable thoughts as anything.

"Ow," he said. "Though you did that earlier, too. Better be careful; Ada Lovelace might do you physical harm if she thinks you're hurting my body."

She laughed, enjoying the pressure of his ribs against hers. "Harm this body?" Her voice was a soft whisper as she stroked her hands up his sides. "Never."

He quickened inside her.

Again? *So soon?* Not that she was complaining.

He moved suddenly, rolling off of her and staring at the ceiling. She frowned. Had she done something to upset him?

His head tilted toward her. "Apparently I can't get enough," he said with a tight chuckle, but his eyes were wary.

Neither can I.

"Do you—should I return to Cat's?"

"Hell, no." He looped an arm around her and pulled her into him, just as his cell phone rang. "Who?" He grabbed it off the side table. "Oh." He slid his finger across it. "Taylor? What's up?"

The female voice burst from the device, loud and upset.

"Slow down. It's okay. No, I'm not doing anything." His eyes shot to Amara's, and he flashed her an apologetic grin.

The words stung. They'd just spent hours in bed and it was nothing? On the other hand, what did she expect him to say? "Hi, sister, I have been bedding the woman with whom you spent an evening."

And it *was* nothing. A physical dalliance. A distraction. A mutual pleasure. No more.

He reached over and smoothed a piece of hair off her cheek as the female voice raged on. She closed her eyes at the delicate touch, and something in her heart hitched. That hadn't been an act of passion; it'd been an act of tenderness. She opened her eyes again. Had he even realized he'd done that? *Perhaps he did that with every woman he bedded.*

"How about I bring you one? No, it's fine. But, um, is it okay if Amara comes, too?"

There was momentary silence from the phone. Was Taylor as shocked as Amara at his suggestion? He wanted her to go with him? *Why?*

The voice chattered again. "Great, okay," Matthew responded. "We'll see you in about half an hour or so." He slid his finger across the phone and set it back on the table. "Uh," he said, his throat bobbing as he swallowed. "I have to go to

Taylor's. Someone stole her laptop."

"Goodness. That's terrible!" Did theft happen often? Was this not a safe area? Then again, London had been full of pickpockets and the like.

"So, do you want to come?"

Amara hesitated. There was no true reason for her to accompany him. Except that she did not wish to leave his company. Plus, she would very much like to see Taylor again. And Charlottesville was the only place she'd seen since arriving. Perhaps it would be of use to study a new town. Yes, that made sense. She should go for her own further edification on American life in the twenty-first century.

"Yes."

He dropped a quick kiss on her nose, then rose from the bed and disposed of the condom. As he stooped to retrieve his trousers, Amara studied the interplay of his muscles, as well as the smoothness of his sides and … ass, as contrasted to the hair adorning his chest. So male. So very different.

So delicious.

She should have indulged in affairs earlier. It was ridiculous, the way she'd abstained. It clearly wasn't her nature—and it hadn't done anything to redeem her reputation. Of course, none of the men in 1813 held a candle to the one standing before her now. He pulled on those funny boxer smalls, then the trou—jeans. Her mouth watered, and she longed to touch, to lick the spot where the denim met his skin.

"Do you need to put on a shirt?" she teased. "Can you not go like that? I find myself rather fond of those jeans, how they enhance what's above … and below."

He arched an eyebrow, a smirk playing across his face. "Only if you go topless, as well."

She threw the pillow at him.

CHAPTER 25

*A*mara's eyes remained glued to the window as her fingers carved themselves into the seat and side door. "Do you have to drive so *fast*?"

"I'm going seventy-two. That's only two miles over the limit." He snickered. "Try not to dig your fingers clear through the metal, will you?"

It was all she could do not to release the contents of her stomach as the world sped by at unheard-of speeds, a blur of green, gray, and yellow. People drove like this every day?

"Hey, you okay? You look a little green."

"My head is spinning."

"Do you need me to stop?"

"No, no." She wanted the trip over as soon as possible.

"It'd help if you'd look ahead, rather than down at the side of the road, you know. That would make me sick, too."

Look farther? Was he mad? But she forced her face away from the blur below to the view in the distance. Her mouth dropped open. "It's beautiful." Everything still moved too quickly, but if she studied the farthest objects she could see, it wasn't so bad. And what she saw was mountains, like she'd never seen in England.

They passed a large, rumbling rectangle, and she squeezed her eyes shut again. "That thing won't hit us, will it?"

"Not if I can help it. I may love my truck, but it wouldn't stand a chance against a semi."

She nodded, keeping her eyes closed a moment longer. Opening them, she risked a glance at him, enjoying the opportunity to soak in his strong profile. His eyes remained on the road, thank God. *Seventy miles an hour.* "What my brother wouldn't have given to travel at such a rate."

Amara's eyes prickled unexpectedly with tears. The last time she'd seen Deveric, his face had been full of life, beaming with pride as his son, Frederick, rode a horse around the paddock. It was hard to accept that he—that her whole family—was long dead. "I miss him."

A single tear escaped, sliding down her cheek. She wiped it away, hoping he hadn't seen. She'd never liked crying. It was sign of weakness, and she was done being weak.

"Your brother?"

She nodded.

"Hey …" His voice was soft as he shifted one hand from the steering wheel onto her leg, rubbing her thigh with his thumb. "You've got the Coopers. And I'm not about to leave you on the side of the road." At the last words, the corners of his mouth pulled down. He turned his head back to the highway, his hand leaving her thigh and grasping the wheel firmly.

Had he regretted saying that? Did he think she'd read more into it than he'd intended? She didn't. There were no strings between them, no stronger connection than a mutual seeking of physical pleasure. *If that were true, you wouldn't be in this truck right now, going to visit his sister.* She bit her lip. Why *was* she here?

Because he'd asked her to come. Why?

She'd said yes. Why?

She didn't want to examine that too closely. She wanted to relax and enjoy being in Matthew's company. As much as she could while they were hurtling through space, at least. With him, she didn't feel judged. He accepted her as she was, with her strong physical passions, her refusal to form an attachment. Of course, he'd refused attachment, as well. That was fine. It made it easier.

"What's your favorite color?"

The question jolted her out of her thoughts. "Purple, I suppose. I've always loved lavender. Lilacs and violets, too. When the lavender was in bloom at Clarehaven, I'd spend hours in the garden, strolling among the blossoms and soaking up the scent."

"What's Clarehaven?"

"My family's estate. My brother Deveric was a duke." *Heavens above, why had she revealed that?* She'd got so comfortable in his presence, she'd let her guard down.

Matthew's head jerked up. "Seriously? A duke? As in, the aristocracy?" When she nodded, he added, "I thought that had mostly died out."

"To a degree, I suppose." But not in her time, not in 1813. It was hard to imagine England without its strongly divided class system. Amara had been part and parcel of it, accepting her position above others without batting an eye. It'd taken Eliza to get her to question that.

"Is *that* why your family lived like you came from an earlier century–trying to recapture your former glory?" His tone was teasing.

"That's one explanation." Hers was not.

He tapped his fingers on the wheel. "So, are you super-wealthy, then?"

Amara fidgeted in her seat. Money was not something one discussed in her society. It was considered uncouth. Did people share such information openly here?

"Sorry, that just came out. It's none of my business."

She straightened her shoulders. "I am a woman of independent means." And proud of it. Though she'd done nothing to earn it. Then again, most of the peerage hadn't, either. They'd inherited it, just as she had.

"I picked well, then," he said, shooting her a wicked grin.

Amara tensed. Would his avowal of no lasting connection change now that he knew of her wealth? She forced herself to breathe out, relaxing her shoulders. No. He was driven to succeed on his own. Matthew Goodson was not the type to live off someone else's largesse, as many of her acquaintance had been. He was no fortune hunter. She knew it in her bones.

When she made no response, he frowned. "I was kidding, you know."

"Yes. I know." She poked him in the side, as he'd done once to her, and as she'd seen Cat do to Ben to lighten the mood. "What is *your* favorite color?"

"Red. Bright, fiery red. I love the passion in the color, the ferocity, the drive."

"Ah. I understand the choice of truck color now."

"Absolutely. How about … favorite food?"

"Swedes."

"Swedes? People from Sweden? You're a cannibal?"

She giggled. "No, sorry. Cat calls them ruta-bagas."

He wrinkled his nose in disgust. "What? Nobody likes rutabagas."

"I do. Our cook, Rowena, fried them with onions. It was heavenly."

"Cook. You had a cook?" He was quiet for a second before that teasing grin returned. "No wonder you don't know your way around a kitchen."

She gasped in faux outrage. "I don't need to, now that I have you." The minute the words were out, she wanted to recall them. She smoothed the hair off her forehead. "That's not what I—"

"No worries," he interrupted, his words a little too quick, a little too smooth.

"Now your favorite."

"Cheese fries."

"Like the potatoes you ate at the restaurant?"

"Yup."

"Ah." She nodded, all seriousness. "A wise choice."

"Favorite animal?"

"Dogs. And I know yours is cats."

"It could be a wombat. You shouldn't assume."

"A wombat? What on earth is a wombat?"

He laughed, a rich belly laugh. "Exactly."

They passed the remainder of the trip sharing more details about themselves. He told of running a marathon in his twenties; she couldn't fathom ever wanting to run nearly that far. She told him of sneaking off to the garden to read and eat the cherry tarts Rowena secretly gave her. "My mother didn't want me to eat them, for fear I'd go to fat."

"What? There's no fat on you, woman." He flicked on the turn signal, the ticking noise beating along in time to the song on the radio. "We're here. Exit 87."

They drove by multiple shopping centers with those ugly gray parking lots, but soon the centers gave way to more scenic greenery, much to Amara's relief. Matthew turned onto a road lined with picturesque houses. At the top of the hill, the houses melded with stately buildings of a light yellow stone.

"Mary Baldwin College," Matthew said. "A women's college."

"Women's college?"

"The student body is comprised of women only. What I wouldn't have given to have access to *that* in my youth."

She rolled her eyes. Men didn't change. *Wait.* There were colleges just for women? "Is the education inferior to that offered men?"

"Not at all. In fact, some argue it's better, with the small class sizes and, well, no distractions from hunks like me." He winked.

Matthew Goodson was flirting with her. And she liked it. She liked it a lot.

After another five minutes, they pulled in behind a large house. Though it was nothing like Clarehaven, it was grander than many a place she'd seen in town. "Taylor lives here?"

"Yeah, she's got one of the apartments on the top floor."

The house had been divided into apartments? That shouldn't surprise her. The Treasure Trove had met the same fate.

Matthew climbed out of the truck, taking a moment to stretch his back before coming around to her side and helping her down. He guided her through a door and up a set of creaky stairs. The steps must have alerted Taylor to their presence, because before they'd even reached the top, she threw open the door.

"Thank God, Matt. Thanks for coming." She looked more angry than upset, her glower broken only by the pinched smile she flashed her brother. "Hi, Amara."

"Hello, Taylor. It is a pleasure to see you again. I am so sorry to hear of your misfortune."

Taylor threw her arms up in the air. "I know, right? You think you live in a safe little town, and then someone goes and steals your laptop."

"Where was it?"

Taylor kicked at the floor. "On my front seat. And, yes, I stupidly left the car door unlocked. It's my fault, I know. But I needed to run in and get my Starbucks. I thought I'd only be a minute."

"You and your coffee habit. You shouldn't waste five bucks on a cup of black water every day."

Matthew's sister stuck her tongue out at him. "We all have our indulgences. You go for the best in computer equipment. I go for lattes."

"Touché."

"Did you bring me one?"

Matthew's brows narrowed in puzzlement before he smacked his hand against his thigh. "Duh, yes. At first I thought you meant a latte. Hold on. I'll be right back." He tipped his head at Amara before ducking out the door.

"He's loaning me a laptop," Taylor said, by way of explanation. "Hey, it's good to see you again. Come, sit down." She crossed the room and dropped onto a rather ugly, overstuffed couch, beckoning Amara to join her. "So, how are you liking Charlottesville?"

Amara swallowed. "It's a lovely city. I particularly like the University grounds." *Because they're the closest thing to home I've found.*

"Me, too. Definitely beautiful. So, before he gets back, what's up between you and my brother?"

There'd been no pause in the words, no forewarning of the

topic, and Amara flinched. "What do you mean?"

"Oh, come on. It's obvious in the way you guys look at each other. Plus, it's not like he brings women here every day."

She and Matthew looked at each other in a certain way? Amara plucked at the edge of her shirt, her head down, her thoughts discombobulated. "He only brought me because I was already at his house."

Taylor's eyebrow arched up, a knowing grin on her face. "Do tell."

Amara wanted to sink into the cushion. "He was … helping me with something," she mumbled, knowing even as she said the words how absurd they sounded.

Before Taylor could comment, Matthew bounded through the door, breathing heavily, a black rectangle under his arm.

"My, my, brother, you didn't have to run." Her eyes danced back and forth between him and Amara. "Unless you had something you couldn't bear to be parted from, of course."

Matthew's face flushed a dull red—as opposed to Amara's cheeks, which burned so hotly she was sure they were the color of his truck.

"Yes, your oh-so-appreciative personality, sister dear."

Laughing, she stood to take the laptop from him, setting it down on a side table. "In all seriousness, thank you, Matty. I need one for school and with finances the way they are right now, well … "

"I'm telling you: ditch the lattes."

She punched him lightly in the shoulder. "So, any chance you guys wanna stay to catch the Shakespeare play? It's Pay-What-You-Will night. Though we'd have to take your truck, Matty. Buffy's gas gauge is on empty."

"Shakespeare?"

Matthew and Taylor both turned at Amara's exclamation.

"They perform Shakespeare here?" He hadn't always been her favorite of the playwrights, but at least he was familiar.

"Yes, it's awesome. The Blackfriars Theater is an exact reproduction of the one in London!"

The one in London? The Globe had burned down two centuries before Amara's time.

"What d'ya think, Amara?" Matthew said. "Would you like to stay, or do you need to get back?"

"I'd be delighted." The theater was one of the few parts of the London Season she'd enjoyed, despite the pointed looks she occasionally had to endure. In London, however, one attended the theater in spectacular gowns. Not sweaters and leggings. "Are we properly attired?"

Taylor waved a hand. "Oh, sure. Lots of people dress casually. Let me just get my coat. We can grab some dinner at Shenandoah Pizza."

Amara's mouth watered. She definitely appreciated pizza.

As they headed out to the truck, Matthew asked, "What's playing, anyway?"

"*Measure for Measure.*"

Amara nearly tripped over her own feet. She'd never cared for that Shakespeare play. She didn't need to see a dark comedy about hidden identities and sexual morality.

She'd lived that hell every day.

But as she slid over in the front seat to make room for Taylor, her thigh settled against Matthews's, and the ever-present spark between them flamed anew.

Forget Shakespeare. Being with Matthew Goodson? Heaven, indeed.

CHAPTER 26

*M*att had been to Blackfriars a handful of times. While he always enjoyed the stellar perform- ances, it was something else to witness it through Amara's eyes. She stared, enraptured, at the stage the entire time.

"They're quite good," she whispered to him at one point, "though it is strange to hear Shakespeare's words spoken with American accents."

He'd chuckled silently. She had a point.

At intermission, as they stood and stretched, Taylor excused herself to the restroom. Matt used the justification of letting his sister pass to lean into Amara, inhaling the exquisite scent of her hair. He stayed there, closer than necessary, long after Taylor had left. His skin prickled at Amara's nearness, and he wanted nothing more than to drop a kiss on her lips right there in the middle of the theater. What would she do?

His hand grazed hers by accident, and it was as if a bolt of lightning hit him, how strong the current between them sizzled. He groaned. She looked at him, but at that moment the actors appeared on the upper balcony, playing instruments and singing in raucous melody.

"Oh, how grand!" Amara clapped along, her face fixed on the actors above her.

Matt, however, remained focused on her. He'd spent the whole day with her. Far more time than he should have. He had work to do. And they weren't anything. Occasional friends with benefits, nothing else. He wanted those benefits right now. She looked so damned adorable, standing there, her cheeks aglow with excitement as she listened to the silly songs.

Taylor returned, and the two women discussed Shakespeare. Matt hadn't a clue what they said; he was lost in his own, confusing thoughts about this woman. For though he'd spent too much time with her, he wanted more. He wanted to take her home and indulge in sexual sport in every room of his apartment. And if she wanted to stay for breakfast or for further driving lessons or anything else, he was fine with that.

And that terrified him.

The rest of the play passed in a blur. Matt barely attended the dialogue, longing instead to pull Amara close and rain kisses on her delicate ear. His eagle-eyed sister would have a field day with that, however. Little escaped her, especially when it came to relationships. Not that he and Amara were in a relationship. But they were something. Weren't they?

Would she be willing to be something more if he expressed interest? She'd seemed as relieved as he to fix their status as "most definitely not committed in any way," but had she been truthful? Or could she have changed her mind in the last week, as he was starting to admit he had?

"What'd you think?" Taylor asked after the cast had taken their final curtain call.

"It was brilliant. I wish my sister Grace was here. She loves anything literary."

"You had a sister?"

Taylor's question was innocuous, but Amara's face crumpled at the words. She sucked in her cheeks, clasping an arm across her stomach.

"Oh, gosh, Amara, I apologize. I wasn't trying to be insensitive." Taylor's blue eyes, so similar to Matthew's, widened in dismay, and she launched herself at Amara, wrapping her arms around her in an awkward hug.

"It is all right. It happened long ago," Amara mumbled, obviously ill at ease. Matt wanted to rip her from his sister and enfold her in his own arms to erase the sadness etched across her features.

Taylor nodded as she released her grip. "My sympathies to you."

By the ride home, the women were back to chatting easily, Taylor doing most of the talking as she analyzed current fashion trends, makeup, and hair styles. "We'll have to go shopping again," she said as Matt pulled into her apartment's lot.

"I'd like that." Genuineness laced Amara's voice.

His sister liked her. That was a good thing, right?

Taylor cracked open the truck door and hopped out before Matt could cut the engine. "No worries, I'll see myself up, Matty. Thanks again for the laptop."

"No problem."

She leaned back into the cab of the truck for a second, a wide grin on her face. "And Matty?"

"Yeah?"

"Captain Obvious."

With that, she slammed the door, practically skipping her way up the sidewalk before launching herself through the entryway.

"Captain What?"

Amara's voice interrupted his churning, spinning thoughts. *What had Taylor meant? What was he missing?*

"Nothing. Just a silly joke." As he shifted into reverse, his phone beeped, the tone indicating a text from Taylor. He pulled it out from the dash, peeking at the words.

Don't let this one go. She's your fish.

Turning the phone over, he slid it back into its holder, thanking God it was dark in the cab so Amara couldn't see the heat creeping up his neck.

Whenever Taylor had gone through a breakup, which was often, he'd always reminded her there were other fish in the sea. One time she'd gotten so pissed at him, she'd screamed, "I don't want just any old fish. I want *my* fish. The one that's perfect for me."

Could his sister be right?

Amara Mattersley was an intriguing mix: both bright and naïve, adventuresome yet inexperienced. Contrasts that made no sense, that had him asking who she was and what she was about. She was fantastic in bed, willing to experiment, and an eager pupil, their latest antics rendering her nearly teacher and him student. Yet there were basic things she didn't know, didn't understand. Like how to drive. How to use most kitchen appliances. Technology. It was as if she were from another century.

He snorted at the thought.

As they wound their way through the streets, Amara kept her face trained out the window. After a few minutes, she said, "Why are the stars so faint here?"

"What do you mean?"

She hesitated. "There seem to be fewer of them than there were in England."

"Light pollution, probably."

"Light pollution?" She looked at him as she repeated the phrase.

"Yeah, the electric lights in town dilute the atmosphere, making the stars appear dimmer."

"Oh." She exhaled, as if in relief. "I'm glad to know they're still there."

"You thought stars had suddenly disappeared?"

She crossed her arms, her chin jutting out mulishly. "Please don't make me feel stupid. I am not stupid. I just don't know all the things you know. Like you surely don't know everything *I* know."

He swallowed. He hadn't meant to offend her. He'd spoken without thinking. "I'm sorry; I didn't mean it like that."

She nodded but said nothing.

"Tell you what," he said as they turned another corner. "I'll take you to Skyline Drive, and you'll see what I mean. It's quite a difference to view the sky from there as compared to the middle of town." When she didn't respond, he added, "Unless you want to get back. I've kept you all day. I shouldn't have taken so much of your time."

"No, I'd be pleased to go. I was merely thinking I had detained *you* far too long; I know how busy you are."

He was quiet a moment, the sound of the tires on pavement the only noise. "I am. Too busy. It's been a long time—years— since I've been stargazing. I think maybe I need it."

The streetlights illuminated the answering smile on her face. "All right, then. Let's go stargazing."

After a comfortable silence on the interstate, Matt took the exit at the top of Afton Mountain, threading his way along Skyline Drive, the scenic highway that wove through the tops of the Blue Ridge Mountains. Within minutes, Amara exclaimed, "They are brighter already! Look, there's Ursa Major."

"You know your constellations."

"A few."

"More than I do, I'm sure. I slept through most of the astronomy section of earth science."

Her sigh caught him by surprise. "You are lucky to have had instruction."

"Didn't you?"

"No."

"How do you know constellation names, then?"

"My brother had books in his library. Copernicus, Galileo, Newton, the Herschels. I read them numerous times. How fascinating are nebulae and comets, and the planets! I would love to look through a telescope, to see the stars and mysteries of the heavens more closely."

"You never have? Not even a toy one?" he teased.

"They make toy telescopes?"

The surprise in her voice indicated she wasn't joking. Another oddity within the mystery that was Amara Mattersley. Should he press her for more information? He was loath to disrupt the peaceful camaraderie between them, though, and she hadn't taken his earlier ribbing well, so he kept quiet.

After a few miles, he pulled into a parking area, grateful for the large open space among the trees. The lot was empty and dark. When he turned off the headlights, the inky blackness swallowed them up, and mild unease crept through him. Not that he'd admit it. It was strange to be in such utter darkness. Even in his apartment at night, lights from various computers and electronics, not to mention the digital clocks, illuminated the room at least a tiny degree.

"Oh, it's heavenly," Amara said, as she got out of the truck. "I missed the darkness more than I knew."

He used the light from his phone to find his way around to her. "Let's sit in the back." He reached his hand out to help her into the truck bed. She clasped his fingers, and the heat radiating between them set his loins on fire. They were out here, alone, just the two of them. Perhaps …

"It's rather cold," she said, her teeth chattering.

"I've got blankets in the cab. Hold on."

He retrieved them, grateful for his mother's insistence he be prepared for emergencies. "I'm not going to freeze to death in the middle of Charlottesville," he'd argued, but she'd insisted.

"You never know. People drive off the sides of roads and aren't discovered for days. Better safe than sorry."

So he drove around with two blankets, several bottles of water, and a box of stale Graham crackers to ease his mother's mind.

Jumping into the back of the truck, he spread one blanket out on the base, then sat down on it. "Here, sit." Amara did, nestling against him. He tucked the other blanket around them, enfolding them in their very own cocoon. "Better now?"

"Yes. Much."

Had she meant the temperature, or was she, too, glad for the physical contact? It felt as if he hadn't been with her, hadn't touched her for days, as if he were thirsting in the desert and she the only thing that would quench him. He leaned against the back of the cab, taking her with him. Both gazed up into the sky.

"Aren't they magnificent?" Amara whispered.

"Magnificent, indeed," he responded.

But he wasn't talking about stars.

CHAPTER 27

mara lay in the shelter of Matthew's arms, reveling in his warmth and nearness as she soaked in nature's majesty above. The stars twinkled in full glory, winking at her as they had since she was a child. She spotted a few familiar constellations: Leo, Cancer, Cassiopeia. What she wouldn't give to see them closely, to know of what they truly were made.

A strange blinking star moved across the sky, and she tensed. "What is that?"

"What?"

"The red star, the one that is moving."

"That's not a star. That's an airplane."

She exhaled. The man must think her the biggest ninny on the planet. There was so much she didn't know. "Oh," she mumbled, pulling her arms more tightly around herself. His fingers stroked a rhythmic pattern up and down her arm, and after a moment she relaxed into him.

They sat there together, enclosed in each other's arms but focused on the stars, for what must have been at least a half hour, if not longer, Amara occasionally pointing out constellations. Not once had Matthew's gentle caress indicated the desire for anything more, and not once had she thought to pursue a more intimate connection, though the idea held appeal. *It is too cold*, part of her said, and while that was certainly true, mostly she didn't wish to interrupt the soothing sensation of simply being with him, without any sexual connection.

It thrilled her. It also frightened her.

No complications. No commitments. That's what they'd agreed; there was nothing deeper between them, would be nothing deeper. A few hours seeking mutual pleasure was fine, but more than that was not what either wanted.

Was it?

"I can't feel my toes," he finally said. "We should probably go."

She scooted away quickly, her own derriere numb from the sitting and the temperature. Once in the cab again, she bundled herself in one of the blankets, her teeth chattering.

"I kept you outside too long," he said, the interior lights revealing a grimace as he started the truck.

"I wanted to be there."

He only nodded as he pulled onto the road. He turned on the radio, which she took as an indication he did not wish to talk. It was fine; her own conflicting thoughts and emotions were all consuming.

What *was* between them? Could she, could they still claim a mere sexual liaison, given they'd spent the entire day in each other's company, most of it not in bed? Then again, Taylor's loss of her laptop had extended the day. Had they remained in Charlottesville, surely they would have parted ways hours ago.

She stole glances at him, the headlights of passing cars occasionally highlighting the contours of his face. She longed to reach out, to stroke the little hairs at the nape of his neck, to rest her hand on his thigh. She longed for things she didn't want to admit.

She was in trouble.

Matt tapped his fingers against the steering wheel in rhythm to the song on the radio, Selena Gomez's *Hands to Myself*, acting for all intents and purposes as if he were totally at ease driving seventy plus miles an hour down the highway with this delectable woman next to him.

In truth, he was anything but. He couldn't stop thinking about her. That in and of itself wasn't unusual, perhaps; Lord knew far too many of his waking hours in the last few weeks had revolved around thoughts of Amara Mattersley. But it'd mostly been thoughts of Amara in bed—of what he wanted to do with her, what they had done, what she'd surprised him with.

Now his thoughts weren't on sex at all. Okay, maybe ten percent on sex, especially considering the song playing, but the rest of his brain wrestled with how much plain old *fun* he'd had with her today, how relaxed he'd felt in her company, how glad he'd been that she'd come with him to Staunton. How pleasurable it'd been to watch her soak up the actors on the stage. How moving it'd been to see her face light up at the miracle of the Milky Way expanding across the sky. How he'd wanted to hold her, sure, but how the motivation had not been lust, but something far closer to … tenderness.

He peeked over at her, her face mostly in shadows, lit just barely by the dash lights. She chewed on her lip, lost in thought. Could she be struggling with the same emotions, the same longings, the same confusion?

Half of him wanted to change up their agreement, to move from friends with benefits to friends who were very clearly something more. The other half of him wanted to run. A relationship didn't fit into his plans. No way, no how. He didn't have time for it, couldn't afford to be distracted. And frankly, he didn't want to get hurt again.

He'd told himself for years he was perfectly satisfied on his own. He didn't want, didn't need anything more. That kind of thing would complicate his life in ways he'd rather avoid. He had his cat; he didn't need any more females in his life.

But looking over at the honey-haired beauty to his side, he was ready to chuck all those reasons against anything deeper right out the window. She was incredibly sexy, to be sure, but she intrigued him in ways beyond the physical. She was highly intelligent, and yet there were great gaps in her areas of knowledge. One moment she was open and friendly, the next biting and defensive. What wounds did she carry beneath that beautiful exterior? And since when had he cared about another's emotional wounds?

His heart skipped a beat, and his breath caught in his throat. He had a feeling he was in serious trouble. The question was, was she in it with him?

CHAPTER 28

"Do you want to come back to my place?" *Please, oh please, come. Share my bed. Be with me.*

Amara was quiet for a moment longer than comfortable. At length, she said, "It's been a wonderful day, Matthew. But I am quite tired. Perhaps returning to Cat's would be best."

He nodded, the pangs of disappointment too strong to ignore. "No problem." The words were casual, but casual was far from how he truly felt. He wanted to take her to bed, to kiss her, caress her, bring her to the ultimate high … and then sleep with her in the true sense of the word. But they'd agreed—no strings, no expectations.

The blocks passed in silence, the streetlights heartbeats of illumination. Before long, he pulled into the Treasure Trove's parking lot. "Looks like someone's still up, at least," he said, nodding at the light in the upper front window as he put the truck into park.

Amara set her hand on his knee. Instantly, his groin quickened, and it took everything he had not to move her hand farther inward, to beg her to come with him, just for the night.

"Thank you, Matthew," she said. "This was a blissful day. I enjoyed the time with your sister." She swallowed. "The theater, the … stars."

He tipped his head. "Agreed. Thank you."

Neither moved.

Finally, Amara gave a half-sigh and opened her door. Matt reached over and grabbed her left hand with his right, his other hand turning her face back to him. He stared into her eyes for a moment, those dark pools he could hardly see save for the bit of light from the headlights he'd left on. He bent in, slowly enough she could pull away, but she didn't, and he touched his lips to hers, a strange sense of joy, of rightness, zinging through him at the sweet connection. They remained like that, their mouths barely touching, until her right hand came off the door handle and into his hair, holding him to her as she opened her mouth, the moan in her throat echoed in his.

He returned the kiss in kind, so damned grateful to have her in his arms. His lips tickled the inside corner of her mouth, then pressed tiny kisses across her cheek and down her jawline to her neck. Soft noises erupted from her, and he moved his hand to the edge of her shirt, his fingers reaching under to stroke her bare skin, its heat sending delicious tremors through his own.

Suddenly, she leaned back, breathing heavily. "I … " She didn't finish the sentence. "I must go."

He sat up. "Of course." Whipping open his door, he jumped down and jogged to her side of the truck, holding his hand out for her to use to descend, and she took it, that same instant sense of connection, of belonging, winging through him. Once on the ground, she withdrew her hand, and disappointment, mixed with something stronger, coursed through him.

It was okay. It was probably only momentary, this ludicrous rush of emotion, of desire that went beyond the physical, probably just a reaction to the not-so-subtle hints from his sister.

"Thank you," she repeated, hesitating for a moment.

He nodded, saying nothing.

She walked to the apartment stairs, ascending them and opening the door without once looking back. As she closed the door behind her, it was as if she'd slammed it in his face— or someplace lower, a region perilously close to his heart.

Amara leaned against the door, her eyes welling with unexpected tears.

"Hey," Cat called as she strolled into the room. "You were gone a long—" She broke off, crossing over to Amara. "Oh, honey, you okay?"

Tears spilled over Amara's cheeks, and she wiped them off hastily, sniffling.

"Come on," Cat said. "Sit with me on the couch."

Amara trailed after her, the tears flowing, embarrassed by her own emotionality. What was *wrong* with her?

Cat scowled, her eyebrows dipping low over her eyes. "What on earth happened? Did Matt do something?" Almost to herself, she muttered, "I've only known him to be a stand-up guy, otherwise I never would have—but how well do I really know—"

Amara shook her head, and Cat ceased talking. "No, he didn't do anything bad." She sniffed again. "He did too many good things." A wail escaped her. "I—I think I have feelings for him." She tried to suck in a breath as another sob overtook her.

An awkward chortle escaped Cat. "I don't see the problem. That seems pretty terrific to me. And not altogether surprising, considering I wrote you guys into a story. Not that that guarantees anything. Ben's always reminding me I provide opportunity, not destiny." She broke off. "Sorry, sometimes even now I struggle to understand these powers gifted to me."

Amara nodded, her nose running. She must look a sight.

"I'll get you a Kleenex." Cat hopped up and grabbed a box of tissues off the side table, handing them to Amara.

She took one, using it to wipe her nose. Paper tissues were such a bewildering idea. She snorted. Not that this was the time for such errant thoughts. "But I don't wish to have feelings for him. I want … I *need* to be independent!"

Cat was silent for a second. "And you think if you get involved with Matthew, you'll lose your independence?"

Amara nodded emphatically, misery leeching out of her every pore. "I do not wish to be dependent on a man in any sense. I saw what that did to women in my era. What it did to my mother."

Her mother had become a harridan in her older years. There was no mincing words about it. Granted, Eliza's arrival had turned that around. Well, not her arrival. That hadn't gone over so well. But the end result—the obvious love Deveric felt for the peculiar American—had finally softened Matilda's heart.

For most of her years, though, Matilda Mattersley had lived a miserable existence, a misery predicated on her husband's betrayals. Deveric thought Amara unaware of their father's numerous mistresses, but she'd long known her parents' relationship had been fraught with as much tension and anger as passion. Her mother had wilted away until nothing but a core of icy bitterness remained, a bitterness no one had ever thought would thaw.

Between that and Amara's own experiences with Drake Evers, dependence on a man held no appeal. It led to heartbreak. Her mother's and her own situation weren't the only she'd witnessed, either. Too many women of her acquaintance had suffered humiliations big and small: broken engagements, public slights. Unwanted pregnancies.

Thank heavens her indiscretion with Drake had not produced a child, for all the other evils it'd wrought upon her. Her dear friend Frances hadn't been so lucky, had found herself with child out of wedlock. She'd quickly married a man twice her age to cover up the potential scandal, a man who soon proved less than a loving new husband. Had he known of Frances's condition before the marriage? If he hadn't and had learned the truth, perhaps that explained his cruel behavior. Though it did not excuse it. Frances had ceased talking of her marriage or husband and had in fact largely bowed out of polite society. Amara hadn't seen her for the better part of a year.

No, Amara wouldn't do that. Wouldn't rant and rail, as her mother had. Wouldn't submit and endure, as Frances had. Wouldn't give her heart and trust so easily, as she had all those years ago. She'd learned her lesson.

Except … except Matthew Goodson called to her like no man ever had. Was it that they'd shared their bodies with each other? Perhaps, in spite of her best intentions, maintaining emotional distance when so physically connected was not possible. Though men of her acquaintance seemed capable of doing so, given their many short-term liaisons. Was it true women could not keep their hearts separate, while men could?

Cat handed her more tissues. "I don't think a healthy relationship and independence are mutually exclusive. In fact, I believe the opposite; you need independence in a relationship for it to be truly solid."

Amara blew her nose in a quite unladylike fashion.

"But I also think," Cat went on, "independence is overrated in modern society." She slanted her eyes at Amara. "I don't know about nineteenth-century England, but here in twenty-first century America, independence is almost a moral virtue, codified in our very national identity. I personally don't think that's so great. I, myself, learned that the hard way. I spent years after my fiancé left vowing to never get involved again. I thought I'd be better, safer, if I remained on my own."

Amara nodded. Cat's last words mirrored her own beliefs.

"Yet I soon discovered, with the help of that manuscript, I wasn't *really* living. I'd been existing. And I'd been missing out on the marvelous possibilities of human relationships. Especially a love connection." Cat pursed her lips. "Not that I'm saying everyone has to have a romantic relationship to be happy or whole, of course. I'm saying ... I learned for me, it's okay to try again, to trust again. And, ironically, I'm totally dependent on Ben, and happy for that to be the case."

Amara's sobs had quieted as Cat spoke and were now down to half-hiccups.

"He's completely dependent on me, too. It's a two-way street, and that's why it works."

Amara's eyes widened. "How is he dependent on you?"

Cat smiled, her face lighting up with emotion. "We need each other to feel whole. We're fine apart, but we feel better together. That's the kind of dependence I like, but it took me a long time to be comfortable with that. Because you're right—dependence brings vulnerability. But what I hadn't recognized was that my supposed independence was a different kind of vulnerability; the kind that results from building up walls and preventing anyone from getting through."

Amara frowned. *How did building walls produce vulnerability?*

Cat waved her hand in the air. "Listen to me, going on and on. I'm sorry, Amara. Sometimes that happens when I get introspective. This is about you. So—what is it about dependence that scares you?"

How typically American, to get right to the point. The bluntness was disconcerting, but one of the things Amara had grown to love most about Eliza. So much better than the facades of her era.

"Women in my time have, or I suppose I should say had, few choices. Marriage was the only one for someone of my station, unless one wished to be relegated a spinster, dependent on male family members' largesse. There were women of means, of course, financially independent women. Widows, usually. They, perhaps, did not feel the constraints as much.

"As the daughter of a duke, I had more leeway than many. Yet from birth I was groomed to make the best match I could, taught that marriage and motherhood were my life's purpose. A life of scholarship was not an option for a woman of my social standing. We received instruction only in what we needed to know to be considered accomplished and in how to run a household."

"That's no small thing," Cat interjected.

Amara's smile was weak. "No, it isn't. Yet we have no control over our finances. All of that lies under men's command."

Cat heaved a huge sigh. "Ugh. Why did I send Eliza there?"

Amara laughed, a true laugh. "I do not know, though the love she and my brother share is undeniable. If there were ever an example of a marriage on equal footing, it would be theirs. But he is the duke, not she. He owns the land, runs the estates, and controls the purse strings. Sure, he's given Eliza *carte blanche*, but most other women are not so lucky." She sighed as she wiped the tears from her eyes. "I am sorry, Cat. I did not wish to burden you with this."

"Nonsense," the older woman said. "We're friends, aren't we? I'm here to help any way I can. And Matthew Goodson's a good man. He's hard working, dedicated, and kind. Ben speaks very highly of him, and that's the reason I brought you to him. And you ... Eliza said you needed someone loyal and true, who'd let you be you, who'd never betray your trust. I believe in my heart Matt's such a man. Though it's ultimately up to you both. I write the stories and create the possibilities, but I'm not God."

Amara slumped against the sofa. "Does it make it better or worse that this is both predestined and yet still ... "

"Free will?"

"Yes."

"I used to think it'd be wonderful to have things, and people, be exactly what and who I wanted them to be—to be in control of them." A wry grin twisted Cat's face. "I've learned otherwise." She stood up, holding her hand out to Amara. "You look exhausted. I'd suggest sleep. We can talk more in the morning."

Amara took the proffered hand and rose, startled when Cat pulled her into a hug, though she couldn't say she disliked it. Cat was right. Perhaps a night's rest would give her better perspective, would make her see she was blowing this out of proportion.

Perhaps tomorrow she and Matthew could resume their mutually pleasurable friendship, and any ideas of something more would have disappeared, much as night melts into day.

And perhaps on the morrow, pigs would also fly.

CHAPTER 29

"I'm taking Washington to Mrs. Postupak's. We'll see you again for dinner," Ben said, planting a kiss on Cat's hair. "Need me to pick up anything from the store on the way home?"

"Chocolate!" Cat grimaced. "You know how much I hate this time of the month."

"You and me both," Ben quipped as he picked up Wash and zipped out the apartment door. Cat stuck her tongue out after him, but the twinkle in her eye rendered the action less harsh.

"Sorry," she said to Amara. "I'm extra moody today; it's that time of the month."

That time of the month? *What did Cat mean?*

"Speaking of which, do you need supplies? I know I gave you a few when you first arrived, but we can get you more. Unless you've done that already."

The blood drained from Amara's face, and an icy sensation stole across her skin. That time of the month. *Her monthlies.* That's what Cat meant.

She hadn't used Cat's offerings, though they seemed much more convenient and pleasant than what she'd had at her disposal at Clarehaven. No, she hadn't used them, because she hadn't bled since she'd arrived. And she should have. Like the rest of her life, her monthlies were occasionally unpredictable, but she'd never gone this long without.

Cat's hand stopped in mid-air before she could brush her hair behind her ears. "What's wrong? You look like you're about to faint."

Amara swallowed, focusing on getting her legs to move one numb step at a time to the sofa. "I haven't … I haven't bled since I've been here." She couldn't meet Cat's eyes.

"You've had a stressful month. Maybe your body's just a little off."

Amara nodded, but nausea flooded her stomach. That first time with Matthew, he hadn't, they hadn't, warded against pregnancy. Though they'd been careful to use condoms in the times since.

"I'm sure there's—" Cat broke off, understanding dawning on her face. "Oh, Amara. Are you saying? Did you and—?"

Amara nodded again, misery enveloping her. Would God really give her the answer to her prayers, to bring her forward to a time where she could create her own independent life, only to have her end up with child?

Then again, God hadn't put her in Matthew's bed.

Or had He? Maybe Cat's stories were too powerful to resist. Both Eliza and Cat insisted the choice was Amara's, but this didn't feel like a choice. It felt like a trap.

Eliza had *wanted* to be with Deveric. And her brother had fallen hard for the bubbly American. Their love certainly seemed genuine. But had Dev had less of a say than he knew? He'd told her he and Eliza needed each other *for the story to work*. He'd been well aware of what, and who, had brought Eliza to him and acted fine with it. But had he been under some sort of spell?

Was she?

Anger bubbled up. Anger at Cat, for bringing her here. Anger at Matthew, for tempting her so. And anger at herself, for giving in.

"Bloody hell," she said, shocking herself with the words, though they felt marvelous to say. She wanted to scream, to rail at Cat, but in her heart she knew the American wasn't at fault. No matter what any story said, Amara had had plenty of chances to turn away from Mr. Goodson, and she hadn't. She'd craved more, in fact. She should have had more control, just like in that garden all those years ago.

"Well," Cat said with a tremulous smile. "You don't know for sure. We need a pregnancy test."

"Pregnancy … test?"

"Yup. You pee on a stick, and it tells you in a few minutes. You can know as soon as a couple days after you miss your period. When was it supposed to come?"

Amara's cheeks burned. In anger, in shame, in embarrassment, in frustration. "My last was directly before I journeyed here."

Cat whistled. "That's plenty of time. Come on, let's go. You need answers."

"But the bookstore … "

"We'll open late. This is far more important."

Thank goodness Cat had been willing to purchase the test. Amara wanted to sink into the floor, mortified that anyone, even a cashier, would know she might possibly be *enceinte.*

Home now, Cat led her into the bathroom, ripping open the box. "You need to pee in a cup, then dip this stick in it for fifteen seconds, or whatever the instructions say, then set it on the counter and wait." She set the purple stick down next to the sink. "I'll fetch a plastic cup; hold on."

As she left the room, Amara clutched her stomach, its meager contents nearly leaving her at the events of the morning. A few days ago, she'd finally admitted to herself she had feelings—unwanted feelings—for Matthew Goodson. Now she had to contemplate whether or not she was carrying his child.

Her head spun, and she sat down on the toilet. Cat returned with the cup, her face radiating kindness and sympathy. Tears stung Amara's eyes.

"Do you want me to stay and help?"

Good God. Amara couldn't imagine anything worse than relieving herself in front of this woman. She shook her head.

"Okay. I'll be right outside. Here if you need me. Whatever the result." Cat closed the door softly as she made her exit.

Amara picked up the stick. What if this revealed she was, in fact, with child? The next few minutes could drastically change the course of her life. She closed her eyes and willed herself to breathe.

You made your bed, Amara. Time to lie in it. She'd survived scandal all those years ago; she could survive this. But as horrendous as scandal had been, it hadn't involved a third person. A child.

She yanked the seat open so hard it banged against the back of the toilet. Tugging her leggings down, she laid the stick on the counter, then grabbed the cup and sat down before she could change her mind. It was awkward, this business with the cup, but once it was done, she placed the cup on the counter before cleaning herself.

After standing up and restoring her clothing, she stared at the cup for a few seconds before grabbing the stick and dutifully following the package instructions.

Two minutes. Two minutes until she knew if her whole life was about to change. Again.

Cat's voice came through the door. "You doing okay?"

Amara pulled it open. If she had to face such life-altering news, she didn't want to do it alone. "I'm waiting," she whispered. "Please, will you wait with me?"

Cat nodded, saying nothing as she moved next to Amara. Both women stared at the stick, the ticking of the clock on the wall the only sound.

It was an eternity.

It was over before she knew it.

Cat gasped, but Amara said nothing, the two lines on the stick staring at her like accusing eyes.

She was pregnant.

Matt rolled over in bed, stretching his back as Lovey kneaded his leg, demanding her breakfast.

"Morning, kitty cat." He felt lighter than he had in a long time. On Saturday, admitting how deep his feelings had grown for Amara had scared the crap out of him. But after taking a few days to think, to reason it out, he felt far more at ease. For one thing, she wasn't the clingy type, always hanging on him, asking for more. If anything, he was the one seeking her out. He'd been the one to text her to schedule a second driving lesson for the weekend, after all.

So what would the harm be in continuing as they were, while opening themselves up to the possibility of more? Who said *more* had to take up all his time? Amara understood the pressures he was under, the work he had to do.

And he didn't have to tell her right away. It'd be wise to explore these feelings, to test them, to see if they were more than infatuation, before he said anything to her. Yes, he'd play it cool … and enjoy the time with Amara while doing so.

He grabbed his phone, checking to see if she'd texted. No such luck. Not that she normally did, but, well, he'd hoped. He glanced at the clock. 8:37. He needed to shower but took a minute to type her a quick message. He didn't want to wait until the weekend to see her again.

Wanna meet for lunch?

Not satisfied, he frowned before adding,

Had a great time last Saturday.

That wasn't too much, right? He wasn't declaring his undying love, but he wasn't ignoring their delightful time, either. Throwing the covers off, he slid into his robe, fed the cat, and then hit the shower, the hot water massaging his torso a reminder of Amara's skin on his, of her mouth gliding over him in the most intoxicating ways. His cock stirred, and he chuckled. "Down, boy. Hopefully later."

Turning off the water, he stepped out, toweling himself dry. Throwing on a pair of Dockers and a button-down shirt, he grabbed his laptop and strolled out the door, whistling a merry tune.

No, no, no. This wasn't supposed to happen.

Amara wanted nothing more than for the earth to open up and swallow her whole. For the second time in her life, her dreams crumbled to dust before her eyes.

Her sister Cecilia would tell her she was being overly dramatic. She was. She didn't care. Having a child may not be the end of the world to someone else, but it was to her. Eliza once suggested Amara hadn't sought out marriage because she didn't want children.

Eliza was right.

Not that Matthew had offered marriage. Or would. Would he? If she'd learned anything in the last month, it was how very different this society was from her own. In her time, Matthew would offer for her, if he were in any position to do so. It was a matter of honor. But in 2016, women bore children out of wedlock on a fairly regular basis, and the fathers did not necessarily feel any sense of obligation toward mother or child. At least according to television.

"Turn off that garbage," Cat teased her once. "It's not reality."

But this was. This was her reality, now.

"Whatever you decide to do, I'll help you." Cat's voice was low in her ear, her hand rubbing Amara's back. It was likely the only thing keeping Amara upright.

A bark of bitter laughter escaped her. "Decide? What choice do I have? I have made my bed, as my mother so often told me. I must truly lie in it now." She crossed her arms over her stomach, as if to deny the truth growing within.

"There are options." Cat's brow creased, her face troubled.

"Options?"

The American bit her lip, her eyes meeting Amara's in the mirror's reflection. "There is adoption. And not all women choose to carry their pregnancies to term."

Amara's eyes widened, though it wasn't as if she hadn't heard of such things in her time—mostly hushed whispers, rumors about herbs and the like. She shook her head. She didn't know what she would do, but it wasn't that.

Her breath came in ragged, harsh measures.

"Are you going to tell Matthew?"

Was it an option not to? Even if it were, she had to tell him. He deserved to know. She could not hide that information from him. "Yes. I suppose I must."

Cat's head bobbed up and down with vigor. "This is his responsibility as much as yours." She paused for a second. "I think you should tell him *everything.*"

"What?" *Everything?*

"Don't you think he should know your past, in all senses of the word, now that you both are this involved?"

"No, Cat. No." Her response was instinctual, panicked. "He wouldn't believe it. That would be the end, no matter … no matter what."

"What do you mean, he wouldn't believe it? We've got Eliza's letters, the photos she sent, the pictures of you with Deveric and Eliza from Eliza's phone. I'd think that would be more than enough."

Amara froze. Why hadn't she thought of Eliza's letters herself? All this time she'd thought she had nothing through which she could prove her origins, only photographs on a phone that she doubted Matthew, with as logical as he was, would accept as authentic.

Still, what good would showing him those things do at this point? Even if he *did* believe her, it didn't change the situation in which she now found herself. And it was more likely to cause additional problems rather than solve them.

"No, promise me you won't tell him. Neither you nor Ben. Let me work this out. One thing at a time. *Please.*"

"Okay, honey, I promise. But at some point, you'll have to address the time-traveling elephant in the room."

Elephant? Amara sat down on the toilet, dropping her head into her hands. She was too overwhelmed to even ask the meaning of Cat's bizarre words.

"We ... he ... We said no strings. It was just for pleasure," she confessed, looking up at Cat.

"Sometimes life has other plans." Cat smiled, though her eyes were suspiciously watery. "And sometimes those plans end up being better than any you could have devised yourself."

Amara said nothing. She doubted it. And now she had to tell Matthew.

CHAPTER 30

Amara hadn't replied to his text by lunch, nor answered her phone. The only logical thing to do was call Cat. Just to make sure nothing was amiss. Mostly likely Amara's battery had died or something. He didn't think she'd intentionally ignore him. They hadn't argued last weekend, had had a great time, right? Though he *had* waited until Tuesday to text her about driving again. Had that been too long? He clenched his jaw. Maybe he shouldn't call. Maybe he should give her space. Besides, he had stuff to do.

After ten more minutes of staring blankly at the screen, he picked the phone up and dialed.

"Treasure Trove, this is Cat speaking. How may I help you?"

"Hey Cat, it's Matt. I was … Is Amara there?"

Cat was silent for a long moment. "Hi, Matt. No, she's not." Her voice was strange.

"Is she okay?"

"Yes, yes," Cat answered instantly, her tone overly bright.

"She went to the Colonnade Club Pavilion on the Lawn."

"Oh, okay. I can catch her later."

A strange noise echoed through the phone. "I'd suggest you catch her there."

"What?"

"Just trust me. Go find her, Matt. Now." She hung up.

He sat, staring at the phone in his hand. What the heck had that been about? Not that he was ever particularly clued in about women, but he had no idea what he'd just missed in that communication. Clearly something big, though. With a sigh, he unfolded himself from his chair and walked out his office door.

What was he about to walk into?

Amara sank into a large armchair in front of the fireplace. No fire crackled in it, but she didn't care. She didn't care about anything. She'd told Cat she needed to go for a walk. Walking always helped to clear her head, and she desperately needed to do so in order to make some decisions. Cat insisted she take her cell phone and begged Amara to keep her updated as to where she was.

Half of Amara had wanted to refuse. Catherine Cooper wasn't her mother. The other half wanted to fall into her arms and weep, grateful for someone who gave a damn, who wanted to help her, and who didn't reject her for the miserable choices she'd made. So when she'd reached the Colonnade Club, she'd dutifully called in her whereabouts, promising to be home in a few hours.

She took in the soothing blue of the walls in this central

room, the furnishings so achingly close in style to those of Clarehaven. She wanted to go home, wanted to flee, wanted to run away from her life.

But she couldn't.

She'd done it once, to get here. Look how that had turned out. And she couldn't return to her era, even if Cat could somehow send her back. Not unwed and expecting. She refused to ever again be a nine days' wonder—or years, rather—to the *ton.*

She was well and truly out of options.

No, you're not, an inner voice chided. *You have means. You can survive this.*

Her phone chimed. Was Cat checking in again? She pulled it out. The words, as well as his name, leapt at her from the screen.

On my way. What's going on?

She dropped the phone, listening to it crack as it hit the floor. Much like her world had cracked apart this morning.

Matt's long legs tore up the pavement as he walked, but it wasn't fast enough. He broke into a run. A deep disquiet had settled over him at Amara's continued silence and Cat's cryptic words, but he couldn't for the life of him figure out what was going on.

He slid around co-eds laughing carelessly, ducked through crowds of students, his pace increasing as he hit the edge of the Lawn. Though the day was crisply cold, he'd broken a sweat—whether from exertion or fear, he wasn't quite sure.

He hesitated at the steps to the Colonnade Club, his hand

on the doorknob. He sucked in a breath and opened the door, stealing in as quietly as possible. Ducking his head around the first doorway, he saw no one. No Amara.

Hurrying along the hallway, he passed a stairwell before entering a parlor room painted blue. There he found her, sitting in a chair, her back rigid. At his footsteps, her eyes rose to his, and he paused.

"Matthew," she said, and she stood, smoothing her hand down over her abdomen.

She looked unsteady, as if she were about to faint, and he raced to her, clutching her by the elbow. "Amara," he said, his voice catching. "Cat said to come. What's wrong?"

Her eyes filled with tears, which spilled over her cheeks. Her mouth formed a horrified O. "I am sorry. So very sorry, Matthew."

He pulled her into him, wrapping his arms around her, his hand smoothing her hair. "Whatever it is, I'll help you, Amara." He had no clue what might have upset her so, but he wasn't about to abandon her.

Her arms clung to him, as if she feared he might disappear, her grip increasing his nervousness even as he relished her body pressed so close. She sobbed into his shoulder for long moments, her chest spasming against his.

The air was quiet, still. No one was there besides them. He was thankful for the unexpected privacy in such a public place. He wanted to get her out, get her away.

She leaned back, sniffling, wiping her eyes with her hands. He didn't let her go, instead touching his forehead to hers as he pressed a kiss to her nose. "Let me help you."

Sucking in a deep breath, she steeled her shoulders, the tension in her body radiating into him.

"I'm pregnant."

CHAPTER 31

*M*att stared at her. No words came. He didn't think he could speak if he tried. He held her for a moment longer, then suddenly dropped his arms, stepping back. "Say what?"

She nodded, misery oozing from her every pore. "Cat showed me how to do a test, and there were lines, and, oh, God, I'm so sorry, Matthew."

He ran a hand over his hair, his other hand on his hip, his chest heaving like he'd run a marathon. "And you're telling me it's mine?"

Her face collapsed, as if he'd struck her. He immediately wanted to call the words back, but he couldn't, could only watch as she disappeared in front of him, walling him away.

On the other hand, it wasn't as if they'd claimed exclusivity. Had she been sleeping with other men? She *had* gotten awfully cozy with that idiotic cowboy. Before he'd dragged her away and home into his bed. Or rather, onto his floor. Without a condom.

No, it was his. He knew it in his gut, in his heart.

"Amara, I'm so—"

She held up a hand, cutting him off. "No need. I see your opinion of me, one that is well deserved. I made the decision to have relations with you. I took this risk upon myself. And I shall be the one to pay the price for it."

Of course she wouldn't. This was *their* problem, not only hers. And yet those words wouldn't come. He couldn't speak, his life-long plans crashing down around him. He'd never wanted children, but even if he had, he wouldn't have wanted them *now*, not with tenure on the line. He'd seen colleagues lose their edge when they'd become parents, the sleepless nights and extra demands undermining their work performance. That wasn't going to be Matt.

He bit out a caustic laugh. *Fuck.* Just a few days ago he'd been mulling over how he hadn't considered a relationship because he hadn't wanted it to affect his professional career. Now here he was, facing impending fatherhood?

She took a step back.

"Amara," he said, inching toward her.

"No."

"No, what?"

"Don't say anything. Your reaction tells me everything I need to know." It was her turn to give a bitter laugh. "And it's no different from mine. I didn't want children. I *don't* want a child."

"Let me expla—"

"No!" she repeated, her voice rising. "You need not. You need not to have any part of this. In my—at one time, you might have had to offer for me, but you needn't do that here, and I assure you, I am not trying to entrap you." She steeled her shoulders, her eyes red-rimmed, but now dry. "You are released from any obligation to me, Mr. Goodson."

With that, she turned and walked out the door, leaving him dumbstruck, his legs rooted to the floor, his eyes on her shattered cell phone.

It matched his shattered life.

Amara rushed across the Lawn, tears seeping from her eyes. She ignored the curious looks from people passing by. She didn't know what she'd expected, but it wasn't that. It wasn't being accused of having relationships with other men. It wasn't silence. It wasn't a laugh so harsh it'd nearly cut her in two.

You didn't react much better when you first saw those lines, Amara Mattersley. And he'd stayed. He hadn't fled. He'd wanted to speak, and she'd cut him off. But what could he say? What could he do? He couldn't repair this, and it was clear he had no more desire than she for a child. No, she might have ruined her own life, but she wasn't going to ruin his, too. She'd work this out, somehow.

She didn't want to return to the Treasure Trove, yet where else could she go? If she contacted Shannon or Jill, she'd have to explain, and that she wasn't willing to do. This situation was shameful enough. She could call Taylor, but to what end? She'd released Matthew from any obligation; contacting his sister would only complicate matters. And it wasn't as if Taylor could remedy things, either.

"Bloody hell." The forceful words felt good leaving her lips, and she nearly said a few of the stronger terms she'd learned in the last month. She walked aimlessly, not sure where she was going, her eyes dry but burning. She missed her sisters. Lord, how she missed her sisters. Grace would be the most understanding, the most sympathetic. Emmeline would likely react as poorly as her mother, focusing on what this would do for her own marriage prospects over what it would do to Amara, though Amara could hardly blame the poor girl; her sisters had lived under the shadow of her scandal for years.

Her disappearance must be a blessing to them. *Must have been, rather.* They were long gone now. What had happened after she'd left? Had they missed her? Cat had shown her the photographs Eliza'd sent, taken long after Amara disappeared. It'd been strange to see her youthful brother at an older age, children at his side, including Frederick, who'd grown into a surprisingly tall and handsome young man, given his frail, tiny stature as a child.

They'd gone on. Had lives without her. She'd come here, to a new life. And she'd fouled it up as surely as she'd fouled up her life then—even more, now that an innocent child was involved.

She stopped in her tracks, looking around. She'd wandered along Main Street for blocks and found herself now at the pedestrian mall to which Matthew had taken her for dinner. There were fewer people today, as the weather was noticeably colder. Nobody paid any attention to her as she walked slowly along one side of the shops, her eyes drifting over to the restaurant where she and Matthew had eaten. Had it only been just under a fortnight since? It felt like an eternity.

A light mist began to fall, and Amara shivered. She should go home. Home? Ha. The Treasure Trove was not her home. She was a stranger there, an interloper. She stood for a few moments, staring unseeingly at the bricks at her feet.

She needed to let Cat know she was okay. The woman

had been nothing but kind. Heavens, the woman was the one who'd given her this chance. The one she'd ruined. She couldn't let Cat worry. She needed to return.

Then she needed to make plans.

Matt couldn't have said how long he remained in the Colonnade Club. He'd sunk into a chair, the one Amara had vacated, after she'd stormed out. His mind swirled, a jumbled, tortured mix of emotions. He'd never wanted kids. Children were unpredictable. He wanted to be in control at all times, to know what was coming, to follow his plan.

The plan just torpedoed by an unexpected pregnancy.

He didn't know what to do.

He should have gone after her, should have chased her, instead of letting her run away, letting her think he wanted nothing to do with her. He didn't know what he wanted, but he certainly *did* know he was a man who honored his responsibilities. It'd gotten him far in college, graduate school, and in his career. Unlike his father, it was who Matt was; someone who honored what he'd committed to.

But you didn't commit to her, nor she to you, a part of him argued. No. It didn't matter that they'd made no promises, that they'd taken precautions. Except that one time. He'd always known if something like this were to happen, he would make it right. Somehow.

He would support whatever decision Amara made. If she wanted to keep the baby, he'd be there to help financially. Tingles raced up his spine. Being a true dad was another thing entirely. He admired how devoted Ben was to Wash, but Matt didn't know if he had that in him. His own father certainly hadn't.

And Matt wanted his life structured exactly as he wished, determined by him and him alone. A child changed that instantly. Permanently.

His breath hitched. *Would* she keep the baby? She was as independent as he, wanting no encumbrances. And he knew well enough the majority of this burden fell on her, no matter what promises he might make.

He tugged at the collar of his shirt, which felt ten times smaller than it had an hour ago. He was to be a father. He, Matthew Adam Goodson.

A door slammed somewhere in the building, jarring him out of his self-absorption.

He needed to find Amara. Now.

Cat nearly tackled Amara as she walked through the front door. "Where have you been? I was so worried!" Several customers watched curiously as Cat enfolded her in a giant hug. "Matt called, saying he couldn't find you. I could tell from his voice you'd talked to him. What happened?" She backed up from Amara, her eyes troubled.

Amara glanced around at the foreign eyes on her. "I do not mean to offend," she whispered, "but may we speak when we are not in the company of others?"

"Of course. Sorry. I've just been worried sick."

"No need. I am fine. But I'd like to rest." Amara didn't wait for a response before crossing to the back stairway and ascending the steps, anxious to hide away in her room. Sleep was not a permanent solution, but a short time free from the worries of the day sounded heavenly.

Elvis, the cat, meowed as she entered the apartment, trotting after her and squeezing through the door to her room before she closed it. Amara'd never paid much attention to cats, particularly. At Clarehaven, they lived outside. But as she settled into bed and the animal curled up at her side, she had to admit the unconditional acceptance and affection from the furry feline was exactly what she needed. If only she could be so accepting of herself.

"You texted she's here?" The words burst out before he could stop them as he sprinted into the Treasure Trove.

Cat looked up from a customer, giving Matt a curt nod and a warning with her eyes. "I'll be with you in a moment."

Good reminder. No need to air his dirty laundry in front of everyone. The store was busier than he'd expected, families and college students milling about. In the corner, Emily whipped up coffee drinks for tired shoppers. For lack of anything else to do, he walked over and ordered one. He wanted to race upstairs, to find Amara right away. But this wasn't his store, wasn't his home. He had to wait.

He sat down on the faded green sofa, cup in hand, and stared into the flames of the fireplace. How was it that life was so different than it'd been just six weeks ago? Not only because of Amara's unexpected, and admittedly unwelcomed, news. But because of her appearance in his life. She'd taken him by storm, this puzzling, adorable woman who'd kissed him on first sight, agreed to a no-strings-attached connection,

wormed her way into his emotions when he wasn't looking—
then turned his world completely upside down with her
announcement today.

One month ago, he'd been fretting to Ben about the new
hiring committee and the falling enrollment in the database
classes. Those concerns seemed laughable now.

The door opened again, and Ben came in, Wash in his
arms. He greeted his wife, pressing a kiss to her lips before
dropping a second on his son's head. The boy reached out
for his mother, his face lighting up as she took him into her
arms.

For a second, Matt pictured himself in Ben's place, Amara
before him, their child between. Panic seized him, as well as
a tiny, unsettling sense of peace, of rightness. Of calm. The
panic he'd expected; the other, not in the least. *Could* that be
his future with Amara, the happiness he saw between Ben
and Cat?

The Coopers, however, had had months to develop their
relationship and build a strong foundation. They'd been
married a year before they'd gotten pregnant. That was vastly
different than considering a future with a woman Matt barely
knew, a mere month after they'd met.

And a future with him was not on her priority list. She'd
released him from all responsibilities, didn't want anything
to do with him. *Had she meant it?* Or had she spoken in the
heat of the moment? She'd been angry and rightly so; he'd
essentially accused her of sleeping around.

He had a lot to make up for.

He waited as Cat chatted with Ben, impatient to speak
with her but not wanting to be rude to his colleague. Ben's
brow suddenly wrinkled, and his brown eyes flashed to
Matt's. With a nod, he left Cat and crossed the room.

"Hello, Matt."

"Hi." Matt stood, as he always did when in the presence of his advisor. This, however, was a decidedly awkward situation.

"How about a beer?"

"Uh—" Matt hesitated. He really wanted to speak to Amara.

"Amara's sleeping. And this might not be the best time for you two to talk. Give her a little time."

Matt's shoulders slumped. Ben knew. This was more embarrassing than the time his high school math teacher had caught him with porn. Matt's cheeks burned as if fire ants were gnawing on them.

"I know we're colleagues, but I'd also like to hope you consider me a friend, Matt."

The words hung in the air, and to Matt's surprise, his eyes welled up. It wasn't that he didn't have friends of his own. He did. One or two. But he could sure use advice from someone with more experience than he in this area. "A beer sounds great."

"St. Maarten's? We can walk, in case it's a two or three—or four—beer kind of night."

"Sure. And Ben?"

"Yeah?"

"Thanks."

The bar was fairly full, which didn't surprise Matt—it was Thursday night, after all, and students liked to start the weekend early. But the atmosphere was comfortable, and the high-backed wood booths lent a sense of privacy.

"So," Ben said, after they'd settled in and ordered.

"Yeah."

"How do you feel about it?"

"I don't know. Stunned. Nervous." He frowned, toying with a paper beer coaster. "Angry."

Ben nodded. "Makes sense."

"But not at Amara," Matt added quickly. "It's not her fault. It's mine. I, uh, forgot the condom the first night."

"It takes two."

"True, but Amara's different than other women in a way I can't quite put my finger on. A little more naïve or something. Not that I'm so clued in."

Ben gave a strangled chuckle. "You got that right."

Matt's eyebrow rose. He took a slug of beer, confused. Was Ben referring to Amara, or to Matt's social awkwardness? Should he ask?

Ben sat back in the booth. "You've got a good head on your shoulders, Matt. I have every confidence you'll figure this out."

"Ha." Matt gave a derisive snort. "Sure wish I did."

CHAPTER 32

*A*mara woke sometime later, the room black and her eyes crusty from tears. She rolled over to look at the bedside clock. Funny how quickly she'd got used to knowing the time at all hours. 3:24 a.m.

Her stomach growled. How could she be hungry? How could her body continue its normal functioning with everything going on? She snorted. How could it not? Another human being was growing inside of her, as unimaginable as that was.

Throwing off the covers, she rose from the bed, scratching Elvis's head as he meowed in protest. Quietly, she padded out to the kitchen and searched for something to eat. A package of muffins sat on the counter, and she helped herself to one, setting it on a plate before sitting down at the table. She'd only eaten a few bites, her mind swirling with the events of the day, when a door squeaked. Was somebody else up?

Muffled steps echoed from the next room, and then Cat peeked around the corner, her mouth pinched in concern. "Mind if I join you?"

"Not at all."

Pulling out a chair, Cat sat down. "How are you?"

Amara shrugged. "I am not sure, to be truthful."

Cat picked at an imaginary crumb on the table. "Ben talked with Matthew last night."

Amara didn't respond.

"Matt's wigging out, sure, but he wants to talk to you. He confessed to Ben he didn't handle your announcement well, and he's sorry."

Amara sighed. "I know he is." She set the muffin down and leaned back in the chair. "But he did not want this. He did not ask for it."

"Neither did you!"

"Of course not, but when I made the decision to be intimate with him, I knew the risks."

"So did he! It takes two, Amara. He's as responsible for this as you are."

"I do not wish to ruin his life, Cat." She turned her head, staring off into the distance, avoiding eye contact.

"Who says a baby will ruin his life? Maybe it's what will save it!"

Amara shook her head. "Babies do not mend things that are broken. I learned that from my brother's first marriage. He thought a child might reconcile him to his wife. It did the opposite."

"But not all—"

Amara held up her hand, cutting Cat off. "Yes, I know, not all would have that experience." She exhaled, wiping the hair from her face. "But let's be honest. Matthew Goodson and I barely know each other. Yes, I understand there are special circumstances. I understand you feel we belong together. That you brought us together for that purpose. I even have feelings for him." She closed her eyes at the admission.

"So what's the problem? My guess is, he has feelings for you, too!"

"But this pregnancy, unexpected and unwanted, changes everything. It traps him. Traps me. We are no longer free to make our own decisions. I ran from 1813 for that very reason, Cat."

Cat said nothing.

"I came here to escape the things that confined women in my era. Marriage. Babies. Dependence on men. I do not wish to be trapped by them now."

"Amara," Cat said, frustration lacing her voice. "Those things do not have to equal being trapped. Did you see *no* happy marriages in your time?"

Amara thought of Deveric and Eliza. They'd been blissfully in love. And it had lasted, as evidenced by Eliza's letters. And her sister, Cecilia. Cecilia had been truly happy. But they were exceptions. Amara's friend Frances, her own mother … Of the women of her social standing who'd married, most had not married for love, but for prestige and social connections. For money. Some of them had ended up in desperate situations, situations Amara never wished to be in.

Yet here she was.

"Look at Ben and me! Can't you see how happy we are? We've both got jobs. A kid. And neither one of us feels trapped. We're exactly where we want to be."

"Yes. I see that," Amara conceded. "But I am not." She stood up and strolled the length of the room, pacing in an effort to dissipate her nervous energy.

"You have time. You don't have to know the answers today."

Amara pinched her eyes shut, exhaling loudly. "I need to go home. To Clarehaven."

"*What?*"

Cat's voice reverberated around the kitchen, and Amara's gaze dashed to Wash's room, hoping his mother's loud, unexpected exclamation wouldn't wake him. She shouldn't have said anything. She'd been mulling the idea over ever since she'd walked away from Matthew.

Cat's next words were a whisper. "You want to go back? To your time?"

Amara shook her head emphatically. "I couldn't. Not now. Even if I wanted to, even if it were possible." She stopped her pacing, staring at Cat. "*Is* it possible?"

Cat hesitated, her eyes not quite meeting Amara's. "I don't know. Maybe. I sent Eliza there, after all."

Amara resumed her rhythmic movements. "It hardly matters. Being an unwed mother may not be the biggest scandal here, but it would ruin me completely in my own society." She snorted. "As a member of such a powerful family, I suppose it's possible people would overlook even that. But I would not do that to a child, to have them labeled a bastard."

"Wow."

"What?"

"It's weird to hear that word used in that sense. Today, when someone says someone's a bastard, it means they're a jerk. It has nothing to do with their parentage." Cat pushed her hair behind her ears. "But if you don't want to go *back*, what did you mean?"

"I want to see if I have any remaining relatives."

"For Pete's sake, you don't need to go all the way to England to find that out. Just Google it!"

Amara smiled, a smile full of pain. "Cat, you've been nothing but kind. Generous to a fault. I see why Eliza loved you so much. But I've not found my place yet. I have nothing and no one. Not really. I long to see my home, to see *something* familiar. I know even if there are Mattersley descendants still living, it's not as if they would take me in. But I need to connect with my past before I can move on with my future."

Cat shook her head. "I am going to say something, and it might make you angry, but it needs to be said. You are running away, exactly as you did in 1813. Perhaps it's time to stay and figure things out here. With Matt. You need to talk with him. He needs to understand, to know why you're reacting this way. He can't do that unless he knows *everything*. And he's sure to believe you if Ben and I vouch for you, tell him our own story, show him the manuscript and your photographs."

"*No!*" Now it was Amara's voice threatening to wake those still sleeping. "You promised neither you nor Mr. Cooper would reveal my ... past."

Cat sighed, rubbing her eyes. "Yes. I promised. Your secrets are safe with me." She yawned. "It's four in the morning. Maybe more sleep will help us both determine what the next step should be."

"Yes, return to your bed. I know you must be up early with your son."

Nodding, Cat stood up. "But you?"

Amara smiled grimly. "I do not think any more sleep will be happening tonight."

She gathered her things as quietly as possible, not that she had much to take with her, and stole out of the apartment twenty minutes later. Cat was right; she *was* running. But she needed to take back some semblance of control, and she was doing so by leaving the country, leaving Charlottesville, leaving Matthew. She wouldn't burden him, wouldn't burn his dreams to the ground the way she'd burned her own.

Ben had left his phone on the table, and she'd used it before she packed to call for a car, a trick she'd learned from reading about something called Uber, where people gave rides in exchange for money. Not so different from hailing a hansom cab. Not that she'd ever done that, either, but there were so many firsts she'd experienced since arriving here, what was one more?

The young man who picked her up cast appreciative eyes at her. But after asking questions and getting only monosyllabic answers, he stopped trying and just drove, the radio the only sound in the car. Amara teared up when *Breakfast at Tiffany's* played. She'd listened to the song with Matthew that one afternoon and liked it so much he downloaded it to her phone for her. She'd played it several times, always thinking of him. Now her phone—Eliza's phone—lay abandoned, broken. She wiped away a silent tear.

When the car reached the airport, Amara's heart nearly leapt into her throat at the enormous machines made visible by the airport lights. She was supposed to ride in one of those? Across the sea? The idea scared her witless, and she nearly changed her mind, but checked herself. What would that prove? She could do this. And she needed to go. She couldn't make decisions here, not with her emotions in such turmoil whenever she saw Matthew. She needed to give him space, to assure him she'd meant it when she said he owed her nothing, that she was not going to burden him with this unwanted development.

Walking into the lobby, she took a deep breath, pulled out

her passport and bankcard Cat had thankfully insisted she get, and approached the first counter she saw. "I need to fly to London."

The woman behind the desk raised her eyebrows. "When?"

"Today," Amara said, nodding firmly. "Preferably as soon as possible."

"Passport?"

Amara handed over the small booklet, and the woman scanned it into the computer, her eyes flying over the screen. Not so different from having papers in England.

After a moment, the woman returned the passport. Typing on the keyboard, she said, "There's a flight leaving in forty minutes, with a connection in Philly, but it's not cheap."

"The price does not matter," Amara said, presenting her bankcard.

"Alrighty, then." The woman swiped the card, smiling as the machine beeped. There came a whirring noise, and the woman reached down, pulling out some papers. "You're on American Airlines 4891 to Philadelphia. Then you've got a nearly four-hour layover before flight 736 takes you to London."

Amara had no clue what a layover was, but she nodded, acting as if everything the woman told her made perfect sense.

"Are you checking luggage?"

Amara paused. What did that mean? "I have this," she said, patting the floppy bag she'd found in a closet. She hoped Cat wouldn't be too angry she'd taken it.

"That's small enough to carry on. Okay, then. Gate 3, after security." The woman pointed to her left.

"Thank you very much." Amara took the papers,

clutching them and her passport as she approached the area marked *Security*. People shuffled through the line, setting their belongings on a moving belt and removing their shoes before walking through a metal doorframe. No one acted as if anything were out of the ordinary, but stripping down to bare feet disconcerted Amara.

Still, a few minutes later, she was through. She found her way to Gate 3 and dropped into a seat, her insides knotting. Closing her eyes, she steeled her resolve. Moments later, she handed over the piece of paper labeled *Boarding Pass* and walked down a hallway before passing through a narrow metal door into a cramped, enclosed space. Her stomach did somersaults. This was an airplane? She disliked it instantly; confined, crowded spaces had never been her favorite. She found her numbered seat and sat down, breathing slowly in an effort to maintain calm. At least she was directly near the window and could see out.

"You okay? You look nervous," came a friendly voice from her side. A rather portly man moved into the seat next to her, smiling as he sat. His leg brushed hers.

"Sorry," he said, a rueful grin on his face. "No one likes to sit next to the fat guy." He shuffled around, searching for his seat belt. "But seriously, are you scared?"

Personal questions from complete strangers still caught her off guard, much less from one in such close proximity. "Don't be," he said, though she hadn't answered. "I fly every week for business. Piece of cake. Never had a problem yet."

This man flew on an airplane every week? How could he stand it, wedging his large form into such a tiny space? Her self-pity dissipated; at least she could sit relatively comfortably. "This is my first time flying," she confessed.

His brows rose. "But you've got a British accent. How'd

you get here if you didn't fly?"

Again with the personal questions. She regretted having said anything. "By … boat." It's how she *would* have come two hundred years ago, had she wanted to visit the Americas. Which she hadn't. Not since Drake.

"Huh. Didn't know they did that anymore." He pulled out his phone. "Well, gotta call the wife before the plane leaves."

Amara rested her head against the seatback, grateful his attention had turned away from her. Minutes later, she clutched at the arms of her seat as the plane began to move. The engines roared, and the machine raced down the runway. Her eyes widened as the earth dropped away from them. Good God, she was in the air. She was flying.

If only Deveric could witness this. He would love it.

Amara, on the other hand, feared she might cast up her accounts, but she couldn't tear herself away from the window. The ground grew smaller and smaller beneath them, the cars resembling ants crawling along pencil-thin pathways.

"It's beautiful, isn't it?" said the man at her side.

It was. After a few more minutes, white wisps drifted around the window, and soon her view was completely obscured. Gracious, what had happened? Were they going to die?

"I love going through the clouds." The man chuckled. "As a kid, I thought we were flying up to heaven."

They broke through, and suddenly she was looking down on a blanket of white, much like the snow drifts that covered Clarehaven's grounds in the winter, only this was softer, wispier. Clouds. She was *above* the clouds. The sun peeked across the billowy horizon, its rays nearly blinding. And yet, they raised joy in her. She'd done it. She was on an airplane, above the clouds.

She was going home.

CHAPTER 33

*M*att groaned as Lovey draped herself on his face. Shoving the cat off, he popped open an eye to stare at the clock. 6:48. Stupid cat. He didn't want to get up yet. He didn't have to be anywhere until nine.

He shook his head, but froze as pain lanced through it. *Damn.* He'd had more to drink last night than he thought if he had a hangover today. Instantly, the events of the previous day washed over him.

Amara. Amara was pregnant.

He grabbed his phone and checked to see if she'd contacted him, then remembered she'd left her broken phone behind.

She could have found another way to reach him, if she'd wanted to. Clearly she hadn't. He shouldn't be surprised; she'd basically walked out of his life yesterday. But surely she'd see that wasn't the answer, would understand this was something the two of them needed to deal with together.

He'd give her space today. Fight or flight syndrome in people was strong, and obviously her urge was to flee, as was his sister's. He'd let her; they had time to figure out what to do. But he'd also let her know he was waiting, for when she was ready.

After feeding the cat, he grabbed a quick shower. He didn't know why he felt so much calmer today. His whole life had changed in an instant, and yet he felt peaceful, as if what should happen would happen, and it'd all work out. He nearly snorted. Likely he was just in denial, but he'd take it for now. Whatever he needed to get through the day.

Pulling on a pair of khaki Dockers and a button-down shirt—his standard teaching uniform—he grabbed socks and headed to the kitchen, settling in with a large cup of coffee courtesy of the Keurig and his laptop. He'd just pulled up his email when his phone rang. Caller ID said it was Cat. He snatched it up. Maybe it was Amara.

"Hello?"

"Matt?" It was Cat. Not Amara. Her voice sounded off.

"Yeah." Who else would answer his phone?

"She's gone."

His stomach dropped. He knew immediately to whom she was referring, of course. "Where?"

"To England. To Clarehaven. She wanted to go … home."

Home? From what she'd said, Amara didn't have a home anymore. What was going on? Why on earth had she left? He closed his eyes, his heart thudding an erratic rhythm against his ribcage. Crap. Things kept getting worse. Would she really do this? Leave without discussing them or this child? "Permanently?"

"I don't know."

"Shit."

"I'm so sorry, Matt. But I thought you should know."

"When did she leave?"

"Sometime after four. She snuck out before Ben and I woke up. She left a note."

Fury rose in him. She'd blindsided him with this news yesterday, then fled. Now she was fleeing even farther, across an ocean? He pinched the top of his nose with his fingers. He didn't know what to do. "Okay," he heard himself say. "Thanks."

"What are you going to do?"

"I don't know," he bit out, unable to hide the anger in his voice. After a tense second, he apologized. "I'm sorry, Cat, the anger isn't for you."

"I know." She paused again. "Matt? I don't have the answers, but I'm here if you need me. This wasn't how this was supposed to work out."

"Tell me about it." He sniggered, a noise of pain mixed with bewilderment. "I, uh, will you let me know if you hear anything from her?"

"Of course."

He set the phone down, staring at it. He had no way of getting into contact with her. *Crap.* What should he do?

His watch beeped, reminding him it was time to go. He had class to teach. He stood and jammed his phone into his pocket, shutting everything behind a wall in his mind as best he could. He had other obligations right now, and unlike Amara, he wasn't one to run from them.

Amara didn't sleep a wink on the plane, in spite of her exhaustion. She disliked being restricted to such a small space for so long, though at least it was less bumpy than a coach ride. Looking out the window at the ocean below brought waves of both terror and elation, almost too much to bear, so she'd copied the man next to her by putting on headphones and watching movies on the screen in the seatback in front of her. Movies. On an airplane. How rich was this?

What would her sisters have thought of modern technology? Would Grace have enjoyed watching acted-out versions of her beloved novels and plays any time she wished? Or would the pages still call more than stage or screen, her imagination supplying the details in a way more satisfying than anyone else's version?

Emmeline would love it, would love the gossipy reality TV shows, including the one Amara was now watching documenting the lives of young, rich English people. She winced at their antics; her scandal had nothing on them. Her mother would roll over in her grave to see people of privilege comporting themselves in such a way.

Amara sighed, glancing around. People of all shapes, sizes, and colors occupied the seats. The front of the airplane held the first-class passengers. Walking through their cabin on her way to her own spot, she'd envied the large chairs. Why hadn't she been offered such a ticket? Then again, she didn't care for the way the passengers seated there avoided eye contact with the people moving past them, as if to deny their existence.

Would she have been any better, if not for Eliza? Eliza'd opened Amara's eyes to the servants Amara had taken for granted, had pretended were invisible, as her mother had taught her. Shame settled on her now for the class divisions she'd accepted as God-given, though it was hard to let go of some of the attitudes of privilege.

A woman worked to soothe a wailing baby, bouncing the

infant on her lap as irritated passengers grumbled or gave pointed glances. No man was there to help her, no husband stepped in in any way.

That will be me.

She touched her hand to her abdomen, grateful that as scandalous as it might be to bear a child out of wedlock, to become a "single mother," as it was termed here, she could afford it. Standing up, she excused herself past her neighbor—a difficult task, considering there was scarcely room between seats, and approached the woman. "Would you like me to hold it?"

The offer startled her as much as the woman. Amara didn't particularly like children. But the empathy flooding her for this poor woman trapped with a screaming child could not be denied. The woman nodded gratefully. "Him. Brady. And I would love to at least use the restroom. Thank you!"

Amara bounced the child up and down on her hip, as she'd occasionally done with her nephew Frederick when he was an infant. The boy stilled, staring at her with wide blue eyes—eyes nearly the same light shade as Matthew's.

She froze. Was she staring into her future, seeing this tiny face before her? She continued to rock him, and after a minute he closed his eyes, his body softening as he relaxed into sleep.

"Oh my. How did you do that?" The boy's mother reappeared at her elbow, the first tremulous smile passing her face at her quiet child. "Here, I'll take him. Thank you."

Amara returned the baby as carefully as she could. Thankfully, the boy didn't wake.

She retreated to the open space near the restroom area, the one place in which she could stand, not ready to take her seat, emotions rushing over her. She was pregnant. She was going to bear a child. Matthew's child. And she was running to escape this scandal of her own making. Would Matthew be grateful or resentful she'd robbed him of his child?

This was the right decision, wasn't it?

A bell dinged, and a flight attendant touched her on her elbow. "Please return to your seat, ma'am. We'll be landing shortly."

Amara dutifully obeyed, sinking into the narrow chair and staring out the window, surprised to see spots of light below. They were over land. Over England. Soon she'd be home.

Except it wasn't truly home anymore.

Matt banged his hand on the keyboard in frustration, unable to focus on the screen before him. Damn her. Damn her! How could she do this to him? How could she tell him she was expecting his child, then run?

He clasped the green paperweight, turning it over and over with his hand. Okay, so he hadn't exactly responded well to her grand proclamation. But she hadn't given him a chance, hadn't let him wrap his mind around any of this before running off.

He glanced at his watch. Eight p.m. Midnight in London, as he knew they hadn't yet moved to Daylight Savings Time. She must be there by now. How could he contact her? Her phone was in his possession—he hadn't been able to leave it on the Colonnade's floor, wanting that piece of her. He debated sending an email to the account he'd set up for her, but would she ever check it?

He sighed. He should go. He wasn't getting anything done. He didn't like this, didn't like not being in control, didn't like his whole life in upheaval. Yes, he should go home. But he didn't want to be alone. Picking up his phone, he dialed.

"Hello?" His sister's voice was breathless, as if he'd interrupted her while she was running. Except Taylor didn't run.

"Tay? It's me. Can I come over? I need to talk."

There was rustling in the background, then a murmur of voices. *Did his sister have someone over?*

"Tonight? Um, sure, okay." More noises. "See you in thirty minutes or so?"

"Yeah. Thanks." He hung up the phone. In thirty minutes, whatever had been going on over there would be easily covered up. Not that it was any of his business. And not that it was something he wanted to talk about tonight. No, tonight he needed to be selfish.

Grabbing his jacket, he jogged down the stairs and out of his office building, making his way to his truck. The stars twinkled in the night sky, and he stopped for a moment, sucking in a painful breath as memories of looking up at the heavens with Amara flooded him. The same heavens that covered England. Weirdly enough, it soothed him to know that while she was so very far away, they still had a connection through the stars.

He shook off that overly cheesy thought and hopped into the truck, revving the engine and peeling out of the nearly empty lot. Now was not the time for tender memories. Now was the time for anger. And planning.

"She's *what?*"

Matt glared at her. "You heard me. Loud and clear."

A wide smile settled on Taylor's face.

"Why are you *smiling?* This is not the time for smiling, damn it. She's pregnant. And she's fled, not just Charlottesville, but the whole damn country. What do I do?"

Taylor's face sobered, and she walked to her overstuffed sofa, plopping down. She patted the cushion next to her, and Matt dropped into it, all of his attention focused on his sister's answer.

"What do you want to do?"

"What do you mean?" He frowned.

"Well, it seems to me you have two choices. One, take the freedom Amara offered, and let her go."

Matt's frown deepened.

"Or, two, go after her."

"To *England?*"

Taylor nodded. Matt leaned back into the sofa, exhaling loudly as his palms traced paths across his thighs.

"The big question is, which do you *want* to do? Moral issues aside, like you worrying about being responsible, as I know you are. Do you *want* Amara in your life or not?"

He closed his eyes, tipping his head back. "But it wouldn't be just Amara anymore; it'd be Amara and child."

"Yup. But the heart of the question is, how do you feel about her?"

He opened one eye and peeked at her. "I barely know her. We spent a few weeks together, a no-strings-attached deal. We never talked future."

She eyed him. "That isn't what I asked." Reaching over, she patted his knee. "If you want my opinion—and if you didn't, you wouldn't be here—I think you care for her far more than you know. I watched you with her, you know, both that first night when I took her shopping, then when you were here. That first night, you were interested. Clear as a bell. But the second? There was something else, something deeper going on. And you both felt it."

Matt's mouth fell open. So *that's* why she'd said Captain Obvious. He'd barely acknowledged to himself that night he might feel something for Amara other than physical desire, might want something more. But his sister had noticed. Had texted him about fish. Had Amara noticed, too? Had she felt the same?

Regardless of what each may or may not feel for the other, there was this ... this baby looming between them. Everything had been placed on fast-forward, whether they wanted it to be or not.

"Matt, I've seen you with other women. But I've never once seen you look at anyone the way you looked at her. Not even Wendy." Taylor's eyes softened, and her hand remained on his knee. "I think you know what you need to do. What you *want* to do."

Matt's chest exploded with feeling, his heart hammering against his rib cage. An odd mixture of longing and fury flooded through him. "Yes, but I can't! I can't go to England, Tay. It's the middle of the semester. I've got responsibilities. Teaching. Research. Finishing this tenure dossier!"

"Yup." Taylor nodded. "All of that's true."

Matt sighed, his eyes meeting hers. They held for a long time. "You think I should go."

Taylor shrugged. *Damn it, why was she so nonchalant about it all?* "Only if you want to. I can't make this decision for you, Matty. But you knew that before you came."

"Fuck."

She giggled. "Yeah, that's what got you into trouble to begin with. Naughty brother."

He snickered as he stood and gathered his coat. "Given the noises I heard on the phone earlier, I'm not the only Goodson being not quite so good lately."

He bellowed with glee at the crimson flooding his sister's face before sobering. "Thank you, Taylor. Truly." Tears flooded his eyes, to his surprise and dismay.

Taylor jumped up, enfolding him in a hug. "You'll figure it out, Matty," she whispered in his ear. "That's why I'm not worried. You'll make the right decision. You always do, big brother."

He held her a moment longer before backing up and giving her a brief nod. He wished he were half as confident in himself as she was.

Ducking out the door, he ambled slowly to his truck, his sister's words roiling around in his head. He put his hand on the handle, glancing at the truck bed. The last time he'd been here with this truck, Amara had been, too, and they'd shared one of the best evenings he'd ever had. One that hadn't ended in sex.

Sighing, his breath foaming in front of him in the cold night air, he whipped open the truck door.

He was going to England.

CHAPTER 34

ondon was familiar, but it was also foreign. London was consolation, but it was chaos, too. After a night spent in an airport hotel—she'd been too exhausted to consider traveling after the flight, plus it'd been past one in the morning by the time she'd cleared customs—she'd taken a taxi into the city, her eyes glued to the window. London had expanded exponentially, yet the closer they neared the West End, the more familiar landmarks she saw, and her heart warmed. They passed Hyde Park, the sight stabbing her with longing for the times she'd strolled there with her sisters and brothers.

They weren't there now. Nobody she knew was. They were all dead. Her stomach roiled as the cab turned off of Piccadilly, wending its way through the narrow streets to Grosvenor Square, the destination she'd requested. The cab rolled to a stop, the driver indicating a fare of fifty pounds. Thank goodness she'd had the foresight to exchange money at the airport. She handed it over without looking at him, her eyes soaking in the square as she alighted from the vehicle.

It was the same, yet not. Unfamiliar stone structures and monuments were scattered about. A monstrous, ugly building —the American Embassy, according to Eliza—dominated the west end, and the row houses lining the square were at once familiar and different, some clearly newer than her era but built in similar style.

"World War II damaged some parts of London," Eliza had warned her. "And the natural passage of time has brought other changes."

The natural passage of time. There was nothing natural about a woman standing now in the very spot she'd stood two hundred years earlier. She clutched at her abdomen, a wave of nausea overtaking her. *Good Lord, don't let me faint.*

People passed her by. Nobody gave her any notice, much less tipped a head in greeting. She sat on a bench and observed the humans around her. She could spy tourists almost instantly: the Americans with their white athletic shoes, people snapping photos with their phones.

I'm a tourist now.

A stranger in a strange land was how Eliza'd described landing in Regency England. That's exactly how Amara felt. She sat a while longer, letting the thoughts and emotions roll over her. She'd done it. She was here. Two hundred years and thousands of miles from anyone who knew her. *Now what?*

Perhaps the decision to come here had been foolish. She snorted. Of course it was. She was a fool. She'd done it again, throwing herself down a path from which there was no easy retreat. How was it she hadn't learned a thing between that night in the garden, so long ago, and her time here? She was alone, *enceinte*, in a city both familiar and strange, with no plan for the future. She buried her head in her hands, letting the tears fall.

"Hey, are you okay?" The voice was a surprise, American in accent, and Amara's eyes rose to lock with those of a young blonde who bore a marked resemblance to Eliza. Amara's mouth dropped. *Was this a sign?* If she believed in signs, that was. Which she didn't. Did she?

She wiped her eyes. "Yes, thank you."

The woman's own brow creased. "You sure? I can listen, if you want."

A man's voice called to the woman, and she glanced over her shoulder. "My husband," she said with an exuberant grin, as she turned back to Amara. "We're on our honeymoon! I finally got to see Grosvenor Square. I've read about it in so many novels!"

Amara couldn't help but smile, too. With her similar looks and bubbly personality, the woman could have been Eliza's sister. Amara would choose to take this as confirmation she was where she was supposed to be. It was better than thinking the opposite. "Truly, I am fine. Return to your husband. And congratulations," Amara said, as she stood up.

The kindly American nodded her head. "Thanks! Being married is *awesome!*" she exclaimed before practically running to a dark-haired man, who dropped a kiss on her lips.

Eliza. And Deveric. It could have been the two of them, standing there before her. But it wasn't.

With a sigh, she shuffled off, determined to see if Claremont House, the family's London residence, still stood. Not that she would know what to do if it did; anyone who lived there wouldn't have a clue as to who she was. But she had to know.

"You're sure?" Matt's brows rose dubiously as he looked at Ben.

"Absolutely. I can cover your classes. Gabe can help, too, if need be."

"We'll even feed your cat," Cat blurted out.

Ben clapped a hand on his shoulder. "You need to do this, Matt. Believe me, I understand." He gave a meaningful glance to his wife, who nodded.

"Is there something you know that I don't?" Matt asked point-blank. Some signs were too big to miss, even for him.

Cat bit her lip. "Amara made me promise to let her talk with you first. I have to honor that. But when you come home, if you still have questions, I'll answer anything I can."

Matt ran a hand over his hair, clasping the back of his head in frustration. He liked Mrs. Cooper, but at the moment, he wanted to wring her neck. Should he press her more? Maybe. Right now, he just wanted to get to Amara. "What if I don't find her?"

"She's going to Clarehaven," Cat said. "It is—was her home."

He blew air out of his cheeks. "And I'm supposed to know where Clarehaven is?"

Ben let out a choked chuckle, earning a glare from Matt. "Sorry. I just thought of what my students always say: 'When in doubt, Google it!'"

"He doesn't need to," broke in Cat. "I already wrote it down." She handed him a piece of paper with an address.

Matt tucked it into his wallet. "You've got my number. Let me know if you hear from her." He tipped his head to them both before sprinting out the door and down the steps. He was going to do it. He was going to leave, right in the middle of the semester. He was doing it.

Because he had to.

The drive to the airport seemed endless, the flight to London an eternity. Every minute inched by when he wanted it to race. He tried to distract himself with onboard movies, settling on a broadcast of the BBC's *Pride and Prejudice*, pretty sure if nothing else, Jane Austen would bore him to sleep.

"Colin Firth is so dreamy," said a voice loud enough for him to hear over the headphones. An attractive blonde across the aisle flashed flirtatious eyes at him. Any other time, she'd have provided a pleasant diversion. But not now, not with thoughts of Amara and his—their—future consuming him.

He barely nodded in return, his eyes flitting back to his screen.

"It's a rare man who enjoys Austen," she said, persistent in her efforts.

"I don't," Matt answered, a wicked smile crossing his face. "I'm only watching it for the men in cravats. They're so sexy, don't you agree?"

It was something his sister always said, whereas Matt had never seen the appeal, never understood what it was about Austen that sent so many women swooning. He was glad he lived in a jeans and T-shirt era; having to dress like those poor guys in those short pants, tight jackets, and confining neckcloths would've driven him nuts.

The woman's face cooled, though she kept the smile. "I get it," she said. "Too bad my brother isn't here. I'm sure he'd love to meet you."

Great. In his efforts to brush her off, he'd succeeded in potentially picking up a male date. Taylor would've had a field day with that. Luckily, the blonde turned away, having gotten his very false hint. He was grateful. Until he looked at his own screen just in time to see Colin Firth dive into a lake. The scene switched to a shot of Elizabeth Bennet, and Matt frowned. The woman's bonnet looked like the one Amara had worn the day they met. The dress was similar, too. He shifted in his seat, discomfort niggling at him, but he shook it off. *Ludicrous.* He was picturing her everywhere, even in a story set hundreds of years ago.

He switched to music. Anything to distract him from the bizarre vision of him as Darcy, strolling off in a cravat toward his own Amara—er, Elizabeth.

Claremont House was gone. In its place were modern structures designed to look older, but they didn't fool Amara. She stood rooted to the spot, staring at the facade of buildings most definitely not her home. It was hard to believe the magnificent abode she and her family had occupied when in Town no longer existed. What had happened?

She walked the streets numbly, making her way to Hyde Park, where she settled on a bench, watching people wander by on cement paths near Rotten Row. Gone were the horses and carriages. Now there were joggers, mothers pushing child carriages, the occasional man or woman in a business suit speaking urgently into cell phones.

The late afternoon sun eased into twilight and with it came immense fatigue, as well as the realization again of what she'd done. She'd left what little was familiar—Cat, Ben, Taylor, Matthew—to flee to a place now as foreign as anywhere else. Tears threatened, but she refused to let them fall. They would solve nothing.

With the approaching dark came fear. Where was she to stay? She hadn't thought this through. She'd just wanted something familiar, known, comfortable.

She hadn't found it.

Standing up, she shook her hair, as if to shake off the worry, the concerns, everything plaguing her. She'd passed several hotels in Mayfair. Surely one of them had a room. Tomorrow, she'd go to Clarehaven. An Internet search on the hotel lobby's computer that morning had told Amara the estate was still privately owned—by the current duchess of Claremont. Maybe the duchess would ... Would what, welcome Amara with open arms because they shared the same name? Not bloody likely.

But perhaps she'd let her see the house. Amara had to ask. She had to be at Clarehaven, to see her childhood home, to make her feel she was real, that this was real.

Then, and only then, would she decide what to do next.

Bleary-eyed, Matt exited the plane, shuffling along behind numerous passengers, including the blonde, who gave him an overly sweet smile, but nothing else. He was wiped out. He'd never been able to sleep on planes, and he wanted nothing more than to fall into a bed somewhere. Well, almost nothing more. He wanted to find Amara.

Shaking his head, he made his way to customs. What was he *doing* here? This was nuts. But what other choice did he have? It's not as if he could leave her alone, without any support. It was his responsibility to come.

As the passport official quizzed him regarding the purpose of his visit, then stamped his passport, Matt admitted to himself he felt more than responsibility, though. He wasn't here merely to fulfill his obligations as an unwilling father. No, he was worried for Amara.

And he missed her. Missed those glowing hazel-green eyes and her silky tresses, missed those delicious curves. Even more, he missed *her*. Her laughter, her strangely charming mixture of intelligence and naiveté. Her independent spirit.

She hadn't asked a thing from him.

She'd enjoyed their time together, though; he was sure of that. They both had. Memories of them entangled on his floor, music pulsating around them, stampeded through his brain, and he had to stop for a moment to catch his breath, his body springing embarrassingly to action. He'd thought it was perfect, exactly what he wanted: a sexy, fun, interesting, smart woman whenever he wanted her. One willing to be alone when he didn't.

But he'd started to want more. He wanted to see her often, wanted her to *want* to be with him. He wanted her to see him as someone who was there for her. Someone on whom she could depend. He'd failed. Instead of being that stand-up guy, he'd gotten her pregnant. And clearly she thought so lowly of him that rather than work through this together she'd fled the frigging country.

Now here he stood on the curb of Heathrow Airport, in England, hailing a cab to search for her. Had someone told him he'd throw aside everything he'd been working towards for a woman, he'd have laughed in their face. Yet, here he was.

He crawled into the cab, not sure where he should go. He needed to get to Clarehaven, but his phone said it was an hour outside of London. It was only 6:30 in the morning now. Should he show up at Clarehaven so early? But he hadn't slept in nearly twenty-four hours. He needed to, to have a clear head before he talked to Amara.

He had no clue if there were hotels near this Clarehaven. "Just take me to a decent hotel," he told the driver. "One near Piccadilly," he added, mentioning one of the few places he'd heard of in London, lest the cabby think him nuts asking for a random hotel in a city this large. The cabby simply nodded and sped away.

Amara woke early, anxious to be off. After settling the bill, she had the desk clerk hail her a cab to take her to Clarehaven. She left the hotel to wait outside, wanting to be in the morning air, though it was chilly. It at least smelled fresh.

She clutched her bag as the cab approached, wondering again if it wouldn't be smarter to go back to the airport, to return to Charlottesville. *But what is there for me?* Cat was a friend, but she wasn't family. She didn't owe Amara anything. And she had her own husband and child. She certainly wouldn't want to take on Amara and her baby—not that Amara would ever burden her in such a way.

This had all gone horribly wrong. What should she do? What *could* she do? She'd come to this century through the circle of stones at Clarehaven. If she went there again, could she return home? Truly home, to Clarehaven in 1813?

If she showed up unwed and expecting, she'd once more be at the center of scandal. *Or maybe not*, another part of her whispered. Amara had allegedly run off with a Royal Navy officer. Ships sank and men were lost all the time. She could easily claim widowhood. A duke's daughter marrying a Navy captain would have raised eyebrows, but it'd be better to be known as a widow than an unmarried mother.

The cab driver opened the rear door for her, and she settled into the seat with a sigh. No, she did not want to return to her time. Not only did more opportunities abound here, but she was an independent woman of wealth now. A woman of no reputation whatsoever in this modern society. No scandal tainted her here. Except for the one growing inside her.

As the cab exited the curb, Amara's gaze drifted absent-mindedly to another cab pulling up. A tall, lean figure alighted from the back, and for a moment Amara stopped breathing. The lithe build, the closely cropped hair; it could be Matthew. The man never turned in her direction to show his face before he entered the hotel, though, and soon they rounded the corner, heading away from the hotel, out of London, home to Clarehaven. Her pulse raced, even as she shook her head. Obviously it wasn't Matthew. He was in Charlottesville, not London. Her mind was playing tricks on her.

She closed her eyes, letting the miles sail by. It wasn't him. Was it?

CHAPTER 35

After securing a room, Matt fell face first into the bed, wishing it'd occurred to him before they were halfway to this hotel that there were undoubtedly hotels right there at the airport. Especially since they'd driven miles east to get here, and his ultimate destination was to the west.

He didn't stir for hours. At a bang in the hallway, he awoke, blinking his eyes as he tried to find the clock. 11:02, the red digits said. No light peeked in around the edges of the closed curtains. 11:02 p.m., then. *Crap*. He hadn't meant to sleep the day away, but he couldn't leave for Clarehaven at this time of night.

He heaved a sigh as he pushed himself up. Might as well shower and shave, then order something to eat. He'd plan for tomorrow, research Clarehaven, figure out how to get there. Figure out what he'd say to Amara if he found her there.

An hour later, he was ensconced back in the bed, laptop on his lap, and a beer to his side, courtesy of room service. He'd Googled the Mattersley family and had found a website delineating the family lineage. It included photos of Clarehaven and several 360-degree views inside the huge home.

This had been Amara's home? This lavish monstrosity, with its numerous rooms?

According to the site, the current owner, Sophie, an umpteenth generation Mattersley and duchess of Claremont, had recently restored the home to its Regency grandeur. From what the family tree showed, this Sophie Mattersley was the last of the Claremont line.

Matt twisted his mouth into a puzzled frown. Sophie was the last of her family? But Amara was a Mattersley. What was going on?

He clicked on a photo of a long hall, the walls of which were packed with portraits of Mattersley ancestors. Clicking on a portrait brought up a larger version of the painting. This was quite the thorough site.

He snickered at the serious expression of a man wearing a starched, pleated collar and a shell-shaped decoration over his groin. Codpiece? Was that the right word? How could the man look so utterly arrogant, so utterly in control, when he was dressed in such ridiculous clothing?

As Matt scrolled through the portraits, the fashion habits changed, though the men bore marked resemblances to each other. Strong genetics, evidently.

The portrait of one Samuel Mattersley showed a tallish gent, back arched proudly, a white wig upon his head, a striking young woman at his side. Around them stood three kids, a boy of perhaps seven or eight, with dark hair and unusually green eyes, and two young girls of similar age to each other. One had dark hair that matched her brother's. The other had hair of honeyed blonde, her face young and innocent as her hazel-green eyes stared out at him.

Something about her caught his attention, something eerily familiar in the curve of her lips, the pert little nose, and those clear eyes. He shook his head. *Good Lord, get a grip.* He was seeing Amara everywhere, even in a painting over two hundred years old. Moving the mouse, he scanned to the label underneath the painting, zooming in as much as he could. Though the words remained blurry, he made out *His Grace Samuel Mattersley, sixth Duke of Claremont, with his wife, Matilda, and children, Deveric, Cecilia, and Amara.*

He shoved the laptop off of his lap, his face draining of blood. *What the hell?* An Amara Mattersley in the late eighteenth century? With a brother named Deveric? Cold sweat pearled on his forehead. Isn't that what Amara said *her* brother's name was?

Then again, in bigwig families like this one, names were often used over and over again. His shoulders relaxed, the tension easing out. Yes, that was it. It was just a family name.

He ran his hands over his face, pulling at his cheeks. Clearly fifteen hours of sleep wasn't enough; he needed more. Because nothing else except sheer exhaustion made it excusable that for a few minutes he'd convinced himself the girl in the painting and the woman in his life were one and the same.

As the cab wound its way up the long, familiar road to Clarehaven, Amara pressed her face against the window, taking in every inch of the landscape in the afternoon light. Much was the same. A familiar row of trees lined the northern edge, trees which led to the pond and ancient circle of stones. Majestic oaks still dotted the landscape, and the house rose, as magnificent as ever, before her.

But there were changes, too. Houses lined the road before the entranceway, houses that hadn't existed in her time. They'd also had to pass through an electric gate to access the front drive. Why was a gate necessary? Did so many people attempt to approach the house?

At least they'd been allowed through and rather quickly, at that. When the cab driver announced her name, per the request from a speaker housed in a post before the gate, the gate immediately opened, much to Amara's surprise. It must be because she shared the same last name as the family that owned the estate. No one here knew of her. No one *could* know of her.

Electric light posts lined the lane as they approached, another difference. The house, too, showed signs of change— not many, but the large garage was obviously new. One open bay contained a shiny, red sports car.

When the cab driver pulled up to the massive walnut front door, it opened, and a young woman clad in well-tailored trousers and a thick sweater descended the stairs, a broad smile on her face. As the woman approached, Amara gasped, taking in the woman's honey-brown hair and hazel eyes, so similar to her own.

The cab driver opened the rear door, and Amara exited as gracefully as she could, given she was on the verge of fainting. She was here, at Clarehaven, the place she'd spent the majority of her formative years. Fumbling in her bag, she produced a handful of large bills and gave them to the man. "Thank you," she said, holding up a hand to indicate no change.

The driver smiled broadly and tipped his head to her. "It's been a pleasure, madam," he said, handing her a card with his number. "Please call if you need a return ride to London."

Amara took it automatically, her eyes sliding to the woman, who hadn't yet said a word. She stood there, studying Amara, an indecipherable expression on her face despite her friendly smile.

Should she tell the driver to stay? Would this woman kick her out in just a few minutes? No, she wouldn't think that way. She'd make the best of this and if the worst came to the worst, she'd determine some other way to get home.

Home? How had she suddenly thought of Charlottesville as home? *This* was home. Except not anymore. *Blast.* This was all so confusing. Amara pulled herself up tall, nodding at the driver to indicate he could go.

As the cab retreated down the lane, she turned to the woman, unsure of her next move. The woman closed the short distance between them, extending her hand. "Hello," she said, as Amara took it and they shook. "I'm Sophie Mattersley. It is quite the pleasure to meet you … Amara."

Had Amara imagined the hesitation in the woman's voice? How had she known Amara's name? Prickles of fear clambered up her spine. *Wait.* The cab driver had announced her. Of course. "Thank you, Your Grace."

Sophie laughed, a light, pleasant sound. "Please. You needn't be so formal. I prefer Sophie. I never wished to be a duchess." A shadow crossed her face, but she shook it off, her smile widening as if by determined effort. "And since you gave your name as Amara *Mattersley*, we must be related. Won't you come in?"

Amara followed the woman up the steps to the house. Her home. Unease inched through her. Why would this woman, a duchess, welcome a complete stranger so readily? And then, as she passed through the door, there was no more time for thought. Her hand flew to her heart as she took in the entryway. It looked exactly the same, the inlaid mosaic floor shining as brightly as ever, the walls lined with the same portraits. Even the wall colors were the same. Had they changed nothing in two hundred years?

Sophie chuckled at Amara's expression. "I take it you like it? I've spent the last few years restoring the house to its Regency glory." She winked—*winked*—at Amara. "From the pictures and paintings I've seen, Clarehaven was at its finest then. What do you think?"

Amara's head swerved sharply as she gaped at Sophie. There was something in the woman's tone of voice, some suggestion of knowledge. Did this woman know who she was? Did she know from *when* she was? Surely that was impossible.

"It is ... magnificent," she finally said, her eyes misting. Oh, how she'd missed it. When here before, in her time, she'd chafed at the restrictions placed upon her. She'd wanted to escape. But nothing felt as good as standing right here, right now.

Matthew Goodson's eyes swam in front of her, those eyes that had pierced hers with tenderness as his body entered hers. She had to amend her previous thought. There were some things that felt as good. That felt a thousand times better.

But she didn't want to think of him, of Charlottesville, of anything other than being in a place at last familiar. And with a woman strangely welcoming. "I thank you for allowing me to visit."

"My greatest pleasure. We *are* family, after all." The woman winked again.

Amara's throat thickened with emotion. This woman didn't know her, yet was being so kind. For the first time since she'd boarded that airplane, hope sprang inside that she could be all right in this new life. A life without Cat or Ben. Without Matthew.

"I …" She wasn't sure what to say. What connection could she claim? She didn't know the Mattersley descendants to the present day. She should have researched that before coming.

"Are you hungry?" Sophie crossed the foyer, the click of her heels echoing in the hallway. The house was so quiet. In Amara's day, it'd been full of people: her family, naturally, but also a veritable army of servants. Now, she heard nothing. Did Sophie live alone? Surely one woman could not maintain such an expansive property as Clarehaven.

Amara followed her. "I would not mind a cup of tea." Her stomach was too knotted to contemplate actual food.

"I'm sure Angie can manage that. And she's made cherry tarts today. An old family recipe. Perhaps you'd care to try one?"

Goosebumps raced up Amara's skin. Cherry tarts? They'd been her brother's favorite. Hers, too, baked from a recipe their cook Rowena had perfected. Had the family used the same recipe all these years?

Amara shook off the eerie chill that had settled on her shoulders. Answers would come in time. For now, she welcomed the idea of sitting down to gather her bearings.

Entering the kitchen, Sophie led Amara to a table off to one side. This room, at least, had changed greatly since 1813. Not that Amara'd spent a lot of time in the kitchens, but the gleaming stainless steel appliances definitely indicated a twenty-first century cooking space.

An older woman with a friendly, round face nodded

toward them both as Sophie sat down and indicated a chair for Amara. Amara lowered herself into it gratefully as she surveyed the room, so familiar and yet so different.

"What would be your pleasure, Your Grace?" Angie said to Sophie. Well, at least someone still stood on formality.

"A cuppa, if you don't mind, Angie, and perhaps a tart or two."

Angie nodded and bustled over to the stove, turning on flames beneath a teapot.

Was she the only one who worked in the kitchen? In Amara's day, Rowena had had numerous kitchen maids to aid her. Then again, there hadn't been refrigerators and microwaves and dishwashers.

"So," Sophie said, that curious smile on her face again. "Tell me about your … journey."

Why did it feel that question was laden with much more than what the simple words asked?

"I traveled from Virginia. I wanted to … research my family's roots."

Angie set a cherry tart down in front of her, and Amara nodded gratefully. She was hungry, in spite of her nerves.

Sophie nodded, waiting. What else could Amara say? "I … I," she fumbled, before stopping.

"I think," Sophie said after a moment, when Amara remained silent, "I know your story."

Amara's eyes went wide, and the piece of tart she'd scooped up on her fork fell back to the plate. "What?"

CHAPTER 36

"Thank you, Angie. I shall take it from here." Sophie looked over at the cook, who'd just poured the boiling water into teacups and set the tea in to steep. Angie nodded before exiting the room. Though they were now alone, Sophie lowered her voice to a whisper. "You are Amara. Sister to Deveric, Duke of Claremont. Am I right?"

Amara nodded automatically. Could there have been another Deveric down the line, a future descendent? Or did Sophie somehow know—

Sophie's voice broke into her panicked musings. "He was my great-something grandfather, his wife Eliza, my something-or-other grandmother. Eliza James Mattersley, who lived in Charlottesville, Virginia. In 2012."

The fork followed the bite of tart. Amara gaped at Sophie, her jaw nearly on the table. Quite unladylike, her mother would chastise, but yet … this woman *knew*. This woman knew exactly who Amara was.

Sophie's eyes sparkled with excitement as her hand flew over to cover Amara's. "How I've waited for this day, hoping you would come. You have no idea! It's been family legend for so long, but I was never quite sure it was true. And now here you are, sitting before me. My relative from two hundred years ago!"

Amara held her hand to her head, her fingers visibly shaking. "I can't—" she said, before swallowing. "I can't believe you know." Relief flooded through her, the torrent of anxiety inside her dissipating in an instant. She didn't have to hide, didn't have to pretend. And Sophie clearly wasn't going to throw her out. She had a place to be.

Until she finds out you're pregnant. Amara frowned. Would that make a difference to Sophie the way it would have to their ancestors?

Sophie leapt up, pacing the kitchen floor, her arms gesticulating enthusiastically. "It's true! All of it. You're here. You're really here! And maybe …" She broke off, biting her lip.

"Maybe?" What had the woman been about to say?

"Nothing, nothing," Sophie said, waving an arm. "Though I would most definitely like to meet Catherine Schreiber, the woman who sent Eliza to my ancestors' time and, well, made me possible. And who brought you here. What a miracle! I can hardly believe it."

"You and me both," Amara murmured. "And she's Catherine Cooper now."

"I can't wait to hear all about you, my ancestors, everything!" Sophie paused in her pacing. "I'm the last of the Mattersley line," she said, her face sobering. "No one else knows this legend. And I'd begun to worry, as I have no children to whom I could pass it on. Though I rather assumed if you *were* going to show, it'd be in this decade, considering 2012 is when Cat first acquired the manuscript.

I'd hoped you might have come a few years earlier. I've been waiting so impatiently."

Amara's head spun. How did this woman know everything?

"But I get ahead of myself. I beg your pardon; I'm just so thrilled! This is the best thing to ever happen." She walked over and positioned herself in the chair across from Amara. "Do you want to tour the house? I'd love to know how I've done with the restorations. Or do you need to rest?"

Now that she'd found a relative and potential friend, the last thing Amara wanted to do was sleep, though fatigue snaked its way through her body. "A tour would be delightful. I wish to know the history—or rather the future, I suppose. I want to know what happened to Clarehaven since my time."

How liberating to openly talk about who, and from when, she was. Cat and Ben knew, naturally, but Sophie was a Mattersley, a family member. Amazing.

"Deveric was an astute estate manager, as you know, and his son Frederick, too, thank goodness."

Freddy. It was hard to imagine her nephew as anything less than the sickly but life-loving little boy she'd known. "Frederick," she murmured.

Sophie nodded, sipping her tea. "We prospered in the nineteenth century. Though your way of life, the British class system, the whole of the peerage, has undergone massive transformation since the Georgian period."

Amara nodded. The industrial revolution and changing social ideas had challenged the long-established power held by the peerage. She'd read about it in books at the Treasure Trove, but Eliza also warned her it was coming, that many of the grand houses would be sold off, pulled down, or opened for tourism, especially with the huge changes that swept through Europe and England after World War I and the economic depression of the 1930s.

"Deveric's and Frederick's foresight, helped along by Eliza's knowledge, enabled us to weather events that destroyed much of rest of this way of life. Not that I mourn it. I never did subscribe to the idea of birth determining worth."

Amara laughed. She couldn't help it. "You sound like Eliza."

"Good. That thrills me! She's legendary in this family for her forward-thinking ways. Though most members had no idea *how* forward, of course." Sophie's eyes sparkled as she took another sip of tea. "Grandmother told me it was Eliza who convinced Deveric to invest in the railways, who got Frederick into steel. It was definitely Eliza who built this family's fortunes."

"And managed to pass some of that fortune to me." The sister-in-law she'd initially wanted to reject, whose intentions she'd doubted, had done so much for her. Amara's eyes welled up.

Sophie squeezed her hand. "May I ask how long you've been here?"

"A little over a month," Amara choked out.

"Less than I would have thought. And what of the man for whom you came forward? I love that idea. It's so romantic, to travel across centuries for your soul mate …"

The tears spilled over, coursing down Amara's face. The look on Matthew's face when she'd walked out of the Colonnade Club, the hurt in those blue eyes, haunted her.

Sophie's brow puckered. "Goodness, I am sorry. I did not mean to upset you, dearest … cousin."

Amara's sobs prevented her from speaking for another few minutes. Eventually, she gulped down great breaths of air, determined to regain control. How vulgar such an expression of excessive emotion must appear to a stranger. For family or not, Sophie was as much a stranger to her as she was to Sophie.

Amara dashed at her cheeks. "No ... soul mate." She looked Sophie straight in the eye. "But I am with child."

To her credit, Sophie's smile didn't falter. "I take it this was unexpected news?" she said after a moment.

Amara nodded, misery crashing over her as she clutched her belly. The source of all her current anguish.

"Did this occur in 1813?"

Amara shook her head, Matthew's face shimmering before her.

"All right, then. We shall just have to work this out." The duchess's eyes took on a steely glint, and the affirmation in her voice, the utter, unexpected support, swelled Amara's sobs to gale-force levels. "You're not the only one in the family to conceive out of wedlock, after all," Sophie continued, patting Amara's knee.

That brought Amara up short. "What?" she hiccupped.

Sophie waved a hand. "A bit of family legend. Great Aunt Lavinia. Had a grand love affair in her early twenties. Totally mad for a French aristocrat. They gallivanted about Europe, passion blazing brightly. Until ..."

"Until?"

Sophia grimaced. "Until his wife showed up. Lavinia told everyone she'd married and that her husband was to follow her to England shortly. No husband did, of course, but few challenged her story." She laughed, a light, tinkling cascade of sound, before her face sobered. "Not that Lavinia's story is important now. Do you want to keep the baby?"

"Yes." Anything else was simply unthinkable. This child was part of her, part of Matthew. Her insides ached, her heart pumping erratically in her chest as icy blue eyes taunted her.

She missed him. Plain and simple. She missed his occasionally awkward conversation, missed his solicitous care, missed his explanations of the modern world. Missed his body nestled against hers under the covers, missed his hips pressing into hers as he moved inside her.

She'd been such a coward, running off, running away from Matthew. But she hadn't wanted to burden him with her own foibles and sins. Cat's words echoed in her head: *It takes two. He is as responsible as you.* No one would have stated such in her own time, of course; the woman took the blame for situations like this. Amara had chosen to lie with him, after all.

"Should we expect the father?" Sophie's eyes held no judgment, merely curiosity.

Amara shook her head. Matthew wouldn't come to England. Chase her across the world, a woman he'd known for such a short period of time, a woman who'd agreed to no attachment, no expectations? A woman he'd accused of having relations with more than one man, who'd screamed at him and then run away?

No. Matthew Goodson would not come to Clarehaven.

Sophie's face softened in sympathy. She rose from her chair, extending her hand. "How about you have a bit of a lie-down? You must be exhausted, what with …" She motioned toward Amara's abdomen. "Then perhaps we can talk in fuller detail. About anything and everything."

Amara dipped her head in agreement and clasped Sophie's hand, allowing the woman to pull her up. A time away to absorb everything, to be on her own, sounded ideal. Something pulled in her midsection and she folded her other arm across it as she trailed behind Sophie. She supposed she'd have to grow accustomed to all sorts of physical changes over the next few months. And other changes for the rest of her life. For she was no longer independent. Her body, her time, her life, now belonged to another human.

Forever.

Images of the young girl in the painting saturated Matt's dreams, mixed with memories of Amara, her face lit up with laughter, with pleasure. He woke the next morning more exhausted than the night before. Perhaps it was jetlag. Or perhaps it was everything catching up to him, the reality of the situation in which he now found himself.

He sat up, running his hand over his head as his ears picked up noises from outside—horns and traffic. But not Charlottesville traffic. No, bloody English traffic.

What was he doing here? This was ludicrous. If by some miracle he found Amara, what was he to say? Should he fall to one knee and propose? Most people didn't marry in this day and age solely on account of a pregnancy, and yet it felt the only logical, honorable course of action. He doubted Amara would accept, however, even if he wanted her to.

Did he? Marriage wasn't on his agenda—at least not for years, if ever. He was too focused on his career to be a good partner. Nor did he wish to repeat his father's mistakes. But the idea of going to sleep next to Amara, of waking up next to her each day, spurred unexpected feelings of excitement and contentment.

It wouldn't be just the two of you, though. There'd be a third. A very noisy, demanding third.

Yes, but that third was a reality now, whether he wished it or not. Wouldn't it be better to raise the child as a family unit rather than a divided household?

Painful personal experience had shown, however, what it was like to have a father not up to the job. To have parents who didn't love each other. And he and Amara didn't love each other.

But he could. He sucked in a breath at the thought, which hit him like a load of bricks. He just might be able to love this feisty, mysterious British miss. Yes, he might be able to love her. Under normal circumstances. With more time.

Groaning, he hoisted himself off the bed. Time was one thing he didn't have. Ben had promised to cover his classes for the week, but more than that was unacceptable. Matt must return.

But first, he had to chase after one very vexing, very missing Amara Mattersley.

After a quick shower, Matt threw his few items into his bag and checked out, hailing a cab to take him to Clarehaven.

"Clarehaven? I drove a young lady there yesterday. Popular place," the cabby tossed over his shoulder, as Matt settled into the back seat.

At the man's words, Matt's body jerked forward. "You took a woman there yesterday? Amara?"

The cabby nodded. "That was her name, matter of fact. A sweet lady." He broke off, his mouth pressing downward.

"What?" Matt said, not able to believe that in a city this

large, he'd hailed the exact same cab Amara had been in the day before. Taylor would tell him it was a sign. If he believed in signs. Which he didn't. Did he?

"Nothing, nothing. She seemed a bit troubled, that's all." His eyes met Matt's in the rear view mirror, studying Matt as if assessing whether or not he were a threat to Amara. After a minute, he gave one crisp nod before shifting into gear and pulling out into the street.

Matt said nothing further, not trusting himself to speak. Amara'd been in this very cab the day before. She *was* at Clarehaven. And in less than an hour's time, he'd have to face her. *Crap. Crap. Crap.* What should he do? What should he say?

He wished Taylor were here. As flighty as she could be, Taylor had a good head on her shoulders, and a keen eye for judging situations from the outside, even if her own choices were sometimes questionable. But she wasn't here. He knew what she'd say, though. "Matt, you have to be true to yourself, but you also have a responsibility. You can't walk away. It wouldn't be right."

No, he couldn't. It didn't matter what he wanted. His sister was right; he had a responsibility, and he wasn't going to abandon Amara or their baby. But would Amara let him be a part of this child's life, a part of her life?

The miles eked by slowly. The English countryside didn't register; all of Matt's attention and energy focused inward. Eventually, they exited the highway, or motorway, as the cab driver termed it, winding along a curvy road through undulating hills speckled with occasional sheep, the fields green and verdant. Dry-stone walls lined property edges, and Matt begrudgingly conceded the land was beautiful. Another ten minutes, and they turned down a narrow lane, going only a short distance before stopping at a gated drive.

"Whom shall I say is calling?" the cab driver asked, as he rolled down his window.

Matt cleared his throat, which had tightened with anxiety. "Matthew Goodson."

There was a pause after the cabby announced his name, then the gates swung open. They coasted down a tree-lined drive toward one of the most enormous homes Matt had ever seen. It was a frigging mansion, easily several times the size of Monticello. Perhaps more, if the house extended far behind its majestic front facade. The thick white columns lining the porch reminded him of UVA's Rotunda.

Suddenly, goosebumps peppered his flesh. He recognized this house. It was the one Amara had searched for on the Internet. *This was Clarehaven? Amara had lived* here? What had she thought of his crummy little apartment? And what on Earth had led her away to room with Cat and Ben in their small place?

He clenched his jaw as the cab stopped at the front entry. The driver jumped out and opened the rear door. Sucking in a breath, Matt unfolded himself from the back of the vehicle, stretching to his full height as the front door of the house— the mansion—opened, and a young woman strode down the front steps.

For a moment, his heart leapt. It was Amara, right there before him. But as the woman neared, he noted subtle differences—the slightly darker hair, slightly browner eyes. The woman could easily have been Amara's sister, however.

Was she Amara's sister?

"Hello," the woman said in a cultured accent, extending her hand to Matt. He almost felt he should turn it over and kiss her knuckles rather than shake it, but he resisted that idiotic notion.

"I'm Sophie Mattersley. May I ask what brings you to Clarehaven?"

"I'm looking for Amara Mattersley," he said bluntly, as he clasped her hand. No sense beating around the bush.

The woman's eyes widened, but she maintained her relaxed body language even as she withdrew her hand, smiling at the cab driver. "What do we owe you, sir?"

Before the man could answer, Matt interrupted. "I've got it." He pulled out several bills and thrust them at the man. "Is that enough?"

The cabby nodded, handing Matt his bag. "Would you like me to wait?"

"No, no," the woman said, that pleasant smile unwavering on her face. "Thank you."

With a nod, the driver reentered the cab and drove off, leaving Matt standing before this stranger, on this estate in the middle of England. *Nuts. This whole situation is nuts.* Matt cleared his throat. "I take it she's here?"

"Yes." She broke off, fidgeting with a bracelet around her wrist, the first sign of any unease on her part.

Matt was drowning in discomfort. "May I see her?"

"She has gone to the stones. Perhaps you'd like to wait here?"

"Stones?"

"An ancient monument on the north end of the property."

"I'd prefer to talk to her now, if you don't mind. Is it far?"

"Nearly ten miles. I'll drive you out if you'd like."

Ten miles? *This estate's property extended out ten miles?* Good Lord, these people had to be nearly as rich as the Queen. "Yes, please."

They rode in strangely comfortable silence in the woman's Porsche. To his surprise, Sophie didn't quiz him, didn't pry into why he was there or what was going on between him and Amara. Had Amara told her? She must have said something, given Sophie's easy acceptance of his appearance.

After a sharp bend, the monument exploded into view. It resembled a tiny Stonehenge, or perhaps that circle of rocks in the Outlander episode his sister had forced him to watch.

"Jamie is so sexy," Taylor'd cooed, mooning over the far-too-pretty man in the kilt.

Matt had rolled his eyes. The time-travel part intrigued him, though. Not because he believed in such nonsense, but because he'd stopped to ponder what it would be like to step back in time a few hundred years. Just a minute of imagining life without indoor plumbing, Chinese delivery, and the Internet had been enough for him to throw up a quick prayer of thanks for the conveniences of the current era.

No, the past certainly wasn't for him.

CHAPTER 37

Sophie stopped the car a short distance away as a honey-haired head poked around the corner of a large rock.

Amara.

His heart leapt at the sight of her, standing there with her arms crossed, puzzlement evident across her features even at this distance. He thrust off his seat belt and whipped the door open, one leg already outside, when Sophie laid a hand on his arm.

He glanced at her.

"Be … careful. Be kind." She said nothing else, merely nodded toward the door.

Matt stared at her for a moment. He couldn't figure her out, this wealthy British woman completely fine with an American stranger showing up and demanding to see … who *was* Amara to Sophie, anyway? He jerked his head away. That wasn't the issue at hand. Amara was. Quickly, he alighted from the car, ducking his head to address her. "Thank you. Are you staying?"

"No." Sophie's smile was peculiar. "Here." She pulled out a card from the dash. "Have you got a mobile?"

He nodded.

"My number is there. Call when you'd like me to retrieve you both."

Matt's eyes flashed to Amara, whose face had gone pale. "Do you think it's a good idea, leaving us alone here?" The words were almost rhetorical. Almost.

Sophie shrugged. "Probably not. On the other hand, there's no place for her to run now."

He tipped his head one more time before standing up and shutting the door firmly behind him. The engine roared to life, and the car backed away, but he didn't see it. His eyes were fixed on the woman in front of him.

Neither moved for a moment, both taking in the sight of the other. At length, Matt broke into a purposeful stride, approaching the woman whose eyes were so wide, so full of fear, she looked like a cornered animal.

"Wh-what are you doing here?" The words were a whisper, ones he barely caught on the current of the wind.

"You dropped a bombshell on me," Matt said, a weird calm lacing his voice. This was right. He was here. It would work out. Somehow. "And I admit, I did not respond as well as I should have. But you ran. You didn't give me a chance, Amara. You didn't give *us* a chance."

"Us?" Her fingers tugged at the edge of her sweater sleeve. "There *is* no us. You—we—made that clear from the start. We were merely indulging in sins of the flesh."

His jaw ticced as anger coursed through him. "Sins? You think what we did was sinful?"

She bit her lip, casting her eyes off to the left. No words came.

He took a few steps closer. "Because it wasn't, Amara. It was the most glorious experience of my life." What they'd shared, both in *and* out of bed, was greater than anything he'd ever had with anyone.

Amara's eyes glistened, but she still refused to look at him. "Regardless, I'm paying for it now. Paying for my lustful nature. For my impulsiveness. For my reckless disregard for everything."

Matt's lips pressed together. "I admit," he said, "this pregnancy was not an expected or welcome one. But, Amara." He reached out, brushing the hair off of her cheek.

She flinched, her eyes flying to his.

"It was an accident. Not a punishment."

A single tear trickled down her cheek and she stepped back, out of his reach. "What do you know? You don't know me. You know nothing of me!" Her voice rose. "Scandal follows me wherever I go. I thought I'd escaped it, coming … there. Here. But I haven't. Not one bit." More tears splashed down her cheeks. "I'm starting to believe I'm cursed."

Matt uttered an expletive under his breath. Running a hand over his hair, he cocked a hip to the side, then settled his arms across his chest. "I do know you. I know you like pizza but not tomatoes. I know you think rutabagas are worth eating but mint ice cream is not—a notion in which you're sorely mistaken, by the way. I know you're far too hard on yourself. I know the noises you make when you sleep. I know the sounds you make when we …" He broke off, giving her a meaningful look. "No, I don't know everything. But I know enough. And I know I want to know more."

"Superficial things, Matthew!" She threw her arms in the air. "And if I told you more about me, you wouldn't believe it. You'd dismiss me as a Bedlamite. Perhaps I am." She clutched her arm across her midsection, pacing back and forth.

"Try me," he said, walking over to her, so close his breath moved the wisps of hair curled around her face. "If I didn't want to know more, if I didn't *want* more, I wouldn't be here. I flew across the ocean for you, Amara."

She gave a half-laugh, half-sob. "You came because of a sense of responsibility to this baby."

"Yes. I admit that. Openly. But that's not the *only* reason. I realized—" He swallowed, his eyes not leaving hers. "I missed you. *You*, Amara. I missed you in my apartment. I missed hearing the odd things you say. I missed you in my bed, yes, but I missed you out of it, too. I missed your stubborn, independent nature, mixed as it is with that strange sense of fragility."

Amara's shoulders shook as tears poured down her cheeks.

"Please," he said, brushing them off with his thumbs. "Give me a chance. Let's talk. About this. Us. Our future."

Great sobs shook her shoulders. "Oh, Matthew," she gasped, leaning into him. "Matthew."

He enfolded her in his arms, one hand rubbing her back, the other weaving fingers through her hair.

"I'm sorry. I'm so sorry … for everything," she mumbled against his shoulder.

He whispered soothing noises, relishing the sweet scent of her. Oh, how he'd missed her. Sure, they had a long way to go. One meeting in a circle of stones was not enough to build a future, but hope surged through his veins. "Not your fault," he murmured into her hair. "It takes two."

She hiccupped. "But before … before we can talk about the future, I have to tell you about the past. *My* past."

Amara's heart pounded wildly. Matthew Goodson was here. He'd flown to England, come to Clarehaven, to find her.

Was she about to lose him again? Could a man as grounded in logic, in science, as Matthew accept the story she had to tell? She no longer had Eliza's phone with its pictures as proof. And Eliza's letters and photographs in Charlottesville, not England. Amara had nothing here beyond words. *Not true*, that damnable voice said again. She had Clarehaven now, which had portraits of her as a child, as a young woman, on its walls.

But would Matthew believe her?

She swallowed, then tipped her head up to imbue confidence in herself. There was no way to know unless she told him. And it was time. "Come with me," she said, as she extricated herself from his embrace.

He frowned but followed her into the stone circle. Reaching the flat stone in the middle, she sat down and patted a spot next to her. He joined her, saying nothing, his eyes questioning, expectant.

"This is where it all began," she said, her hands tingling with nerves. "I sat here and wished ... wished to be in Eliza's time, in the twenty-first century, so that I could have independence, get an education. So that I could escape my past."

Matthew's expression didn't change. Perhaps she hadn't been clear enough. "I sat here in 1813, Matthew."

At that, an eyebrow tipped up, and a chuckle escaped him. When she didn't laugh in return, his face sobered, both eyebrows arching. "Say what?"

She swallowed, hard. "I came to America from England, yes. But I came from 1813, not 2016."

He exhaled heavily. "I don't know what's going on, Amara, but I don't appreciate this kind of joke." His lips folded into a pinched line.

She leapt up from the stone, pacing in front of him. "I'm not joking! This." She waved an arm about. "Clarehaven. It was my home. Two hundred years ago." Stopping for a moment, she looked at him again, the anger and doubt in his eyes piercing her. "Remember Eliza James, Cat's friend? The one who married my brother?"

Matt raised a brow, confusion written across his face. "A little. I met her once at the bookstore, before she moved."

"Moved where?"

"To England," he answered slowly.

"And have they heard from her since?"

His jaw tightened. "I'm hardly privy to every detail of their personal life, Amara."

"But you've seen the painting above the Treasure Trove's fireplace of the woman in the gown, bedecked with a tiara?"

"Of course."

"You know that's Eliza, right?"

"Cat mentioned that one day, but I figured it was one of those tourist things, like getting a sepia-toned photograph when visiting the Old West."

"It's not. That's Eliza, here. After she married my brother, Deveric Mattersley. Seventh Duke of Claremont."

Matthew clutched his temples but remained on the rock. "Okay. You're telling me that not only did you come forward from the past, but that Cat's friend did the reverse? That time travel is possible, and that the Coopers know about it?"

Amara nodded vigorously. "I don't blame you for your skepticism. I was highly skeptical, too, until Eliza showed me her telephone, with pictures of things I'd never even imagined."

Matthew cleared his throat but said nothing, even as Amara

continued to walk back and forth in front of him. She stopped, crossing her arms over her chest. "Do you believe me?"

He stared at her, those ice-blue eyes sending waves of both heat and cold through her. At length, he stood up, pulling his cell phone out of his pocket. "I think I'd like to return to the house."

Amara raced to him, grabbing at his arm. "I know it's a lot to take in, Matthew. But it's the truth. My truth. And … there's more."

He sighed, his fingers pausing on the phone. "More? What more could there possibly be beyond time travel?"

"You should know, need to know, Cat has a manuscript, one with powers that lets her match people. Create love stories. It's how it works. For me to come forward, I had to come forward … for love." She brushed the hair back from her face. "Not that it's predestined, or one doesn't have a choice. Both people can choose, *have* to choose, if they want it to work. But it sparks the attraction. It's why you're attracted to me. This—us. It's not real. It's created. So it's fine if you walk away. It's not your fault. It's mine, for asking for it."

Matthew ran his fingers over his hair, incredulity written across his face. "Now you're claiming I'm under some sort of love spell connecting me to a woman from two hundred years ago?"

Amara nodded.

"Are you high? What are you on?" He pressed numbers on the phone, fury radiating from him as he yanked it up to his ear. "Sophie? Yeah, ready. As soon as possible."

He jammed the phone back into his pocket, turning away from Amara.

She hesitated. Should she go to him? What purpose would it serve? She'd told him the truth. It was up to him to determine what he was going to do with it. If he accepted it. Which, given the hostility emanating from him, seemed highly unlikely.

"God damn it, Amara." His voice was half a yell as he whirled to her. "You think you have to come up with something as ridiculous as this to tell me you don't want to be with me? What in the hell?" He stalked toward her, eyes blazing, tension across every muscle.

He stopped mere inches away, the heat of his skin lashing against her. "You're telling me that you and I, that the connection we had—have—isn't *real*?" His mouth was a hair's breadth from hers, but he didn't touch her, didn't connect. "You're telling me any feelings between us are fake, conjured?"

She leaned into him. She couldn't help it. She wanted so badly to feel his arms around her. She knew it was a spell, a created connection, and yet she wanted it to be real. *It was real between Deveric and Eliza*. The thought emblazoned itself across her brain. Cat had created the possibility, the attraction, but Eliza and Deveric had chosen to follow it—to a marvelous end, a love the likes of which Amara had never seen.

But that didn't mean it would work that way for Amara and Matthew. *You didn't want it to, remember?* She'd used Cat's magic to get here, but she'd had no intention of actually falling for this man standing before her, so close it was if their breath was one. If she just moved a fraction of an inch.

And she did, touching her lips tentatively to his, wanting to feel him, to see if their connection was genuine, if it *was* more than a magical story Cat had written. He exploded against her, his lips crushing hers as his hands pressed against her back, holding her to him. They tasted each other, savored each other, sounds of pleasure and pain and longing and hurt issuing back and forth between them. He ran a hand up into her hair, practically growling as his mouth dueled with hers. His other hand pulled her hips in against him, and she could feel his hard length against her.

He broke off, chest heaving against hers, eyes pulsating with desire ... and rage.

"You're telling me that isn't real?"

Matt's head spun. He wanted to forget everything, let it all go, and simply sink into the deliciousness of Amara Mattersley. But even as she'd gasped and moaned beneath him, thoughts of everything she'd just told him intruded, and he'd suddenly released her, backing up a step.

"Well?" he demanded now, his voice rough, angry, his body tense.

"I—" Amara looked down at the ground, her whole frame shaking.

He spun away from her, staring out at the stones lining the circle in which they stood. *What Taylor wouldn't give to be here.* His sister was obsessed with Stonehenge; seeing it in person was number one on her bucket list.

He growled. Why was he thinking of his sister?

Because it was easier than dealing with the woman behind him.

Time travel? What kind of idiot did she think he was?

An unexpected image of Amara that first evening struck him—in that unusual dress, a bonnet on her head. Her peculiarities of speech and mannerisms. The lack of technological experience he'd dismissed with Amish jokes ...

Could it be?

340

He shook his head. Dr. Matthew Goodson dealt in what was rational, in black and white, in what was tangibly before him. It's what worked, it's what made sense, and it's what he was going to hold onto now. He didn't know what the true story was, but time travel wasn't part of it.

His eyes swept over the stones. It was admittedly a beautiful spot. Purple flowers wound themselves around the base of the rocks, and a gentle breeze tickled his skin as the sun warmed him. In spite of his anger, his confusion, the space conveyed a palpable sense of peace. Of hope.

His shoulders stiffened at the unmistakable sound of a car approaching. Amara hadn't said anything in the last few minutes. What was she doing? He turned, his heart still pounding—and then cracking ever so slightly at her tear-streaked face. She looked so wretched, so miserable. He wanted nothing more than to take her back into his arms. But first, he needed answers.

Sophie pulled up before them in a silver SUV, remaining in the driver's seat a moment before gracefully exiting the vehicle. She cocked her head at Amara. "I take it, it didn't go well?"

Amara cast a glance at Matt before shaking her head in response. "I told him my … history. He doesn't believe me."

Matt whirled to stare at Sophie, though he addressed his words to Amara. "Wait. You're telling me Sophie knows your claims? That she *believes* them?"

Sophie nodded. "I understand it's a lot to take in, Mr. Goodson. Why don't you come back to Clarehaven? We can sit for a cup of tea and talk things over. I'm sure you have many questions."

Matt ran his hand over his hair again. *Damn it, what was happening? Had the whole world gone mad?* Or just he?

The image of the painting he'd seen online last night flashed through his head. He'd thought then the girl in the portrait—the portrait hanging on Clarehaven's walls—was Amara. Just for a moment. Could it be?

Shaking his head, he stalked toward the automobile without looking at Amara. He'd go with them—what choice did he have?—but he'd be damned if he made this easy on either of them. Plus, his mind was a whirl of confusion.

He settled into the rear seat as best he could, surprised when Amara crawled in next to him, rather than taking the front next to Sophie. He shot her a harsh glare, then looked away out the window. Even so, the nervousness radiating from her was unmistakable, and after a moment he let his leg loll to the side on the pretense of not having enough room— which was, in fact, the truth; stuffing 6'3" of a man into the back of a car was never easy, even in a large SUV. His knee touched Amara's, and she gasped softly. He didn't meet her gaze, his own eyes fixed on the scenery flashing by.

But he didn't remove his leg, either.

Misery welled up in Amara. It'd all gone so wrong, but what had she expected? What had she wanted? Seeing Matthew standing there before her on Clarehaven's grounds, her first impulse had been to launch herself into his arms—a desire she'd immediately squashed. She'd come here to deal with her mistakes, not entrap a man with them, a man already entrapped by a manuscript, a spell, about which he knew nothing.

She needed to be independent, not look to a man for

salvation. But as Matthew's thigh rubbed against hers, it was hard not to wish to be saved.

It'd be so much easier to give over to the attraction, to the feelings she must acknowledge had long been growing for him. But attraction faded. And how could she ever trust, ever believe he wanted her for her, between the manuscript and … and the baby?

Her abdomen cramped, a sharp pain, and she settled an arm over it as they pulled into Clarehaven's garage. She groaned as a second pain hit, and Matthew looked over, concern creasing his face. "Are you okay?" His voice was distant, polite, but his eyes betrayed him.

"Yes, fine," she answered in a similar, reserved voice. "I'm sure it's nothing."

Both exited the car and followed silently after Sophie. As they neared the door, a third pain struck Amara, so intense she doubled over.

"What the? Sophie!" Matthew's panicked voice hit her ear as his arms went around her, lifting her against his chest. "Something's wrong!"

CHAPTER 38

atthew can lift me? She nearly giggled at the errant, silly thought. He was tall, of course, even taller than her brothers, but lean, and she'd never thought of herself as little. His scent, that familiar, seductive combination of woods and man, settled over her, and she nestled into him, soaking up the smell. Another pain stabbed through her, however, and she moaned in his arms.

"Her room is upstairs. Follow me," Sophie commanded, her voice calmly efficient, showing none of the fear Amara felt—the same fear she'd heard in Matthew's voice.

He carried Amara up the grand staircase and into the bedroom Sophie indicated, laying her on the bed in the middle before smoothing her hair from her forehead. Suddenly, Sophie gasped behind him.

Matthew stood and whirled, and Amara lifted her lids enough to see Sophie press her hands against her mouth, her eyes focused on Amara's lower body. Matthew followed her gaze, and his face whitened. At the same time, Amara noticed the wetness between her legs, a wetness she hadn't felt since … since her last monthlies.

With effort, she propped herself up on her elbows to see what they saw—a reddish stain, growing larger now, on her tan leggings. Mortification enveloped her.

"I'll call the doctor," Sophie said, spinning and racing out of the room.

Matthew swooped in to Amara's side, his hands tracing her face carefully, tenderly. "Oh, Amara." His forehead beaded with perspiration, and he kept his eyes trained on her face.

"Not good with blood?" she said with a weak smile.

He went from white to a slight shade of green. "Normally, I'm fine. But this is … this is you … and …"

"I understand. Would you mind fetching a towel, lest I ruin the bed?" She couldn't believe how calmly the words came out. It was as if she were removed from her own body, a mere observer of the situation. Everything felt surreal, beyond reality.

Everything of the last month was *beyond reality.*

"Of course." Matthew jumped up, looking around the room before spying a bathroom off to the side. He disappeared inside, reemerging with several large bath towels. Returning to the bed, he carefully propped her to the side, all business as he settled the towels under her pelvis before gently rolling her back.

"Are you in any pain?" His brow wrinkled with worry, those icy eyes burning into hers. He took one of her hands in his, rubbing his thumb back and forth across her palm.

"No. Not now. But I can feel … " Tears welled up in her eyes as the import of what was happening finally hit her. She was losing the baby. Her and Matthew's baby. Wetness seeped out of her eyes, flooding her cheeks and the pillowcase around her.

Matthew's own eyes spilled over, one tear splashing down onto her skin.

"I'm so sorry, Matthew. I didn't want, we didn't want, but I still didn't mean for this—"

He clutched her hand more tightly, shushing her as he smoothed her hair away from her face again. "It's not your fault, Amara. It's not your fault."

But it was.

Was this God's ultimate punishment for her transgressions? For her past? For her breaking the laws of nature in hopes of escaping to a better future?

She'd never wanted to have children. Yet knowing she was losing this baby, pain seared her like never before. Not physical pain; after those first few jabs, nothing hurt now. No, not physical pain. Emotional pain, emotional devastation worse than she'd ever suffered, even worse than being caught half-naked with a man in a garden all those years ago.

"It is," she whispered, her eyes drifting shut. "It *is* my fault." She hiccupped a sob. "I didn't want this baby. I wanted freedom. Independence. And now I'm paying for my selfish desires. Selfish. So selfish."

"Amara, no!"

She heard his voice as if from a distance, heard more words, but couldn't distinguish them as she relaxed into the welcome blackness enveloping her, dragging her out of her own personal hell.

"No," he whispered again. How could she believe she was to blame for a miscarriage? "This is *not* your fault," he insisted, but her eyes were closed, her breathing regular. He checked her vitals, not sure if she'd simply fallen asleep or passed out. The rhythmic rise and fall of her chest reassured him, though. More tears streamed down Matt's face as he held her hand in his. He hadn't wanted a baby, either. Both of them freely acknowledged that. But he certainly hadn't wanted this. He sneaked a glance at her pelvis. The red stain felt like a stab to his own heart.

Sophie ran back into the room. "A doctor will be here shortly. How is she?"

Doctors still made house calls in England? Though he supposed when one had wealth, a doctor might well go anywhere summoned. "Out for the moment."

Matt made no effort to hide his tears from Sophie. He felt weirdly comfortable with her, though they'd known each other less than a day. Because she looked so much like Amara? "But she's …" He gestured toward Amara's abdomen, swallowing hard.

"Yes. She will be fine, Matthew." Sophie walked to him, settling a kind hand on his shoulder. "Women miscarry quite frequently."

"But like this? With this much—"

"It'll be all right," she interrupted. "We—you—must trust in that."

A bustling in the hallway caught their attention, and a young woman entered the room, followed by a portly older man with a black bag in his hand. The woman exchanged a few words with Sophie, then left.

"Good afternoon. Doctor Lowenstein, at your service. Let me see to the young lady, if you would." The doctor nodded at Matt, who sprang up, moving a few feet away. "It might be best if you leave the room," the man added, when Matt moved no farther.

"Not a chance," Matt said, surprising himself. He didn't want to witness what was happening, but it went against every grain in his body to leave Amara right now. "I have some medical training," he added, as if to bolster his case for staying.

The doctor shrugged, turning back to his patient. He efficiently stripped away her leggings—surprisingly strong for an older gentleman—and gently examined her, pulsating carefully on her abdomen before checking her internally. For that part, at least, Matt averted his eyes.

After a few moments, the doctor sighed. "How far along was she?"

Matt looked to Amara. "Can't have been far. We only met a month ago."

"I'm sorry to say what you most likely already know, but she has miscarried."

The words, pronounced with such matter-of-factness, sparked both anger and a fresh wave of sorrow in Matt. How could the man sound so calm when the woman before him was bleeding so profusely?

Because it's not his baby.

"Will she be okay?"

"Yes. The bleeding is heavy, but that is to be expected. I will give her a high dose of ibuprofen to help staunch it, but if this continues for more than a few hours, you must take her to Accident and Emergency at the local hospital."

Hours? Good God. "She could bleed out before then!"

"I think she would prefer to stay here, Mr. Goodson," broke in Sophie from his side. She gave him a pointed glance. "A hospital, especially one as *modern* as what we have in Winchester," she said, "might feel overwhelming at a time like this."

He couldn't mistake the emphasis on modern. So Sophie truly believed Amara had come from another time. Or was keeping up the pretense, for some reason. He ran a hand through his hair as he paced the room. He wanted answers. Needed answers. But first, he needed to ensure Amara was going to be all right. "You will stay here," he said to the doctor, a command more than a question.

The older man frowned, adjusting his belt. "I cannot. I have other patients to whom I must attend. But I will leave my number, should you need to contact me, and will check in again when I can."

Matt growled in protest.

"She will be fine, Mr. Goodson," Sophie insisted, smiling in apology at the doctor as he took his leave.

Matt rubbed his hand over his face, nodding once in their direction.

But would he?

An hour later, Matt paced the halls of Clarehaven, not taking in his surroundings, his thoughts on the pale woman lying in the bed upstairs … and on the loss she—they—had suffered.

It hit him hard. He'd barely started to come to terms with the whole idea of being a father, and it—no, he or she—was gone. Like that. His eyes overflowed, but he didn't care. He was alone. Sophie had offered to stay with him, but he'd asked for time to himself.

He wondered idly where she was now. With Amara?

No doubt he should be there, too, but he didn't want to disturb her if she was still sleeping. And in truth, he didn't know what to say. Didn't know what he felt. He didn't want this to be one of the times where the wrong thing came out of his mouth, as so frequently happened. This was not one of the situations in which such a *faux pas* might be forgiven.

He stopped to study a portrait of a heavyset man with a starched collar around his neck. It was the same portrait he'd seen on the web, right down to the codpiece. How had the poor man breathed with a neckpiece that tight? Yet he gave off a confident air, certain of his position, his wealth, his life; something no ridiculous collar could take away.

Exhaling, Matt moved to the next portrait, this one also of a man, leaner than the first, though the resemblance was strong. This man sported a long, white, curly wig. He looked equally ridiculous, in Matt's opinion. He glanced at the label: His Grace James Samuel Deveric Mattersley, fourth Duke of Claremont.

Mattersley. Amara Mattersley. She belonged to this family, this family that stretched back generations. He surveyed the hallway, taking in its lavish decorations and ornate furnishings. What was it like to grow up with so much wealth, so much security? These people hadn't ever had to go on food stamps, like his family had.

"That's my great-great-great-great-great grandfather. Or something like that. A whole bunch of greats." Sophie's voice was soft and warm as she approached.

He looked up, not bothering to dash the moisture from his cheeks. "I can't imagine knowing my roots that far back." A lame thing to say, but it was the only thing he could think of.

She cocked her head to the side. "How are you? You've had quite the day, I would say."

He nodded, his gaze darting down the hallway. "But not as bad as hers." His lips pulled into a pained line.

"True. But it's your loss, too."

He didn't want to hear the words, wanted to block them and this woman out. They'd barely met. She didn't know him. Talking about such intimate things, especially when she bore such an uncanny resemblance to Amara? It was almost too much. Almost. He had questions, needed answers. And she was standing here. Slowly, his eyes fixed on hers. "You know the story she told me?"

"You mean the one about her coming forward from 1813?"

He gulped at how easily that rolled off her tongue. "Yeah."

"It's true." Sophie gave a shrug, as if to say her impossible words were of no consequence. "Though I'm sure it's hard for you to believe. I've had a lifetime to know the family secret and grow accustomed to it."

"Family secret?" he echoed, unable to manage anything else.

"Yes. That Great-Grandmother-Whatever Eliza was actually born in this time. 1983, to be exact. But she traveled back to 1812, to marry my grandfather-some-generations removed. Deveric. He was a handsome one, I have to admit."

Matt's eyes nearly popped out of his head, but she kept talking. "And Amara? She came forward from 1813. Something about a scandal, though it's nothing anybody would bat an eyelash at now, poor thing. Times were much different then."

Again with the insouciant shrug, whereas to him it was if the bottom of the world were falling out. "You're telling me time travel is real, and that your family has done it. Twice."

"Yes."

Matt looked around for a chair. He needed to sit before his legs buckled beneath him.

"I'll show you." She beckoned him farther down the hallway, pointing to a large painting on the wall. "That's Deveric and Eliza the month they were married. The little boy is Frederick, Dev's son with his first wife, Mirabelle. And the puppy he's squeezing is Pirate. I love that they included the dog in a family portrait."

Matt studied the painting. It looked like any other old portrait to him, and yet that was definitely the same woman in the picture hanging over the Treasure Trove's fireplace mantel. And the man ... something in his features was awfully familiar. Amara-like.

"Here's the whole family," she said, drawing him along to the next portrait, which showed the same couple and child he'd seen before, though this time Eliza's hand rested on her belly, as if she were ... as if she were pregnant. Matt swallowed the lump in his throat as he examined the people around them, including an older lady with a rather formidable expression.

His eyes drifted to the woman on the far right, and his whole body froze. It was Amara. No mistaking it. The same gorgeous honey hair and hazel-green eyes, that long, graceful neck, the sweet little mouth. He gasped.

"Yes," Sophie said, as if his reaction were nothing out of the ordinary. "That's Amara, in 1813. And that's her mother, Matilda, the Dowager Duchess." Sophie indicated the dragon-like lady he'd noticed first. Her lips turned up a hint at the edges, rendering her mildly less forbidding. "There's Amara's brother, Chance." She pointed to a handsome young man. "And her sisters, Grace, Emmeline, and Rebecca."

Matt put his hand to his head. "You're telling me the Amara I know—the one in that room right now—is the same one in this painting. That this is her family? From two hundred years ago?"

"Yes." Sophie's eyes were calm, patient. "And at least a part of you believes it, too, or you wouldn't be reacting as you are. You'd have dismissed me out of hand."

"I still want to."

"Yes, I'm sure you do!" A chuckle escaped the woman. "Here's another, though Amara was gone by then." Sophie pointed to a painting of Deveric and Eliza again, though this time Eliza was holding an infant in her arm. A small girl stood next to the same boy, Frederick, though he was obviously older now, nearly a teen.

"But what did she tell her family? Did they—do you—all know?"

"No. Only the daughters, and of those, just one. We didn't want the secret to get out, you understand."

"No. I don't. I don't understand."

"I'm sure not. Let's retire to the kitchen and have a cup of tea, and I'll explain whatever you wish to know."

He nodded, trailing after her like a zombie, not comprehending anything around him. It was too much.

"Amara told her family via a letter she'd eloped to India with a Navy captain, though naturally she didn't. She came here. Or rather, she came to you," Sophie said, as they entered a cozy room from which the smell of fresh bread emanated. His mouth watered in response. He hadn't eaten all day.

"And no one challenged it?"

"I suspect Deveric and Eliza covered for her, but it's not as if they had instant, ever-available contact like we do now, you know." She sliced the loaf of bread on the counter and brought it over to a table, gesturing to him to sit down. "I'll fetch the marmalade." She set a few small jars on the table. "I hope this is sufficient."

"It's fine." He grabbed a slice and bit into it, relishing the taste. For several moments, the sound of him chewing was the only sound in the room. "Tell me more," he finally said, taking a sip of the tea she'd poured for him while he ate.

"This American, Catherine, has a manuscript that allows her to create love stories, even across the ages."

"Cat's a ... real-life cupid? But with words instead of arrows?"

Sophie nodded. "That's how I understand it. She writes stories that bring people together—though Granny Eliza was always quick to note the two people involved had a choice. The attraction would be there, but only they could decide if it'd blossom into a life-long love."

Matt swallowed, his throat suddenly dry in spite of the tea. "So Cat wrote a story in which Amara comes forward to this time, to be with *me*?"

"Must be."

He sat, his stomach knotted as if in a big ball of yarn. None of this made any sense. And yet ... "Why *me*?"

Sophie smiled, a gentle smile. "That's not for me to know, but my guess is this Cat thought you and Amara a good match."

"But Amara wants nothing to do with a relationship! She's said so numerous times. And, frankly, neither do I." As the words left his mouth, his heart jerked, protesting his lie. He *hadn't* wanted a relationship; that much was true. But he did now. His thoughts drifted to the woman lying in the bed upstairs. "I should check on her. I should be with her."

Sophie's eyes softened. "We have just met," she said. "Both you and I, and I and Amara. But I feel as if I know you. I sense you are a good man, Matthew Goodson."

Matt said nothing, his lips pressing together. If only he felt that way himself.

CHAPTER 39

Amara blinked, the sound of voices calling her out of her fog.

"Thank you for coming back, Doctor Lowenstein. I appreciate it."

"The blood loss has slowed considerably, and her vitals are good."

Someone exhaled. "Was there any way to prevent this?" The voice was deep, familiar. Worried.

She blinked again, focusing her eyes on the figures to the side of the bed. *Matthew.* Matthew was here.

"Doubtful. I don't know her full medical history, but unfortunately pregnancy losses in the first trimester are fairly common, especially in the first eight weeks."

Pregnancy ... loss? Her hand drifted to her stomach as she struggled toward full consciousness. Suddenly, the image of red against beige flooded her mind, and her eyes jerked open. Blood. There'd been so much blood. A noise escaped her.

"Amara!" Matthew rushed to her side, grabbing her hand in his large warm one, his eyes troubled but full of concern.

"How are you?"

She swallowed, her eyes misting. "We … I lost the baby, didn't I?"

His jaw ticced, his lips flattening. "Yes."

One tear slipped out of the corner of her eye. "Then why are you still here?"

"Why am I—?" he thundered, jumping up. He looked at the older man. "If you'll excuse us."

"Certainly." The doctor hurried out the door, closing it gently behind him.

Matthew turned back to Amara, his eyes blazing with fury and pain. "You think I only came here because of the baby? And now that it—he—she—is gone, you think I'd just *leave?*"

She flinched at the raw emotion in his voice, even as a small part of her heart stitched itself back together at his words. Tears spilled over her cheeks. "I'm sorry, Matthew. I'm so sorry … for all of it."

His face slipped, the anger instantly replaced by sorrow, and he sat down by her side, clasping her hand with one of his, using his other to smooth her brow. "Oh, Amara," he said. "I am so sorry, too. For what you've gone through. I know you didn't want to have children, but—"

"No," she choked out in a half-sob. "I didn't. So why do I feel so devastated?"

He squeezed her hand. "Probably for the same reasons I do. We didn't want this, yet I'd wrapped my mind around it. And now …"

"And now …" She turned away from him, her eyes focusing on the sunny yellow wall across the room. He was silent, though his thumb still rubbed hers.

"I beg your forgiveness," she said, though she didn't look at him, "for running away. I thought coming here would give you your freedom, would give me my freedom. But some things are too big to run away from. I needed to take responsibility for my actions. I got myself into this. I can't … I couldn't … I shouldn't run away from that."

"Amara," he said, tipping her face towards his. "We both got ourselves into this. This is not, nor should it have ever been, something for you to shoulder alone. I am so very sorry for the way I reacted when you first told me. I should not have cast doubt on you. I should have—"

She raised her arm, touching a finger to his lips. "Shh. I understand."

"No. You don't." His jaw tightened again. "My oldest brother, Eric, had a girlfriend who claimed he got her pregnant. They married, had the baby. My brother grew close with the little girl. Then the woman dropped the bombshell that not only was he not the father, but that she was leaving him for the man who was."

Amara's jaw dropped. She couldn't imagine such a thing. *How horrendous.* Had anyone among her peers done likewise it would have been far worse a scandal than any she'd ever caused. Before she could say anything, he went on.

"And I've never wanted children, because I saw what a burden we were, especially to my mother after my dad left." He paused for a moment, pain creasing his forehead. "I vowed I would get a good job, earn lots of money. I watched my mother face down the sheer terror of not being able to provide for us, time and again. I never want to feel that."

His sudden, wicked smile startled Amara, whose own mouth had turned down at the ache in his voice. "And, in truth, I never liked kids. Too noisy, demanding, irritating." He rubbed his hand over hers, the smile fading. "But I was ready, anyway, Amara. I would have been here for our child."

For our child. Not for her; for the child. The child who would never be. Now that there was no child, he was free. They were free.

Amara was silent, her thoughts racing. Matthew insisted he was here for more than merely the baby, but it wasn't as if they had claims on each other. They'd made that clear from the start. What was also clear was that she brought complications wherever she went. 1813, 2016 … the result was the same. Scandalous behavior and negative consequences. With men.

She should have stuck to her original plan, the plan to come forward, yes, but to live an independent life, free of involvement with anyone of the opposite sex. Involvement brought trouble. Pain. Problems. This proved it all over again.

His thumb repeatedly traced over her palm. A faint hum buzzed between them, a palpable attraction, connection, even in the face of loss. *Because of loss*, her mind whispered. He wouldn't be here otherwise. He'd wanted to leave her at the stones; she was sure of it.

And their attraction was artificial, not real. Not that she wouldn't have noticed a man like Matthew in her own time. He was certainly handsome, especially with those wicked blue eyes. But the constant ache for him was nothing more than the result of Cat's manuscript, of the story she'd written, the spell she'd woven. Cat created attraction; she'd said so herself.

And that's what this was. Attraction. Sexual desire. She didn't *love* Matthew Goodson. Yes, she admired his form, had certainly enjoyed herself in his bed. And though she appreciated many of his character traits, it by no means meant she had made the mistake of falling in love with him.

Falling in love meant risk. The possibility of heartbreak. And the loss of independence she so desperately craved.

No, she was most definitely *not* in love with Matthew Goodson. And if her heart ached, it was merely on account of all that had happened this day.

She closed her eyes, and Matthew's thumb stilled on her hand. "Amara?" His voice was soft but urgent, full of concern.

"I wish to be alone," she said, turning her head away, refusing to meet his gaze. She didn't want to argue. She wanted to ignore. To forget. To sleep.

He hesitated. "I understand. But I'll be here if you need me. We will talk more later."

The words sounded as much a threat as a promise.

Matt paused outside the door, leaning against the wall. His breath came in ragged spurts, the anguish at the loss of the baby—their baby—smacking into his ribs. And to see Amara there, so fragile-looking, so sad, her eyes rimmed with purple circles, her cheeks sunken. He wanted nothing but to go back in, hold her close, and promise everything would be all right. Even if it wouldn't be.

The depth of his feeling shocked him. It went against every fiber of his body to walk out of that room and leave her behind, and yet he needed to honor her wishes. It just felt … *wrong*. He should be in there. Doing something.

Taylor's voice echoed in his mind. "Just like a man," she would have said. "Always wanting to fix things. Some things you just can't fix, Matty."

He wasn't sure what to do now.

He strode to the staircase, his thoughts on Amara as he made his way down to the long hall with all the portraits, unsure of where else to go. What he wouldn't give to undo what had happened. Damn that forgotten condom. It'd messed everything up. *He'd* messed everything up.

They'd been having a great time, the two of them, in a carefree, casual kind of relationship. And yet, at some point, it'd become more. He'd looked forward to seeing her. And when he did, his day felt complete. When he didn't, something was missing. There'd been times in his office he'd caught himself staring off into space, the focus and drive that had been his cornerstone for so many years suddenly absent. He'd attributed it to the newness, the excitement of it all. But now, as he passed rows and rows of portraits, he wondered if it hadn't grown into something deeper when he wasn't paying attention.

A portrait to his left caught his eye, and he stopped, nearly stumbling over his own feet. It was the one he'd seen on the Internet, the one showing her as a young child. And there was no doubt it was Amara. He'd accepted that much.

The time travel explanation made sense of many things he hadn't understood before: the clothing, the unfamiliarity with common experiences, the newness of cars and driving. His gut told him it was true. Not that he was one to normally go by emotion over logic and fact, but Sophie's story, Amara's own confessions, her behavior upon first arrival, the paintings here. It was proof enough, wasn't it?

Not that he wasn't going to corner Cat and Ben the first chance he got. They had some explaining to do.

He stood, his eyes on the child in the portrait, imagining for a moment it wasn't Amara, but the daughter they might have had. His stomach clenched and his throat went dry, anger and grief battling for dominance in his head.

Why had this happened? And what did it mean for his—

for their—future?

Footsteps echoed from the other end of the hallway. Looking up, he spied Sophie approaching, her brow wrinkled in concern. "Is everything all right? At least as all right as it can be?"

"Yes." His tone was brisk, businesslike, lest he betray the well of emotions flooding him. "Amara is fine. The doctor says she'll make a full recovery. She wanted to sleep, so I left. At her request." He didn't know why he felt the need to assert the last, but he did.

Sophie's face relaxed. "Good. I shall not disturb her, then. It's growing late; I'm guessing you might like to retire yourself? I had your bag moved into a guestroom. I hope that wasn't too presumptive."

She'd let him stay? Rather than question her—he didn't want her to change her mind—he nodded. He was exhausted.

"Come, I believe Angie has some chicken waiting for you."

"Thank you, Sophie. For everything today. For your kindness to a stranger."

Sophie smiled. "What's the expression? A stranger is merely a friend one hasn't met yet. Besides, I like having people here. It gets lonely in this old mausoleum by myself." A hint of something shadowed her face, but she shook it away. "Now, then. To the kitchen."

"To the kitchen."

Together, they walked off.

But Matt left his heart in the room above him.

CHAPTER 40

Amara woke to the sound of raindrops against the window, a muddled, gray light permeating the room. It matched her mood. For a blissful second, her cares and sorrows didn't exist, until full consciousness brought the events of the previous day flooding back.

Her hand inched across her abdomen, which no longer hurt, thank goodness, though the doctor had told her to expect the bleeding to last for a good week or so. He'd returned after Matthew had left and explained all in great detail to her, assuring her she would still be able to have children if she so chose. Her cheeks had burned at his frank talk, and she'd been glad when he'd taken his leave, promising to check on her should need arise. She turned her head to the window, watching water trail across the glass. Funny how her eyes felt so dry this morning, the rest of her so hollow. Numb.

Noises echoed in the hallway. Matthew. Matthew was still here. The thought pinched her brows together. She did not want to interact with him. She'd prefer to stay in this cocoon of nothingness, this shelter from the storms raging outside—and within.

Why hadn't he left? There was no reason for him to remain now that there was no baby. Would he try to stay? Would he want to? Would he confuse grief for affection? Try to convince her—and himself—there was more between them than there was?

For there was nothing between them. A few weeks of sinful indulgence, for which she was now paying the price. Her family would be appalled; her mother most certainly would have disowned her, the sister of a duke openly cavorting in bed with a man.

Her hand moved from her stomach to her heart, as if she could hold in the painful thumping, each beat reminding her of the ticking of a clock. Time had run out on her. She'd tried to escape her past but merely ended up repeating it. She'd been intimate with a man with no promises, no future. *Though*, a stubborn part of her mind insisted, *it's what she and Matthew both said they'd wanted*. She'd not been played the fool this time, as with Drake. No, she'd gone into this with open eyes and a protected heart.

So why did she feel so broken? *Because of the baby*. Guilt gnawed at her insides. The baby had paid the price for her sins. The doctor, Sophie, even Matthew had tried to convince her this was a common occurrence, that a number of women lost pregnancies for no apparent reason, but Amara knew the reason. It was her punishment for the mistakes she'd made, the sins she'd committed.

She should have been the demure, respectable, respectful daughter she was expected to be. Instead, she'd broken the rules, sought independence she didn't deserve, had tried to achieve a life beyond her. She'd even defied the natural order of things by time traveling to chase after that dream.

Shame bore down on her, pinning her to the bed. The

rhythm of the rain did nothing to soothe her, reminding her instead of her mother's tears when Amara had been caught *in flagrante delicto* in that garden, of her own tears when she'd realized the level to which Drake had betrayed her.

A knock sounded at the door, interrupting her morose train of thought. She nearly ignored it, but the courtesy bred of years had her call out, "Come in."

Matthew poked his head around the door, his expression uncertain, before he walked in, his tall, lithe frame garbed in a becoming green sweater and a pair of jeans. A hesitant smile graced his face as he approached the bed. "How are you?"

She did not return his smile. In fact, she turned her gaze back to the window, so that she wouldn't have to look at him. Looking at him brought a pain she didn't want to feel, didn't want to consider. "I am fine."

Matthew sat on the edge of the bed, his unexpected action drawing her eyes to his. Reaching forward, he made to smooth the hair off her head, but she jerked away. Hurt shadowed his eyes for a fraction of a second, but he pasted on a smile. "I wanted to check on you. I hope you were able to sleep."

"Some."

"Have you had anything to eat?"

"I'm not hungry." She closed her eyes.

Silence reigned for a few moments.

"Amara."

She paused. "Yes?"

"I … we … this is not your fault."

"I know." The words came out automatically, though she didn't believe them.

"No, truly. This is *not* your fault. If anything, it's mine."

At that, her eyes popped open. "*Your* fault?"

He nodded, misery creeping over his face. "If I hadn't forgotten a condom ..."

A bitter sigh escaped her. "No. This is my punishment. To atone for my manifold sins."

"What?" His incredulous tone echoed in the small chamber. "You can't be serious."

Amara turned her head back toward the window, water tracing its way down her cheeks in patterns similar to those on the panes. "Yes, I am. I came forward to escape my past. The past in which I was intimate with a man, then publicly shamed. Yet what did I do once here? I became intimate with a man. Quickly. And while public shaming is not as prevalent as in my era, I am once again bearing the brunt of my own foolish choices."

"Amara." Matthew's voice cracked as his hand sought hers under the blanket. She did not resist his grip, but nor did she return it. "No. You're not making sense. I don't know what happened in ... in your previous life. And I don't care; it doesn't matter to me. What does matter is who you are now, and that woman is someone I've grown to care for very much."

"No."

Matthew's next words were a growl. "What do you mean, no?"

"No." She turned her face back to him. "I don't believe you care for me. That was never part of the arrangement. I think you are confusing your sense of duty and grief about this baby with caring for me."

Matthew stood up, his body rigid with anger. His face was a mask of fury, its own thunderstorm. "How dare you tell me how I feel? You may speak for yourself, Amara, though I think grief is twisting what *you* feel. But you may not speak for me." His chest heaved as he breathed great, ragged gasps of air. "You think I came just for the baby. But I did not. I did not, Amara Mattersley. Did it play into things? Of course. How could it not? But I came, leaving my own country, my job, my students, everything, for something I only figured out the second I saw you again, standing among those stones, though I tried to deny it." He leaned down, boring into her eyes with his.

"I came here because I love you, damn it!"

CHAPTER 41

Amara gasped at his outburst, but Matt didn't care. How dare this woman, this infuriating, exasperating, challenging, frustrating, delectable woman, announce to him his feelings for her weren't real?

A part of him knew it was a defense mechanism, a barrier against pain, much like the barriers he'd erected when his family had fallen apart. Half of him wanted to shake some sense into her, for her to see they had so much more than a mere physical connection.

The other half wanted to punch the wall, as much over frustration with himself as with her. If only he'd realized his heart was engaged far earlier, perhaps they wouldn't be here now, looking at each other as enemies, as … strangers.

This woman had shared his bed, his days, his nights. This woman had his heart, yet she acted now as if he were an acquaintance at best, perhaps even an annoyance. *She's not in her right mind, Goodson. She can't be, not so soon. And neither are you.* But the truth did little to ease the sting.

He retreated from the bed, pacing back and forth, his

hands on his hips. "If only I'd seen it sooner. It took you leaving for me to see, for me to know. And now you're telling me what we had is *nothing*?"

"Oh, Matthew." Her tone was lost, sad.

"I admit, I didn't want you to be pregnant. I didn't want a baby. But the idea of a part of you and a part of me, infinitely blended together? It pierced my heart, Amara. In a good way. And what I know, what I'm sure of, is in spite of this crazy time-travel thing, in spite of it *all*, I want *you*."

Amara's shoulders convulsed, but she said nothing, closing her eyes against him again, her whole face a mask of heartache.

He wanted to go to her, to touch her, but if he did, would she bat him away, reject him? He couldn't risk it. Having declared his love for a woman for the first time in his life—for he'd certainly never spoken those words to Wendy—he was feeling mighty vulnerable already, especially since Amara had in no way, shape, or form reciprocated.

He continued pacing, waiting for her to speak. Long stretches of time passed. Finally, he stood still, willing her to open her eyes, to say *something*. When she did, however, he wished she hadn't.

For all she said was, "Go home, Matthew."

The ride to the airport passed in a haze. Matt sat, rigid, his eyes on the scenery rushing by, but he didn't take anything in. His mind was on the woman he'd left behind, the woman at Clarehaven. Amara.

He'd run into Sophie, of course. Bag in hand, other hand

on the door handle, he'd whipped open the front door just as steps hurried toward him.

"Matthew, wait!"

He hadn't wanted to stop, had wanted to let his fury power him forward, but he couldn't be rude to his hostess. She'd been so kind, welcoming him, a complete stranger, into her home, encouraging him with Amara. So he'd paused, his shoulders slumping.

"You're going?"

"Yes. Amara has asked me to leave. Demanded, rather."

"Oh, Matthew."

He could hear the sorrow in her voice, a sorrow that matched his own.

"You should stay."

The empathy on her face was nearly his undoing. He swallowed. "She doesn't want me."

A scoffing noise emanated from her throat, and his eyes widened. "She does. She just … With everything happening, physically as well as emotionally …"

"Yes. Which is why I'm giving her space."

Sophie sighed. "I wish you'd stay. You're more than welcome."

Matt gave her a sad smile. "Thank you, Sophie. You've been more than generous. But this is something Amara must work out for herself. I've told her where I stand. She needs to decide where she does." His eyes moved to the floor. "Take care of her, Sophie."

With that, he'd strode through the door into the pouring rain.

Now, as he sat in the back of the cab, his mind pitched forth a thousand misgivings. Maybe he should turn around, should go back. Sophie was right; Amara had been through more than he could ever imagine in the last few days—his sudden appearance, her confessions about her origins, the loss of their baby …

His heart spasmed, grief ricocheting throughout his chest. Their baby. The sheer sense of loss decimated him. The image of Amara, lying small and pale against that large bed, was an image he'd never forget. A curse escaped his lips. What was he doing in this cab, leaving behind the woman he loved?

He was doing what she'd asked. What she'd demanded. He was leaving. He wasn't going to force something that wasn't wanted.

The cab eased through the tangled approach to Heathrow, pulling up to the departures entrance. Matt sat, even as the driver opened the door for him.

"Sir?" The voice broke through his haze, and Matt quickly extricated himself from the cab, apologizing to the driver and handing him a few extra pounds.

With a purposeful stride, he stalked to the ticket counter, his mind refusing to let his doubts turn him around. He needed to go home, as much for the work awaiting him as because Amara told him to. He'd left in the middle of the week, in the middle of the semester. He'd dropped everything, driven by the urge to reach Amara, to make it right.

Instead, he'd done everything wrong.

After a short wait, he had his boarding pass in hand, and he headed to his gate. Once there, he sat down and pulled out his laptop, opening up the paper he'd been writing, determined to immerse himself in what was comfortable and familiar, in what had never rejected him or let him down: work.

Before he knew it, they were boarding. As the plane took off and the buildings gave way to fields below, his throat constricted. He searched the ground, wondering if they were flying anywhere near Clarehaven. Near Amara. Near his heart.

Sophie was right. He should have stayed. Should have let the emotion settle and approached things more rationally. Should have fought for Amara.

But hadn't he done that in coming in the first place? In dropping everything and rushing off to a foreign country? In finding her and baring his heart and soul?

And she'd rejected him.

It was up to her now. Amara had to decide what she wanted and whether Matt figured into her plans at all.

He closed his eyes and leaned back into the tiny, uncomfortable seat, ignoring the appreciative glances of the pudgy brunette next to him. He needed to clear his head. And to get himself back where he belonged: home, in Charlottesville, secure in his apartment with Lovey, working on algorithms and papers and with all that was orderly and controllable.

Amara slung an arm across her eyes to block the sun in a way her mother would never have approved. Who had opened the curtains? Moving her arm slightly, she opened one eye, blinking against the brightness.

She was alone. *Thank heavens.* A fire crackled in the hearth across from her bed, telling her someone had been in. Why had they set the fire? It wasn't as if it were necessary; central heat was one of the numerous updates Clarehaven had received.

With the only light coming from the window and the fire, and with the furnishings nearly unchanged since her era, Amara could almost imagine she was in her own time. Her heart clenched as she fantasized of throwing open the door to find Grace or Emmeline or even Becca waiting outside, ready for the day's adventures. Not that their options would have been anything but mundane. They would have strolled the grounds or gardens, or spent hours writing letters, or played the pianoforte, or perhaps read one of Grace's novels. Still, to see Deveric. Eliza. Even her mother. For a moment, the longing was so intense, Amara thought she'd burst. She tossed in the bed, not wanting to rise to face the day.

And she didn't have to. She could do what she wished, when she wished.

What *did* she wish?

Matthew's face swam before her, and his words of the day before, his declaration of love, echoed in her ears. He'd told her he loved her. But did he? Could he? How? They hadn't known each other long—though many a couple from her era had betrothed themselves on slighter acquaintance. And what they had shared, what was it, really? An intense physical connection. A few fun days. But love? No. He didn't love her. He felt guilty. Responsible. That was all.

But he'd come for her. He'd left his work, his world, and flown to England. To find her. It was more than Drake Evers had done. It was the opposite. Drake had run away; Matthew had run to her.

Yes, but Drake never got you pregnant. A stroke of luck, of course, and she doubted he'd have done anything if he had. Matthew, at least, had tried to do the right thing. Hadn't he?

She groaned, rolling over in the bed. What a mess. She'd come forward to this century seeking independence.

Freedom. And what had she accomplished instead? She'd ended up pregnant.

Shame settled deep on her shoulders. She'd done the one thing she'd been raised never to do: give herself to a man and end up in trouble. And she'd done it twice. Her hand drifted to her abdomen. The blood still flowed, but otherwise she felt no different. She was no longer with child, however. Guilt, deeper than the shame, ate at her innards, covering her like a shroud.

She hadn't wanted the baby, had wished it away. And now it was gone. Her fingers traced the expanse of her stomach. How had this happened? How had her life become a worse tangle of shame, of scandal, than it had been in her own time? Was she cursed, doomed to make mistake after mistake, never achieving the happiness, the satisfaction Deveric and Eliza had found? Or her sister Cecilia? Cat and Ben exuded that same joy, the joy of being with someone who truly loved them.

Loved them. Matthew had insisted he loved her. Right before she sent him away. How could she believe him? It was such a jumbled tangle: their intimate encounters, this unwished-for child. And Cat's manuscript. Surely the only thing Matthew Goodson felt for her, besides a sense of obligation, stemmed from the magic that had brought them together in the first place.

Fresh tears streamed down her face as a soft knock came at the door.

"Amara? It's me."

Amara sniffed, wiping at her eyes. She wanted to pretend she was sleeping and hadn't heard Sophie's voice, but she couldn't do that, not to the woman who'd willingly opened Clarehaven to her. Not to the woman who was her last, if distant, living relation.

"Come in." Hopefully the light was low enough Sophie wouldn't see the evidence of Amara's misery.

The door cracked open, and Sophie poked her head through, surveying the room before stepping inside and shutting the door. Crossing to the bed, she dropped into the chair next to it. "Oh, darling."

That's all it took. Tears sprang unbidden to Amara's eyes again, cascading down her face to soil her pillow.

Sophie reached out, her hand clasping Amara's. "I'm so sorry about the baby."

Of course. Sophie assumed these tears, this grief was about the baby. Which it was, in part. But her heart had cracked open and wept tears now of its own for the other losses in her life. For all the hurt and pain she'd ever endured. For her own dreadful decisions that had led her to Drake Evers. To 2016. To Matthew.

She sucked in gulps of air, the sobs racking her shoulders. "Move over."

Amara froze in stunned surprise but then did as told, shifting over as Sophie climbed onto the mattress and lay down on her side, face-to-face with Amara. It reminded Amara so much of conversations she'd had with her sisters in the same manner that fresh pain stabbed her. What a horrible mess she'd made.

Sophie stroked the hair away from Amara's face, tucking strands behind her ear. "You're going to be all right. You are strong, Amara. And this is not the end of your story."

Amara's brow knitted even as some of the tension leaked out of her shoulders at the soothing words. What did Sophie mean, her story? Had she meant that literally or figuratively? "How … what do you mean?"

"I mean though it may not seem possible, there is life beyond this deepest grief. The sun will come up, the days will pass, and at some point, not today, but in a week, or a month, or heavens, even a year, you will realize you are ready for whatever is to come next. For there is always something next."

Amara studied her, this woman at once so familiar and yet still largely a stranger. She spoke with conviction behind her words. What had brought such wisdom? What had Sophie suffered?

As if Sophie had read her mind, she spoke. "Someday I'll tell you, but this is not about me. This is about you. And Matthew."

"He left."

"Yes, he did. But he told me that's because you demanded he do so."

"He could have stayed."

Sophie snorted. "That man is in love with you. Do you think he was going to deny any request you made, especially when he saw you in such pain? Pain he thinks he caused?"

"Pain *he* caused?"

"Of course! He claims this is his fault, both you getting pregnant, and you … you miscarrying. That you did so because of your conversation at the stones."

"What?" Amara sat straight up. How could he think losing the baby was *his* fault?

Sophie eyed her. "It makes about as much sense as you thinking it's *your* fault, doesn't it?"

"But it is—" Amara broke off. "You don't understand. You don't know me. It *is* my fault. The result of the foolish decisions I made and keep making. I didn't want this child, and so …"

"It doesn't work like that. If it did, unwanted pregnancies wouldn't be an issue. You didn't do anything. This happens at a higher rate than most people know. Because we learn so early now if a woman is pregnant, pregnancies that might never have been suspected in your era are known about from practically the day they happen."

Amara's eyes rounded. "You speak as if … "

"As if I've had a miscarriage myself?" Sophie's eyes closed, anguish shadowing her face for the briefest of moments. "Yes." Her words were crisp, businesslike as she rushed ahead. "But that is far in the past, and I know it was not meant to be. Not like you and Matthew."

"Matthew and me. We are only meant to be together because Cat wrote her story that way."

Sophie frowned. "You don't believe that, do you?"

A bitter chuckle escaped Amara's throat. "What exactly do we have in common, Sophie? He is a professor, a highly educated man, focused on his career and his computers and his future. Our life experiences are vastly different. And besides, he said himself he wanted no relationship, no entanglements."

Sophie opened her mouth as if to speak, but Amara continued, her voice rising. "I am a duke's daughter, a duke's sister, relatively well-educated for my time but not for this one, a woman embroiled in scandal then as well as now, with little to offer. And no desire for a relationship. I wanted independence, a future of my own determining. *That* is why I came forward to this time. Not for a man. For myself."

"You speak as if independence and love are incompatible. But what of Deveric and Eliza?"

"What of them?"

"From her letters and descriptions passed down through

376

the generations, Eliza strikes me as the independent sort."

"The woman traveled through time specifically to marry my brother. How is that possibly independent?"

"Well, did she change who she was for him? Did she give up her own mind, her own activities, her own life?"

Amara frowned. "Of course she did. She left behind everyone and everything she knew."

"True. But because she *wanted* to. And from the stories I've heard, she wasn't particularly submissive once she found him."

Amara giggled in spite of herself. That much was true. Eliza had wanted Deveric, but she hadn't been willing to settle, had always been who she was, much to Amara's mother's consternation and the other sisters' delight.

And she'd been willing to leave when things weren't working out.

The giggle left. "But she *wanted* a man. I don't."

Sophie reached out, tracing her fingers softly down Amara's cheek. "You keep insisting that. If that's how you truly feel, all right." Suddenly, she rolled off the bed and stood up. "I should let you rest." Moving toward the door, she paused after opening it. "But, Amara? Don't let your past determine your future."

As the door shut, Amara stared at it.

What did Sophie mean?

CHAPTER 42

The flight passed in a blur of anguish and regret. He shouldn't have left, shouldn't have abandoned Amara there, alone. But what else could he have done? She'd asked him to go, and he wasn't going to press himself on her. He'd already done enough damage. Besides, she wasn't alone. She had Sophie.

Who did he have? Taylor? This wasn't exactly a situation he could explain to his sister, which was one of the reasons he hadn't contacted her. Ben? He had to have known the truth about Amara, about the time travel. About the manuscript. Matt longed to kick something as he shuffled behind the passengers ahead of him. The Coopers had both known, and more than that, had intentionally thrown Amara and him together. Anger surged through him at the situation, at the mess he found himself in, at what he and Amara had both suffered.

Stalking to his truck, he threw himself in the driver's seat. He wanted answers.

And he wanted them now.

Matt didn't even stop at his apartment, so desperate was he to confront Ben and Cat about their duplicity, about their involvement in the whole mess. Jerking to a stop in front of the Treasure Trove, he threw the truck in park and leapt out of the driver's seat, his long legs taking the stairs two at a time. Yanking open the door, he stalked through, startling a young woman to his right. Ignoring her, he strode to the back of the room, where Cat stood behind the register, helping a customer. At the sound of his heavy footfalls, she glanced up, her eyes widening with each step he took.

Reaching the desk, he stopped, forcing himself to breathe before he blew up. His eyes, however, never left her tall form, all of his frustration and rage focused on her.

Cat smiled at the older gentleman in front of her, showing no outward sign of disturbance, but her hand shook as she handed him his purchases. "Tell Moira hello," she said.

The man tipped his head to her. "I sure will, young lady. And give that fine little boy of yours a squeeze from ol' Fred."

With a laugh, Cat answered, "Will do." As the man ambled away, her gaze moved to Matt. "Hello, Matthew," she said, tucking a piece of hair behind her ear.

"Hello?" he ground out, his voice a furious whisper, still conscious of the woman browsing at the front of the store. "That's all you have to say after interfering in, after *ruining* my life?"

Cat held up her hands. "Whoa. Those are some serious accusations."

Matt clenched his teeth together, his jaw ticing. "Yes. And you've got some serious explaining to do. You and Ben both."

Cat exhaled loudly, blowing her bangs out of her eyes with a nod. "I'm happy to do that. After business hours?"

The noise that emerged from Matt's throat was a cross between a growl and a curse. He looked at his watch. "Fine. You've got ten minutes."

Cat turned to the clock behind her. "Heavens, is it that late already?" She fidgeted nervously with a pen.

The front door opened, and Matt turned as Ben held the door for the young woman, who slipped out with a nod. Walking through, Ben's eyes fell on the two figures at the back, and a grin broke out on his face. He headed toward them. "Hello, my love. And to you, Matt. It's nice to see you—" He broke off as Cat shook her head.

Matt's chin jutted out as he stared at his advisor, his colleague, the man he'd begun to consider a friend.

Ben's footsteps slowed. "I take it your time in England didn't go well? Did you not find Amara?"

"Oh, I found her all right. At Clarehaven. Her home. Her *ancestral* home."

Cat and Ben said nothing.

"The home she lived in before coming to Charlottesville," he continued, though he was sure they knew the details. "*In 1813*. Ring any bells?"

Cat swallowed. "I wanted to tell you, Matt." She glanced at her husband, gnawing on her lip. "*We* wanted to. Amara begged us not to. Said it was hers to tell if you were to know."

Matt snorted, a bellow of anger.

"Believe me, I've second-guessed honoring that promise since you left," Ben added, but stopped when Matt's glare shifted to him, his hands curling into fists.

Cat cleared her throat, drawing his attention. "So you know about the time travel. Did she tell—?"

Matt cut her off. "Did she tell me about the manuscript? Yes. And about the *story* you wrote to bring her forward. To me. The story linking us together, even though neither one of us wanted that. Neither one of us asked for that."

He ran a hand over his hair, clasping the back of his head. "What gave you the right?" His tone was half fury, half agony. "How *dare* you interfere with my life like this? Or Amara's?"

Cat's brow creased. "I … we—"

"We did it for you, Matt," Ben said, moving behind the desk. He slung an arm around Cat's shoulders, pulling her close. Cat visibly relaxed, and for a second, pangs of envy raced through Matt. *No!* He wasn't going to focus on his sorrow, on his pain at losing Amara, on how much he missed her. His anger was his focus now, and rightfully so.

"You remind me so much of me a few years ago," Ben continued. "Smart. Driven. A workaholic. A lonely workaholic."

"Lonely?" The word burst out of Matt.

"Perhaps it was presumptive." Ben held up his free hand palm forward to concede guilt. "But I remember how empty my life was, though I didn't think so at the time. And when we read Eliza's letter, her plea for Amara, well, I thought—"

"—*We* thought," interjected Cat.

"We thought she'd be a good fit for you. Someone to draw you out of yourself, away from the screen. Someone who might just be your other half."

"And I had no say?" Matt's brows furrowed, rage surging through him again.

"Of course you did! You had as much say as you would with any woman expressing interest in you. You could have said no at any time!" Cat burst out.

"Really? With a magical story linking us together, not to mention you throwing her at me every chance you got?"

"My stories provide possibilities. They're not written in stone. The attraction may be stronger, yes, but I've no doubt you've resisted acting on attractions before."

An image of his teaching assistant, a cute redhead, from last semester's class sprang to mind. She'd made it clear she was interested in him. Matt had considered it briefly but hadn't pursued it. She was a student, and he'd never cross that line. Still, this was different. Wasn't it? He blew air out from his cheeks, then sucked in a deep breath.

After a moment of silence, Cat reached a hand forward, as if to soothe him. "What happened in England, Matt?"

His eyes filled with tears, and he ducked his head so they wouldn't see. "I want to see this manuscript. This—*our*— story."

"Of course. But won't you tell us what happened? Is Amara okay?"

He lifted his head to the ceiling, his nostrils flaring as he willed the tears not to fall. One defied him anyway, slipping down his cheek.

Cat sucked in a breath but said nothing.

"She … we lost the baby. And when I told her I loved her, she told me to go home." He wiped the moisture from his cheeks, then settled his hands on his hips, glowering at Cat and Ben, even as more tears threatened to spill.

"Oh, Matthew. Oh. I am so sorry. About the baby. About everything." Cat's own eyes glistened with moisture, and she clasped her hands over her mouth.

"I am, too." Ben's voice exuded sympathy. He walked out from behind the counter and set a hand on Matt's arm. "You told her you loved her?"

"Yes. Because I do, damn it. And it's your fault." He yanked his arm away. The words were harsh, but some of the anger had left his voice. He could blame Cat and Ben until the cows came home, but in his heart he knew it wouldn't change anything. Whatever the circumstances, however Amara came to be in his life, he loved her now.

And she'd rejected him.

"Give her time."

Matt huffed. "Time?"

"Yes, time. Believe me, I know how difficult all of this is to absorb, to come to terms with. When Cat first told me, I didn't contact her again for weeks." Ben's eyes didn't leave his. "I wrestled with it. I wanted to reject it. I was angry, bewildered, doubting, confused. I was all of those things. But I came back. I came back, because I knew I was falling in love with her, and I needed to see what was there, if there was a possibility."

He walked over and planted a kiss on his wife's mouth. "I'm so glad I did. I had no idea how empty my life was without Cat. And, well, she's converted me into a bit of a cupid, wanting to give others the same opportunity, the same chance at love that we had. I admit, knowing she has the power to set the spark is kinda heady."

"But as we said before, the people involved *always* have a choice," Cat added quickly. "It's up to the couple to kindle the full flame."

Matt's shoulders eased a little. "Show me the story. And the letter to you."

Cat nodded. "Ben, will you lock up? I'll call the sitter and make sure she can keep Wash longer."

"Sure," Ben answered, heading toward the front door. Cat gestured to the stairs leading up to their apartment. "Come on up."

Matt followed her, his head spinning. He settled himself

on the sofa at her bidding while she called the sitter. After a brief conversation, she nodded at Matt. "I'll be right back."

She returned a moment later, a plain black book and several envelopes in her hand. She handed him the book first. "This is the manuscript, passed down to me from my grandmother."

He opened the book, surprised by the richly illuminated pages contained within the simple binding.

"Please be careful and don't touch the pages directly; it is quite old. I mostly read from the photocopies I had made. But I wanted to show you it's for real."

"And it says?"

"It says I can create love stories."

He looked up, raising an eyebrow. "I'm sure it says more than that. It's a short book, but it's not that short."

Cat shoved a lock of hair behind her ears. "The rest are records of such love stories—a history, so to speak. A man deeply wronged the original author. She was determined it never happen again, to her or to her sisters. Somehow, she created this, created the magic. The manuscript is quite vague on how that actually occurred. Intentionally, I assume; she likely didn't want to be accused of witchcraft. Most of the truths about the manuscript and its powers have been handed down orally, for generations."

"But how did you come to have it?"

"Apparently that woman from so long ago was one of my relatives."

Just as Amara's relatives had handed down her story. He wrinkled his brow. "This is crazy. A magical medieval manuscript working as a love potion?"

"Kind of. It gave me powers, but I have to write the stories. Nuts, right? But I tested it out. It worked." She chewed her lip for a second before rushing on. "Then Eliza, my Austen-loving friend, asked me to send her to Regency England, to get a chance with a duke. I didn't think it'd work, what with the time travel and all, but it did."

She waved the letters in her hand. "And Eliza was thoughtful enough, thank God, to write me tons of letters, telling me about her new life. She sent forward books and other things, too. Including a plea on behalf of her duke's sister. Amara." She handed him an envelope. "Amara didn't write this letter; Eliza did. But she went into detail about Deveric's poor sister, how she'd been duped by some rascal and tainted with scandal ever since." Cat shook her head. "So glad social mores aren't so stringent today. Anyway, Amara wanted a chance at a new life, a life where she had the freedom to make choices she'd never have in her own era."

Cat paced in front of him as he drew the letter from the envelope. "The only problem was," she continued, "I couldn't just bring her forward willy-nilly, no matter how much I wanted to. I needed to bring her forward for love, or at least the possibility of love. That's the limitation of the manuscript—I can only create opportunities in love. Nothing else. In truth, I didn't think it would work."

A nervous trill of laughter escaped her as Ben walked through the door and crossed to her side. "I mean, at least Eliza *knew* whom to wish upon," Cat continued. "I had no way of writing to Eliza and Amara to give them any instructions. I could only do exactly what she asked in the letter."

Matt's eyes scanned the page, the words written in old-fashioned ink but with a modern slant and a modern tone. *I'll have her go to the stones,* it began, *just as you had me do, so she can wish on her forever love and hopefully come forward to you.*

Cat said something else, but he didn't hear her as he read on.

She says she doesn't want love, but I think that's just hurt talking, Cat. She got caught being intimate with a man she thought loved her and was going to propose. Until he told her he was already married. When they were discovered, he fled, leaving her to deal with the aftermath by herself. Can you imagine? I mean, it'd be embarrassing in our own time to be discovered in public, sure, but here? Here it's the kiss of death, especially to a duke's daughter. Stupid double standard, requiring women to remain virtuous while men sleep around. Never did like that part of this era.

Anyway, babbling again, just like your old friend. Like I said, I'll send her to the stones and have her wish to come forward. Three times, like in the Wizard of Oz. But no ruby slippers, though we could certainly afford some.

I hope you can think of someone who'd be a good fit. Someone who could love her, but also give her breathing room. Someone who'd support her in her goals for a better education, for a more independent life.

Deveric and I will do our best to ensure she's well cared for financially. Hopefully that will pan out over the next two hundred years! If not, perhaps you can sell some of the Dickens books I sent on her behalf.

She's feisty, defiant, prickly … and hurting. She doesn't fit here, Cat, just like I didn't really fit there. I think she's meant to be in the twenty-first century, with all it can offer her. Thanks for giving her the chance. Here's praying it will work again!

Much Love, Eliza

Feisty? Prickly? Not when he'd last seen her, lying so pale and weak against that bed. *She did command you leave, though.*

He'd done that to her, robbed her of her spirit, hadn't he? By impregnating her, then reacting as he had. He'd hurt her again, left her like the asshole described in the letter. Shame ate at him. Yes, he'd gone to her in the end, but late. Too late. With shaking fingers, he handed the letter back to Cat. "And your story?"

She nodded, passing him a second piece of paper. It was brief.

As requested by my dearest friend Eliza James, now Eliza Mattersley, Duchess of Claremont (what a thrill that still is to write!), Amara Mattersley will go to the ancient stones at Clarehaven, where she'll wish to be in the future with her true love. I know she won't know specifically on whom she's wishing, like Eliza did, but, well, maybe this magic stuff will still work. She'll appear here February 14th, 2016—Valentine's Day, for what could be more romantic than that? She'll arrive around 7:00 p.m., when Matthew Goodson is over for his weekly meeting with Ben.

For Matt seems a great match for Amara. He's brilliant, kind, respectful, and hard working. Too hard working. Ben worries for Matt, thinks Matt has no life beyond work. Wouldn't a woman from another century, an era before cell phones and computers, be perfect for a man who never looks up from his screen? And wouldn't a man who adores his sister as much as Matt does, according to Ben (who met her at a social event), be the kind of guy who'd want Amara to be happy, to have her own independent life? Everything in my gut says yes.

They both have a choice, of course, just as Eliza and Deveric did. I'll bring them together, but they'll decide whether or not they belong together. Here's hoping it works.

If not, I can always pair her with William. Ha, ha. – Catherine Schreiber Cooper

Matt scowled. "Who's this William?"

Cat and Ben exchanged a glance, one Matt couldn't read. "He was someone I went on a date with. Before Ben."

"Two dates."

"What?" Cat looked at her husband.

"Two dates," Ben repeated. "And I envied him on both of them."

"Well," Cat answered, pressing her lips to his nose. "They were good dates, I admit. But you were the one with whom I'm meant to be."

Matt cleared his throat. "Why now?"

Cat turned back to him, her forehead wrinkling in confusion. "What do you mean?"

"You said Eliza went back in 2012. Why wait until 2016 to bring Amara forward?"

Cat gave a guilty smile. "Well, first I was enjoying my time with Ben. Perhaps that was selfish. Then I got pregnant. I didn't have the time or energy I'd need to give to Amara when I was caring for a baby. Talk about sleep deprivation." She sat down next to Matt. "In fact, I was going to wait until Wash was a little older. I figured it didn't make a difference to Amara; she'd go to the stones in her own time and come forward whenever I said. At least I hoped it'd work like that. But I've watched you every Sunday night when you're with Ben. I sensed a loneliness in you, a desperation, especially this year. It seemed the time." She looked him full in the face, her gray eyes searching his. "Was I wrong?"

He tensed. He didn't care for being described as lonely, much less desperate. And yet … he had to admit she was right. "No. You weren't wrong." The words were a whisper.

He buried his head in his hands. He'd been living half a life, immersing himself in work to avoid his past. And Amara had come forward to avoid hers, leaving everything and everyone she knew in a desperate attempt to be free from her own history.

He could relate to that.

But the mess they'd created together? *It wasn't a mess until you made it one.* It wasn't a mess until the pregnancy.

The days they'd spent together in his apartment? Easy. The afternoon spent listening to music? He'd loved it. The night under the stars after Shakespeare? Heaven. The hours they'd spent in bed, Amara in his arms, those hazel-green eyes staring up into his as their bodies moved together? Pure bliss.

No, most of it hadn't been a mess at all.

And it wasn't just the physical. They'd spent hours talking. He'd shared more with her than any other person, including his sister. Why hadn't he seen it then? Why had it taken this blasted turn of events to show him how he felt about her? And what could he do now? He'd followed her to England. He'd accepted her time-travel story, even though every logical inch of him protested. And why?

Because he loved her. He loved her, body and soul. But he'd come too late to that realization, hadn't he? Because in the meantime, she'd lost the baby, and then sent him home.

He closed his eyes, his chest burning. "I don't know what to do," he whispered.

"Give it time," Ben said, compassion lacing his voice. "And let her know how you feel."

"She knows how I feel."

"Let her know again."

Matt popped an eye open. "But she's in England."

Ben gave a wry smile. "Yes. In England. In 2016. In the time of phones and email and texting and Skype."

Matt brightened. Amara might not have a phone, but Sophie did, and he had her number. "You're right." He stood up, stretching his back, which ached from the long airplane ride. He shook a finger at them. "I'm still pissed at you," he grumbled, before a corner of his mouth popped up. "And yet grateful, too."

"Understandably."

"I've gotta go." Without any further good-bye, Matt jetted out the side door and down to his truck, anxious now to get home, to do what he could to make this right. He paused only to text a quick message to Sophie before throwing the car into drive, hope filling his heart for the first time in days.

CHAPTER 43

*A*mara sat on the flat platform in the middle of the circle of stones, her eyes taking in every detail of the weathered rocks, the violets growing at their base, the rays of the morning sun streaming through heating her back. Her hands traced the coarse texture beneath her. *This is where it had all started.* Her heart pounded in her chest. *And this is where it could all end.*

She'd spent an hour strolling the halls of Clarehaven, taking in each and every detail, before wandering the gardens. Sophie had clucked at her, worried at the exertion so shortly after her miscarriage, but Amara had to move, had to see, had to think. And she didn't want to do it lying in that godforsaken room, the one that had mocked her two hundred years ago when she'd retreated to it after the scandal, and the one that mocked her now with its memories of Matthew. Of Matthew standing by her as she lost their baby. Of the tenderness in his eyes after he'd vowed his love for her. Of the devastation on Matthew's face when she'd sent him away.

Yes, the last place she wanted to be was in that room.

She turned now to face the sun, letting it beat down on her cheeks, warming her in the cold spring air. She'd asked Sophie to drive her here, and the darling woman had complied, almost no questions asked except the one. "Are you going back?"

"I don't know," Amara had answered. "Check on me in an hour?"

Sophie had given her a sad smile. "I hope you'll be here."

"Whether I am or not, Sophie Mattersley, I'm grateful for everything you've done for me. You are a kind-hearted, wonderful soul, and I wish you every happiness."

Sophie sucked in her cheeks in surprise at Amara's words. "You, too," was all she'd choked out before hopping back into the car and driving off.

It'd been close to an hour, Amara was sure. She'd sat here, contemplating what to do. She'd considered trying to wish herself back to 1813. It was tempting to run away again, though she'd be less running away and more returning to the problems she'd wanted to escape in the first place.

No, she couldn't go back. Even if it were possible without another story from Cat, which she doubted. It was time to stop running. To be the independent woman she'd vowed she'd be. To take responsibility for her own life, her own choices.

And she didn't want to go. There was too much here, too many wonderful things. Hot showers. Airplanes. The Internet. Television. Pizza. It wasn't a perfect society, no, not with some of the things she'd seen on TV, not with things she'd witnessed with her own eyes. But hers wasn't, either, and there were far more opportunities for her in 2016 than there'd ever be for her in the past.

Did she want to stay at Clarehaven, though? Sophie would let her, she was sure. The woman was lonely, living in this cavernous house by herself. She liked Amara, and Amara liked her. It would be easy, in a way, to sink back into a version of her old life here.

A cloud moved over the sun, and the world went suddenly darker, colder. Amara shivered. Yes, she could stay here. But she didn't want to. She wanted to return to Charlottesville. To Matthew. She missed him. Missed him desperately. And she missed him because …

Because she loved him.

The revelation hit her not like a ton of bricks, but like the slow unfurling of the first spring's bloom—a welcome sight after a long, harsh cold.

She loved Matthew Goodson.

Warmth spread through her as the sun emerged from the clouds, but it wasn't only external warmth. No, it was an internal peace, an acceptance. She loved Matthew.

She loved his quiet strength, his humor. The way he'd come after her to England. He hadn't abandoned her, not like Drake. She'd abandoned him, and yet he'd come anyway. And he'd stayed by her side through her revelations about her past and through the loss of their baby.

He hadn't left. Not until she'd commanded him to. And he'd respected her wishes enough to leave, even after declaring his love for her. She'd initially thought that proof his feelings were misinterpreted, or at least stemmed from guilt or a sense of responsibility. Not love.

But now she saw it was the opposite. He'd loved her enough to let her go when she'd said that's what she wanted.

She reached for the phone in her pocket. Sophie's cell phone. Sophie had insisted she bring it. "In case you want to come home earlier than an hour. You can call the house phone," she'd said with a smile.

Pulling it out, Amara tapped the screen, frowning when it did nothing. Was it broken? She swiped her fingers across the glass. Nothing happened. Panic filled her until she realized how silly that was—even if the phone was broken, it wasn't as if she couldn't walk back to Clarehaven. She'd done it before.

She traced her finger around the edge of the gadget, stopping when it bumped a button on the top. The power button. Amara sat up, pressing it firmly. Had the stupid thing just been off?

The phone beeped as it turned on, and Amara glanced at the screen. A text message with Matthew's name popped out at her. She moved to the words below, and her breath caught.

> I shouldn't have left. Please tell her I love her. I'm here when she's ready.

Amara's heart raced, beating an erratic rhythm. The phone said it was 10:03. How long ago had he sent that? Before she could think about it, she typed out a response as fast as she could—which still wasn't very fast, her fingers tripping over the tiny keyboard.

> I shhouldn't hav3e told yu to.

She clicked send and closed her eyes. The time to decide was now. Did she want to stay here, in England? With Sophie, at Clarehaven? Or did she want to go home?

Home. She'd just described Charlottesville as home.

Yes, she needed to go home. Clarehaven had been her home once, but it wasn't any longer. It was known and dear, and being here had been a balm to her wounded soul. But it wasn't her home, not anymore.

She wanted to go back to the two-bedroom apartment she'd shared with Matthew for those few days. Back to the kitchen with its baffling appliances, and the tiny bathroom with the heavenly shower. And the big bed in Matthew's room. But mostly, she wanted to go back to Matthew.

She didn't know what the future held. She just knew she needed Matthew Goodson in it.

Matt stared at the phone in his hand. He'd sent his message last night, without thinking. After getting home, he'd fallen into bed, exhausted, clinging to the hope that the reason he hadn't gotten a response was that it was late in England, well past midnight, and not that he'd never hear anything.

Moments ago, his phone had dinged. Though it was only barely after six, he'd been lying awake for nearly an hour, putting off getting up by petting Lovey. He was drained from the events of the past few days—hell, the past month. When the text signal chimed, though, he'd grabbed his cell so fast he'd scared the cat off the bed.

Given the typos, it was clearly Amara, not Sophie, who'd responded. Why did she have Sophie's phone?

Who cares? She'd answered him.

Should he return to England? He could go back to the airport, catch another flight. No. No, he couldn't. The ball was in Amara's court. He'd chased her halfway around the world, for Pete's sake. He'd accepted her for who she was, wild time-traveling story and all, and bared his heart to her.

If his sister Taylor knew the extent of the crazy antics

her brother had undertaken in the last few days, she'd never believe it. Not of Matt. Predictable, routinized, work-focused Matt. He'd dropped everything and raced off to England. After a woman.

And he hadn't told Taylor any of it. But he should, and soon. He needed her wisdom.

He snorted as he rolled out of bed, still clutching the cell. He almost didn't recognize himself anymore. Who was this man flying by the seat of his pants? Who'd accepted time travel as if it were as natural as any other scientific principle? Who'd fallen head over heels in love with a woman, so much that he was willing to put his job, his career, at risk to chase after her?

Should he answer her? What could he say?

The phone beeped in his hand, and a second message appeared on the screen.

I"m comning home.

"You're sure?" Sophie's forehead wrinkled in concern.

"Yes. I am." Amara took one last look at the room before stepping through the doorway and closing the door firmly behind her.

Sophie spoke again as the two women descended the grand staircase. "I'm thrilled for you, absolutely. But may I ask what brought this on? Last I knew, you'd sent the man away."

Amara gave a crisp nod of her head. "I've spent the last few hours thinking. Truly thinking."

She paused as they reached the foyer, letting her eyes fall on each familiar detail—the marble busts, the mosaic-tiled floor. Every aspect was the same as it had been in her era—except for the electric chandelier, of course, and the light switches on the wall.

"I had assumed, or decided, rather, based on my own experiences, that loving a man, that life with a man, was not compatible with the kind of independence I wanted, the independence I never had in my own time."

Sophie nodded, her eyes focused on Amara, but said nothing.

"By trying to keep Matthew at arm's length, I thought I was protecting myself, my plans … my heart. But he wasn't the one stifling me. I was. I saw him only as a potential downfall, someone who'd become an obstacle to my goals if I let myself feel anything for him."

Amara grasped the front door and flung it open wide. She paused at the threshold. "When I learned I was expecting a child, it was everything I'd ever feared. I'd been lucky to escape such a fate with Drake. Now here I was, two hundred years later, making the same mistake."

She hesitated at the top step, her words trailing off as she surveyed Clarehaven's grounds.

"Mistake?" Sophie prompted.

"Yes. I let desire rule and found myself embroiled in scandal. A seduction in a garden then; a child conceived out of wedlock now. It felt the same. Worse. Everything I'd left England to avoid—the shame, the scandal, the lack of options—came crashing back. History was repeating itself. And it was all my doing."

"Amara, that doesn't make any sense." Sophie descended the outside stairs behind Amara, who'd walked ahead of her, angling for the massive garage. "It's not like you—"

Amara waved a hand. "It made sense to me. From my experiences. My worldview."

She stopped, turning toward Sophie with a frown. "And that was the problem. I'm not in 1813 anymore. No one judges me here. Except myself. I put myself back into that prison of scandal, of recriminations, of judgment. And I'm the one who threw away the key."

Sophie stopped as Amara paused in her steps. "And now?"

"Now I see, I truly see, there *can* be freedom, there *can* be equality in love. Matthew has shown me more consideration than any man. He gave me freedom in Virginia. Yes, he reacted badly to the pregnancy news. But so did I. I ran. I ran, as I always had, wanting to hide, to bury, to ignore."

Amara's feet moved again, quickening her pace toward the garage. "Then he came. He came for me, Sophie. He left everything to come for me. Even when I told him the truth about me and who I was, *when* I was, he stayed. When we lost the baby, he stayed. He professed to love me. And I kicked him out. I abandoned *him*. It wasn't the other way around."

She opened the car door and climbed in, as Sophie went around to the right side, gracefully settling herself behind the steering wheel. Fastening her seatbelt, Amara turned to Sophie. "And now, I'm changing history. My history. I'm going home."

Sophie's brows rose at the last comment. "Clarehaven will always be your home."

Amara laid her fingers on Sophie's leg. "Thank you. That means more to me than you know. You opened your home, and yourself, to me from the moment I arrived. It was more than I expected and more than I can ever repay."

"Don't be silly," Sophie said, waving a dismissive hand before backing out. "We are family, after all."

"Yes. We are. But I don't belong here. Not anymore." At Sophie's sigh, she added, "Please know, you are welcome in Charlottesville anytime."

"Perhaps I'll come," Sophie said, sadness in her smile. Then her eyes twinkled mischievously. "Perhaps this Cat can write a story for me, as well."

"Yes. She can."

Both women fell silent as the miles raced by.

"I shall miss you, Amara Mattersley." Sophie enfolded her in a tight hug.

"And I, you, Sophie. I may be your aunt some generations removed, but you are like a sister." Amara squeezed her eyes shut as she returned the hug. "Thank you."

"No, thank *you*. You livened up my rather boring existence. And you've given me new faith in love."

"I have?"

Sophie released her, nodding vigorously. "You came across centuries for it. The least I can do is hope to find someone in my own era."

"I didn't—"

"Yes," Sophie said, her voice artificially stern. "You did. Now go get on that airplane and fly home to him. And text me once you're there, so I know you're safe."

"Yes, Mother." Her tone was wry, but Amara's heart constricted. It was harder to leave Sophie than she could've imagined. But her future wasn't here. It was across an ocean, and she could hardly wait to get back to it. "Farewell, Sophie."

"No. This isn't good-bye. This is 'see you later.'" With

one final squeeze on her arm, Sophie released her, turning quickly and striding away.

Amara watched her go before rushing to her gate, anxious to be back in Charlottesville. Her step was light, her heart full of hope … and anticipation.

She couldn't wait to get home to Matthew.

She only hoped he would welcome her.

Chapter 44

The knock on the door woke Matt, and he opened one eye, blinking wearily at the clock. 9:52 p.m. What on earth? He'd fallen asleep before ten?

The knock sounded again, more insistent. Who could that be?

Lovey meowed in protest as Matt rose from the bed and slipped on his robe. Suddenly, it hit him. *Amara.* It could be Amara. He tore out of the bedroom, skidding to a halt in front of the door. He worked the locks, then threw it open.

And there she stood, her hair askew, her eyes red-rimmed. She'd never looked more beautiful.

"Hello," she said, her voice quaking. Nervousness?

"Hello."

"I caught the first flight I could. I'm sorry for the late—"

He didn't let her finish, pulling her in through the doorway and into his arms, his lips crashing down on hers as he slammed the door behind her. She squeaked in response, but then laced her arms up around his neck, weaving her hands through his hair, pulling him even closer.

They kissed, at first heatedly, intensely, as if each feared the other would disappear. Then the kisses dissolved into a tenderer, more leisurely embrace. At length, she pulled away slightly, but not before dropping a kiss on his jaw. "I'm so sorry for sending you away, Matthew."

"Shh." He traced her mouth with his finger, his eyes widening when she lightly bit the tip. "I'm sorry for all of it. Forgetting a condom. The mess I made with you when you told me. The—the miscarriage."

He swallowed, grief pounding through his temples. "But I'm not sorry for you. I'm not sorry I met you. I don't care how it happened. I don't care if Cat wove us together with some sort of spell. She was right; I needed it to happen. I needed you."

His hands rose to frame her face. "I was living half a life before I met you, Amara. I thought I was happy. I had my job, my machines." He waved a hand toward the computers lining the living room. "But I wasn't. I was hiding. Determined not to get hurt again, like Wendy hurt me. Like my father hurt me. And in doing so, I avoided everything. Until you."

"Oh, Matthew. I did the same. I told myself I wanted to come here for independence, for a new future. But mostly I was running from my past. Hiding from my mistakes, too. When I repeated them here, I ran again." She traced his jaw with her hand, her fingers trailing over the stubble. "I wish I'd realized sooner you weren't what was sabotaging my desires. *I* was."

She leaned up to press her lips against his, but released him again quickly. "I thought I couldn't have love. On occasion I wanted it, after seeing Deveric and Eliza. But it wasn't for me, not if it meant losing my freedom. My independence. Myself. When Eliza described this future, her education, the choices available, I had to come. But I thought the last thing I wanted, the last thing I needed, was love."

She gave him a grin that quickly turned saucy. "I admit freely, I liked the benefits this freedom gave me. My time with you here. But I couldn't see a way to make a relationship work without giving up my own dreams. I thought love meant entrapment. Like it had with Drake Evers."

She ran her fingers over his eyebrow, then smoothed them into his hair again. "But you … you are not Drake. You are not like any man I have ever known. You let me be me. And I love you for it."

Matt's pupils flared. "Say it again."

"I love you, Mr. Matthew Goodson."

A meow at their feet interrupted them as Matt dipped to kiss her again, and they laughed, the insistent feline weaving her way in and out of Amara's legs.

"Guess I'm not the only one who missed you." He swung her into his arms, carrying her down the hallway.

"Matthew," Amara said, her eyes anxious. "I can't yet. I'm still bleeding, and …"

"It's all right, Amara. I wasn't expecting anything. We have a lifetime for that. I just want to hold you … and never let you go."

She relaxed into him, delighting in the warmth of his body against hers, the soft texture of his robe tickling her cheek. He laid her on the bed, then shed the robe as she settled herself under the blanket.

"You're naked!" she shrieked, though her eyes drank in the sight of him.

"So I am. You know I sleep like this. Just in case a sexy siren should slip into bed with me." He crawled onto the mattress, sliding under the blanket with her, and rolled onto his side, pulling her against him so that his large frame encircled her, his arm settling over her waist, his hand resting just below her breasts.

"And does that happen often?" she challenged.

"Once in a lifetime, dearest Amara. Once in a lifetime."

Together, they fell asleep.

EPILOGUE

February 14th, 2017

"It's been exactly a year. Have you finally forgiven me?" Cat arched a brow at Matthew, who was helping himself to a second serving of the lasagna before him.

"Forgive you? I celebrate you. Without you, I wouldn't have found the love of my life."

Amara beamed at him before taking a sip of her water.

"How are classes going, Amara?" Taylor asked.

"Without a doubt, they are challenging, but it's helpful to have a live-in tutor. Though I'm a wee bit better versed in the history of England than he." She blew a kiss at Matthew.

From the other side of the table, Wash beat a steady rhythm with his spoon on his plate, grinning when his mom and dad turned to him. "More bread!"

"Washington, banging your spoon is not polite." Cat chastised, but love shone from her eyes.

Ben reached over and handed his son a breadstick.

"Ben, that's his second one."

Ben winked. "The boy knows what he likes, and he likes bread. I can hardly fault him. Plus, it will keep him quiet while Matt and Amara talk their future plans."

Amara's eyes flew to Matthew. "Er, well," she stammered. "We haven't … I mean, we're taking things one day at a time."

Matthew grinned at Ben, sending him a brief nod. Pulling his napkin from his lap, he set it on the table before carefully kneeling on one knee before Amara.

He grinned as her eyes grew wide, her hands flying to her face. "What are you—"

"Amara Mattersley, you're right. We are taking things one day at a time. But I'd like to do it together, for every day of the rest of our lives. Will you do me the honor of becoming my wife?"

Amara's mouth dropped open, and her glance skittered to Cat and Ben, then Taylor. Had they known Matthew was planning this? Cat's watery eyes and Ben's wide smile gave her the answer. Taylor pumped a fist in exultation. Amara looked back at Matthew, those ice-blue eyes wide, love—and nervousness—written across his face.

Her own eyes prickled suspiciously, and her skin tingled with exhilaration, and fear and hope and love. "Yes. Yes, of course."

Cat whooped, Taylor hollered, and Wash banged his spoon again as Matthew bounced up and pulled her into his arms, his mouth finding hers and searing it with a kiss.

After a moment, Ben cleared his throat. "If you don't mind," he said, his voice teasing. "There are children present."

Amara broke apart from Matthew, a giggle escaping her.

Matthew snickered in return, before diving in for another

kiss. "I hope it's okay I did this in front of Cat and Ben," he whispered. "But I thought since they were the two who hatched the plan to bring us together …"

"… It's only fitting they see their success." Amara nodded.

Cat and Ben clapped, Wash following suit.

Taylor bounded over and hugged Amara. "Now we'll really be sisters."

"Thank you," Amara said to Cat. "Thank you for sending Eliza to my brother. She brought him light when he was lost in the darkness. And thank you for bringing me to Matthew. Without him … " A tear slipped out of her eye. "Without him, I wouldn't have seen that the past is not the future."

Matthew pressed his lips to her forehead. "And without you … I shudder to think. I had no future. Not really."

"Oh, you do," Ben broke in. "I got word today the department unanimously approved your tenure application, and that the dean's ready and anxious to send it to the higher ups right away. I'm not supposed to tell you that." He shrugged his shoulders. "But I don't think you'll be giving away our secrets … "

Matthew's face broke out into the widest grin. Amara hugged him. "Your future is secure," she said, love shining from her eyes. "Though I have enough money that we never have to worry, you know."

Matthew pursed his lips. "A kept man," he said. "I could get used to that. But my future was secured the minute you said yes. I love you, Amara Mattersley. For all of your past, present, and future."

"Yes," she breathed against his lips. "Our past, present, and future."

Fall in love with the magic in
A Man of Character and *A Matter of Time*, the first
two books in the **Magic of Love** series:

A Man of Character

Available now at **http://bit.ly/AManOfCharacter**

***What would you do if you discovered the men you were
dating were fictional characters you'd created long ago?***

Thirty-five-year-old Catherine Schreiber has shelved love for
good. Keeping her ailing bookstore afloat takes all her time,
and she's perfectly fine with that. So when several men ask
her out in short order, she's not sure what to do…especially
since something about them seems eerily familiar.

A startling revelation—that these men are fictional
characters she'd created and forgotten years ago—forces Cat
to reevaluate her world and the people in it. Because these
characters are alive. Here. Now. And most definitely in the
flesh.

Her best friend, Eliza, a romance novel junkie craving her
own Happily Ever After, is thrilled by the possibilities. The
power to create Mr. Perfect—who could pass that up? But
can a relationship be real if it's fiction?

Caught between fantasy and reality, Cat must decide
which—or whom—she wants more.

A Matter of Time

Available now at http://bit.ly/AMatterOfTime

Can a man with a past and a woman from the future forge a love for all time?

Nobody would blame widowed doctoral student Eliza James for giving up on Happily Ever After; at twenty-nine, she's suffered more loss than most people do in a lifetime. But Eliza's convinced her own hero is still out there, waiting for her, just like in the beloved romance novels she devours. Every Jane Austen-loving girl deserves a Darcy, right?

Only Eliza doesn't dream of a modern-day affair: she wants the whole Regency experience. When a magical manuscript thrusts her back two hundred years into the arms and life of one Deveric Mattersley, Duke of Claremont, however, Eliza realizes some fantasies aren't all they're cracked up to be, especially when her duke proves himself less than a Prince Charming.

Convinced he's at fault for the death of his wife, Deveric Mattersley has no interest in women, much less marriage. Determined to atone for his sins, he decrees himself content to focus on running his family's estates and on raising his son—until the mysterious Mrs. James appears. Who is she?

What does she want? And why does she make Dev's blood run hot in a way no woman ever has?

A charming time-travel Regency romance full of wit and humor, *A Matter of Time* reminds us that, like books, you can't judge people by their covers, and that love often comes when least expected.

And coming 2017, the first in Margaret Locke's new (non-magical) Regency series, *Put Up Your Dukes*:

The Demon Duke

Shy and bookish Grace Mattersley much prefers reading to social just-about-anything. Her family may be pressuring her to take on the London Season, but she has other ideas. Like reading every book she can get her hands on. And perhaps even writing one, in the vein of that Lady Author's fine *Sense and Sensibility*.

What she has no idea about is how to deal with Damon Blackbourne, Duke of Malford.

Banished to Yorkshire as a boy for faults his father failed to beat out of him, Damon has no use for English society and had vowed never to return to his family's estate at Thorne Hill, much less London. However, when his father and brother die in a freak carriage accident, it falls on Damon to take up the mantle of the dukedom, and to introduce his sisters to London Society–his worst nightmare come to life.

He never planned on Grace.

The beautiful debutante stirs him body and soul with her deep chocolate eyes and hesitant smiles. Until she stumbles across his secret.

Will she betray him to the world?

ACKNOWLEDGMENTS

"Here's the thing: the book that will most change your life is the book you write." – Seth Godin

That has certainly proven true for me. The list of people to whom I am indebted grows longer, not shorter, with each successive book. I count this as the highest of privileges, to have so many friends, fellow writers, and readers supporting me and cheering me on.

To the Shenandoah Valley Writers Critique Group for their insights and encouragement as I whipped this book into shape from its humble 2015 National Novel Writing Month (NaNoWriMo) beginnings.

To beta readers Phyllis A. Duncan, Vanessa Hinman, Josette Keelor, and Heather Raffa, for their sharp eyes and highly valued feedback.

To my bestie, Kary Phillips, for, well, being my best friend, and for possessing editing and proofing skills of the highest caliber.

To my brilliant editor, Tessa Shapcott, for her invaluable guidance in honing and shaping my stories and characters so that they shine brighter than anything I could ever formulate on my own.

To Joy Lankshear of Lankshear Design, for her eye-catching covers and interior formatting that make me—er, I mean my books—look exquisite.

To RWA's Beau Monde, for constantly offering helpful answers to my many naïve questions. I quest to get it right, but of course any errors remain my own.

To my kids, for putting up with me when I'm on deadline.

To Brett, for the same. And for being my own Captain Obvious. I love you, Schmuck Boy.

About Margaret

Don't tell her mom, but Margaret Locke started reading romance at the age of ten. She'd worked her way through all of the children's books available in the local bookmobile, so turned to the adult section, where she spied a book with a woman in a flowing green dress on the cover. The back said something about a pirate. She was hooked (and still wishes she could remember the name of that fateful book!).

Her delight in witty repartee between hero and heroine, in the age-old dance of attraction vs. resistance, in the emotional satisfaction of a cleverly achieved Happily Ever After followed her through high school, college, even grad school. But it wasn't until she turned forty that she finally made good on her teenage vow to write said novels, not merely read them.

Margaret lives in the beautiful Shenandoah Valley in Virginia with her fantastic husband, two fabulous kids, and two fat cats. You can usually find her in front of some sort of screen (electronic or window); she's come to terms with the fact that she's not an outdoors person.

Margaret loves to interact with fellow readers and authors! You may find her here:

Blog/Website: **http://margaretlocke.com**
Facebook: **http://www.facebook.com/AuthorMargaretLocke**
GoodReads: **http://www.goodreads.com/MargaretLocke**
Instagram: **http://www.instagram.com/margaret_locke**
Pinterest: **http://www.pinterest.com/Margaret_Locke**
Twitter: **http://www.twitter.com/Margaret_Locke**
Amazon Author Page: **http://www.amazon.com/Margaret-Locke/e/B00W62NPC0**

Interested in being the first to know about Margaret's upcoming releases, or hearing about other insider information not shared on her website? Sign up for her newsletter!
http://bit.ly/MLockeNewsletter

What did you think of *A Scandalous Matter*?

Would you kindly consider leaving a review on Amazon (http://bit.ly/AScandalousMatter) or GoodReads (http://bit.ly/GR-ASM)?

Word-of-mouth is the best way for authors to reach readers, and the online version of word-of-mouth is reviews. Thanks so much!